THE LAST ODYSSEY

THE LAST ODYSSEY

A THRILLER

JAMES ROLLINS

WM
WILLIAM MORROW
An Imprint of HarperCollins*Publishers*

FIRST EDITION

Library of Congress Cataloging-in-Publication Data has been applied for.

ISBN 978-0-06-289289-8 (hardcover)
ISBN 978-0-06-289296-6 (international edition)

20 21 22 23 24 DIX/LSC 10 9 8 7 6 5 4 3 2 1

To readers everywhere, to those who still seek out lost worlds and greater truths hidden within scribbles of ink on paper. Thank you for joining me on this journey.

Acknowledgments

It's said that Homer once wrote, "The journey is the thing." And the path from idea to published novel is its own rocky road. My odyssey in finishing this book was made all the easier through the help of an esteemed (and patient) cadre of first readers, reviewers, and cheerleaders. Collectively known as the Warped Spacers, they include Chris Crowe, Lee Garrett, Matt Bishop, Matt Orr, Leonard Little, Judy Prey, Caroline Williams, John Vester, and Amy Rogers. And a special thanks to Steve Prey for the Arctic map. But I also have to single out David Sylvian for making me look good across the digital universe. And Cherei McCarter, who has shared with me a bevy of intriguing concepts and curiosities, several of which are found in these pages. And William Craig Reed for his valuable help with submarine warfare hardware. Of course, none of this would happen without an astounding team of industry professionals whom I defy anyone to surpass. To everyone at William Morrow, thank you for always having my back, especially Liate Stehlik, Danielle Bartlett, Kaitlin Harri, Josh Marwell, Richard Aquan, and Ana Maria Allessi. Last, of course, a special acknowledgment to the people instrumental to all levels of production: my esteemed editor, Lyssa Keusch, and her industrious colleague Mireya Chiriboga; and for all their hard work, my agents, Russ Galen and Danny Baror (along with his daughter Heather Baror). And as always, I must stress that any and all errors of fact or detail in this book, of which hopefully there are not too many, fall squarely on my own shoulders.

Map of Greenland

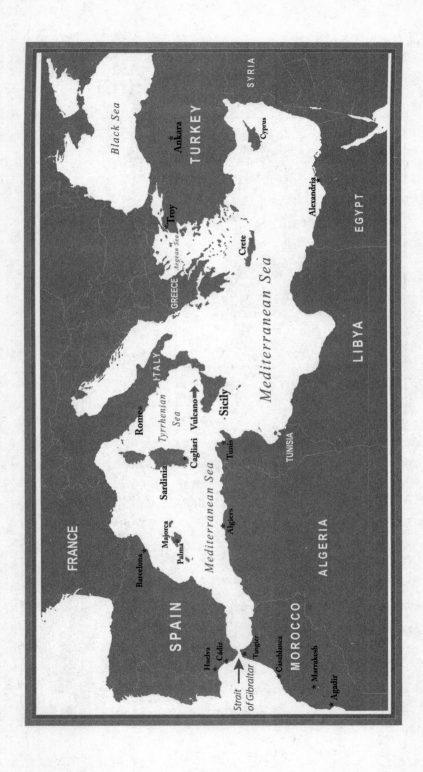

Notes from the Historical Record

History is a fluid enterprise. Stories of events change depending on the viewpoint. It is often the victor who gets to tell the tale and cement myth into fact.

Take the twin epics of Homer—the *Iliad* and the *Odyssey*—two lyric poems that recount the Trojan War and its aftermath. These stories were believed to have been composed during the eighth century B.C., though most historians today doubt Homer even existed. This bard who sung tales of gods and monsters was likely just a convenient pseudonym, representing the many minstrels who recounted this turbulent story.

Still, to what degree were these two epics based on historical events and how much was pure fantasy?

For centuries, historians dismissed even the existence of Troy—a great city besieged by the Greeks and brought low by the trickery of the Trojan Horse, as recounted in the *Iliad*. Troy was believed to be a mythical place, a fantasy brought to life by Homer. Then in the late nineteenth century, a German amateur archaeologist named Heinrich Schliemann dug into a large hill at the Turkish site of Hisarlik and exposed the ruins of a great city. It would take many years, but eventually this buried complex was indeed identified as the lost city of Troy.

And just like that, myth became history.

But what about Homer's *Odyssey*, the story of the great war hero Odysseus and his treacherous ten-year journey back to his island home of Ithaca? Here is a tale of hardship and ruin, of colossal monsters and witches, of god-sent storms and sirens who drove men mad. Surely none of this tale could be based on fact. Still, historians and archeologists continue to sift through the *Odyssey*, searching for clues, trying to map the route of Odysseus's ship, even assigning geographical sites to places mentioned in this epic poem.

Case in point. A little over a decade ago, a British management consultant named Robert Bittlestone used modern-day geological tools to identify the site of Odysseus's hometown of Ithaca, where the great warrior would return at the end of his epic journey. Archeologists had already dismissed the present-day island of Ithaca as this site, as the island failed to match Homer's description in the *Odyssey*. Instead, Bittlestone proposed a new theory supported by evidence, pinpointing the Greek peninsula of Paliki as the true location of ancient Ithaca. His evidence was so convincing that James Diggle, a Cambridge University professor of Greek and Latin, declared, "It's irresistible, and supported by geology . . . once you go over the terrain, there is an extraordinary match."[*] Bittlestone's conclusions were also supported by other scholars of ancient antiquity.[†]

Thus we have proof that the events recounted in the *Odyssey* have a true historical starting point (the city of Troy) and an end point (Ithaca). Such discoveries beg the question: *What about everything in between? How much of Homer's epic poems of gods and monsters could also be true?*

It is now readily accepted that, despite the question of Homer's identity, these stories *do* seem to recount a great war that truly happened. In fact, these two epics shine a light into an era known as the Greek Dark Ages, a turbulent time that saw the collapse of three Bronze Age civilizations: the Greek Mycenaeans, the Anatolian Hittites, and the Egyptians. How and why did this happen? Recent discoveries reveal that a series of battles *did* sweep the Mediterranean region. The fighting was so widespread that

[*]   Fergus M. Bordewich, "Odyssey's End: The Search for Ancient Ithaca," *Smithsonian Magazine*, April 2006.
[†]   Nicholas Kristof, "Odysseus Lies Here," *New York Times*, March 10, 2012.

some historians declared this to be the first great global war, even calling it World War Zero. Much of this dark struggle still remains shrouded in mystery, though some archaeologists now believe there was a *fourth* civilization involved in this fighting, a civilization that defeated the other three—then vanished into the past.

If true, who were these lost people? Could Homer's stories offer clues to their origin and where they went? The answers can be found within these pages and will shed light on a new world war threatening us today. So, consider yourselves forewarned—not all stories of gods and monsters are fiction.

Notes from the Scientific Record

We are a curious lot, us humans. Unfortunately, our curiosity sometimes leads us into more trouble than it does benefit us. Especially when it comes to *inventions*. The wheel came into widespread use around 3500 B.C., and since then, we've not stopped innovating to both improve our lives and to better understand it. The old adage "necessity is the mother of all invention" remains as true today as it did back in 3500 B.C.

But is this sustainable? Will we reach a time when advancement stagnates? Some believe we've already reached that tipping point. Tyler Cowen, an economist at George Mason University, penned a manifesto, *The Great Stagnation*, stating that we've reached our apex of innovation by having already taken full advantage of cheap energy and industrial-age breakthroughs. He thinks our time of rapid advancement is coming to an end.

Or will it? There certainly have been periods of technological stagnation, mostly because individual societies actively *choose* to stop innovating. The Chinese did it after the Ming Era; the Arab world followed suit during the fourteenth century. Still, it seems whenever one part of the world douses the flame of innovation, another picks it up. When the Arab world was sinking into darkness, the countries of Europe started the Renaissance, carrying forward the torch that the Islamic world had forsaken.

To illustrate, from the eighth to the fourteenth century—known as the Islamic Golden Age—Arab scientists proved themselves to be masters of design and innovation. One of the most prominent was Ismail al-Jazari (1136–1206), who invented all manner of tools from water clocks to sophisticated automatons. The components and techniques of construction were beyond anything seen before. Al-Jazari's greatest masterwork was a volume titled *The Book of Knowledge of Ingenious Mechanical Devices* and contained diagrams for more than a hundred inventions. He would become known as "the Leonardo da Vinci of the Arab World."

In fact, it is believed that Leonardo was influenced—even "borrowed"—from the works of al-Jazari, who died two centuries before Leonardo was born. By doing so, Leonardo carried forward the torch of innovation that had been abandoned by the Islamic world after its golden age dimmed. In fact, al-Jazari's influence over Leonardo has proven to be far greater than anyone imagined—as you will soon discover.

Still, such is the path of innovation: passed from one hand to another, from one country to another, from one century to another.

Finally, let's return to that old adage "necessity is the mother of all invention." If true, this begs the question: What has fired up invention and innovation more than anything else?

The answer lies in a single word.

War.

THE LAST ODYSSEY

βουλοίμην κ’ ἐπάρουρος ἐὼν θητευέμεν ἄλλῳ,
ἀνδρὶ παρ’ ἀκλήρῳ, ᾧ μὴ βίοτος πολὺς εἴη,
ἢ πᾶσιν νεκύεσσι καταφθιμένοισιν ἀνάσσειν.

"I would rather be a paid servant in a poor man's house and be above ground than king of kings among the dead."

—WORDS FROM THE GHOST OF ACHILLES IN HOMER'S *ODYSSEY*

Happy will they be who lend ear to the words of the Dead.

—LEONARDO DA VINCI

The artist leaned closer to the decapitated head. The macabre decoration stood spiked atop the table of his studio, perfectly lit by the morning's brightness. In fact, he had chosen this apartment at the Belvedere due to this wonderful light. The villa stood within the Vatican, on grounds considered holy. Still, without a tremor of hesitation, he expertly dissected the skin off the dead girl's cheek. The poor lass had died before her seventeenth birthday.

A tragedy, but one that nonetheless made her an excellent specimen.

He exposed the fine musculature under her skin and squinted at the delicate fibers that ran from her cheekbone down to the corner of her slack lips. He spent the next hour carefully tweezing muscles and noting how the pale lips moved in response to his efforts. He paused only to scratch at a parchment, recording each movement with deft strokes of his left hand. He noted the tiny shifts of the dead woman's nostril, the way the conformation of the cheek changed, the wrinkling of her lower eyelid.

Once satisfied, he stood with a creak of his back and stepped to the plank of wood resting on its easel. He picked up a horsehair brush and studied the left side of his subject's unfinished face, her countenance forever fixed at a three-quarter turn. Without his subject here, he had to proceed from memory. For the moment, he ignored the fall of her painted tresses, the drape of her gown. Instead he dabbed his brush in oil and adjusted a shadow near her lip, using the knowledge he had just gained from his dissection.

Satisfied, he stepped back.

Better . . . much better.

Twelve years ago, while he had been living in Florence, a rich merchant, Francesco del Giocondo, had commissioned him to paint a portrait of his young wife, the beautiful and enigmatic Lisa. Since then, he had carried her unfinished portrait with him: from Florence to Milan to Rome. Even still, he was not ready to let her go.

That upstart Michelangelo—who sometimes shared these apartments at the Belvedere—ridiculed his reluctance at finishing this painting, mocking such dedication with all the weight of youthful arrogance.

Still, it mattered not. He met those painted eyes staring back at him. The cold morning sunlight streamed through the second-story windows and set her skin to glowing, heightened by the dying embers of the small hearth that warmed the room.

Over the years, with every bit of knowledge gained, I've made you all the more beautiful.

But he was not yet done.

The door to his studio opened behind him. The complaint of hinges reminded him of other duties, other, more urgent commissions that would yet again pull him from her smile. His fingers tightened on his brush in irritation.

Only the soft, apologetic voice of his apprentice dimmed his frustration. "Master Leonardo," Francesco said, "I've gathered all you requested in the palace library."

He sighed, set down his brush, and turned his back on his Lisa once again. "*Grazie*, Francesco."

As Leonardo stepped toward his furred winter cloak hanging beside the door, Francesco's gaze discovered the half-skinned head atop the worktable. The young man's eyes widened, his face paled, but he refrained from commenting.

"Quit gaping, Francesco. Surely by now such sights should not unnerve you." He donned his cloak and headed toward the door. "If you wish to become a master artist, you must seek knowledge wherever you can acquire it."

Francesco nodded and followed Leonardo out the door.

The pair headed down the stone steps and out the door that led to the Belvedere courtyard. A winter's frost had turned the yard's grassy sward brittle and white. The crisp air smelled of woodsmoke. Scaffolding enclosed the incomplete wings of the courtyard to either side.

As they hurried across, Leonardo appreciated this moment in time, as if history were waiting for one era to pass to the next. This sense of impending change thrilled him, energized him, lit a hopeful fire in his chest.

At last, with his nose burning from the cold, he and Francesco reached the towering Apostolic Palace. The building's chapel had recently been painted by that damnable Michelangelo.

Irritation at this thought warmed away the winter's chill. Last year, Leonardo had snuck into the chapel, well after midnight, armed with a lamp. He had studied the young man's work in secret, refusing to give Michelangelo the satisfaction of his appreciation. He remembered craning his neck, awed by the ceiling. He could not help but respect the genius on display, recognizing the innovative use of perspective in such a large volume of space. He had taken several notes, drawing what knowledge he could from Michelangelo's handiwork.

Leonardo's ongoing bitterness with the young artist reminded him of his own admonishment to Francesco: *You must seek knowledge wherever you can acquire it.* But that did not mean one had to acknowledge the source.

He stomped up the palace stairs, nodded to the posted guards, and shoved inside.

Perhaps sensing his frustration, Francesco led the way toward the wing that housed the Vatican library, where he had worked throughout the night, scouring dusty shelves and closets, all to gather the materials Leonardo wished to study for his next commission.

Time was running short.

Leonardo was scheduled to leave in three days to accompany Pope Leo X north to Bologna, to meet with the French king—François I—who had recently sacked Milan. Matters of state were to be settled at this coming meeting, but the king had ordered Leonardo to attend. A letter had accompanied this odd demand.

It seemed the king—who knew of Leonardo's talent—wanted him to produce a great work to commemorate the French victory. Details were included. King François wanted him to craft a gold mechanical lion, one capable not only of walking on its own, but whose clockwork mechanism would open its chest, revealing a hidden bouquet of lilies inside, the sigil of the French king.

Francesco—ever his companion—guessed his thoughts. "Do you truly think you can design such a golden artifice?"

Leonardo glanced over to the young man. "Is that doubt I hear in your voice, Francesco? Do you question my ingenuity?"

The young man stammered, his cheeks going crimson. "Of . . . of course not, master."

Leonardo smiled. "Good, because there's enough doubt inside me. Arrogance only carries one so far. Great works are born of equal parts divine brilliance and earthly humbleness."

"Humble?" Francesco lifted a brow. "You?"

Leonardo chuckled. The boy knew him well. "It's best to show arrogance to the public. To convince the world at large of your confidence in all endeavors."

"And in private?"

"That is when you should know your truest self. One must be humble enough to recognize one's limitations, to know when further knowledge is needed." He remembered gawking up at Michelangelo's lamplit ceiling and what it had taught him. "That is where true genius begins. Armed with enough knowledge and ingenuity, a man can do anything."

He hurried toward the library, ready to prove that statement.

10:02 A.M.

Let me have done well.

Francesco held the door open for his master, then followed Leonardo into the papal library. He prayed his efforts did not disappoint the great man.

As he trailed his mentor, the musty smell of old leather and moldering pages greeted their entry to the main vault. Wood shelves climbed to the rafters, interspersed with the pale ghosts of marble statues. Ahead, a lone lamp brightened a wide desk, neatly stacked with books, loose papers, even a pyramid of scrolls.

Leonardo crossed to the desk. "You certainly have been busy, Francesco."

"I did my best," he sighed. "That Arab volume you wanted proved especially difficult to track down."

Leonardo glanced back, his brows raised. "You found it?"

With a measure of pride, Francesco pointed to the thick tome at the center of the gathered material. While its leather cover was worn and blackened with age, the gilt lettering of the title remained bright, shining in the lamp's glow. The writing flowed in Arabic, lettered quite beautifully.

Leonardo's finger hovered over the title—كتاب في معرفة الحيل الهندسية—and read it aloud. "*Kitab fi ma'rifat al-hiyal al-handasiya.*"

Francesco translated it in a hushed voice. "*The Book of Knowledge of Ingenious Mechanical Devices.*"

"It was written two centuries ago," Leonardo said. "Can you imagine such a time, the golden age of Islam, when science and learning were held in the highest regard?"

"I would love to travel to such places sometime."

"Ah, my dear Francesco, you are too late. Those lands have fallen into darkness, rife with wars, savage in their ignorance. You would not enjoy it." His fingers came to rest atop the cover. "Thankfully, its ancient knowledge was preserved."

Leonardo opened the book, parting it at a random page. The black ink flowed in a river of Arabic around an illuminated drawing of a fountain, with water streaming from the beak of a peacock into a complicated contraption of gears and pulleys. Francesco knew the remainder of the book was full of such illustrations of other devices, many of them automatons like the French king wanted his master to design.

"The author was Ismail al-Jazari," Leonardo said. "A brilliant artist and the chief engineer for the Artuklu Palace. I suspect there is much I can learn from this book to help me design the French king's golden lion."

A new voice rose behind them. "Perhaps there is another book that will also help you."

Leonardo and Francesco both turned to the library door that they had inadvertently left ajar. A short but robust figure stood at the entrance. His simple white cassock and skullcap shone in the wan light. With the alacrity of youth, Francesco dropped to one knee and bowed his head. Leonardo barely managed to crouch before the figure spoke again.

"Enough of that. Stand, you two."

Francesco straightened but kept his head bowed. "Your Holiness."

Pope Leo X crossed toward them, abandoning a pair of guards at the door. He cradled a thick book in his arms. "I heard about your apprentice rooting through our libraries. And the purpose behind his search. It seems you intend to do your best to please our new guest to the north."

"I've heard King François can be quite demanding," Leonardo admitted.

"And militant," the pope added pointedly. "A tendency I'd prefer he kept to the north. Which means not disappointing his royal highness lest he consider venturing farther south with his soldiers. To avoid that, I thought I'd lend the services of my own staff to your pursuit."

Pope Leo stepped to the table and placed the heavy volume down. "This was found within the Holy Scrinium."

Francesco stiffened in surprise. The Holy Scrinium was the private library of the popes, said to contain amazing volumes, both religious and otherwise, dating back to the founding of Christendom.

"This was acquired during the First Crusade," the pontiff explained as he set the book on the desk. "A Persian volume of mechanical devices from the ninth century of our Lord. I thought it might be of use, much like the volume your apprentice obtained."

Plainly curious, Leonardo opened the book's nondescript cover, its outer title long worn away. Inside, he discovered the name of the author and turned sharply to the pontiff.

"Banū Mūsā," he said, reading the name aloud.

His Holiness nodded, translating the same. "The Sons of Moses."

Francesco opened his mouth with a question, then closed it, too abashed to speak.

Leonardo answered anyway, turning slightly toward Francesco. "The Sons of Moses were three Persian brothers who lived four centuries before Ismail al-Jazari. Al-Jazari acknowledges them by name in his book for their inspiration. I didn't think any copies of this work still existed."

"I don't understand," Francesco whispered, drawing closer. "What is this volume?"

Leonardo placed his hand upon the ancient text. "A true wonder. *The Book of Ingenious Devices*."

"But . . . ? " Francesco looked at the neighboring book, the one he had painstakingly acquired.

"Yes," Leonardo acknowledged, "our esteemed Al-Jazari named his work after this older volume, changing the title only slightly. It's said these three brothers—the Sons of Moses—spent decades collecting and preserving Greek and Roman texts following the fall of the Roman Empire. Over time these brothers built upon the knowledge found within those texts to craft their own book of inventions."

The pope joined them at the desk. "But it wasn't just *scientific* knowledge that interested these brothers." The pontiff flipped to the end of the book and pulled free a folio of loose pages. "What do you make of these?"

Leonardo squinted at the yellowed pages and lines of cursive ink and shook his head. "It's clearly Arabic. But I'm far from fluent. With time, maybe I could—"

The pope's hand waved dismissively. "I've Arab scholars in my employ. They were able to translate the pages. It appears to be the eleventh book of a larger poetic work. The opening lines state *'When we had got down to the seashore, we drew our ship into the water and got her mast and sails into her.'"*

Francesco frowned. *Why did that sound familiar?*

The pontiff continued, reciting the translation from memory. " *'We also put the sheep on board and took our places, weeping and in great distress of mind. Circe, that great and cunning goddess—'* "

Francesco gasped, cutting off the pope, such was his shock.

The name Circe . . . that could only mean one thing.

Leonardo shifted the pages closer and confirmed it. "Are you saying this is a translation of Homer's *Odyssey*?"

His Holiness nodded, appearing amused. "Into Arabic, some nine centuries ago."

If true, Francesco knew this could be the earliest *written* version of Homer's poem. He found his voice again. "But why is this chapter here, tucked in an ancient book of Persian mechanical devices?"

"Perhaps for this reason."

The pope exposed the last page of the folio. An intricate illustration had been hastily inked there. It appeared to be a mechanical map complicated by gears and threaded wires and marked with scrawled Arabic notes. The terrain looked to encompass the breadth of the Mediterranean and beyond. Still, the mechanical map looked incomplete, a work in progress.

"What is it?" Francesco asked.

The pope turned to Leonardo. "It is what I hope *you* can discover, my dear friend. The translators here could only discern a few hints."

"Like what?" Leonardo's eyes shone brightly, the man clearly enraptured by this mystery.

"The first clue." The pope tapped the Arabic pages of Homer's *Odyssey.* "This part of the epic poem tells of Odysseus's voyage to the Underworld, to the lands of Hades and Persephone, to the Greek version of Hell."

Francesco frowned, not understanding.

The pope pointed to the illustrated device and explained. "It seems the Sons of Moses were trying to craft a tool to lead them there." He stared hard at Leonardo. "To the Underworld."

Leonardo made a scoffing noise. "Preposterous."

A chill swept through Francesco. "Why would these brothers seek such a place?"

The pope shrugged. "No one knows, but it is worrisome."

"How so?" Leonardo asked.

The pope faced them, letting him read the sincerity in his eyes, and pointed to the last line below the illustration.

"Because it says here . . . the Sons of Moses found it. They found the entrance to Hell."

FIRST

THE STORM ATLAS

The sea is a boundless expanse whereon great ships look like tiny specks; naught but the heavens above and the waters beneath; when calm, the sailor's heart is broken; when tempestuous, his senses reel. Trust it little. Fear it much. Man at sea is but a worm on a bit of wood, now engulfed, now scared to death.

—AMRU BIN AL-'AS, THE ARAB CONQUEROR OF EGYPT, 640 A.D.

1

The sea fog hid the monster ahead.

As the skiff vanished into the ghostly bank, the morning light dimmed to a grim twilight. Even the rumble of the skiff's outboard motor was muffled by that heavy pall. Within seconds, the temperature dropped precipitously—from a few degrees below zero to a cold that felt like inhaling icy daggers.

Dr. Elena Cargill coughed to keep her lungs from seizing in her chest. She tried to retreat deeper into her bright blue parka, which was zippered over a dry suit to protect her against the deadly cold waters around them. Every loose bit of her white-blond hair was tucked into a thick woolen cap, with a matching scarf around her neck.

What am I doing here?

Yesterday she had been sweating on a dig in northern Egypt, where she and her team had been meticulously unearthing a coastal village that had been half-swallowed by the Mediterranean four millennia ago. It had been a rare honor to lead the joint U.S.-Egyptian team, especially for someone whose thirtieth birthday was still two months off—not that she hadn't earned her place. She had dual PhDs in paleoanthropology and archaeology and had since distinguished herself in the field. In fact, in order to work on the dig, she had declined a teaching position at her alma mater, Columbia University.

Still, she suspected being chosen as team leader was not all due to her academic accomplishments and fieldwork. Her father was Senator Kent Cargill, representing the great state of Massachusetts. Though her father had insisted he had not pulled any strings, he was also a career politician, serving his fourth term, which meant lying came second nature to him. Plus, he was the current chairman of the Committee on Foreign Relations. Whether he said anything or not, his seat on the Senate likely influenced the decision-making process.

How could it not?

Then came this sudden summons to fly to the frozen wilds of Greenland. At least this request had not come from her father but from a colleague, a friend who made a personal plea for her to come inspect a discovery made there. Curiosity more than friendship drew her away from the dig in Egypt, especially the last words from her colleague: *You'll want to see this. You may get to rewrite history.*

So yesterday she had flown from Egypt to Iceland, then took a turboprop plane from Reykjavik to the small village of Tasiilaq, on the southeast coast of Greenland. There she had overnighted at one of the town's two hotels. Over a dinner of seafood stew, she had tried to inquire about the discovery made here, but she got only blank stares or silent shakes of a head.

It seemed only a few locals knew about the new discovery—and none of them were talking. Even this morning, she remained none the wiser.

She now sat on a boat with three strangers, all men, sailing across a dead-calmed fjord into a fog as dense as cold paste. Her friend had left a text this morning, promising to join her in Tasiilaq this afternoon in order to get Elena's assessment on whatever had been discovered here.

Which meant, for now, she was on her own, and clearly out of her depth.

She jumped as a loud roar carried over the water, shivering the flat seas around the skiff. It was as if the monster ahead had sensed their approach. She had heard similar rumblings throughout the night, making it hard to sleep, heightening the tension.

Seated ahead of her, an auburn-bearded mountain of a man twisted back to face her. His cheeks and nose were ice-burned a ruddy red. His yellow parka was unzipped, as if he were oblivious to the cold. He had been introduced as a Canadian climatologist, but she couldn't remember his name. Something Scottish sounding. In her head, she thought of him as McViking. From his cold-toughened face, she had a hard time judging his age. Anywhere from the mid-twenties to early forties.

He waved an arm ahead of him. "Glacialquake," he explained as the rumbling faded away. "Nothing to worry about. Just ice calving and shattering off the face of Helheim Glacier. That mass of ice ahead of us is one of the world's fastest-moving glaciers, flowing some thirty meters a day into the ocean. Last year, a huge chunk of it broke away. Some four miles wide, a mile across, and half a mile thick."

Elena tried to picture an iceberg roughly the size of lower Manhattan floating past their little boat.

The climatologist stared off into the fog. "The quake from that single break lasted a full day and was registered by seismometers around the world."

"And that's supposed to reassure me?" she asked with a shiver.

"Sorry." His face cracked into a huge smile, his green eyes twinkling even in the foggy pall, which immediately made him look far younger. She guessed now he was only a couple of years older than her. She also suddenly remembered his name: Douglas MacNab.

"It's all that activity that drew me up here two years ago," he admitted. "Figured I'd better study it while I still can."

"What do you mean?"

"I've been working with NASA's Operation IceBridge, which uses radar, laser altimeters, and high-resolution cameras to monitor Greenland's glaciers. Specifically Helheim, which has retreated nearly three miles over the past two decades and shrunk three hundred feet in thickness. Helheim acts as a bellwether for all of Greenland. The entire place is melting six times faster than three decades ago."

"And if all of the ice here vanished?"

He shrugged. "The meltwater from Greenland alone would lift sea levels by over twenty feet."

That's over two stories. She pictured her dig site in Egypt and the ancient ruins, half-drowned by the Mediterranean. Would that be the fate soon of many coastal cities?

A new voice intruded from the starboard side of the skiff. "Mac, quit being such an alarmist." The thin, dark-haired man seated across from her sighed heavily. If there was a single word to describe him, it would be *angular.* He looked to be all sharp edges, from elbows and knees to the jut of his chin and high cheekbones.

"Even with current warming trends," the man continued, "what you just described won't happen for centuries, if ever. I've seen your data, and NASA's, and run my own correlations and extrapolations. When it comes to climate and the cyclic nature of planetary temperature, the number of variables in play are too many to make firm—"

"C'mon, Nelson. I wouldn't exactly consider your assessment to be unbiased. Allied Global Mining signs your paychecks."

Elena studied the geologist anew. When she had been introduced to Conrad Nelson, he had made no mention of being employed by a mining company.

"And who funds your grant, Mac?" Nelson countered. "A consortium of environmental groups. That surely has no impact on *your* evaluation."

"Data is data."

"Really? Data can't be skewed? It can't be manipulated to support a biased position?"

"Of course, it can."

Nelson sat straighter, clearly believing he'd made his point, but his opponent wasn't done.

"I've seen AGM do it all the time," MacNab finished.

Nelson raised a middle finger. "Then evaluate this."

"Hmm, looks to me like you're admitting I'm number one."

Nelson scoffed and lowered his arm. "Like I warned you, data can be misinterpreted."

The fog bank suddenly brightened around them and shredded to either side, revealing what lay ahead.

Nelson made his final point. "Look over there. Tell me we're running out of glacier anytime soon."

A hundred yards away the world ended in a wall of ice. The front of the glacier stretched as far as the eye could see. Its shattered face looked like the fortifications of a frozen castle, with hoar-frost encrusted parapets and crumbling towers. The morning sunlight fractured against its surface, revealing a spectrum running from the palest blue to a menacing blackness. Even the air scintillated with tiny ice particles, glittering and flashing as they approached.

"It's massive," Elena said, though the word failed to capture the breadth of the monster.

Mac's smile widened. "Aye. Helheim stretches four miles wide and runs over a hundred miles inland. In places, the ice is over a mile deep. It's one of the largest glaciers draining into the North Atlantic."

"Yet, here it still stands," Nelson said. "As it will for centuries."

"Not when Greenland is losing three hundred gigatons of ice every year."

"Doesn't mean anything. Greenland's ice sheet has ebbed and flowed. From one ice age to another."

Elena tuned out the rest of their argument, especially as it grew more technical. Despite the ongoing debate, she sensed these two men were not enemies. Clearly the two enjoyed their sparring. It took a rare soul to survive this harsh place, which likely forged a commonality of spirit and ruggedness that bonded everyone, including these two scientists on opposite sides of the divide on climate change.

Instead, she turned her attention to her surroundings. She studied the silent bergs filling the channel. The skiff's pilot—an Inuit elder with a leathery round face and unreadable black eyes—expertly navigated them through the maze, while puffing on an ivory pipe, giving each berg a wide berth. She soon discovered why. As one seemingly tiny iceberg capsized, flipping fully over, swinging up a massive shelf of ice, revealing how much of its true mass lurked beneath the blue-black surface. If they'd been near the berg at the time, it would have taken out their boat.

It was a reminder of the hidden dangers here.

Even the glacier's name hinted at the threat.

"Helheim . . ." she mumbled. "The realm of Hel."

Mac heard her. "Exactly. The glacier was named after the Viking's World of the Dead."

"Who gave it that name?"

Nelson blew out a heavy breath. "Who knows? Probably some Nordic researcher with a sardonic sense of humor and a love of Norse mythology."

"I think the source goes back much further," Mac said. "The Inuit believe some glaciers are malignant. Passing warnings from one generation to another. Helheim is one such place. They believe this glacier is home to the *Tuurngaq*, which means 'killing spirit.' Their version of demons."

Their pilot removed his pipe, spat into the sea, and mumbled a warning. "No use that name."

Apparently, such superstitions had not fully died away.

Mac lowered his voice. "I'll wager those old stories were the true source for someone choosing to name this glacier Helheim."

Elena searched around and asked the question nagging at her since she climbed aboard the boat. "Where exactly are we going?"

Mac pointed to a black arch in the ice wall. They were close enough now to make out an opening, a shadowy rift cut into the glacier face. It was framed in azure ice that seemed to glow from within.

"Last week, a large berg calved off there, exposing a huge meltwater channel."

She noted a stream running out of the rift, strong enough to push back the floating icy sludge that rimmed the bottom of the glacier. As they approached, the metal sides of the boat sliced through the loose broken ice with a scream of knives on steel. It set her teeth on edge. A new coldness settled into her bones as she suddenly recognized the trajectory of their boat and the lack of any beach in sight.

"Are . . . are we going to travel *inside* the glacier?" she asked.

Mac nodded. "Straight into the heart of Helheim."

In other words, down to the World of the Dead.

9:54 A.M.

Douglas MacNab kept wary watch on his passenger as they approached the face of the glacier. He cast sidelong glances back at Dr. Cargill, noting how much paler her countenance had grown, how her fingers had tightened on the boat's gunwale.

Hang in there, kid. It'll be worth it.

When he had first been told an archaeologist—a woman—was coming to Greenland from Egypt, he hadn't known what to expect. He vacillated between picturing a female Indiana Jones and some bespectacled academic who would prove to be ill-fitted for such a harsh landscape. He assessed the reality to be somewhere in between. The woman was plainly overwhelmed, but she did not balk. Past the trepidation in her eyes, he recognized a stubborn curiosity.

He also hadn't expected someone so pretty. She was not overly curvaceous or photoshopped polished. Her form was lithe, but muscular, her lips full, her high cheeks rosy in the cold. Small lines crinkled the corners of her eyes, maybe from too much squinting into a desert sun or maybe from long hours of academic reading. Either way, it gave her a studious look, like a stern schoolteacher. He also found himself unduly fascinated by the lock of ice-blond hair poking out from the edge of her woolen cap.

"Mac, eyes forward," Nelson warned him. "Unless you want us to run into a submerged berg."

Mac stiffened and turned fully forward, both to hide the heat rising to his face and to peer into the depths ahead of their skiff. The blue waters had turned a murky brown due to the silty melt of the glacier.

He returned to his job in the bow, watching for any hidden dangers, both in the waters below and across the surrounding calving face. But he knew John Okalik, their Inuit pilot, had a far sharper eye when it came to reading the ice. The native had been plying these treacherous waters since he was a boy, nearly five decades. And his family for generations before that.

Still, Mac kept a closer eye as they drew up to the mouth of the melt-water opening. It stretched ten yards across and climbed twice as high. Another steel-sided boat came into view. It was tucked to one side and roped in place via ice stakes pounded into the wall. Two men sat there with huge-barreled rifles in their laps.

John stood up at the stern and chatted quickly with the pair, relatives of his, which pretty much defined everyone from the village of Tasiilaq.

As they spoke, Mac looked back and forth, trying to follow the conversation. He was somewhat fluent in Kalaallisut, the main Inuit language of Greenland, but the men here were using the dialect of their local tribe, the Tunumiit.

Their pilot finally settled back to his seat by the tiller.

"So, John, we're good?" Mac asked.

"My cousins say yes. River still open."

John goosed the motor and slipped past the other boat to enter the meltwater channel. The grumble of the outboard amplified in the enclosed space as the skiff fought the current.

Mac noted Elena staring back at the shrinking arch of sunlight—and at the armed pair. "Why the guards?" she asked. "Do we have to worry about polar bears swimming out there?"

It was a reasonable guess. There remained a persistent threat of those giant white carnivores, especially with their astounding ability to swim long distances—though the shrinking Arctic ice pack was straining even their considerable ability.

"Not bears," Mac answered her. "Once we get to the site, you'll understand."

"Where—?"

"It's not much farther," he promised. "And I think it's best you see it without any expectations." He glanced to Nelson. "It's how we discovered it. I came in here three days ago with Nelson, mostly for the adventure of it, but also to better understand what's going on underneath Helheim's frozen white face. Drilling out mile-deep cores and analyzing the ancient gasses trapped in the old ice can only give you so much information. Here was a rare chance to travel to the source, to the heart of the glacier."

Nelson spoke as he struggled to open his watertight pack. "I came along to take samples at this depth, searching for any mineral treasures ground up by this massive ice shovel carving its way across the face of Greenland."

"What's even out here?" Elena asked him.

Nelson grunted as he finally tugged open the wax-sealed zipper. "Greenland's true wealth lies not in the amount of freshwater trapped as ice, but what is hiding beneath it. A cornucopia of untapped riches. Gold, diamonds and rubies, huge veins of copper and nickel. Rare earth elements. It promises to be a huge boon to Greenland and those that live here."

"Not to mention filling the deep pockets of AGM," Mac added pointedly.

Nelson dismissed this with a derisive snort as he extracted a handheld device and set about calibrating it.

Elena turned her attention to the tunnel. The blue ice grew ever darker as they continued deeper. "How far does this tunnel go?"

"All the way to the rocky coastline," Mac said. "We're traveling through a tongue of ice that extends three-quarters of a mile out from the shore."

10:02 A.M.

Oh, god . . .

Elena's breathing grew heavier with this news. She tried to imagine the weight of ice above her head, remembering Mac's description of a berg the size of lower Manhattan calving off this glacier.

What if that happened while we're inside here?

It eventually became so dark Mac switched on a light at the bow of the boat, casting a beam far down the tunnel, igniting the ice to a bluish glow, revealing darker veins within, like some ancient map, marking traceries of mineral deposits scoured from the distant coast.

She took a deep breath, doing her best to calm her nerves. While she had no problem crawling her way into tombs, this was different. Ice was everywhere. She tasted it on her tongue, drew it in with every breath. It encircled her completely. She was inside the ice; the ice was inside her.

Finally, a glow appeared out of the darkness, beyond the reach of the bow lamp.

Mac glanced back to her, confirming what she hoped. "We're almost there."

With a final whine of the motor, the skiff rode up the river to where blue ice ended in an archway of black rock. The meltwater channel continued farther, flowing down a series of cascades formed of broken stones and ice. But a single battery-powered lamp pole marked the end of their journey, a lone lighthouse in a frozen world.

Elena gasped at the sight illuminated before her. It was as if this lighthouse had lured a ship to this cold harbor.

"This is impossible," she managed to eke out.

John angled their skiff to an eddy at the side of the river, where Mac roped their bow to a stake screwed into the ice wall.

Elena stood up, balancing herself, oblivious to the dangers of the icy waters. She craned her neck to take in the breadth of the huge wooden ship, its keel and planks turned black with age.

"How could this be here?" she mumbled.

Mac helped her from the boat to a spit of wet rock. "If I had to guess, the sailors sought shelter in what was once a sea cave." He waved an arm to the black rock that hung over their heads. "They must have gotten trapped here, become frozen in place, until eventually the ice swallowed them completely."

"How long ago was that?" Elena asked.

"From the age of the ice," Nelson said, as he climbed out to join them, "we estimate it was shipwrecked around the ninth century."

Mac stared back at her. "Everyone thought Christopher Columbus discovered the New World in 1492. Then he lost that title when it was discovered the Vikings had settled in Greenland and northern Canada in the late tenth century."

"If you're correct about the age, it would mean this ship landed a full century earlier," Elena said. "And this is no Viking ship."

"That's what we thought, too, but we're no experts."

Nelson nodded. "That's why you're here."

Elena now understood. While she had a dual degree in paleoanthropology and archaeology, her specialty was in *nautical* archaeology. It was why she was picked to unearth the Egyptian port city swallowed by the Mediterranean. Her field of interest was in pushing back the date when humankind first dared to ply the seas. She remained endlessly fascinated by such endeavors and the engineering history behind each advancement. It was a passion likely instilled in her as a girl, when she and her father used to sail each summer off Martha's Vineyard. She still cherished those childhood memories, those rare moments when the two could spend quality time together. Even in college, she had been part of her university's crew team, rowing scull to an Ivy League championship.

"Any guesses as to where this ship came from?" Mac asked.

"I don't have to guess." She headed toward the exposed stern of the boat. The forward bow was still encased in ice. "Look at how the sheathing planks are stitched together. Even the bindings are coconut rope. It's all a very characteristic design."

"Did you say *coconut*?"

She nodded and stepped toward where a pair of masts had broken long ago and now stuck out of the cave like two flags. The torn remnants of their sails were still preserved. "Those two lateen sails . . . they're made of palm-leaf matting."

Nelson frowned. "Coconut and palm leaves. So definitely *not* Vikings."

"No, this is a Sambuk. One of the largest dhows of the Arab world. This one appears to even have a deck up there, which makes it one of the rare oceanic merchant vessels of the Arab world."

"If you're right," Mac said, "which I don't doubt, then this discovery could prove it was Arabs, not Vikings, who first set foot here."

She wasn't ready to assert that. Not until she could carbon-date the vessel. Still, her friend—the colleague who had urged her to come here—had been right. This discovery had the potential to rewrite history.

Nelson followed her, waving his handheld device. "Unfortunately, these poor sailors never made it back home to tell their story."

"Or at least, *one* didn't," Mac added. "We found only a single body aboard the ship. No telling what happened to the rest."

Elena turned sharply back, nearly blinded as Mac flicked on a flashlight. "So, you've been inside?"

Mac pointed toward where a boulder had cracked open the side of the hull. "It's the other reason you were recommended. This isn't all we discovered. Follow me."

He led the way to the trapped ship and twisted sideways to fold his large form through the crack in the hull. "Careful where you step and try not to brush against any supports. We're lucky this boat wasn't crushed flat by the ice. The roof of this cave must have protected it all this time."

Elena climbed in after Mac, with Nelson trailing. John stayed with the boat, still smoking his pipe. With the motor switched off, the place was now deathly quiet, as if the world were holding its breath. As her ears adjusted, though, she could still hear the ice. The walls moaned and sighed. A low grinding echoed throughout the tunnels as if some massive beast were gnashing its teeth.

The reminder of the danger tempered her excitement—but not enough to stop her from exploring the ancient ship.

Mac's flashlight illuminated the main hold, which was supported by ice-blackened timbers. They crossed quickly through this dead forest. The air had a vague oily smell, like mineral spirits or gasoline. To either side, giant earthenware jars stood shoulder-high, lining the curve of the walls.

One had shattered long ago, looking as if it had exploded from the inside. She caught a stronger whiff of wet asphalt as she passed it, but any evaluation of the contents would have to wait.

Clearly her guide had a goal in mind.

Mac led them toward the boat's bow, where steps led up to a door in a wooden wall. "We guessed this was the captain's quarters."

He climbed and entered first, bowing low to pass through. Once inside, he stepped aside and offered his hand to help her up. She took it, already feeling weak-kneed by the breathless excitement of it all. Along with a measure of terror.

She joined Mac in the windowless quarters. Shelves lined either side, where books and scrolls had long decayed into moldering ruins. A desk filled the forward part of the tiny cabin, abutting the arch of the ship's wooden prow.

"Might want to brace yourself for this," Mac warned.

He shifted his large bulk so she would approach the desk. She took a step forward, then back again. A chair stood before the desk. But it was not empty. A figure sat there, nestled in a fur cloak made from the hide of a polar bear. His upper body lay collapsed across the desktop, his cheek resting against the surface.

She took a deep steadying breath. She had examined mummies during her time in Egypt, even dissected a few. But the body here was far more disturbing. The skin had turned to blackened leather, nearly the same hue as the ancient desktop. It looked as if body and desk were one. Yet, at the same time, the body appeared perfectly preserved, down to the eyelashes framing the white globes. She almost expected him to blink.

"It seems the captain went down with the ship," Nelson said distractedly, his focus on his handheld device.

"Maybe he wanted to protect this." Mac shifted his beam to follow the corpse's arms draped atop the desk. Skeletal hands framed a large square metal box, easily two feet wide on each side and half a foot thick. Its surface was stained as black as everything else and looked to be hinged on the far side.

"What is it?" Elena drew alongside Mac, taking some comfort from the solidness of his presence.

"You tell me."

He reached across the body and lifted the lid. Light blazed forth from within—but as she blinked away the glare, she realized the brightness was only the flashlight's beam reflecting off the golden inner surface.

Shocked at what was revealed, she leaned closer. "It's a map." She studied the three-dimensional rendering of seas and oceans, of continents and islands. She traced the main body of water in the center, which was rendered in priceless blue lapis lazuli. "That has to be the Mediterranean."

The revealed map encompassed not only the breadth of the sea but all of Northern Africa, the Middle East, and the full measure of the European continent and surrounding oceans. The map extended out into the Atlantic, but not as far as Iceland or Greenland.

These sailors traveled beyond the edge of their map.

But why? Were they explorers searching for new lands? Had they been blown off course? Were they fleeing a threat? A hundred other questions filled her head.

At the top of the gold map, an elaborate silver device was imbedded there. It was spherical, six inches in diameter, half buried in the gold map. Its surface was divided by curved clockwork arms and encircled by longitudinal and latitudinal bands, all inscribed with Arabic symbols and numbers.

"What is it?" Mac asked, having noted her attention.

"It's an astrolabe. A device used by navigators and astronomers to help determine both a ship's time and position, even identify stars and planets." She glanced back to Mac. "Most of the earliest astrolabes were simple in design, just flat discs. This spherical design . . . it's centuries ahead of its time."

"And that's not all," Mac said. "Watch this."

He reached to where the dead captain's hand rested near the flank of the box. He flicked a lever there, and a ticking arose from inside. The astrolabe began to slowly turn on its own, driven by a hidden mechanism.

Movement drew her eyes to the gemstone rendering of the Mediterranean. A tiny silver ship began to glide away from what was modern-day Turkey and across the blue sea.

"What do you make of that?" he asked.

She shook her head, as mystified as Mac.

Nelson cleared his throat. "Guys. Maybe we'd better leave that be."

They both turned to him. His gaze was fixed on the screen of his handheld device. He thumbed a dial, and a quiet clicking rose from it.

"What's wrong?" Mac asked.

"I mentioned all the resources buried here in Greenland, waiting to be extracted. I failed to mention one. *Uranium*." He lifted his device higher. "I forgot to bring a Geiger counter the first time we came down here and thought I'd use this opportunity to correct that mistake."

Elena stared upward, trying to peer through the deck to the rock and ice beyond. "Are you saying we're standing in the middle of a uranium deposit?"

"No. This is the first time I got a reading. After Mac opened the box." He reached down and held the Geiger counter closer to the map. The clicking became more rapid and louder. "That device is radioactive."

Mac swore and quickly slammed the box closed.

They all retreated.

"How hot is it?" Mac asked.

"About the equivalent of a chest X-ray for every minute you're exposed."

"Then let's leave it here for now." Mac herded them back into the ship's hold. "We'll continue to keep guards posted at the channel entrance in case word of this treasure reaches the wrong ears. We can come back later with some lead shielding and extract the device. Get it somewhere safe."

They clambered out of the frozen ship and back to the shore of the icy river. Mac's plan made sense, but Elena hated any delay. She stared longingly back at the stranded ship, anxious to know its history.

As she turned around, a thunderous boom shook through the channel. The river sloshed its banks. Chunks of ice crashed into the water.

She hurried closer to Mac. "Another glacialquake?"

"No . . ."

As the blast echoed away, a new noise reached them. Rapid popping, like a chain of firecrackers going off.

She stared up at Mac.

"That's gunfire," he said and took her hand. "We're under attack."

2

Who the hell thought this was a good idea?

Joe Kowalski huffed loudly and sank his large bulk deeper into the steaming heat of the hot spring. Sweat pebbled his brow. His fingertips had desiccated into sickly prunes. Curling his lip with distaste, he inhaled the rotten-egg odor of the sulfurous waters. He feared he'd stink like this all day.

So much for a romantic detour.

That was the excuse his girlfriend, Maria Crandall, had given for stopping at the Blue Lagoon. The resort lay nestled within a black lava field, dotted with mounds of mossy green. It was also positioned halfway between Iceland's Keflavík International Airport—where they had landed an hour ago—and the smaller domestic airfield just at the edge of Reykjavik, which offered the only flights to Greenland. Unfortunately, the next scheduled departure wasn't for another three hours.

So, Maria had suggested this side trip while they waited.

With a sigh, he rolled his forearm out of the water to check the time—then shook his head at his bare wrist. His missing watch reminded him of the three warnings given to them upon checking into this corner of the resort, called the Retreat.

First, they were told that in order to preserve the purity of the waters, they would be required to shower naked before entering the baths. It was the only part of the experience he had appreciated. He remembered soaping every square inch of Maria's sleek body in their private changing room's shower, appreciating her curves as she leaned on one long leg, the way she twisted her wet blond hair into a pile atop her head, how her breasts would lift with each . . .

Nope. He shifted his bulk. *Best think of something else right now.*

This was a public pool.

To distract himself, he remembered *why* he was even here in the first place.

The second warning about this resort concerned cell phones. Such devices were forbidden within the confines of the interconnected pools. Kowalski was fine with this. Especially considering it had been an unwelcome call from his boss, Director Painter Crowe, that had set him on this path from sultry Africa to the icy freeze of Greenland.

He and Maria had been visiting the Congo, where they were scheduled to spend a week at Virunga National Park. Maria had been hoping to visit— or at the very least, *spot*—Baako, the western lowland gorilla she had released into the wild two years ago. He had hoped for the same. The big hairy lug had left an ape-sized hole in his heart. So, he had to hide his disappointment when Painter had called about some discovery in Iceland and wanted Maria's input. Maria had dual degrees in genomics and behavioral sciences, with a specialty in all things prehistoric. It seemed an ancient ship with a priceless treasure had been found deep within the ice of Greenland. Maria was immediately intrigued and suggested they recruit a former colleague of hers from Columbia University, a friend who specialized in nautical archaeology.

They were due to meet up with her in Greenland as soon as they landed. He almost checked the time again, then remembered the third warning about this place. The geothermal seawater was rich in caustic silica and risked damaging anything metallic. That meant any chains, rings, watches would have to be left in the changing room. Which included his cheap Timex.

But that wasn't the most disappointing item he had to abandon.

He sulked deeper into the water.

He had thought the reunion with Baako might have made for the perfect moment. Then that got screwed up. So, when Maria suggested a romantic detour to these hot springs, it sounded like a great fallback position. He had pictured palm trees, bubbling baths, glasses of champagne. He scowled at the reality: an interconnected series of concrete swimming pools filled with sulfurous waters, all surrounded by severe cliffs of black volcanic rock.

He shook his head.

Maybe it's not meant to be.

Maria was certainly out of his league.

He was just a navy seaman who had stumbled his way into an elite covert group tied to DARPA. His fellow Sigma teammates had been pulled from various special forces groups and retrained in scientific fields. He only had a GED and an innate skill at blowing things up, which cast him as the unit's demolitions expert. Though he was proud of his role, he could also not escape a deep vein of insecurity—of being a fraud. Sigma's symbol was the Greek letter Σ, which represented the "sum of the best," the merging of brain and brawn, of soldier and scientist. But Kowalski knew Sigma counted far more on the thickness of his bicep than on the sharpness of his mind.

And I can accept that.

But he feared someone else would not.

A sharp whistle drew his attention to Maria's slim figure as she swam on her back, scissor-kicking her legs to propel her toward him. She impressively held aloft a drink in each raised arm.

"How about giving a girl a hand, big guy?"

He smirked and gave her a slow clap. "You know you ought to throw away your lab coat and start waitressing. Especially in that bikini. You'll make a fortune."

She slid up beside him and sat on the submerged bench, not spilling a drop from either glass. "Take this."

He accepted the tall glass filled with some sickly green concoction. "I'm guessing this is not beer."

"Sorry. It's all healthy living here."

"So, you got me a mug of algae."

"It's fresh. They scraped it off the bottom of the pool this morning."

He glanced at her to see if she was serious.

She rolled her eyes and leaned against him. "It's a smoothie, jackass. Kale, spinach, I think . . ."

He held his glass away. "I think I'd rather have the pool algae."

"There might be some in there actually. But they blended it with *bananas*. Which only seemed appropriate, considering . . ." She lifted her glass and tapped it against his. "To Baako."

He sniffed the contents with a grimace. "Ugh. I don't think even a starving gorilla would drink this."

"Not even when I bribed the bartender into adding three shots of rum to yours?"

"Really . . . ?" He reconsidered his drink and took a sip. He tasted the banana—then the sweet burn of rum on his tongue and up his nose. He nodded his approval.

Not half bad.

She took a deep swig from hers and turned those deep blue eyes toward him. "Of course, I had them put *four* shots in mine."

He gave her a wounded look.

Her hand slid up his bare legs and under the edge of his trunks. "I can't let you get *too* intoxicated. I have plans for you when we get back to that shower. And I know you can't hold your liquor for sh—"

"Excuse me," a voice said behind them.

Kowalski hadn't even heard the slim man in a Blue Lagoon polo approach behind them. He hated being caught off guard, especially now.

"What is it, bub?" he barked a tad harshly.

The man lowered a tray with a cell phone resting atop it. "I'm sorry to disturb you, but the caller said it was an emergency."

Kowalski met Maria's eyes over the tray.

The caller could only be one person.

Maria slid her hand off his thigh. "The director seems determined to keep interrupting us."

More like cock-blocking.

Kowalski took the phone and held it to his ear. "What's wrong now?"

12:40 P.M.

Back in the private changing room, Maria buffed her hair dry with a towel. She avoided the dryer on the dressing table, fearing the loud blower would keep them from hearing the ring of the satellite phone.

A few minutes ago, Director Crowe had used the resort's house line to tell them there was trouble in Greenland and to expect a fuller briefing on Joe's encrypted phone once they got somewhere private.

But she had already heard enough.

Trouble in Greenland . . .

Fearing the worst, her breath had grown tight in her chest. She had been the one to suggest Elena check out the shipwreck.

If anything's happened to her . . .

In the mirror, she watched Joe as he climbed back into his black jeans. Crossing to the rest of his clothes, he scratched at the damp mat of hair on his chest that did little to hide the mass of his pectorals and the well-defined ridges of his abdomen. With a grunt, he hauled on a gray hoodie and slapped a Yankees ball cap over the stubble of his shaved head.

As he turned back to her, she tried to read the hard planes of his face, the firmness of his lips under the slight crook of his nose. But all she sensed was an impatience that equaled her own. He stepped to the dressing table, his six-foot-plus frame looming next to her. She elbowed him back a step, both to reach her own blouse and to give herself more room to breathe. Joe filled whatever room he entered. Sometimes it was too much.

"You okay?" he asked.

She hid the warmth rising to her cheeks as she buttoned her shirt. "Just worried. I hate this waiting."

"She'll be okay."

"You don't know that," she snapped back.

She shoved her feet into a pair of worn hiking boots, her anxiety burning toward anger. She knew Joe was just trying to reassure her, to protect her feelings, but it was a trait that was beginning to grate on her.

When they'd first met two years ago, she had found the guy exciting—dangerous even—certainly unlike the men she had dated before. Then again, her pool of candidates in the academic world had been limited to a more intellectual set—until this huge beast burst into her world. Loud, brash, addicted to the foulest cigars. She had never imagined herself attracted to such a man. But he made her laugh—often and deeply. And sure, the physicality of the guy was intoxicating. The sex was mind-blowing.

But was that all there was?

During that tumultuous first meeting, she had caught hints of a hidden depth to the man, especially in his interactions with the young gorilla Baako. There was a tenderness that showed through small cracks of his tough demeanor, especially when he communicated in sign language to the gorilla. The two had become like father and son. But over the past months, those tender cracks had seemed to seal up. It was one of the reasons she had suggested Joe accompany her on this trip to Africa. She had hoped a reunion with Baako might break through whatever callus had formed, to let what was buried and hidden shine forth again.

But that had not happened.

It made her wonder if there was any future here?

And more important—do I even want that?

She had grown up with an identical twin sister, Lena. Though Maria loved the intimacy of a relationship that could only come from two who shared the same womb, the same DNA, she also fought against that genetic codependency. She craved independence, to be her own person, to be free of anyone's shadow.

Then Joe came into her life. A man who naturally cast a huge shadow—and not just physically. Of late, he had become more and more overprotective, bordering on possessive.

To make matters worse, he had seemed more closed off these past weeks, barely speaking to her beyond grunts. Maybe the novelty of their relationship had subsided, and he'd become bored with her.

Or am I bored with him?

Before she could give this more thought, the satellite phone rang loudly.

Joe snatched up the device and moved next to her. He bent low so she could eavesdrop. "You've got us both," Joe said. "What the hell's happening out there?"

"I don't mean to alarm you, but ten minutes ago, we received a report of gunfire, maybe an explosion at the glacier where Dr. Cargill was investigating the archaeological site."

Maria tensed. *Oh, god . . .*

"But the entire coast is socked in with a thick fog, so we've got no visuals. It could just be hunters or someone scaring off a polar bear. Still, I'm not taking any chances. The closest village—Tasiilaq—has a small police force, but they're involved with a search-and-rescue mission far inland. Still, the one officer left in town was dispatched to investigate."

"What do you want us to do?"

"I want your boots on the ground out there ASAP. I contacted the navy. Although the U.S. had decommissioned its base in Iceland, we were recently granted permission to station a few P-8 Poseidon maritime patrol planes to monitor Russian submarine activity up in the Arctic."

"Let me guess," Joe said. "We're hitching a ride."

"A Poseidon is fueling on the tarmac at the international airport. The jet can get you to the Kulusk airport—which is fifteen miles from Tasiilaq—in forty-five minutes. There a helicopter will be waiting to take you over to the glacier, weather permitting."

Maria heard the director's stress on those last two words. "What about the weather?"

"Patterns are rapidly shifting out there. An unseasonal piteraq is building inland and could strike the coast in the next two to three hours."

"What's a piteraq?" she asked.

"A fierce windstorm. They can blow a hundred miles per hour with gusts twice that. If it strikes, it'll ground all aircraft along the entire coast."

Joe snorted. "And you want us to duck under that hurricane before it shuts down the place."

"You're the only ones who can get there in time," Painter admitted. "In the meantime, I'm mobilizing everyone here in D.C. in case things go sideways. I'm hoping that won't be the case."

"But you're not taking any chances," Maria added.

"And you know why."

She did. Dr. Elena Cargill was not just a good friend; she was also a senator's daughter. Maria shifted to catch Joe's eye, to let him see her fear, her guilt.

And I put her in harm's way.

3

Elena shivered in the cold darkness of the ancient dhow's hold. Terror had driven her heart into her throat, while her mind spun with a dizzying array of possible escape scenarios: *flee farther up the river channel, hide in a crack in the ice, try to swim past who was coming.*

She came to only one conclusion.

We're trapped.

Mac and the geologist Nelson sheltered in the ship with her. They flanked the crack in the hull, while John lay on his stomach between them, armed with their only weapon. As gunfire echoed to them, the Inuit had slipped a shotgun from under the seat in the skiff's stern before they all retreated here.

Now it had gone deadly quiet.

The blasts had stopped a minute ago, but she was under no misconception that the attackers had been driven off. From the ferocity of the firefight, there had to be a score of assailants. And from the loud explosion that shook ice, the thieves had come with more than just assault rifles. Likely grenades. Finally, a loud scream had punctuated the end of the assault, which made John flinch, a reminder that the man's cousins had been guarding the channel's entrance.

With a deadly focus, John kept his cheek fixed to the stock of his shotgun, the double barrels aimed down the length of the meltwater channel. Next to him lay a leather bandolier holding red shells. *Eleven total.* Not counting the two rounds already loaded in the chambers. Mac had told her each shell was a solid lead slug versus being full of loose shot. The rounds were designed to punch a hole through a polar bear.

Still, even this formidable weapon would not hold off a large force.

They needed another plan.

Nelson finally offered one, a possibility she had not even considered. "Why don't we just give the bastards that gold map?" he said. "Place it out at the water's edge for them to take. As priceless as it is, it's still not worth us dying over."

Elena balked at this. She hated to lose such a significant historical artifact. "Will handing it over make them leave? They might believe there's more treasure than just that map."

"She's right," Mac said. "There's no telling who leaked the news of our discovery or how inflated the story got before it reached these thieves' ears."

"Still, it's worth trying, isn't it?" Nelson pressed. "From our hiding place, we can do our best to convince them that there is no other treasure. And if our words don't work, there's always John's loud and deadly counterpoint. They may prefer to haul ass out of here with something worth millions versus another protracted fight."

"True," Mac conceded and glanced over to Elena. He kept a palm shielded over the beam of his flashlight, but she read his apologetic look. "As Nelson said, it's worth trying. It's not like we have a lot of cards to play here."

Elena crossed her arms, still unconvinced but plainly outvoted.

"Okay, then let's grab it," Nelson said. "Before it's too late."

The geologist headed toward the ship's bow, drawing Elena with him.

Mac held back long enough to reassure John. "We'll be right back."

When Mac joined them, he lowered his hand from his flashlight. Elena blinked away the sudden glare. Stumbling a step, she crushed a potsherd under her boot heel. She instinctively cringed at the damage. An archaeologist's primary goal was to preserve what history had kept safe for centuries.

She stared down at the scatter of other pieces of broken pottery across the bottom of the hold. Her gaze swept toward one of the towering earthenware pots that lined the boat's hold. While this pot had broken a long time ago, the others appeared to be intact, topped by clay lids.

Mac noted her attention. "We examined them. They're sealed with wax." He pointed his flashlight to the shattered one. "From the petroleum smell still lingering there, I'm guessing they're filled with some type of fuel. Maybe whale oil. We didn't want to break one to find out."

She appreciated his caution and prayed she lived long enough to discover if he was right. As she started to turn away, a soft tapping drew her attention back to one of the intact pots. It sounded like something was inside.

What the hell?

"Let's go," Nelson urged, clearly deaf to the noise.

Mac swung his light away and followed. She kept with them, shaking her head, dismissing the tapping as an acoustic trick in the darkness.

Probably just water dripping on the deck overhead.

She and the two men hurried toward the captain's cabin.

Nelson reached it first, climbed the stairs, and entered the cramped room. He quickly crossed to the closed metal box atop the desk.

Elena lingered in the doorway, remembering the geologist's warning about the radioactive nature of the device. Its internal gears were still *ticking* as it rested on the desktop. When they had fled earlier, they must have left its tiny lever turned to the "on" position.

As Nelson reached the desk, Elena warned him. "Maybe we should turn the device off. I don't think it should be moved while it's operating. Any jarring could damage the internal mechanism."

Nelson scowled. "What does it matter? So, the thieves leave with a broken map. I'm not going to cry over their loss. I expect they'll just strip it and melt the gold and silver down for a quick sale."

Mac passed Elena his flashlight and shoved up next to Nelson. "Still, let's turn the thing off."

In their haste, the two men got in each other's way. Nelson ended up elbowing the frost-mummified body of the captain. The chair toppled, taking the corpse with it.

Elena cringed at the crash, at the leaden thud of frozen flesh. With the impact, something flew off the captain's lap and landed near her toes. She crouched and picked up a rectangular package. It was wrapped in sealskin, with the edges hardened with old wax. Clearly someone had tried to preserve the contents against the elements, and the captain had kept it close, all but cradling it with his own body as he died.

Sensing it was important, she pushed it into her coat and tugged her waterproof zipper higher. She straightened and watched Nelson and Mac lift the large map box. From her low vantage, she spotted a bronze rod pop up from the desk's surface, apparently spring-loaded and held in place by the weight of the gold map.

Uh-oh . . .

She had read of booby traps being sprung by careless trespassers in Egyptian tombs. She tried to warn them. "Don't mo—"

A loud gong sounded inside the desk.

Startled, both men tried to back away. Nelson lost hold of one corner of the heavy box. It tilted wildly in his arms. The unlatched lid fell open.

Time slowed as Elena watched the delicate silver astrolabe roll out of its cradle in the map and drop toward the floor. Mac spotted it fall. He crashed to one knee, balanced the box on his thigh, and caught the softball-sized sphere in one large hand.

He expelled a huge sigh of relief.

In the stunned silence that followed, a new noise erupted. The Geiger counter hanging from Nelson's belt burst forth with rapid clicking, far more furious than before.

"Close it up!" Nelson shouted.

Mac shoved the astrolabe into his parka's pocket, and the two men regained a secure hold on the box. Nelson flipped the lid shut, but the Geiger's clicking continued unabated. They all shared scared glances. Had the booby trap ignited something volatile in the heart of the device?

Mac nodded toward the cabin's door and got them moving. "Let's get this dumped outside before it blows up or something."

Elena led the way, guiding with the flashlight. The beam lit the dark depths of the ship's hold. Motion drew her eye to the roof. Large bronze hammers, hidden among the deck rafters, swung down on levered wooden beams. One after the other they slammed into the tall earthenware pots. The hammerheads punched holes in the sides. Cracks splintered outward from the impacts.

As she stood there, a black oily liquid flooded out of the giant pots, spilling across the curved bottom of the boat.

"Go, go, go!" Mac shouted.

Elena got moving again and rushed forward. As she crossed the ship's hold, the flashlight illuminated phosphorescent green veins streaming through the black oil. There was an unnaturalness to that sheen. Definitely not whale oil.

This was confirmed when Nelson's Geiger counter clicked even faster, matching the pounding of her heart.

"Christ, it's glowing," Mac said.

It took Elena another breath to understand. As the men passed with the radioactive box, the oil responded. The green veins shone with a sickly radiance, as if the emissions from the map were exciting an unstable component in the oil.

Elena slowed, but Nelson forced her from behind. "Keep moving!" he shouted. "Just get the hell out of here!"

"Wait," she said. "Listen."

Above the ticking of the Geiger counter, a strange sound echoed throughout the hold. She had heard it before. A quiet tapping. It seemed to rise from several of the pots now and sounded more like *scratching*—as if something was trying to claw its way out of those pots.

She stared back at the men. "What is—?"

A loud boom made her jump and swing around.

Across the hold, John fired his shotgun again.

Oh, no.

Mac set the box down. "You both stay here," he warned and skirted low toward the crack in the hull.

Clutching the flashlight, Elena watched the toxic oil seep toward her. Despite the Geiger's clicking, all she heard was that macabre scratching, like scabrous nails on a chalkboard. Goose bumps pebbled her arms. She did not know what they had triggered with that booby trap, but in her bones, she knew one certain truth.

We should not be here.

10:59 A.M.

Mac dropped flat next to John.

The Inuit elder loaded two more shells into the shotgun's breech without looking down. His gaze remained fixed on the cascading flow of the neighboring meltwater channel. Multiple glows lit the icy depths, marking the presence of divers. Closer at hand, a dark body bled on the icy shore, outfitted in an insulated dry suit.

The bastards swam here.

Or at least, a forward assault party.

Mac heard the rev of an engine deeper down the channel, growing louder with every breath. Clearly others were coming, dashing any hope that John's cousins had survived.

To either side of the channel, two of the underwater glows grew brighter. Black assault rifles rose low in the azure waters and strafed the side of the ancient ship. But the icy timbers held fast.

John blasted toward one of the snipers, but the shooter sank away, while the other focused his fire at the Inuit elder. Rounds peppered closer, ricocheting off the rocks. John rolled and aimed toward the source, but the second assailant was already sinking back into the depths. Elsewhere, another trio of lights brightened the water.

Mac knew the combatants could keep up this deadly game of underwater Whac-A-Mole until John ran out of shells. He placed a hand on his friend's shoulder. "Leave it," he warned. "Save your ammo until it can do the most good."

John grunted in acknowledgment as he reloaded.

Mac settled next to him.

Let's see how this plays out.

Clearly these were not simply thieves. This team was too organized, too well outfitted.

The grumble of an approaching motor filled the tunnel. A black Zodiac pontoon boat sped into view—then hung in place in the current, hovering just at the edge of the meager light.

A bullhorn blasted from it.

"HAND OVER THE STORM ATLAS AND YOU WILL LIVE!"

Mac frowned. He pictured the gold map. Was that the Storm Atlas? If the attackers already had a name for it, they clearly knew far more about it than Mac's group.

So, definitely not ordinary thieves.

This was further confirmed by the next command: "HAVE DR. CARGILL CARRY IT TO MY MEN."

Mac flinched. How did the bastards know Elena was here?

"FOLLOW THESE SIMPLE INSTRUCTIONS, AND ALL WILL END WELL."

Yeah, right. Try telling that to John's cousins.

"YOU HAVE ONE MINUTE TO DECIDE."

A scuffle and scrape behind him drew his attention. Elena and Nelson came forward, hauling the map box between them.

"I'll do it," Elena said. "It's not like we have much choice. They can easily take it if they want to."

Nelson nodded. "We don't have the firepower to stop them."

Mac rolled to face the pair. "That atlas—or whatever it's called—is the only reason they haven't come in here guns blazing. They clearly don't want to damage it. But once they have possession of it . . ."

"Then all bets are off," Elena finished.

"Still, we can buy extra time by cooperating," Nelson said. "Every minute we're still breathing, we have a chance. Otherwise, we're dead already."

Mac considered this. If nothing else, the enemy seemed to want Elena, maybe for her knowledge, maybe because she was a senator's daughter and they planned to use her as leverage. Either way, if the shit hit the fan, she might still live. And besides, Mac could think of no other solution. Especially with everything happening so fast. And maybe Nelson was right. With more time, he might think of something.

The bullhorn sounded a final warning. "TEN SECONDS!"

Okay, he definitely needed *more* than ten seconds—but one step at a time.

"Fine," Mac conceded. "We'll play along."

For now.

11:12 A.M.

Elena struggled with the box as she crossed from the ship toward the water's edge. The large map weighed at least seventy to eighty pounds, far too much for her to manage on her own, so Nelson had agreed to accompany her. Despite her terror, a corner of her mind dwelled on the mystery in her hands.

The Storm Atlas. Why was it called that? And how did these strangers know its name?

Curiosity tempered her terror—but only slightly.

As she and Nelson neared the meltwater river, a trio of divers rose from the icy stream. Assault rifles were fixed to their cheeks. Tiny lamps flanked their masks, shining brightly in the dim light.

The centermost figure approached. Once close enough, he waved his weapon's barrel from Nelson to the ancient dhow. "Put down. Go now."

"All right, all right," the geologist mumbled.

She and Nelson lowered the map box to the rocky shore. The geologist gave her a worried look and retreated toward the dark shelter of the ship. As he did, the gunman aimed his rifle at her chest. He didn't need to tell her to stay.

She stood, shivering.

One of the attackers, standing calf-deep in the current, lifted a wrist radio to his lips. She heard a smattering of what sounded like Arabic. Though fluent in a handful of dialects, she could not make out the man's words due to the rumbling cascade behind her.

In response to his call, the motor of the pontoon boat growled to a higher pitch. The vessel shot forward, aiming straight for her. As it neared, she counted five on board. All outfitted in dry suits. One manned the tiller in the stern. Two leaned out over the black pontoons with deadly rifles raised. Between them, in the bow, stood a mismatched pair. A wall of muscle towered over a smaller, slim figure with a bullhorn in hand.

Clearly the team leader.

As the nose of the Zodiac reached the water's edge, the leader tossed the bullhorn aside and leaped gracefully to shore. Only now did Elena realize it was a woman. The tight-fitting black wetsuit left little doubt as to her gender. A neoprene hood covered most of her head, but from her ample cheekbones, dark eyes, and a caramel complexion, she had to be Middle Eastern.

Elena glanced back at the ancient dhow, then to the map.

Is that why this group—clearly all Middle Eastern—knew so much about this treasure?

She couldn't help but be intrigued by the historical mystery here.

Without a word, the dark woman came forward, dropped to one knee, and opened the box. Gleaming gold greeted her. Elena studied the map once again. It seemed to have reverted to its original state. The tiny silver boat had returned to a port in what appeared to be the coastline of Turkey. Looking down from above, she suddenly guessed that city.

"Troy," she whispered aloud.

The woman turned to her, cocking her head slightly, her dark eyes twinkling.

"It seems whoever brought you here had not been misguided."

Elena took little solace from this assessment. She noted the scar that split the woman's lower lip and carved a pale path down her chin, along her throat, and vanished under the edge of her wetsuit. It made her no less attractive. Still, Elena sensed a palpable danger wafting from her, like the radiation off the golden map.

Both were beautiful but deadly.

The woman's penetrating eyes fixed on Elena. "Where is it?" she asked.

"What are you talking about?"

The team leader pointed to the hollow space in the map that once held the silver sphere of the astrolabe. In the depths of the empty cradle, bronze gears shone brightly. Elena pictured those cogs and wheels turning the astrolabe like the hands of an intricate clock.

"Where is the Daedalus Key?" the woman pressed.

The Daedalus Key?

Elena let her confusion show in her face and used it to reinforce her lie. "I don't know what you mean. That's all we found."

The leader straightened and commanded in Arabic to someone behind Elena. Elena made out one phrase. *Taelimuha.* Which meant "teach her."

She turned and found a hulking figure standing silently at her shoulder. She had not even heard the large bodyguard leave the Zodiac. He stood over seven feet, and surely suffered from some form of genetic gigantism. His face was all crags and scars. His brow heavy and thick. His eyes as dead and cold as those of a great white.

The man balled a fist and slammed it into Elena's side.

She cried out and crumpled to the ground. Sharp pain radiated outward, making it hard to breathe. The tears she had been trying to hold in check burst forth hotly.

The woman stared down at her. "Do not lie again." She then pointed to the ship and barked to her men in Arabic, loud enough for Elena to easily translate. "Secure the key. Kill them all."

4

Too wired to sit, Kowalski paced the length of the P-8 Poseidon's cabin. It was his fourth circuit over the past twenty minutes.

He finally reached the "wine racks" at the stern of the aircraft, which held rows of cylindrical sonobuoys. He leaned on a barrel-sized rotary launcher that shot the buoys into the seas to assist the maritime patrol plane in monitoring Russian subs in the area. He tapped a finger on the launcher's canister. His other hand—still in a pocket of his long leather duster—crinkled the cellophane around a Cuban cigar.

Maybe they won't catch me back here if I took a couple puffs . . .

No one was around. The large jet had a crew of only nine, all of them stationed up front. With the crew busy at their monitors, it was aggravatingly quiet aboard the plane, which only got on his nerves.

Across the length of the bird, he spotted the Poseidon's commander exit the cockpit and head toward the monitoring stations amidships. He stopped to say something to Maria, who was belted into a seat beside one of the two observer's windows. The man laughed at something she said. His hand rested too long on the back of her seat.

Kowalski felt a bit of heat rise in his neck. The commander was young, smiled often, and looked way too much like Tom Cruise in *Top Gun*.

He left his cigar in his pocket and headed aft.

He marched past the sections of the plane that housed its avionic compartments and antisubmarine armaments. He ended up meeting the commander at the row of five seats lining the port side, where a team of four men and one woman were bent over various glowing screens, monitoring the aircraft's sophisticated APY-10 multi-mode search radar and ALQ-240 Electronic Support Measures Suite.

Earlier, upon learning that he was former navy, the tactical coordinator of the group had tried to explain to Kowalski some of the equipment and its capabilities. He barely understood every third word. It reminded him how much of an old sea dog he actually was. Apparently modern warfare had outgrown him.

The commander nodded to Kowalski. "I just came back to tell you we'll be landing in ten minutes, so it's best if you join Dr. Crandall and get strapped in. We're due to hit some weather along the coast."

As if the gods had heard him, the jet bucked underfoot. Kowalski kept his feet by grabbing a seatback. The commander seemed to have managed to stay upright by merely smiling wider.

Bastard...

"Like I said," the commander warned, "time to buckle up."

Kowalski straightened and began to shoulder past the man when the tactical coordinator turned in his seat and slipped off a set of large earphones.

"Commander Pullman, I just received a report from another Poseidon heading back to Reykjavik. They picked up a possible bogie, running periscope depth along the coast ahead. But with the storm behind them and the seas full of broken ice, they lost it and never made a full ID. They're asking us to run a search pattern before landing."

Kowalski checked his watch. "No good. You can play cat-and-mouse with the Russkies another time. We need to be on the ground ASAP."

The smile on the commander's face turned into a grimace. "Let me remind you this is *my* aircraft. You're only hitching a ride."

The jet bounced again, throwing Kowalski fully off his feet. Even Pullman grabbed the seats to either side. He certainly wasn't smiling now.

The pilot radioed back, his voice strained. "The storm ahead is ramping up into a real monster. And fast. Everybody strap down."

Kowalski stared challengingly at the commander. "Looks like Mother Nature just demoted you."

Pullman scowled and turned to the tactical coordinator. "Radio your contact. Tell them 'no go' on that search pattern."

"Yes, sir."

Before the officer could turn away, Pullman added, "As a precaution, run all three launchers. Drop a row of sonobuoys from here to the coast." He glanced back to Kowalski. "We may not be able to stay airborne, but that doesn't mean we can't keep listening."

Kowalski shrugged and pushed past the commander.

Bub, do whatever you need to save face.

He crossed forward and dropped heavily into the seat next to Maria.

"What was that all about back there?" she asked.

"Just making sure no one gets sidetracked."

She twisted and tried to look back. Her hand found his and squeezed hard. "Is that likely to happen?"

"Not on my watch."

She settled back around with a sigh. She tried to remove her hand, but he caught it and held it firmly. Her skin was hot, but her face remained pale. He easily read the anxiety and guilt in her glassy eyes. He knew better than to offer empty platitudes, to try to reassure her about the safety of her friend. He could only offer the facts.

"We'll be on the ground soon," he promised.

Hopefully before it's too late.

5

Mac watched Elena crumple alongside the meltwater stream after being kidney-punched by that dull-eyed behemoth.

Goddamn bastards.

He took a step toward the crack in the hull, ready to go to her aid, to defend her.

Nelson grabbed his shoulder. "There's nothing you can do." He then snagged a fistful of Mac's parka and yanked him back. "And it looks like we've got company coming."

Outside, an order was shouted in Arabic. The assault team responded by running low toward the stranded dhow, flanking to either side. One strafed the crack in the hull with a rifle to cover the others' approach.

John fired both barrels at the shooter. The gunman flew backward, struck square in the chest. His body crashed into the river. Then John rolled to the side as return fire pounded where he'd been. He escaped unscathed and joined Mac and Nelson. Outside, John's shots had forced the attackers to approach with more caution.

Not that it would buy them much time.

"We need a place to hole up." Nelson pointed across the dark hold. "Maybe barricade ourselves inside the captain's cabin."

With no better idea, Mac pointed his flashlight and shoved his friend forward. "Go."

All three of them rushed toward the bow. The tramp of their footfalls turned to splashes as they reached the oil pooled in the bottom of the ship. With the map now outside, the liquid had gone dark again.

But this raised another question.

"Maybe this crap's flammable," Mac suggested as they splashed along. "If we set it on fire, it could act as a barrier, maybe drive the others off."

"Or get us all killed," Nelson said. "Remember, this is a *wooden* ship. So, let's leave arson as a last resort."

As Nelson spoke, the giant clay pot behind him brightened with a now-familiar greenish glow. It shone through the cracks and hammer-pounded hole. Mac spotted shadows moving within that sheen, accompanied by a scrabbling of sharp nails on hard clay.

Mac stopped and squinted.

What the hell . . .

Something was definitely in there. But what? How could anything still be alive after so many centuries? Had it somehow been preserved in the foul oil? He remembered the hammers falling. He pictured the flowing oil, like a pregnant woman's water breaking. What was about to be born?

"Quit gawking," Nelson blurted out. "I need your light over—"

"Quiet," Mac warned.

But it was too late.

As if hearing the man, the glow flared brighter behind Nelson, and the pot shattered outward, letting loose what it held. Like some exploding nest of spiders, a riot of crablike creatures burst outward, hundreds of them. Each the size of a saucer plate—ringed by long articulated legs. They raced blindly in all directions, scrabbling up the sides of the hull, across the rafters, even diving into the oil. As they moved, their joints bled with the same green ichor coursing through the oil, as if fueled by that malignant substance.

In that ghastly glow, Mac saw that those hard carapaces weren't made of chitin or shell—but solid *bronze*. He gasped at the realization. These were not *living* creatures, but beasts crafted and built, forged in malevolent fires and fueled by some volatile ichor.

As if to prove this, one of the things burst into flame—then another, and another. The green fluid seemed to be reacting to the damp air. Yet, it was not a perishing flame. The fiery creatures continued to race, bumping against others, setting others aflame.

One sped along the underside of a rafter and reached a thick icicle and spiraled down its length. Intense heat melted the ice, but instead of water dripping down—droplets of fire rained into the black pool below, as if the fuel inside the beasts could set even water on fire.

Impossible . . .

Mac struggled with the hellish sight, frozen by the horror of the spectacle.

Nelson's reaction was more vigorous. He screamed and stumbled forward. Mac caught him under an arm. His cry still echoed across the hold, seemingly with enough force to shatter another two pots. They exploded forth with hundreds more of the tiny bronze monstrosities. The new batch of creatures raced crazily across walls and rafters.

Nelson writhed, pawing at his back. "Get it off . . ."

Mac turned his friend's body and spotted a fiery bronze crab latched on to his back. Sharp legs had impaled his coat and scrabbled furiously, ripping and burning their way through Gore-Tex and goose down, seeking the flesh beneath.

Before Mac could help, another crab climbed into view on Nelson's shoulder and leaped onto the man's throat. Mac tried to bat it away with his flashlight, but its legs had already dug deep into the tender flesh. Skin blackened and smoked around where they were imbedded.

Nelson contorted in agony, his jaw stretched wide. An animalistic gurgle emerged from his throat. Smoke wafted from his lips. Mac thought about the bastard on the icicle, turning water to fire.

What would it do to *blood*?

With his heart pounding in his ears, Mac tossed his flashlight toward the cabin and grabbed the carapace of the burrowed creature on Nelson's throat. He ripped it free and flung it away. Boiling blood and flames flew after it. Nelson sagged in his arms, groaning, only semiconscious from the pain and shock. Mac covered the wound with his palm, patted at the edges where flames still flickered from beneath blackened, cracked skin.

"Help me," Mac croaked out.

John had kept close, warily waving his shotgun around. He splashed forward and used the butt of his weapon to knock the creature off Nelson's back before it reached flesh.

Together they hauled Nelson toward the captain's cabin.

But ahead, lit by the glow of his tossed flashlight, the wooden floor of the ship was crawling with a horde of the fiery bronze beasts. More sped along walls or clung to rafters. There was no way they'd get through them without being overwhelmed.

Yet, he noticed that the beasts gave the black pool a wide berth. It was likely the only reason he and John hadn't already been attacked. Unfortunately, Nelson had been standing too close to the first clay pot when it exploded. Two of the creatures must have been thrown toward him, landing on the nearest island in the black sea.

Mac pictured the hammers smashing into the pots, the oil flowing out. Did that black oil act as some sort of insulation? Did it need to be drained out of the jars to allow these creatures to animate back to life?

As they neared the pool's edge, Mac tested a theory. He swept his leg through the oil and cast a black swell toward the closest crab. The wave fell thickly over the creature, and immediately doused its golden flames. It scrabbled a final oily path—then stopped moving.

John looked at him.

It was something, but how could this knowledge help them? The remaining distance was too far to splash a safe passage through them. Maybe they could roll in the oil as a repellant. But did they dare take that risk?

The decision was taken away from them with the deafening blasts of a rifle. Mac ducked low as rounds pelted into the oil and ricocheted off the walls. John gasped as a red burn bloomed across his cheek from a graze. Mac felt a tug on his left arm. Goose down fluttered from a hole blasted through his parka. Nelson's head cracked hard against the side of Mac's skull. Mac felt the wash of hot blood, the sting of shattered bone.

With horror, he turned and saw that half his friend's face was gone.

Still, he cradled the body and dropped flat into the oil.

John did the same.

Mac turned toward the stern as more gunmen flowed inside and spread out. John twisted, trying to raise his shotgun.

"Don't," Mac warned.

The rifle blasts had been far louder than Nelson's earlier scream—and triggered a more profound reaction. All around, pots shook with deadly potency, then one after the other, they shattered, releasing the monsters inside.

The mass scrambled furiously on their jointed legs toward the new arrivals. Green ichor flared into golden flames. Panicked at the sight, the gunmen fired at the bronze horde—which only attracted them more. They raced across every surface, scurrying over one another in their haste to reach their targets.

They're drawn by noise . . .

Mac realized now that the bronze crabs had *no* eyes. Blind, they clearly responded to sound. He looked back toward the captain's cabin. The creatures there had also heard the commotion and set off in fiery golden streams across the walls and rafters, aiming for the gun blasts and screams. One lost its footing above and tumbled into the pool. Its flames snuffed out as it struck the oil.

Mac finally released Nelson's body with a grimace of guilt and sorrow. He nudged John toward the dark cabin. This was their only chance to reach that refuge. The two men rose from the oil and ran low toward the cabin door.

Mac reached it first and waved John inside and retrieved his flashlight.

He looked back across the hold, now lit by a hellish glow, punctuated by spats of gunfire. Those who had entered the ship thrashed and screamed. Their bodies covered in clawing, digging bronze. Their flesh burning, smoking; their blood boiling inside them.

Aghast, Mac retreated into the cold, dark cabin. He pulled the door closed behind him, but not before a huge pot to his left—twice the size of the others—cracked open and something massive shouldered into view. His brain struggled to comprehend those moving plates of bronze, the razored maw full of flames, the piston of its legs.

Then John drew him back and closed the door on the unholy sight. He shifted a bronze bar in place, closing them in, locking the monsters out.

No, not monsters.

John met his eyes and named them. *"Tuurngaq."*

Mac nodded, knowing it to be true.

Demons.

11:40 A.M.

Elena huddled on the rubberized bottom of the Zodiac. The pontoon boat had retreated from shore and hovered in the meltwater current. As she stared back, she shivered with far more than the cold.

Across the way, the ancient dhow burned. Smoke choked the view as flames danced deeper in the darkness. Closer at hand, thin ribbons of golden fire flowed from the ruins of the ship and drained into the meltwater stream. There they formed flaming rafts along the banks and spread fiery fingers toward them.

The woman at the bow barked to the helmsman. He nodded and swung the Zodiac away. They dared not risk those flames. Even now the intense heat was melting the ice overhead. Ancient glacial waters showered down, but rather than dousing the flames, the rainfall seemed to stoke the fire below.

By now, Helheim Glacier responded to the acid burning at its heart.

Ice cracked and popped all around them. Perhaps knowing the tunnel could implode at any moment, the helmsman sped the Zodiac faster.

Elena stared back toward the dhow as their boat skidded around a bend. Before she lost sight of the ancient ship, something pushed through the smoke. She prayed it was Mac, somehow miraculously still alive. But what appeared instead, shrouded in a pall of smoke, was a massively shouldered beast, its ruddy bulk glowing with an inner fire. She caught a glimpse of horns—then the sight vanished as the Zodiac rounded the bend.

She settled back around and hugged her knees to her chest.

She felt leaden, in shock after the horrors of the past few minutes.

Moments ago, as the map had been loaded aboard the boat, she had heard Nelson scream. All eyes had turned to the eerie glow emanating from the hold of the ship. The team leader had silently pointed to the boat, and the assault team rushed through the crack in the hull. Once inside, gunfire chattered hollowly.

Elena had covered her ears, picturing Mac, Nelson, John.

Then came the screams.

Even her palms could not block the terror and blood in those cries. One of the gunmen reappeared, crashing blindly to his knees outside the crack in the hull. He looked like he had donned a suit of fiery bronze armor, but these plates shifted and clawed at his body, ripping through neoprene and skin. Blood boiled from the tears. His body arched back savagely, cracking spine and bone—then exploded in a ruin of blackened flesh and bright flames.

The team leader's hulking bodyguard grabbed his charge by the shoulder and drew her and the remaining men to the Zodiac. The woman resisted at first, even taking a step toward the dhow, but by then the ship was burning, flames spreading. She scowled, turned her back, and waved them all into the boat and out into the meltwater channel.

The woman was not taking any chances at losing the hard-fought treasure, even if the map wasn't intact. As the Zodiac sped along the icy river, dark eyes found Elena. As the woman silently stared, she used two fingers to pull back the neoprene hood of her wetsuit and shake out a fall of hair as black as a raven's wing. Elena saw gears turning behind that hard, calculating gaze, clearly contemplating what to do with her prisoner.

The woman finally turned away as the Zodiac shot free of the glacier and into open air. Winds immediately assaulted them. Whitecaps ridged the waters of the fjord. A fog still clung to the sea, but its thick cloak had shredded apart.

A storm was coming.

As the Zodiac bounced through the chop, the destination came into view through the scraps of fog. A black conning tower stuck out of the blue sea. As the Zodiac rushed toward it, the submarine rose enough to expose a deck sluicing with seawater. The helmsman drove the Zodiac's bow onto that wet deck, lodging it there.

The leader hopped out and gave swift orders. Two men hauled the heavy map box, while the giant came for Elena. She avoided his touch, shrugging away from his hand, and climbed out on her own.

With everyone offloaded, the helmsman abandoned the Zodiac and kicked it out to sea. Then he raised an assault rifle and strafed the pontoons, causing it to start slipping beneath the waves. As it spun away, Elena felt the rising rumble of the sub's engines through the deck plates. It seemed the team was not wasting any time evacuating the area.

Except to attend to one last task.

Elena heard a muffled boom and felt the deck buck underfoot. A foaming streak cut through the whitecaps and sped away. *Torpedo.* She clutched a hand to her throat and stared toward the face of Helheim Glacier. A moment later, ice blasted high into the stormy air, the concussive force felt even from this distance. A huge section of glacier calved away, dropping like a white guillotine across the opening to the meltwater channel.

As the berg struck the sea, a huge wave swept toward them.

"Come," the woman ordered.

Elena considered leaping into the water instead.

As if sensing her hesitation, the team leader faced her. "There is much you need to know." Her eyes bore into her. "Much you will *want* to know."

Elena balled a fist, ready to tell the woman to fuck off. But she pictured the map and the mystery of it all. The woman was right.

I want to know.

Elena turned and headed toward the conning tower, while still keeping her fist clenched. Intellectual curiosity might motivate her, but now she had another goal, too. She pictured Mac's grinning face, the amused glint in Nelson's eyes, John's stoic strength.

I will get my revenge.

6

Elena still lived . . .

Maria tried to take comfort from this bit of hope, but the rest of the local policeman's report was dire.

She sat with her hands wrapped around a steaming mug of coffee in the Red Hotel's cozy dining space. The room consisted of a handful of tables and chairs, a small library space, and a high shelf lined with a rainbow of snow boots, both new and antique. With its bright red clapboard exterior and large windows that looked out on an expansive view of King Oscar's Harbour, she might have been charmed by the place, but not under these circumstances.

The dining room was crammed with a score of locals. It seemed the torpedo's blast had been heard by everyone, and the entire village wanted information.

All eyes were on the only witness.

"The tunnel is gone," Officer Hans Jørgen reported from across the table. The man wore an open fur-lined Sherpa jacket, over his uniform's khakis. His Danish ancestry could be heard in his accent and evident in his short-cropped blond hair. "The torpedo took out the entire face of the glacier. Collapsed a huge section."

"Can you describe anything else about the submarine?" Commander Pullman asked. After landing in Greenland, word had reached the military jet about a submarine being spotted in the area. The commander had insisted on joining Maria and Joe aboard the helicopter that ferried them to the village. The rest of his crew had remained behind to secure the aircraft as gale-force winds pounded down from the mountains. "Did you spot any insignias on the conning tower? See any letters or numbers painted on it?"

Jørgen shook his head. "Like I said, I only reached the glacier's fjord in time to see the explosion. My patrol boat was still three kilometers off. I was lucky to pick out the sub through my binoculars before it submerged."

Maria squeezed her mug. "And you're sure you saw Dr. Cargill being taken aboard."

He nodded. "She was easy to pick out in her bright blue parka. The rest of the sub's crew wore black neoprene."

She turned to Pullman. "Is there any way to track that sub's path?"

He cast an accusing glance toward Joe, who sat with a cigar smoldering between his teeth. "Not much I can do from the ground. Still, we're monitoring the sonobuoys we dropped. Luckily, our Poseidon was outfitted with the newest Multistatic Active Coherent buoys. They can generate sonar pulses for days and have a long-range capability. The buoys alone may offer some guidance. But if we could get airborne . . ."

He shrugged at the obvious.

That's not happening anytime soon.

The short helicopter ride here had been like flying inside a paint shaker. The winds had picked up steadily, growing wilder by the minute. During the flight, the pilot had gripped his controls with white knuckles, his lips moving in a silent prayer. By the time they landed, his hair was plastered to his scalp with sweat.

We're not going anywhere.

Someone called out from the gallery of locals. "And what about the others?" he shouted. "The three who went with that woman?"

"*Aap!*" someone joined in, pressing the same inquiry in Inuit.

Jørgen turned to the crowd. "*Utoqqatserpunga,*" he said apologetically. "I don't know. I only saw Dr. Cargill."

Joe puffed out a cloud of smoke. "Either they're dead," he said bluntly, "or the blast trapped them inside that hunk of ice."

Pullman leaned closer to the table and lowered his voice. "If they're alive, they might know what happened and tell us who took Dr. Cargill."

"That's a big *if,*" Kowalski said.

Jørgen nodded. "Alive or not, there's no way anyone can reach them."

"I can," someone said from the crowd. A skinny figure dressed in a hide jacket and boots pushed forward. He looked to be no more than fourteen. His thick black hair was cut in a firm line over a smooth forehead.

Jørgen swung around. "Nuka, the channel is collapsed. There's no way to get back inside."

"Yes, there is," the young kid insisted with a defiant confidence.

Jørgen looked ready to object, but Joe cut him off. "How?"

"I'll show you." He thumbed toward the exit, where the winds howled and rattled the door in its frame.

"Forget it," Jørgen warned. "No one is going out into the teeth of this piteraq."

"*Naa.* I'm going." Nuka turned toward the door. "It's my grandfather out there."

Maria now understood the teenager's obstinance, reading the fear and determination in the young man's face. His grandfather was the Inuit elder—John Okalik—who guided Elena's party into the glacier.

Joe stood up and stamped out his half-smoked cigar, which he only did in the direst circumstance. "Kid, I'm going with you."

Maria turned to him. "Joe—"

He waved away the rest of her words. "Damned if I'm gonna sit around and do nothing but listen to the wind try to rip the roof off this place." He faced her. "If there's even the tiniest of a chance those guys are alive, I'll dig them out with a backhoe if I have to. They're the only ones who know what happened to your friend."

She reached out and touched his arm. "I know. I was about to say that *I'm coming with you.*"

He stiffened. "Wait. That's not what I meant. Maybe it's best if—"

She cut him off and stood. "Nope. Your reasoning was very convincing."

Joe stared hard at her, clearly judging how far to push it. He came to the right decision and simply shrugged.

Jørgen looked between the two of them. "You're both crazy."

"I've been called far worse." Joe waved to Nuka. "Show us what you got, kid."

Nuka headed toward the door. "Let's go. I know my grandfather is still alive. But not for long if we don't hurry."

"You'd better be right." Joe clapped the boy's thin shoulder. "I'm not freezing my ass off for nothing."

12:22 P.M.

"We have to risk it," Mac said.

Standing waist-deep in frigid water, he slid the bronze bar away from the door of the captain's cabin. He turned to John, who nodded.

Better to die on our own terms.

Half an hour ago, a massive explosion had rocked through the glacier. Mac had expected to be crushed under tons of ice. But as echoes of the blast died away, he and John found themselves still alive. Then the waters began to flood into the cabin, indicating the meltwater river had been dammed up by a collapse of ice from the blast.

Mac could guess what had happened. The bastards must've blown the entrance into the glacier, slamming the door on their way out.

Rather than allowing them to drown, like two trapped rats, Mac took a deep breath and pushed the door open. It took effort due to the rising waters. He cringed, expecting to be ambushed by hordes of fiery crabs. Instead, his flashlight revealed half of the stern was gone. The remaining hold was a smoldering ruin lit by a few fiery timbers. Flames also pooled in rafts atop the water.

Through the dense smoke, handfuls of crabs glowed ruddily in the darkness. They crouched on blazing bits of flotsam or sat atop boulders of ice. A pair even rode a corpse floating in the water. Most appeared not to be moving, their fires ebbing. A few scrabbled feebly.

Whatever volatile compound it was that fueled the creatures, it seemed to be losing its potency. Mac searched for the rest of the mass of crabs, but they were nowhere to be seen. Maybe the sudden flooding was too much for them to handle, and they all drowned away.

Still, as he led the way slowly into the hold, he warily kept his distance from those he could see.

John tapped Mac's shoulder and pointed to where a section of the hull had broken open. He then pointed up. Mac nodded.

We need to get out of this water.

Both of them wore dry suits under their outerwear, but it didn't stop the cold from penetrating down to their bones. Mac clenched his jaw to keep his teeth from chattering. His legs and feet were already numb, making it hard to traverse the uneven floor hidden under the black water.

Finally, they reached the breach in the hull and climbed the ship's broken ribs, steering clear of any timbers that still burned. Once up top, they found that the forward half of the deck was still intact, the nose of the ship still solidly imbedded in ice.

From this high vantage, Mac surveyed his surroundings. As he did, a slab of ice broke off the roof and crashed into the water. A huge wave sloshed against the side of the ship, stirring the flaming pools and washing more bodies into view.

Mac tried not to think about his friend Nelson.

Now's not the time for mourning.

The icefall was a reminder of a more immediate danger.

While holed up in the cabin, secondary quakes and thunderous cracking had continued sporadically as the weight of the glacier pressed down upon this fragile pocket. Mac knew the truth. After a decade working up here, he could read ice like a book.

This place won't hold out much longer. It could collapse at any time.

Still, it might not matter in the end. Ahead of them, the meltwater river had transformed into a lake. And with more and more water flowing in here, the level climbed steadily toward their position. The rising waters also squeezed the thick smoke into an ever-shrinking pocket of air, making it hard to breathe.

John coughed hoarsely.

Unfortunately, something heard him.

An angry bellow rose out of the smoky pall on the ship's starboard side. With his heart in his throat, Mac shifted to the deck rail. He remembered the crabs hadn't been the *only* creature to emerge from those oil-filled pots.

He stared down. Large sections of the roof had collapsed, littering the shoreline and building a breakwater pile of ice and rock between the ship and the cascade flooding the chamber.

Something moved down in that maze.

Flames lit its path through the smoke, offering glimpses of a hulking form. Drawn by John's cough, it pounded toward their position, then vanished into the thicker pall surrounding the ship.

Mac held his breath, afraid even his exhalation would be heard. His eyes strained to pierce the darkness.

Where is—

Something crashed into the side of the dhow, hard enough to shake the entire ship. Mac fell to one knee. John kept upright, his shotgun fixed to his shoulder, the double barrels pointing down into the darkness.

The creature roared its frustration below, casting flames from its maw, revealing jaws lined with fiery razors. Curved bronze horns mounted its brutish head. As it bellowed, it had lifted onto its hind legs, kicking the air with its front legs, which displayed a row of curved blades along their backsides.

Then it crashed back down to all fours and vanished into the smoky darkness.

Mac listened as the killing machine—half bull, half bear—paced back and forth below.

Another section of ice cracked from the roof and splashed into the rising lake. Mac shared a frightened look with John.

We can't stay here.

If that thing didn't kill them, the cold, the water, or the ice would. They needed another way out, a way past that fiery bull.

But how?

12:55 P.M.

"No way!" Kowalski screamed into the gale-force winds.

The rescue party huddled on the lee side of a row of three red snowmobiles. They shared the space with a sled and its team of dogs, thick-furred husky mixes. The dogs had scraped little nests in the glacier's ice and curled there, breaths steaming the air, oblivious to the cold.

Nuka had used the team to guide the trio of snowmobiles across the glacier. He had explained his choice of transportation: *The dogs know the safest path across the ice. Too easy to fall through a hidden hole. You learn to trust their eyes, their noses.*

After leaving the hotel at Tasiilaq, the group had boarded a Ram 2500 truck with giant knobby tires and traveled a treacherous gravel road to reach the top of Helheim Glacier. The storm pounded them continually, battering the truck with gusts that threatened to tip it over. Once at the glacier's edge, they parked next to a huddle of small blue-painted shacks and a dozen parked snowmobiles. It seemed Nuka's family operated a tour company, offering trips across the glacier.

Maria had asked where the kid's parents were. He told them that his mother and father were members of Tasiilaq's search-and-rescue unit. They were gone, dealing with an emergency inland, which had also pulled most of the experienced crew from the village.

Kowalski looked at who they were left with.

The second string . . .

Despite his previous misgivings, Jørgen had come along. So had a pair of natives: two stocky older men, said to be relatives of the family, which probably could be said of everyone in the village. The two were rigging a rope to the back of one of the snowmobiles.

Nuka coiled the loose length over one shoulder. He pointed past the rubber track of the snowmobile. "That's the only way into the heart of the glacier. Down through the moulin."

"No way," Kowalski repeated.

He leaned out from the shelter of the snowmobiles. The wind came close to tearing the set of goggles from his face. Nuka had lent them to him, along with a helmet and a thick parka that was too small for his large frame. The sleeves didn't even reach his wrists.

Ten yards off, the white surface of the glacier had been cut deeply by a blue stream. The water wended down from the higher elevations and vanished down a ten-foot-wide hole, spiraling away into the depths of the glacier.

A *moulin,* the kid had called it.

Kowalski shook his head.

More like a half-frozen whirlpool.

"You're going down that hole on a rope?" Kowalski scoffed.

Nuka had already donned a dry suit that covered his entire body, even a mask for his face. "I've made such climbs before."

Maria shifted closer. "How do you know *this* moulin connects to the same river that had been flowing out of Helheim?"

"Dr. MacNab told me," Nuka said. "When I'm not running tourists, I sometimes help Mac chart the flows and channels up here. It's a job that never really ends, with everything melting and moving all the time."

Kowalski straightened. "If you're right about it leading down there, then I should go with you."

Nuka crinkled his nose with disdain. "You're too fat."

Kowalski stared down at his stomach, both insulted and shocked at the kid's bluntness, which made him almost like the kid. "It's all muscle."

"Uh-huh. Even if you could fit through any tight squeezes down there"—he pointed to Kowalski's exposed wrists—"my spare suit will never fit you."

"What about me?" Maria asked. She stood up next to Nuka. "You and I are about the same size."

He eyed her up and down, then shrugged. "Yeah, sure."

"Like hell." Kowalski literally put his foot down, blocking her.

She ignored him. "Grab me a suit," she ordered the kid. She then turned to Kowalski. "My sister and I caved for years, as part of our research. My rope work and rappelling skills are more than up for this task."

Kowalski pointed to the moulin. "Does that look like solid rock to you?"

"Joe, I'm not letting Nuka go down there by himself."

He understood her concern, but he wasn't happy about it.

Nuka passed Maria an insulated dry suit. She lifted it up and stared across the men huddled in the shelter. "And it's not like any of you are fitting in this thing."

Recognizing a battle he could not win, he held out a hand. "Fine. Let me help you into the damned thing."

Maria danced a bit in the cold as she stripped her outerwear and snuggled into the thick suit. She combed back her hair and pulled the hood over her head. "How do I look? And be honest." She waved to Nuka, who was hunkered against the wind, feeding a rope into the moulin, letting the current carry the weighted end down its throat. "Who's wearing it best?"

Kowalski pulled her into a hug. "You both look like stranded seals."

He felt her shiver in his arms and knew it wasn't all due to the frigid winds. For the millionth time, he couldn't believe this woman gave him a second look, let alone two years of her time.

"If you don't let me go, I'll never get to save anyone."

He held her at arm's length. "Don't be a hero."

She smiled. "Add a cape to this spandex, and I bet I'd look like Wonder Woman."

"You're always Wonder Woman to me."

"That's swee—"

"Especially in bed."

"Okay, now you ruined it." She stepped away. "Hold the fort until I'm back. We'll radio our progress."

Kowalski watched her cross out of the shelter of snowmobiles and walk awkwardly toward Nuka, her boots locked into steel crampons for the climb down. When she reached the moulin, she glanced back.

He and Maria were fluent in sign language. Knowing he wouldn't be heard over the wind, he raised a hand with his pinkie and thumb outstretched, then pointed at her.

[*I love you*]

She turned away, clearly missing his message. Nuka had already rigged a second line. He hooked the new rope's belay to her hip harness. He then double-checked all the knots and gear. Once satisfied, he lowered himself down into the moulin on his line, bracing his legs and spiked feet against the walls.

Maria followed, vanishing after him.

Kowalski stared at that frozen whirlpool. He hoped this wasn't a waste of time, and a risky one at that. While he certainly wanted the others to be rescued, he held fast to one prayer.

Just come back to me.

7

Maria's foot slipped off the slick side of the moulin. As she fell, the belay and rope caught her. She swung wildly until her hip hit the ice.

"You okay?" Nuka called from five yards below, hanging on his own line, his words muffled by his face mask.

She reestablished her foothold. "Yep," she said with more confidence than she truly felt.

She realized she might have exaggerated her skill to Joe. She hadn't rappelled in years, and apparently it wasn't like riding a bike. She was rusty. Or maybe it was the unusual nature of this descent. She did her best to avoid the thin stream corkscrewing around her. Still, water constantly sprayed her mask, making it hard to see. Also, the ice proved to be both rock-hard and slippery. To her, the descent was less like rappelling and more like ice-skating.

"Tunnel angles away from here," Nuka called up. "Should make it easier."

She wiped the spray from her mask and looked down. The first section of the descent had been nearly vertical, but the light attached to Nuka's mask revealed the shaft heading off at a thirty-degree angle.

Thank god . . .

She happily dropped to that section, closing the distance to join Nuka. The tunnel ahead squeezed to half its size, but it was still manageable if they stayed single file.

But for how long? And would their ropes even reach the bottom?

They both had ice axes strapped to their backs, but Maria had no desire to attempt a free descent beyond the end of the rope.

As they continued, the chute grew steadily less steep, but the water also deepened underfoot, requiring them to brace their legs to either side of the strong current.

After another several yards, Nuka stopped and shifted his mask aside and sniffed the air. "Is that smoke?"

Smoke?

Maria stopped and did the same. The fresh air froze the hairs in her nostrils, but she noted a hint of woodsmoke. She knew there could be only one source of combustible material down here. She pictured the ancient ship.

Had it been set on fire by whoever took Elena?

She didn't know, but the scent suggested they must be close. She waved Nuka on. "Let's keep going."

"Um, that's gonna be a problem." Nuka reached down and fished the loose end of his rope from the frigid current. He held it up. "We've reached the end of the line."

She scooted next to him. "What now?"

But she knew what his answer would be.

He began freeing his harness from the belaying device. "Like you said. We're close." Once free, he unhooked his ice ax. "And it's not too steep. I can probably just hike the rest of the way if I'm careful."

"Not alone, you're not."

Despite her earlier trepidation, she felt confident enough to go a bit farther. If the tunnel became any more treacherous, they could always use their axes and crampons to reach the rope again.

"Help me off my line," she said.

After he did, he stared up at her. With his mask pushed to the top of his head, his eyes shone brightly, enough for her to read his fear and relief. "Thanks."

"Just get going before I change my mind."

He set off, demonstrating the proper method. He kept his legs wide, taking each step with care, making sure his crampons had a good grip. He held the ax low in both hands, ready to jam it into the ice if he slipped.

She followed, matching him step for step.

It was tedious, but they made slow progress. Effort and tension had her sweating inside her dry suit.

"I think I see a glow ahead," Nuka said.

She straightened and tried to peek past the kid—and promptly lost her footing. Caught off guard, she crashed into the main current, which immediately caught her body and shoved her forward. She hit Nuka and knocked his legs out from under him.

Tangled together, their ice axes were useless.

The current sped them a short run, then spilled them down a painful cascade into a wider chamber. Once in the larger space, the stream spread and lost some of its force. It split ahead, dividing around a jagged berg of blue ice.

Nuka grabbed her around the waist and hauled her to the left to avoid hitting the obstruction. He then used their combined momentum to roll them out of the river and onto a frozen bank of rock.

She patted the solid ground.

Rock . . .

They must have reached the glacier's bottom. Maria sat up, gasping, the wind knocked out of her. Across the dark chamber, the shadowy husk of a ship smoldered in the gloom.

We made it.

Her relief was short-lived.

A shout rose from the ship, full of panic.

"Run! Get the hell out of there!"

1:33 P.M.

A moment ago, Mac had thought his eyes were playing tricks on him. He thought he'd seen ghost lights flickering by the meltwater cascade flowing into the chamber. Then he heard an eerie echo of voices. The Inuit believed some glaciers were haunted, and after learning their *Tuurngaq*—their demons—were fiery and real, he did not discount the possibility of ghosts.

Then a pair of figures, as solid as the ice and rock, came sliding and tumbling into view. From the dhow's deck, he saw them roll out of the stream and onto the shoreline.

But he wasn't the only one to note their trespass.

Below the ship's rail, the shadowy bull had been pacing alongside the hull. As the two newcomers crashed into the cave, flames huffed from its nostrils, flaring brightly in the gloom. Its bronze head pivoted in their direction. Heavy legs pounded as it headed toward the commotion.

Mac did his best to warn them—not that it did much good.

A call answered him. "Dr. MacNab? Mac? Is that you?"

Mac recognized that nasal-crack of puberty. He turned to John, who stood straighter, also recognizing the voice.

Mac cupped his mouth and shouted. "Nuka! There's a dangerous creature down there. Drawn by sound. Maybe light, too. So douse your lamps. Stay quiet."

To try to lure the beast back here, Mac pounded his foot on the ancient planks. The bull responded and slowed its pace.

Until Nuka called again. "We have ropes over here! A way to climb out!"

Mac groaned inwardly.

What don't kids today know about staying quiet?

Again the bull headed toward the cascading water. Mac hammered the planks harder, but the beast ignored the sound this time. Perhaps it was intelligent enough to know there were easier, more accessible targets out there.

He needed a new plan—one that was probably foolhardy.

"Nuka!" Mac yelled. "Just shut the hell up. Retreat into the tunnel. We'll try to get to you."

He then turned to John.

"Looks like it's time to take the bull by the horns."

1:35 P.M.

Clutching her ice ax in both hands, Maria stayed low and backed up-stream along the waterway. Its babbling made it difficult to hear. Her eyes searched the dark shoreline, which was a maze of broken ice and glacier-carved rock.

Nuka followed her.

What could be living down here? Had a polar bear been trapped with the men?

From the terror in the man's voice, she knew it had to be something else, something far worse than a polar bear.

But what?

They finally reached the moulin's tunnel again. She crouched to enter when a gun blasted hollowly over by the smoking shipwreck.

She jumped. So did Nuka.

Closer at hand, maybe ten yards away, the smoky darkness bloomed with fire. For the briefest instant, she caught a glimpse of something bulky, plated in armor. But a broken cliff of ice blocked most of her view—then the lurking monstrosity retreated, trailing flames, and headed back toward the ship.

Nuka turned to her, his expression shocked.

Whatever it was, it had been almost on top of them.

She retreated deeper into the tunnel, drawing Nuka with her.

Another gun blast rocked through the chamber.

She prayed the others knew what they were doing.

For all our sakes.

1:37 P.M.

Back inside the ship, Mac stood waist-deep in icy water and stared across the dark hold as John reloaded. Both men hid behind tall shards of the giant shattered pots. Mac turned his attention to the smoldering ruins of the dhow's stern, searching for their nemesis.

C'mon, you bastard, where are you?

After failing to lure the bull with his pounding, Mac knew they needed to pull out their big gun. The first shotgun blast should have been impossible to ignore. Still, he had held his breath, fearing it wouldn't work. Then he'd heard the heavy tread of its approach back to the ship. He signaled John, who emptied his second barrel through the roof.

The two blasts in the closed space left his ears ringing. *What if it didn't take the bait?* He turned to John, ready to nod for another blast—then a roar drew his attention to the stern.

The bull rounded the back of the ship and waded into the hold, impossibly trailing flames in the water. Its overlapping bronze plates shifted as it shouldered toward them. Its head swiveled, threatening with its curved horns. Flames huffed from its wide nostrils. Its jaw gaped, revealing rows upon rows of razor-edged plates.

Dear god . . .

Mac's blood turned to ice. Even hidden, he felt exposed and vulnerable. He wanted to push farther into the shelter, but he was paralyzed with fear, immobilized by the horror.

John must have noted his panic and whistled to him.

The bull jerked toward his Inuit friend, drawn by the noise.

No, no, no . . .

Mac finally acted, returning to his plan. He flicked on his flashlight and threw it toward the open door of the captain's cabin. The light cartwheeled through the air and into the tiny chamber. It hit the far wall and clattered loudly, spinning on the desktop.

The bull roared, casting out flumes of fire from its throat. It charged toward the cabin, either lured by the sound, or maybe it *could* see. The beast did have a set of black-diamond eyes, lit by an inner fire, but they could be merely decorative.

Either way, the bull lowered its horns and barreled through the water, leaving a fiery wake in its path, along with the stench of burning oil. It leaped headlong into the cabin and smashed into the desk, splintering it to ruin, then struck the curved prow hard enough to jolt the entire ship.

Mac and John were already moving. John shifted to the center of the hold, while Mac headed to the cabin. Once in position, John fired both barrels into the back of the bull. The solid-shot shells pounded into its rump with resounding clangs but only dented its surface.

Still, the impact of those massive slugs hammered the beast in place and gave Mac a chance to reach the open door. He set his shoulder against it and shoved it closed. John joined him and grabbed the brass bar they had set outside. Together they jammed the brace between the door and floor planks.

Inside, the bull thrashed and roared, but the confined space gave it little room to maneuver or get up a head of steam to smash out.

Or so we better hope.

"Go!" Mac yelled.

The two of them splashed their way out of the ship. They clambered to the rocky shore and sprinted through the maze of boulders and bergs. It quickly became too dark to see as they left the flaming pools of the lake behind them.

"Nuka!" Mac shouted. "Get those lamps back on!"

Lights flared in the distance.

Then a huge crack of timbers exploded behind them. Mac glanced back to see the bull burst through the side of the hull. It bounded high, lit by angry flames. It landed with a skid of sparks and thundered toward them, cloaked in fire and smoke.

"Haul ass," Mac urged John.

Together they ran for the cascading water. Upon reaching it, they scrambled up the wet rock toward the lighted tunnel. Inside, he spotted two figures crowded together a short way up.

"Keep going!" he yelled to them.

The heavy tread of the bull closed in behind them. It shattered through ice and bounced off boulders in its haste to run down its prey.

Mac pushed John into the tunnel, then crowded in behind him.

Nuka slid back and passed an ice ax to Mac. He pantomimed hacking into the ice. "Dig and move!"

Got it.

John managed to scale the slick tunnel with a skill ingrained into his DNA. Mac followed, clawing at the ice with the ax and dragging himself up. It was slow going. The others were leaving him behind.

Not going to make it.

He was right.

The bull reached the tunnel and slammed headlong into it. Jammed there, it roared at Mac, sending gouts of flame at him. Its jagged maw snapped at his scrambling feet.

Panicked, he let his ax slip. He belly-flopped into the current and washed back toward the bull.

"Stay down!" Nuka hollered.

Twin blasts deafened him. He felt the passage of the shotgun slugs over his head. The rounds struck the bull between the horns and punched it back into the tunnel, buying Mac enough time to plant his ice ax again and regain his footing.

He set off quickly, knowing the bull would be back.

It roared behind him.

A woman shouted to him, "We're almost to the ropes!"

Mac didn't know who this lady was, but he obeyed. He set a harder pace. By the time he reached the others, Nuka and the stranger had secured their hip harnesses to belaying devices.

Nuka pointed to the back of their two harnesses. "Grab hold."

John latched on to the woman's harness; Mac locked his fingers on to Nuka's.

"Hold tight," the lady warned. "It's gonna be a bumpy ride."

1:42 P.M.

Maria pressed the radio to her lips. "Now . . . as fast as you can!"

She stared up the dark throat of the moulin. She clutched the rope with both hands. A slight vibration was the only warning. The slack in the line snapped taut—and the four of them were jerked forward and dragged bodily up the slick chute.

Earlier, while waiting tensely, Maria had radioed topside, letting them know they would need an immediate evacuation. With their two ropes secured to the tow hitch of a snowmobile, she saw no reason to climb on their own when they had the horsepower to be pulled up.

An angry bellow chased them.

Maria glanced back. Even now, the fiery creature tried to force its way after them.

"Screw you," MacNab called back.

Maria let out a sigh of relief—until the tunnel began to cave in. Whether from the thrashing of the beast or the concussions of the shotgun blasts, something finally gave way. The tunnel below cracked, and the chute imploded with an explosive clap of ice.

The roaring finally ended.

The continuing collapse chased them up the moulin. She stared ahead and sent a silent prayer to those above.

Don't spare those horses.

After a few more breaths, they reached the wider vertical shaft. The snap of the line tossed them hard against the wall. With the impact, the Inuit elder lost his handhold on her belt. He swung wildly by one arm. Secure in her harness, she let go of the rope and grabbed his hide jacket with both hands.

"I got you."

She clutched with all her strength until iron arms hooked around her waist and hauled her and Nuka's grandfather free of the moulin.

She let the elder go and lay on her back.

Joe's windburned face stared down at her. "What did I tell you about not playing hero?"

She shrugged. "I think I was only a supporting character here."

Joe helped her sit up. The others were safely out, too. She stared over at the red-bearded climatologist.

"Mind telling me what that was all about?" she asked.

"I will. Over a beer. Lots of beer."

Joe nodded at this wisdom. "Best plan I heard in a long time."

Maria held up a hand, knowing this could not wait. "First, what about Elena? Do you know who took her?"

"Dr. Cargill? She's still alive?"

"As far as we know. I'll fill you in on the details over those beers. But do you know who took her and what they wanted?"

"I have no idea who they were. But they're definitely not from around here. They were speaking Arabic."

Arabic?

"As to *what* they wanted, I'm not entirely sure. Definitely wanted the gold map. They called it the Storm Atlas, as if they already knew what it was."

Maria frowned. *A Storm Atlas?*

"Oh." He reached to a pocket and removed a softball-sized silver sphere. It looked to be inscribed and covered with complicated-looking dials and compasses. "They also wanted this."

SECOND

THE DAEDALUS KEY

Quod est ante pedes nemo spectat, caeli scrutantur plagas.
No one regards what is before his feet; we all gaze at the stars.

—*IPHIGENIA*, A TRAGEDY BY QUINTUS ENNIUS (239–169 B.C.)

8

Commander Grayson Pierce had survived countless brushes with death, but nothing had prepared him for fatherhood—especially living with a tiger mom.

"It's not going to happen," he warned from the living room's sofa.

"It will."

Seichan sat cross-legged on the Persian rug, like some Eurasian queen. She had pushed the coffee table aside and held their baby boy under his arms. She did her best to get the child to balance on legs made of Jell-O. Jackson Randall Pierce wasn't cooperating. He cooed and babbled and tried to reach his toes.

Gray tapped the well-thumbed book on the end table. "Says here not to expect a baby to walk until nine months to a year. Maybe longer."

"That's only an average." She pointed her chin toward a stack of printouts. "Look. There are many articles about babies who started walking by six months. It's rare but not unheard-of."

"Jack is only *five* months old. In two days."

"So? He's already sitting up on his own, even crawling a little. That's ahead of schedule. And I got him sleeping through the night two months ago. You said *that* couldn't be done."

"Not true. I seem to recall I said, *please, dear god, won't this kid ever sleep.*"

"Well, I did it."

Gray considered whether he should unplug their wireless router. Seichan spent too much time on the Internet reading all she could about child-rearing and treated motherhood as a blood sport. She was determined that Jack would reach every milestone sooner than the books said, using those accomplishments as proof she was the best mother on the planet.

And this was a woman who once doubted her maternal instincts.

Of course, she was a former assassin, brutally trained to be heartless and cold-blooded. So, he understood her misgivings. He had enough worries about his own parenting skills. At first, her dogged determination amused him, but as it continued, he had grown concerned. After Jack's birth, the two of them had taken an extended period of parental leave from Sigma. Gray was scheduled to return to duty next month, after Jack's six-month birthday party, which apparently was something that needed to be done.

Gray slid to the floor until his knees pressed against hers. He took little Jack, sniffed his Pampers, and from the odiferous emanation, decided this walking lesson was over. But a diaper change could wait a few moments. He scooped Jack under one arm and shifted next to Seichan. They settled together against the chair behind them. Jack fussed in his arms, but he kissed that mop of dark hair, which got the boy to settle—at least for the moment.

Seichan stretched her legs and leaned against him. He pulled her closer with his free arm, where she snuggled against him. She wore a pair of black yoga pants and a matching bikini-strap top. Her long mane was tied in a ponytail that draped to her midback. He smelled the musky scent of her skin. She and Kat had gone to an early yoga class. Not that Seichan needed the stretching and breathing exercises. The determined woman had shed her baby fat in six weeks, returning to her sculpted fighting form.

Gray looked down at his own belly, which had filled out a little.

I should've followed her example.

Still, considering their months of sleep deprivation and Jack's unpredictable schedule, Gray cut himself some slack. Kat's husband, Monk, had been inviting him to play basketball or to spot him at the gym, but Gray had mostly declined, enjoying this period of domesticity. Plus, he always felt a twinge of guilt leaving Seichan alone with Jack. He wanted to pull his weight as best he could.

Maybe I'm trying to prove something as much as Seichan.

Over the past six months, Kat and Monk had come over often with their rambunctious girls, Harriet and Penny. While they never stated it openly, Gray suspected the visits were to make sure Gray and Seichan did not become too isolated, as could often happen with first-time parents, whose lives end up revolving around the baby, leaving time for little else. Perhaps Monk and Kat were also demonstrating by example how to balance married life, parenthood, and a demanding job. The pair certainly kept them abreast of events at Sigma command, almost as if to entice them to return early.

The satellite phone Gray had left on the end table chimed.

He groaned, not wanting to get it. But Jack, half-drowsing, heard it too and began to sniffle his way toward a full wail. He passed the baby to Seichan.

"Needs a diaper change," he said.

"Not so fast. When you start breastfeeding, we'll talk about excusing you from diaper duty."

He grinned and rolled to the phone. "Fine. It's probably Monk seeing if I want to join him for a game of pickup at the park."

"You should go." She eyed his midsection. "Really."

He rolled his eyes and picked up the satellite phone. He answered it and was surprised to hear Captain Kathryn Bryant's voice.

"Kat, do you want to speak to Seichan?"

"No, I'm calling you on behalf of the director. I know you're still on leave, but we're monitoring a situation over here. And someone involved has asked specifically for you."

He felt a familiar fire stoke in his blood. "Who?"

"It's a long story. We'll fill you in when you get here."

He covered the phone and turned to Seichan. "Something's up over at Sigma. They want me over there."

"Really?" The gold flecks shone brighter in her green eyes, plainly intrigued, maybe envious. Still, she waved him off. "Go. Get out of here."

He lifted the phone, but Seichan raised a hand.

"*After* you change Jack's diaper."

He smiled.

Definitely a tiger mom . . .

10:02 A.M.
Washington, D.C.

"Welcome back to the lion's den," Painter Crowe said.

Gray stepped into the director's office. Nothing had changed over the past five months. The windowless room was spartan. The only pieces of furniture were a couple of chairs and a wide mahogany desk in the center of the room; the only decoration was a Remington bronze seated on a pedestal in the corner. It featured an exhausted Native American warrior slumped atop a horse, a reminder of the director's heritage and a testament to the cost of battle for any soldier.

Painter stood before a trio of flat-screen monitors that glowed on three of the walls. The director had shed a navy suit jacket, which now hung over the back of his chair. The sleeves of his starched white shirt were rolled to his elbows, a sign that he'd likely been up for hours if not all night. The entire command center, buried under the Smithsonian Castle on the National Mall, buzzed with activity. Even Kat down the hall had only waved to him as he passed Sigma's intelligence nest. She had been bent over a monitor with her second-in-command.

Something definitely has everyone stirred up.

Envy and irritation flickered through him. Before going on paternity leave, he had always been in the thick of things, one of Sigma's top field operatives. Now he felt like someone stumbling into the middle of a story. Not only was he out of the loop, but he felt out of step with the rhythm here.

He didn't like it.

As Painter crossed toward his desk, Gray noted the flat-screen that the director had been studying. It showed a topographic map of Greenland's eastern coast. A pattern of red Vs crisscrossed the neighboring sea. Call signs next to them suggested they were military planes.

"Take a seat," Painter said. "Kat will join us in a moment after she loops in a video call."

Gray sank into a chair, as the director settled behind his desk. Though more than a decade older, Painter kept his frame trim and muscular. There was never any waste to the man. The only notable change was that he'd grown his jet-black hair longer, nearly to his collar. His face was more deeply tanned, highlighting his Native American heritage.

Gray knew the source for these physical changes. Monk had told him that Painter had spent a break with his wife, Lisa, on a horse trek through Arizona, such was the carefree life of a married couple without kids.

I remember such times . . .

Though it felt like a lifetime ago.

Director Crowe had returned last week—apparently arriving in time to deal with this crisis. Before Painter spoke, he combed a single snowy lock behind one ear, like tucking in an eagle's feather, and sized Gray up.

"Fatherhood seems to agree with you," he finally said.

"You should've seen me a couple months ago." Gray rubbed the dark stubble on his chin. He remembered the beard he'd briefly sported. For a while, he'd been too exhausted to shave, his hygiene routine intermittent at best. Even now, he wore a pair of black jeans pulled from the hamper and a hooded gray sweatshirt.

Painter nodded. "Still, thanks for interrupting your leave."

"What's going on?"

"Apparently a situation in Greenland has blown up in our faces. A few days ago, we got word of the discovery of a shipwreck buried within the heart of a glacier."

Painter picked up a remote and swiveled his chair. He pointed to the flat-screen monitor to his left. A poor, pixelated image appeared on the screen, showing a broken-masted ship half trapped in ice.

"A pair of researchers up there—a climatologist and geologist—discovered it by accident. Along with a treasure inside."

Painter clicked the remote and showed a photo of a gold map in a dark box with a spherical object imbedded in it.

Gray stood up and crossed over to get a better look. "I don't understand. Why does this discovery concern Sigma?"

"I'll get to that in a moment. Just know we needed to confirm the discovery's authenticity and secure it quickly. After a few inquiries, I learned that Maria Crandall knew a colleague, a nautical archaeologist working in Egypt, who we convinced to investigate the ship."

"Maria? Kowalski's girlfriend?"

"That's right. Those two were already in Africa. I had them follow behind the archaeologist, so that if what was discovered was authenticated, they'd be able to secure it and extract it."

Gray began to suspect why this situation in Greenland had *blown up*, as Painter described.

If Kowalski was involved . . .

Painter continued, sharing a tale of a deadly ambush, the theft of a map, and the kidnapping of an archaeologist. But the story also told of something unleashed from the hold of the ship, something horrific and impossible.

"Details are still coming in," Painter admitted. "A brutal storm made communication with Greenland sketchy. Now that the weather's let up, we have five Poseidons flying a search grid, hunting for that submarine."

Gray glanced over to the Greenland map with its crimson Vs moving slowly over the Arctic Ocean. He pointed to one veering away from the others. "Did they pick up a trail?"

Painter glanced back. "No. A set of sonobuoys detected the sub as it headed north along the coast. It traveled beyond the buoys' range, but from the trajectory and speed, we suspect it sought the cover of the Arctic ice cap."

"From under there, it can travel anywhere without being seen."

"Exactly."

"You said the assault team spoke Arabic. Do we have any intel on who they might be?"

"Not as of yet. Kat has every international intelligence agency trying to answer that question. She was able to determine that Conrad Nelson— the murdered geologist—shared the photos I showed you with his employers, Allied Global Mining. After that, anyone there could have shared them far and wide."

"Where they reached the wrong eyes."

"And the *right* ones. Those same photos drew another agency's attention. They asked for our help and drew Sigma into this mess." He glanced significantly at Gray. "It's that group who asked for *your* assistance."

"Me? Why?"

"They want—"

Painter was cut off as sharp voices carried from the hall. Gray recognized Kat's voice, trying to calm someone. The man with her sounded both flabbergasted and angry, his accent distinctly Bostonian: "Who the hell knew all this was down here? Right under our noses."

Painter stood up and checked his watch. "He's early." He sighed to Gray. "The president asked that Sigma personally accommodate his visit, especially considering the circumstance."

Gray frowned. Only a handful of people outside of DARPA knew of Sigma's existence, let alone the presence of these covert headquarters at the edge of the National Mall.

Kat arrived first, leaning on a cane. Though mostly recovered from her ordeal last Christmas, she still remained weak on her left side. She was dressed in navy blues with an emerald frog pin in her lapel, a remembrance of teammates lost.

She moved aside to let the visitor enter. "This way, Senator."

Into the office stepped a tall, broad-shouldered man, outfitted in a trim Armani suit with a blue tie and black leather shoes polished to a sheen. Gray suddenly felt way underdressed in his jeans and hoodie, especially considering who had just arrived.

Painter came around his desk and shook the man's hand. "Senator Cargill, welcome to Sigma command."

Gray inwardly kicked himself. Earlier, engrossed in Painter's story, he had failed to make the connection. It was perhaps a testament to how rusty he'd gotten during his leave. The name of the kidnapped archaeologist— Dr. Elena Cargill—had not clicked with him.

Is this the reason Sigma is all riled up?

Senator Kent Cargill took in the room with a glance. His focus briefly fixed on the map of Greenland, then returned to Painter. The fifty-year-old man stood over six feet tall, all lean muscle, honed by two combat infantry tours in the Middle East, one during Desert Storm. His dark blond hair was slightly curled, disheveled but in a manner that made him seem approachable.

Few in the country didn't know his face. Some considered him the JFK of the new millennium, especially with his Bostonian accent. Like Kennedy, he was also Roman Catholic, but unlike the former president, he was not polarizing. People on both sides of the political aisle loved him. He was devout in his faith, but open-minded. He was firm in his convictions, but willing to compromise. A rarity on Capitol Hill. There was talk of him running for president, to fill the soon-to-be-empty White House.

Gray shared a look with Painter. It was the director who had recruited Elena to investigate the ship in Greenland, who put her in harm's way and got her kidnapped as a result.

Senator Cargill's eyes were cold and hard, and in this matter, *uncompromising*.

"Where the hell is my daughter?"

9

Looks like I've come nearly full circle.

Elena stared out the private jet's window at the sun glinting off blue seas, the spread of islands. Having researched this region for her entire career, she had no trouble identifying landmarks, enough to roughly estimate her location.

I'm back in the Mediterranean . . . likely over the Aegean Sea.

She guessed a little over twenty-four hours had passed since she had been taken aboard that infernal submarine. But she couldn't be certain. Her captors had locked her in a cabin with a lone bunk, where without portholes she could not sense the passage of time. They had fed her and treated her brusquely but not cruelly. Despite the tension, she had napped fitfully—only to be shocked awake when the entire sub shook violently.

Panicked, heart pounding, she had feared they'd been torpedoed or blasted by a depth charge. Then that hulking brute of a bodyguard had come and hauled her out of the cabin and over to the sub's command center. Bright sunlight flowed down through the open hatch of the conning tower, along with a blast of freezing air. She was forced at gunpoint up the ladder, where she discovered a featureless world of windblown snow and

blindingly white ice. She realized the earlier crash had been the sub cracking through the Arctic ice cap.

Not far from the sub, a turboprop plane sat on a makeshift runway
scraped into the ice. After she and six members of the assault team had
offloaded, the submarine quickly submerged, plainly not wanting to be
spotted. She was transferred to the turboprop, which took them to a nondescript island. There she had been forced into this jet.

Movement drew her attention back to present. The assault team leader
came down the cabin's aisle. The jet's interior was appointed in rich fin-
ishes of ash wood and blond leather. A bar at the back was lined with Bac-
carat crystal. She only knew that because of the fancy water goblet resting
on the table between her and the seat facing her. Clearly the attack in
Greenland had nothing to do with the value of the ancient map's precious
metals.

Something bigger was afoot.

The woman dropped into the seat opposite. Elena noted how drawn
and silent the team leader had become. The caramel of her features had
paled; her eyes looked haunted. After the rush of escaping Greenland,
she clearly must have been dwelling on the events, digesting them more
fully, trying to come to terms with the horrors unleashed from the ancient
dhow's hold.

"We will be landing soon," the woman said.

Elena stared back at her, too curious to stay silent, willing to risk
punishment, suspecting that now might be the time to get some answers.
"Who are you?"

The leader answered with a stretch of silence, studying Elena, as if
judging whether she was worthy of such knowledge. She finally spoke.
"You can call me Bint Mūsā."

Elena translated the name. "Daughter of Moses."

She got a nod of confirmation. The woman absently traced a finger
along the scar. "A title that is hard-earned."

Elena swallowed, not doubting the woman. She also fought to keep
her face expressionless. She was suddenly too conscious of the pressure at

her lower back. So far, the others had not discovered what she had kept hidden. Apparently assuming she was no threat, they had only patted her down, making sure she had no weapons, and confiscated her phone before locking her up in the sub.

They had failed to find the small sealskin-wrapped package tucked in an inner pocket of her parka, the artifact she had taken from the ship captain's corpse. While aboard the submarine, anxious and needing a distraction, she had risked examining the object. She cracked its wax seal, parted the old skin, and found two preserved chapbooks inside, with leather covers stitched together with thick cords.

She had been too afraid of damaging the brittle books to open them, but long ago their titles had been burned into the ancient leather and remained legible. Both were inscribed in cursive Arabic. The first was a single word—ملحمة—which meant *Odyssey*. At the time, she wondered if it could be a written translation of Homer's epic poem, but she could not risk opening it to find out.

Especially as the second title was even more intriguing.

Even now that line of Arabic burned in her mind's eye, along with its translation.

The Testament of the Fourth Son of Moses.

Elena had imagined it must be the dead captain's log, an account of how his ship ended up in a sea cave along the coast of Greenland, why it had stayed there, and where it had come from to be carrying such horrific cargo. She had wanted to crack that journal open, but she feared damaging such a vital historical record, the final words of a *Son of Moses*.

She stared at the scarred woman across from her, who claimed the title of *Daughter of Moses*. What could be the connection? She had no doubt there was one. Her kidnappers certainly seemed to know far more about the dhow and the golden map than anyone else.

The pilot radioed back to the passenger compartment, speaking Turkish, which surprised Elena, considering everyone else spoke Arabic. "We'll be landing in ten minutes. Fasten your seat belts."

Elena had already done that, so she turned to the window and stared

below. A coastline appeared ahead. If she was right about the blue waters below being the Aegean Sea, she guessed that the rocky shore ahead
marked the coast of Turkey. To keep her fears in check, she tried to determine *where* along the coastline they were headed. She searched for landmarks, took account of the sun's position, and felt a chill, born of certainty
and trepidation.

A wide waterway cut to the northeast. *That has to be the Dardanelles
Strait.* In classical antiquity, it was named the Hellespont, or the Sea of
Helle. The strait cut through northwestern Turkey and connected to the
Sea of Marmara.

*It seems I truly have traveled full circle . . . from Helheim to the Sea of
Helle.*

She returned her attention to the approaching coastline. She recognized that deep carve of a bay, the towering cliffs sweeping to either side.
She had recently seen a depiction of this port. She pictured the golden
map's tiny silver ship resting along this very stretch of coast. Back at the
dhow, she remembered naming this place and getting confirmation from
the woman seated across from her.

The plane reached the coast and dropped lower.

Acres of ancient walls and foundations came into view below, further
solidifying her conviction.

She knew this place.

It's the ruins of Troy.

She glanced back to the woman, to Bint Mūsā, this Daughter of Moses. Dark eyes studied Elena in turn.

What the hell is going on?

10

Gray dropped back into the leather chair in front of the director's desk. "We'd better find his daughter."

Senator Kent Cargill had just left, escorted by Kat.

Painter remained standing, his expression pained. "Agreed. We don't need to make an enemy of this man, especially if he ends up in the White House."

The director had spent the past forty minutes updating the senator on their search efforts and the plans going forward, involving intelligence and policing agencies around the world. Cargill took in these details, asked pertinent questions, and offered his resources as head of the Committee on Foreign Relations in the Senate.

Gray had simply listened, letting these two men discuss everything. He had expected the panicked father—a senator surely used to getting his way—to throw his weight around, to butt heads with the director, to make demands. And certainly, Cargill's eyes were haunted, his lips drawn and pale with worry, but the man stayed on task, perhaps knowing that the best chance to recover his daughter would not be served by bluster and threats.

Gray tried to imagine how he'd act if someone kidnapped Jack. *I'd be knocking walls down.* Considering the senator's judicious calm in the face of such a crisis, he would make a great president. There was steel in his spine, and he had a mind as sharp as a bear trap.

As to Sigma's culpability in involving his daughter, he readily acknowledged his daughter was headstrong and as passionate about her work as he was. There was even a glimmer of interest when Painter told him about the ancient dhow discovered buried in the ice of Greenland, a discovery that could prove Arab explorers reached the New World centuries before the Vikings.

Cargill had shaken his head upon hearing all of this and admitted with a sniff of amusement: *Once Elena caught wind of this, you couldn't have kept my daughter away.*

Now that matters had been resolved with mutual respect, Painter rounded his desk and returned to his chair. He sank down and stared pointedly at Gray. "As you can see, we definitely need our *best* people on this case."

Gray understood the implied request and hoped that description still applied to him.

"But I'm not the only one who would like to enlist your help," Painter said, reminding Gray about their earlier discussion.

"Who are you talking about?"

"I told you before that the photos taken by the geologist were distributed to his employers and likely spread far and wide."

"Reaching the wrong eyes. Got it. But what did you mean by these images reaching the *right* ones? You mentioned another agency getting wind of all of this. Who?"

Before Painter could answer, Kat knocked on the door frame behind him and entered. "Now that our esteemed guest is gone," she said, "I've reestablished the videoconference call."

She crossed around to Painter's computer and raised a questioning eyebrow at the director, who nodded permission for her to use his desktop. She typed rapidly, and the flat-screen behind him flickered, an image juddered, then firmed into the features of a man. The figure appeared to be leaning on a desk, his face near the webcam on his end.

His green eyes twinkled with amusement. He wiped a fall of black hair aside, a match to his priestly frock. The white of his Roman collar flashed on the screen.

It was Finn Bailey—*Father* Finn Bailey.

Gray immediately understood *who* had requested his involvement.

"I see our prodigal son has returned," the priest said with a distinct Irish brogue, clearly having a full view of Painter's office on his screen. "Welcome back, Commander Pierce."

Gray ignored Bailey and turned to Painter. "The other entity that heard about the discovery, that saw the geologist's photos . . . it was the Vatican."

"Not in its entirety," Bailey answered from the screen. "Only those of us in its *intelligenza*."

Gray sensed a much larger story about to unfold. Few were aware that the Vatican had its own intelligence agency, its own spy network. For decades—if not centuries—it secretly sent out operatives to infiltrate hate groups, secret societies, hostile countries, wherever the concerns of the Vatican were threatened. Basically, they were James Bonds in clerical collars—but without the license to kill.

Gray's history with this organization went back eleven years, when he'd first met Monsignor Vigor Verona, a former member of the *intelligenza*, an honorable man who would go on to save Gray's life and whose niece had once captured his heart. Both were now gone, sacrificing themselves to save the world.

Just seeing Father Bailey woke that old pain. The priest—who was no older than Gray—had been a former student of Monsignor Verona at the Pontifical Institute of Christian Archaeology in Rome and eventually recruited into the Vatican's *intelligenza*. Due to this past connection to his dear friend, Gray was willing to hear this priest out, but a part of him still found the man grating, too full of himself, too assured that he filled out the shoes of his former mentor.

Never, Gray thought. *You'll never be Vigor.*

Aloud, he asked, "What does any of this have to do with the Vatican?"

"Ah," Bailey said, "that's a long story, one too long to relate at the moment. I think it's best if we start with the present. A week ago, our organization was alerted to a set of photos circulating about a discovery in Greenland. We recognized the importance of this find, specifically the gold map and silver astrolabe, and how it tied to a mystery going back centuries here at the Vatican."

"What mystery?" Gray asked.

Bailey raised a hand. "Suffice it to say, we wished to have the discovery authenticated and the treasure brought here. That was our priority, but as you can imagine, there are not a lot of Catholic churches in Greenland, let alone a member of our *intelligenza.*"

"So they asked for our help," Painter filled in.

"We believed this matter needed to be addressed quickly," Bailey explained, "especially as word was likely to spread."

Kat straightened up from the computer. "Which tragically proved to be the case."

"Do you know anything about the ones who stole the map?" Gray asked. "Who kidnapped Dr. Elena Cargill?"

"Unfortunately, we do not. But we do know those thieves were not entirely successful in their pillaging of the site."

Gray frowned. "What do you mean?"

Painter answered, "The climatologist on site, Douglas MacNab, was able to secure the spherical astrolabe after it was accidentally dislodged from the map. The man said the group that attacked them wanted it, called it the Daedalus Key."

The Daedalus Key?

"We don't know why they call it that," Bailey admitted. "But one of our members—a colleague at the Pontifical Institute of Christian Archaeology—is familiar with such devices, these spherical astrolabes. They are a rarity. And we can guess why those thieves wanted it so desperately."

"Why?" Gray asked.

"I'll let the monsignor explain."

Bailey reached forward to his keyboard, and the webcam image widened, revealing a figure standing to his left. Gray stiffened in his seat. His reaction was not only because Bailey had failed to mention anyone else was in the room, listening in on the conversation. It again went to this priest's brash nature.

Even Painter looked perturbed. Kat simply went cold-eyed.

Gray leaned forward, doing his best to cover his initial shock. Maybe it was Bailey's use of the title *monsignor*. But for the briefest moment, Gray thought it was Vigor Verona standing there, some ghostly apparition, but as the man stepped closer, Gray recognized it was only a resemblance. The monsignor wore the same formalwear of his station. He was also roughly the same age as Vigor had been—maybe late sixties, early seventies—with a similar fringe of gray hair framing his bald tonsure.

"This is Monsignor Sebastian Roe, a professor at the university and a longtime member of our *intelligenza*. You may speak freely in front of him."

Like we had any choice prior to this moment.

The monsignor took Bailey's place and smiled shyly. "From your expressions, I see Father Bailey had not informed you all of my presence." He cast a scolding look at the priest. "I think I remember someone once telling me that *young men think old men fools, and old men know young men to be.*"

Gray could not help but smile. The guy even talked like Vigor.

Monsignor Roe turned his attention back to those on his screen. "You'll also have to forgive if I'm a bit didactic. I've been teaching for four decades and I think I can't help it when I'm speaking to a group."

He cleared his throat and began to explain. "To understand the importance of what was secured from that frozen ship, you must first understand its rarity. No one knows *who* invented the first astrolabe, a device that's part cosmic map and part analog computer, capable of determining the position of stars and constellations, the rising and setting of the sun, even nautical directions. But most believe the first astrolabe was invented by the Greeks during the second century B.C. Maybe by Apollonius or Hipparchus."

Roe waved this last detail aside. "Anyway, it was a *crude* version. Later, astrolabes were refined to their finest form in the Middle East during the Islamic Golden Age. Still, even then, these astrolabes were flat, planar in nature. Let me show you."

He tapped at the keyboard, and a window popped up in one corner of the screen, showing a gilded flat plate covered in hands, dials, and inscriptions.

"This is how all astrolabes looked up until the ninth century. Then the first *spherical* astrolabe was invented, likely by Al-Nayrizi, a Muslim mathematician. But to this day, only a *single* example of such a device has ever been found. It sits at the History of Science Museum at Oxford University."

He reached and clicked again to bring up the image of a tarnished brass globe engraved with symbols, Arabic numbers, constellations, and all encircled by arched arms and etched bands.

"This artifact dates back to the fifteenth century, to the Middle Ages, and was likely made in Syria. But it's what's written on the bottom that is the most intriguing." He brought up an image of the lower half of the globe, where faint inscriptions could be seen.

"What's written here reads *The Work of Mūsā*."

Gray stood up to get a closer look. "Mūsā? Is that the name of the artist?"

Roe seemed to stare straight at Gray from the screen. "So it has been believed, but I think if you read deep into the history of—"

Bailey stepped forward and cut him off. "Like I mentioned, let's return to what's going on *today* before we get too lost in the past."

Gray narrowed his eyes, sensing Bailey was keeping something significant up the sleeves of his priestly frock.

"What was recovered in Greenland," Bailey continued, "is only the *second* such astrolabe ever found. That alone makes it valuable, but it is also a significant cog in the mechanical map that was taken from that ship. It is in fact its *key*. That's why we requested it be brought to Rome for any chance of knowing what it portends, where it might point to."

Painter stood and stepped over to the map of Greenland, where an ongoing search for the missing submarine continued, depicted in real time. He pointed out the single red V that had veered off from the others and headed east across the Atlantic.

"Kowalski, Maria, and Dr. MacNab are aboard this Poseidon jet. They're already on their way to bring the artifact to the Vatican."

"We'd like you to join us here, Commander Pierce," Bailey said. "That silver astrolabe is only the first piece of a larger puzzle, but some pieces are still missing. We could use your unique insight to help us pull it all together."

Now it's beginning to make sense.

Gray knew he had been recruited into Sigma for this very talent, far more than for his military prowess. While growing up, Gray had always been pulled between opposites. His mother had taught at a Catholic high school, but she was also an accomplished biologist. His father was a Welshman living in Texas, a roughneck oilman disabled in midlife and forced to assume the role of a housewife. It was maybe this upbringing that made him look at things differently, to try to balance extremes. Or maybe it was something genetic, ingrained in his DNA, that allowed him to see patterns that no one else could.

This is why Bailey asked for me.

"Before I agree to travel to Rome," Gray said, "you seem to have some general sense of where this map leads. I want to know."

Bailey's eyes sparkled brighter. "Surely you've already figured that out, Commander Pierce. Otherwise, maybe it's best if you stay home."

Gray wondered if it was a mortal sin to punch a priest, but Bailey was right. He already had a good idea. "That ship was carrying a cargo beyond comprehension," he said. "Something horrific, fueled by a volatile radio-active compound—"

Roe nodded. "We've discussed it. We believe it's a form of Greek fi—"

Bailey lifted a hand. "Let's not interrupt Commander Pierce's assessment."

Roe shook his head, clearly growing as irritated with the young upstart as Gray was, but the monsignor simply crossed his arms.

Gray continued: "The mechanical map must have been engineered to act as some sort of navigational tool. To lead to the source of the ship's deadly cargo."

Bailey's smile widened. "Precisely. And as a way to lure you away from your parental responsibilities, I will tell you the name of that source."

Gray let out an exasperated sigh, growing tired of this game of secrets. "What is it?"

"The map's builders named the place Tartarus."

Painter frowned. "Tartarus? As in the Greek version of Hell?"

Gray remembered the director's description of what had been unleashed from that ship's hold. The name was certainly apt.

Bailey nodded. "But keep in mind that Tartarus was not only the Greek's abyss of torment and suffering. It was also the corner of Hades where the Titans were imprisoned. The monstrous gods who preceded the Olympians. Creatures of immense power, beings of fire and destruction."

The priest let this description hang in the air.

Kat turned to Painter. "Whether metaphorical or not, this unknown site is clearly a cache of some unknown fuel source, not to mention diabolical weapons. If Father Bailey's colleagues in the *intelligenza* know of this place, then whoever kidnapped Elena Cargill—who seems to know far more about this than anyone—must also be aware of this legend."

Gray nodded. "They intend to find that place and plunder its resources."

Painter turned to him. "We can't let that happen."

"Which is why we'd like Commander Pierce to join us in Rome," Bailey said. "I suspect time is of the essence. Especially, as Captain Bryant has so wisely stated, our unknown enemy is already better informed than we are."

Painter stared at Gray.

"Before I agree to go," Gray said, "there's someone I have to consult with first."

And she's not going to be happy.

12:33 P.M.
Takoma Park, Maryland

Seichan cursed as she fit the shield over her left breast. *Should've bought a double pump.* She shifted in the kitchen chair, her back supported by a pillow. She had fed Jack an hour ago and put him down for a noon nap in his crib, but she knew he could wake at any moment.

While Jack slept, she stared at a series of digital photos as they slowly faded from one to another to another in an electronic frame: *Jack as a new-born with a hospital bonnet on his head, then a month later in a sailor onesie, another with a grin that filled his entire face, then in the arms of Gray, who wore a proud papa expression.*

A warmth spread through her, and she switched sides.

Another image appeared: *Gray in swim trunks, lifting a giggling Jack from a baby pool in the backyard.* She stared at his muscular physique, the flash of his ice-blue eyes in the sunlight, the wet mop of his dark hair. She loved Jack dearly, achingly so, but she also recognized that parental responsibilities, not to mention sleep deprivation, had diminished the level of intimacy between her and Gray. But, of course, Jack's addition had also added a lot to their relationship, too.

She knew all too well that life was evolution; romantic bonds changed over time. If they didn't, stagnation could kill a relationship as surely as any infidelity.

As one image faded to the next, she remembered when she and Gray had first met. It had been in a biological research lab in Fort Detrick. She had shot him. She clearly remembered that moment, but it now felt like a different person had pulled that trigger. It felt like watching a movie versus a real event in her own life.

Back then, she had been an assassin with a terrorist organization. She had eventually betrayed them and helped bring the group down. Afterward, alone and abandoned, she found a refuge with Sigma, then a home with Gray.

Still, she could not discount the fact that a hard core existed within herself, one that persisted, one she could not deny. From a young age, she had been brutalized into a killer. A part of her still craved that adrenaline spike in her blood.

She again heard that gunshot, watched Gray fall in her mind's eye. Other deaths—far bloodier—flashed through her. She didn't feel horror, only a familiar coldness, bordering on satisfaction.

Nearby, the digital image faded into a picture of her, gently kissing the soft fontanel atop her baby's head.

Who is that woman?

Who am I?

She didn't entirely know—and she feared the answer. To make matters worse, over the past several weeks, she felt like she was losing herself. And if she did, what could she offer Gray? What kind of mother would she be to Jack? To distract herself, she did her best to focus on the task at hand, a skill honed into her as an assassin. She concentrated on raising Jack, putting all her energy there, because that was easier than looking in the mirror.

But that was no longer working.

Something was building inside her, along with a new fear.

Until I know who I am, maybe Jack would be better without me.

Noting that her milk production had dwindled, she turned off the pump and set about detaching the bottle and screwing on the lid.

As she did, the front door opened, and Gray called her name.

"In the kitchen!" she yelled back, her voice cracking a bit.

About time you're back.

His boots thumped across the hardwood floor, then he pushed through the swinging door to join her. He was sweaty, his breath quick. His very presence filled the kitchen. Even his scent washed away the sweet perfume of milk with a ripe musky masculinity.

"I have something to discuss with you. Sigma wants me to—"

"I know," she interrupted, standing up. "Kat called me and filled me in. You need to go."

"Are you sure?"

"Yes, I'm sure. Because I'm going with you."

Gray stiffened. "But what about—?"

"Kat's going to watch Jack. Monk's already on his way over to pick him up. Harriet and Penny are beyond thrilled." She crossed to the refrigerator and put the two bottles at the back, adding to the lineup there. "I've been pumping regularly over the past weeks. I've got plenty here for four days, and more milk in the freezer for good measure."

She turned and met his eyes.

I need this.

She had expected him to balk, but instead, his eyes flashed with an excited glint. It had been a long time since she'd seen that thrill shining there. She felt her heart respond, pounding harder as she realized a deeper truth.

We need this.

Gray reached out and pulled her closer. "We could be heading into Hell. Maybe even literally."

She stared up at him and smiled, wider than she had in a long time.

"I'm counting on it."

11

The forty-eighth Mūsā to carry that holy title left the Kocatepe Mosque, the largest house of prayer in Ankara. It was where he always prayed when he visited Turkey's capital. He had just finished the Maghrib prayer, the sunset prayer, performing all three *rak'at*, the two *sunnahs*, and both non-obligatory *nafls*.

Now is not a time for half-measures.

He headed across the plaza, leaving the massive bulk of the mosque and its four thin minarets behind him. He was followed by the trio who served him, the three *Banū Mūsā*, the Sons of Moses. They were not in fact his blood, as such titles had to be earned through butchery and trials by fire. In fact, he had no children. His second wife remained at her family estate outside of Istanbul. It had been an arranged marriage, one necessary for his position. Afterward, they seldom spoke, even more rarely touched, just enough to consecrate their wedding bed.

His true family were these Sons of Moses who guarded him. They each carried a pair of Caracal F semiautomatic pistols in shoulder harnesses over their suit jackets. Eyes watched for any threats to his person.

He was led to his armor-plated limousine, where two *Bint Mūsā*, the fierce and deadly Daughters of Moses, guarded the vehicle, similarly armed, but also with throwing knives sheathed at their wrists.

One opened the door for him, and he climbed into the backseat.

The Sons joined him, while the Daughters slid into the front, one taking the wheel and engaging the idling engine. The long limousine slid into the evening traffic and headed through the brightly lit city. They were due at the airport in another hour, but first he had one last obligation in Ankara.

He settled back in his seat, but his heart still thrummed in his chest. Anxiety and excitement kept his muscles tense.

After so many centuries . . .

A long line of men took the title of Mūsā, going back to the ninth century, to the first of his name, Mūsā ibn Shākir, a great astronomer who was born in Khorasan in northeast Persia. He had four sons—though most historians only knew of *three*—who, due to their intelligence, studied at the famous House of Wisdom in Baghdad, during a time when Islam shone with a golden brightness. Following the fall of Rome, the sons spent their lives traveling far, gathering rare texts from Italy and Greece, preserving them, building upon the knowledge found in them. They would produce wondrous works, constructing canals and crafting ingenious devices, along with writing dozens of books.

But only a select few knew the secret history of the Banū Mūsā brothers, how *four* had become *three*, how one of Mūsā ibn Shākir's sons betrayed the others, stole their greatest treasure and the secret it protected, destroying all records, leaving no trace to follow. For this treachery, his name was stricken from their books, his history in the family erased.

It was as if Hunayn ibn Mūsā had never existed.

Still, what that brother stole, what he sought to keep from the world, was not forgotten by a sect within Baghdad's House of Wisdom. They kept that knowledge hidden, from generation to generation, from one caliphate to another, from one country to another. Forty-seven men had led this cabal in the past, each taking the title of *Mūsā*, knowing that someday what was lost would be found again.

And that time was upon the world now.

I am the forty-eighth Mūsā—and I will be the last.

He had suffered much to achieve this position, a birthright forged in blood and grief. His first wife—his dearest Esra—and his baby boy were killed by a Kurdish bomb. He eventually hunted the insurgents down, and in the dead of night, slaughtered those responsible, along with their wives and children. Still, all that blood could not wash away his grief.

Instead, he gathered a new set of Sons and Daughters to his side, those hardened to the cause. He intended not only to make all of Kurdistan suffer, but to ignite the entire region. With tensions throughout the Middle East at their highest, the time to bring about Armageddon had come. The return of what was lost was a portentous omen.

Into this powder keg, I will not just toss a match—I will cast forth a thousand flaming torches.

He considered what had befallen the team in Greenland, the horrors that had slaughtered them. It was proof that what Hunayn had sought to keep hidden did truly exist. With such knowledge, Mūsā knew what he must do, what he knew in his heart was always his destiny.

I will find the entrance to Hell, break open those gates, and unleash Armageddon.

He had always sensed the end-times were upon the world. From the unnatural disasters, the pollution of the planet, the endless wars, and most important of all, the moral decay around the globe. The signs were all around. Recognizing this, Mūsā had studied the Islamic apocalyptic writings and read the hadiths—words attributed to Prophet Muhammad— that spoke of the Last Days, when Isa, whom the Christians named Jesus, would return.

He closed his eyes and silently recited a much-quoted apocalyptic hadith: *The Son of Mary will soon descend among you as a just ruler; he will break the cross and kill the swine.* Unlike Christendom's view of the end-times, Islam believed that when Jesus returned, he would shun Christians and side with Muslims. He would end his own worship by destroying the cross and prohibiting the eating of a pig's flesh, as was already dictated by Muslim law.

And Jesus would not come alone.

Preceding his momentous return would be the arrival of a twelfth imam, a divine caliph and descendant of Muhammad, who would purge away injustice, battle Satan, and burn the world clean.

That figure was called *Mahdi*, whose name means *the guided one*.

Over the past centuries, many men—false prophets—had claimed to be the twelfth imam, but Mūsā knew the truth. He knew with certainty that there was only one who could purge the world. And the discovery in Greenland—during the reign of the forty-eighth Mūsā—was surely proof.

I will find the gates of Hell, steal Satan's flame, and cleanse the world with fire.

Then his title would forever change.

From Mūsā to Mahdi.

He had always known in his bones that this was his true destiny.

The phone in his pocket rang and vibrated. He retrieved it, already expecting this call. The voice that answered confirmed it.

"My esteemed Mūsā, our plane has landed on the coast," Bint Mūsā stated firmly, speaking Arabic as was traditional within their group, respecting the original tongue spoken by their ancient founders. "We are on our way to the House of Wisdom."

"Very good. And the map is secure? The archaeologist in hand?"

"Yes, but as I've informed you, we regretfully failed to retrieve the Daedalus Key."

Mūsā heard the anguish at this failure, a misstep that would normally deserve punishment, but this Daughter had recovered much and suffered horrible losses. He would grant her mercy—and hope.

"Fear not, my Daughter, we will obtain the Daedalus Key. Plans are already in motion."

A sigh of relief followed. "I am grateful to hear such glorious news."

"I will meet you at the House of Wisdom by midnight."

He hung up the phone, ready to attend to his last obligation in Ankara. The limousine turned onto Atatürk Boulevard. The car traveled the tree-lined street to a set of tall gates in a stone wall. An American flag decorated the entrance to the U.S. embassy.

The gates stood wide, flanked by guards.

As the limo parked at the curb, Mūsā climbed out. Classical music drifted through the open doors to the compound, where a party was already under way in the courtyard.

The U.S. deputy chief of mission approached, his hand outstretched. "*Hoş geldiniz*," he greeted in Turkish. "Ambassador Firat, we're thrilled you were in town and could attend our soiree tonight."

"Most gracious." He shook the man's hand. "As the ambassador to your beautiful country, how could I not?"

Escorted by the deputy, Mūsā headed through the gates, stepping onto foreign territory while in his own land.

Soon all such borders will be burned away.

From the courtyard, he glanced back to his limo, full of his Sons and Daughters. He turned around with a smile, knowing others of his family were already preparing for the next step in his plans.

To secure the Daedalus Key.

12

Kowalski frowned and sat up straighter as the Land Rover turned off the main highway that circled Rome and headed to the southwest. Leaving the glow of the city behind, the SUV sped away and climbed toward dark hills dotted with the lights of small villages. Black clouds obliterated the stars as a summer thunderstorm threatened. Thunder echoed down from the highlands sounding like distant cannon fire.

"Where are we going?" he asked from the backseat, turning away from the lights of Rome. "I thought we were going to where the pope lives."

"We are," Maria answered with an exasperated sigh next to him.

"Isn't that back in Rome? At the Vatican?"

"Yes, but like I told you, we're going to the pope's *summer* palace. In a town called Castel Gandolfo, sixteen miles to the south. It's up in the hills outside Rome. That's where Director Crowe wants us to take the astrolabe, and where we'll meet with Father Bailey and Monsignor Roe."

Kowalski settled back down, too tired to press the matter. He was glad Maria had been on that conference call with Crowe. He was no good with details, especially after days of tension and too little sleep. By the time they were finally able to escape Greenland, the ferocious windstorm had blown itself out, and their destination had changed. Rather than heading back to the States, they had been diverted to Italy, ordered to take the silver astrolabe here. No one bothered to explain why. But an order was an order. And if nothing else, the change put a burr under Pullman's saddle. The Poseidon's commander had been none too happy to be called away from hunting for that missing submarine and return again to his role as a glorified Uber driver.

Twenty minutes ago, the jet had touched down on the outskirts of Rome, at Guidonia Air Base, an Italian Air Force facility. Pullman nearly shoved them out the door.

Or at least, me.

A black Land Rover Defender with the word CARABINIERI stenciled in white on the side had been waiting on the tarmac. The driver, a young MP named Reynaldo, was dressed in a dark navy uniform with a matching beret. Kowalski had looked enviously at the man's holstered Beretta 92. Without any weapons, Kowalski felt naked.

Douglas MacNab leaned forward from the SUV's third row. "Maria, when are your teammates due to arrive?"

"Crack of dawn," she answered.

Kowalski rankled at this reminder. It was like Director Crowe couldn't trust him to deal with this mess on his own. Instead he had to send backup.

Suddenly worried, he glanced back to Mac, making sure the bearded climatologist hadn't left the case aboard the jet when they'd been rushed off. He was relieved to see the silver valise resting on the seat next to him. Due to low-level radioactivity, the astrolabe had been secured inside that lead-lined case. A yellow-and-red hazard label had been slapped onto its side, intended to keep anyone curious from opening it.

Not that Mac was going to let it out of his sight.

The climatologist had insisted on accompanying the astrolabe, his reasoning solid: *My friend died over this,* he had argued, *and Elena was kidnapped on my watch. Until I know what's really going on, this damned thing ain't leaving my side.*

Kowalski would've been satisfied with a simple *finders keepers* as an explanation, but he appreciated Mac's stubbornness and determination to get to the bottom of all of this.

He hoped it didn't get the guy killed.

The Land Rover climbed along a twisting two-lane rural highway, slowing down periodically when it passed through a village. As the SUV accelerated out of a place called Frattocchie, the summer storm finally found them. One moment the road was dry, then around a bend, rain whipped the vehicle in thick windblown sheets. Fat droplets pelted the roof. The windshield wipers beat wildly.

"Bad weather seems to be plaguing us," Mac said from the back.

Maria checked the map on her cell phone. "We're only three miles from Castel Gandolfo. We should be there soon."

As they continued, the storm steadily worsened. Visibility shrank toward the SUV's front bumper. Reynaldo cursed and was forced to slow down—and luckily, he did. Around another blind turn, they came upon a lumber truck that had jackknifed across both lanes, hazards blinking. The driver braked hard to avoid a collision.

So much for getting to that village anytime soon . . .

With the Land Rover idling, the driver swore in Italian and pushed open his door. "I'll find out what the problem is," he promised.

As the MP stepped out, the driver's-side window exploded. His body flew backward, pounded by a barrage of gunfire. A trio of black-clad men armed with stubby carbines burst around the tail of the truck and rushed forward.

Kowalski was already moving with the first gunshot. He shoved Maria down, vaulted over the seatback, and dropped behind the wheel. He kept low as gunfire strafed the windshield, shattering and splintering it. Not bothering to close the damaged door, he yanked on the gearshift and pounded the accelerator. All four tires gripped the wet road, and the Land Rover flew forward.

He crashed headlong into the side of the truck, pinning and crushing two of the shooters. A third rolled out of the way. Kowalski knew he had seconds before the bastard collected himself and fired.

He shoved the SUV into reverse and sped backward.

Lights flashed in his rearview mirror as two motorcycles dashed from side roads onto the highway. Riders lifted submachine guns as the bikes accelerated toward them, cutting off his exit.

No surprise there.

Kowalski braked hard—right next to Reynaldo's bloody body. With the driver's door still hanging open, he hung from the wheel and reached down with his free arm. He thumbed the flap on the MP's holster and yanked the Beretta free. Then he used all his core to pop upright in the seat.

Time for a little payback.

He lifted the pistol, balanced in both hands, and floored the gas pedal. With its gear still in reverse, the Rover sped backward. Kowalski aimed forward. The gunman by the truck had regained his feet on the rain-drenched road. Kowalski fired twice through the windshield. The bastard's body jerked the same number of times, both rounds striking center mass.

As the man fell, Kowalski kept the accelerator floored.

"Stay down!" he hollered to his passengers.

The SUV flew backward, forcing the motorcycles to split to either side. Through the shattered driver's window, he emptied the clip at the bike on the left side. Rounds sparked off metal. The rider in back tumbled away. The motorcycle careened wildly off the road, hit a boulder, and cartwheeled through the air and crashed into a tree.

The other cycle spun expertly on the road and came back at them, already firing, forcing Kowalski to keep low.

But he had not been the target.

The front right tire blew, sending the Rover into a spin on the wet road. Kowalski dropped the empty pistol and grabbed the wheel with both hands, as warning lights flashed across the dash. He regained control more by sheer will than by the grip of the SUV's tires. With the Rover now headed back the way it had come, he hit the accelerator and raced away from the motorcycle as it gave chase.

He might have made it, except that another lumber truck came barreling out of the storm at them. It purposely jackknifed across the road, blocking their escape. But not before a black SUV sped around it and raced to close the distance.

Goddamned bastards had backup upon backup.

"We're not getting out of this," Maria called from the back.

Like hell.

He swerved off the road and bounced headlong into an open field. Unfortunately, the heavy downpour had turned the fallow field into a muddy bog. Kowalski fought the Rover as best he could on its three good tires, but halfway across the field, it became mired in the mud, wheels spinning uselessly.

Kowalski swore and checked the rearview mirror. The other SUV had fared no better, even worse in fact. It had made the mistake of attempting to follow the Rover's tracks. The freshly churned-up mud proved more treacherous, quickly burying the vehicle up to its axles.

Men were already emptying out.

More came from the road.

"It's a footrace from here," Kowalski warned. "Everybody out."

As they all bailed from the Rover, Maria gasped. Kowalski turned. Mac clambered out next to her, his face a mask of pain. He had a hand clamped on his left shoulder. Blood seeped out faster than the rain could wash away. He had been struck sometime during the barrage, but the man hadn't made a sound.

Maria went to help him.

Instead, Mac nodded to the open door. "The case."

She understood and retrieved the lead-lined box. A fresh barrage of gunfire ripped the grassy field and pinged off the back of the Rover.

Kowalski pointed to a dark line of trees ahead. He prayed it marked the edge of a forest they could get lost in. "Go!"

They set off across the boggy field, the mud sucking at their boots. They kept the bulk of the Rover between them and their pursuers, but that meager protection would not last long. Still, they reached the trees safely and stumbled into cover. Unfortunately, they could not catch a break. The trees were thick pines, densely packed, but it was only a small copse.

Beyond the tiny patch, the ground fell away toward a black lake a mile off, framed by volcanic cliffs. Closer at hand, lights glowed in the storm, marking a town.

"That's Castel Gandolfo," Maria said. "Sitting above Lake Albano."

So close, yet so far.

"Almost made it," Mac said with a groan. Clearly the man had spent the last of his energy—and a good amount of his blood—getting here. He was going no farther.

Maria grimaced as she stared at the man, recognizing his plight, then turned to Kowalski. "You could still do it," she said.

"Do what?" he asked, though he already knew.

She held out the case. "You need to get this over to that village. You're the only one who could make that run."

"I'm not leaving you."

"I'll only slow you down. Besides—" She glanced to Mac. "I'm not leaving him, alone and bleeding."

He knew she was right and knew she would never leave the injured man. Still, he balked.

She pointed down the slope to a steaming vent where a thin stream ran down toward the distant lake. "There's a small cave there. Probably a hot spring. We'll hole up inside there. You haul ass for that village."

Shouts rose behind them. The enemy was closing in.

He stared at Maria, his heart hammering in his ears. He did the only thing he could—and took the case.

10:48 P.M.

Maria and Mac huddled deeper into the steamy warmth of the shallow cave. She cringed as footfalls and voices sounded to the left, but none of the pursuers spotted their hiding place.

All eyes seemed to be on Joe. She spotted his shadowy form bounding down the slope, using bushes and boulders as cover. A thin stream bubbled out of the back of the cave and flowed between her and Mac. The injured man sat with his knees at his chin in order to cram his big body into the small space. He shivered despite the heat, probably close to shock from blood loss and pain.

Sirens echoed over the hills as local police responded to the gunfire. She prayed the enemy heard it, too. That it made them call off the chase. Maria wanted to raise more of an alarm. She cradled her phone in her hand, ready to call for help, both to alert Castel Gandolfo of Joe's desperate run and to summon medical help for Mac.

But not yet.

She had to make sure no one heard her or saw the shine of her phone's screen. So, she waited breathlessly until all of the pursuers had chased their prey down the slope of the volcanic caldera. Once she could no longer spot Joe or his hunters, she lifted her phone.

Mac whispered to her. "Do you think he'll make it?"

"If anyone can, he can. And if not—"

She refused to even think about that, too guilt-ridden, too fraught with fear. She stared out through the steam to the cold rainy night, trying to spot Joe.

What have I done?

10:49 P.M.

His breath heaving, Kowalski stumbled down the grassy, rock-strewn slope to a gravel path. The case thumped against his thigh as he gulped a big lungful of wet air and prepared for another sprint. Across the footpath, maybe fifty yards away, he spotted the reflection of black water, its surface pebbled by heavy raindrops.

Lake Albano.

To his left, the path—likely part of a hiking trail around the lake— led toward the lights of Castel Gandolfo.

Gotta go for it.

He set off again, getting a second wind from knowing that his flight had drawn the enemy after him, away from Maria and Mac, everyone chasing this damned football. But he knew he was more of a defensive guard than a running back. He was built to hit hard, to bring an opponent down, not to sprint for the goalposts.

Still, sometimes a linebacker did make a touchdown.

Determined to prove this, he pounded harder along the path. Ahead, he could already make out windows and the dark outlines of stone walls and tiled roofs.

I can do this.

Then the world exploded with light. Startled and blinded, he skidded to a halt. Winds whipped more savagely, as if a tornado had caught him.

But it wasn't a tornado.

Gunfire chattered from above. Gravel erupted across his path as he blinked away the glare and shielded his eyes against the bright light.

He craned his neck up at the helicopter hovering overhead. It seemed the enemy had called in even more backup, this time air support. He stared again at those lights, knowing this particular linebacker had been tackled a few yards short of the goal.

He sank to his knees, put the case on the path, and lifted his arms.

Seconds later, above the beat of the helicopter's rotors, he heard the heavy tread of boots on gravel. He turned only to have the butt of a rifle slam into the bridge of his nose. Bone crunched, and his vision flared with a crimson flash of pain. As he fell on his side, a deeper darkness fell over him.

He fought to stay conscious—but even here, he was failing.

He felt the gust from the rotors as the helicopter lowered to collect its prize. He heard sirens but knew help would not arrive in time. Still, the enemy seemed to hear them, too. Shadows swirled around him; voices barked Arabic.

Closer at hand, someone grabbed the case.

He tried to reach for it, but his arm was kicked away.

No longer able to hold his head up, it fell to the gravel. He tasted blood, smelled it. Even his fading vision ran red, but he saw enough.

The case was unlatched and opened.

Kowalski stared at the empty box and coughed out a laugh.

Smart, girl . . . clearly too smart for me.

11:04 P.M.

Maria lowered her phone as the helicopter lifted and sped away. She suddenly could not breathe. Her chest heaved, but she could not catch any air. It had taken the last of her will, all of her energy to call Painter, to do her best to relate what had happened. He was already rousing forces in the area, but it would be too little, too late for one of them.

Joe . . .

She had heard the gunfire and feared the worst.

What have I done?

It had been her mantra after sending Joe on his futile run. She hadn't told him of her subterfuge, needing him to believe he carried the astrolabe with him. She wanted him to run with all his strength, both to draw the hunters away and for his own survival. If he had made it to Castel Gandolfo, then he and the artifact would be safe.

But if he didn't make it—

She parted her jacket and revealed the silver astrolabe in her lap. She had taken it from the case while running for the tree line and hidden it in her coat. Her specialty was behavioral science, mostly dealing with primates, but it applied here, too. She knew in the heat of the hunt that the enemy would pursue Joe. It was instinctual behavior of a predator spiked on adrenaline to chase running prey.

So, she had turned that to her advantage.

Still, the knowledge did nothing to assuage her guilt.

She took deep, gulping breaths.

I'm sorry, Joe.

13

Gray crossed the barricaded square. Ahead rose a four-story yellow building with shuttered windows and a set of massive wooden doors. The portico marked the entrance to the Pontifical Palace, the pope's private summer home. When the pontiff was not in residence, it also served as a museum.

Though that was not true today.

After last night's attack, the palace had been converted into a fortified bunker. The entire picturesque village of Castel Gandolfo—with its cobblestone streets, souvenir shops, and tiny cafés—was locked down. Military vehicles were parked along the quaint streets. The barricaded square was patrolled by gunmen in body armor and helmets. They were part of the *Gendarmeria Corpo della Città del Vaticano*, the Vatican's police force, assigned not only to investigate crime but also trained in counterterrorism. Like Vatican City proper in Rome, the hundred acres of the summer palace were not Italian territory but belonged to the pope.

Gray and Seichan had their identifications examined at two checkpoints. They had been patted down and electronically wanded at the barricade.

When they reached the tall portico doors, a man in a dark blue blazer waved them closer and asked for their papers again. From his cold countenance and the firm muscles bulging against the tailored Italian fabric, he was military, too. He was flanked by a matching pair of men, all of them wearing radio earpieces. Gray also noted the Heckler & Koch MP7 submachine guns half-hidden under their jackets and the holstered SIG P320 pistols, along with radio earpieces.

Despite the lack of their usual uniforms of Medici blue, red, and yellow, Gray knew who these loyal soldiers were. *Swiss Guards.* But not the regular patrols. Only the most elite of these Swiss soldiers were allowed to serve incognito, the equivalent of the pope's Secret Service.

As Gray waited with his arms crossed, he stared across the square. Dawn already glowed rosy to the east, though the sun was not yet up. Even with the small army gathered here, his eyes searched for any threat. He drew in deep breaths, anxious to keep moving. These constant roadblocks grated on him. It had been an interminable flight here, followed by the long drive from the air base.

Seichan touched his arm. "He'll be okay," she said, zeroing in on the source of his agitation.

While en route, Gray had been getting regular updates on the search for Kowalski. No body had been found where his teammate had been ambushed. Only blood and machine gun shells. Even now, scuba crews scoured the dark green waters of the nearby volcanic lake, looking for a body.

Finally, the guard passed back their identifications. "I am Major Bossard," he said with a stiff Swiss accent. "I will be your escort. You will not leave my sight while on Vatican land. Follow me."

He led them through the doors into the heart of the Pontifical Palace. They were brusquely marched along marble-lined halls, past the busts of popes, and through a luxurious greeting parlor with plush antique furniture. Gray noted velvet ropes marked off several areas, evidence that tourists were herded through these same spaces.

But he wasn't here for a tour.

Bossard finally led them through a set of doors to a wide balcony that overlooked a meticulously manicured hedge maze. The grounds here were larger than Vatican City, covering not only the palace and its gardens but also a small forest that hid an ancient Roman amphitheater, and a seventy-five-acre dairy farm.

A table had been set to take advantage of the garden view.

Three people pushed back and stood from the remains of a breakfast and greeted them.

Maria Crandall rushed forward and hugged Seichan. "Thank god you're both here," she said breathlessly.

Father Bailey came and shook Gray's hand. His eyes showed no twinkle of amusement now, only a grim determination. "I certainly agree with Dr. Crandall's statement."

Monsignor Roe stayed at the table and nodded to them. The older priest had shed his formal finery and simply wore jeans, a black buttoned shirt, and a light jacket against the morning's chill.

Gray noted one person was missing. "How is Dr. MacNab doing?"

Maria answered, "He's recovering. He's being cared for at a medical ward in one of the pontifical villas. He lost a fair amount of blood, but luckily the wound was only a deep graze."

"Any more word on Kowalski?" Seichan asked. Her well-intentioned words clearly tore open a wound in Maria.

She crossed her arms and turned slightly away. "Nothing," she mumbled.

"Then he must be alive," Gray concluded.

Maria glanced back to him. "Why do you think that?"

"As quickly as the attackers were chased off, if they had killed Kowalski, they would've left him where he fell. There would be no advantage in taking his body or hiding it. In fact, your bit of subterfuge likely saved Kowalski's life."

She straightened, plainly needing this reassurance. "What do you mean?"

"If those bastards had grabbed the astrolabe during the ambush—

either at the highway or along that lakeside trail—they would have no need
to keep any of you alive. They certainly would have shot Kowalski on the
spot. Instead, once they found the case empty, they would have grabbed
him. They would want to interrogate him, to find out what he knows."

"How can you be sure?"

Gray shrugged. "Because it's what I would've done."

Maria slowly uncrossed her arms. Some of the fear faded from her
face, but not the guilt. "How did those bastards even know we were coming up here?"

How indeed?

Gray turned to Father Bailey. "*Why* are we up here? Why did we need
to bring the astrolabe to the pope's summer palace?"

Bailey waved them to the table. "You should eat."

Gray grabbed the priest's arm before he could turn away. "Why?" he
pressed.

Major Bossard stepped forward, a palm resting on his holstered pistol.

Bailey waved the guard down and answered, "We're here because
Monsignor Roe requested it." He shook his arm free. "If you'll kindly join
us, maybe he'll explain his reasoning."

Gray exhaled his frustration and followed the priest.

As they settled to a table laden with platters of scrambled eggs, hearty
breads, and delicate pastries, Monsignor Roe cast an apologetic look all
around. "*Perdonami.* Perhaps in hindsight I should not have chosen this
location."

"It's not your fault," Gray said. "But why did you want us at the summer palace?"

Roe sighed, clearly trying to gather his thoughts. He finally said,
"What do you know of the Holy Scrinium?"

Gray frowned at the strangeness of this question and shook his head.
He had never heard the term.

Roe explained: "The first Vatican Library was officially established in
1475. Then in the seventeenth century, Pope Leo XIII separated out its
most vital volumes and records into a separate archive, the *Archivio Segreto
Vaticano.*"

"The Vatican's Secret Archives," Gray said.

The monsignor sighed. "*Si*, but before there was a Vatican Library, long before the Secret Archives, there was the Holy Scrinium. It was the pope's personal library. Founded by Pope Julius in the fourth century. It traveled with the popes that succeeded him, never leaving their sides. The archive contained books and theological writings dating back to the founding of Christendom."

Gray guessed where this was going. "The Holy Scrinium still exists."

Roe gave a bow of his head. "It is the true *secret* library of the Church."

Bailey leaned forward. "Monsignor Roe is the prefect of the Scrinium. Its official caretaker."

Roe explained his position. "The Holy Scrinium contains treasures too rare and important to be shared, too heretical to be shown, even too dangerous. It's why the astrolabe had to be brought *here*."

Gray looked back at the bulk of the summer palace as the newly risen sun turned its yellow walls to rose gold. "Are you saying the Holy Scrinium is hidden here?"

"No," Roe said. "Not exactly."

6:04 A.M.

Where are we going?

Seichan followed the others across the rooftop of the Pontifical Palace.

From this height, a panoramic view opened up on the full breadth of Lake Albano and the surrounding wooded hillsides and volcanic slopes. A cold breeze blew off the lake. She smelled a scent of orange and lavender in the wind.

No wonder the popes picked this place to escape Rome's stifling heat.

On the rooftop, sections of the view were blocked by a pair of huge silver domes, two astronomical observatories.

Monsignor Roe explained to Gray. "These observatories are mostly showpieces today. Two new ones were installed a mile to the south, in a converted nunnery. We're just finishing up a summer school program over there, in astronomy and astrophysics. Proof that science continues and will always be part of our religious life here."

The two men strode ahead of her, alongside Maria, while the Swiss guard, Major Bossard, trailed behind the group.

Definitely not letting us out of his sight.

As she stepped around a chimney, she felt a heaviness in her bosom, a constant reminder of Jack, of the responsibilities she had left behind. She had already called Kat three times, making sure all was well, that Jack was settling okay, nursing fine without her.

Monk is in heaven, Kat had assured her. *After being surrounded by females, he finally has another man in the house. He already bought Jack a little catcher's mitt. You may never get that boy back.*

Despite these words of reassurance, Seichan could not escape the guilt—not for abandoning Jack, but for the thrill inside her. She had never felt freer or lighter. After first carrying the child for nine months, then caring for Jack day and night, she had never felt truly alone. For the first time in what seemed like years, she was her own person, her own self again.

Until she felt that increasing fullness again, noting that she would have to pump soon. A reminder that she was still physically bonded to another.

This is just a temporary reprieve.

Before she could dwell on this, they finally reached a set of stairs leading up to a doorway into one of the domes.

As they climbed the steps, Gray peered at the huge structure. "I don't understand. What does an observatory have to do with a secret library?"

"Actually, there's been a library on these premises going back to the early nineteen hundreds, when Pope Pius the Tenth moved treasures of astronomical interest from the Vatican Library to here. Including original works by Copernicus, Galileo, and Newton."

Maria followed behind the monsignor. "Is that why you wanted the ancient astrolabe brought here, to an *astronomical* library?"

Roe glanced back at her as he reached the top of the stairs. "Unfortunately, no, it's not that library where the astrolabe needs to be."

The monsignor opened the door and led the way through a small anteroom into a vast domed space. It smelled of oil and lemon polish. A huge telescope stood angled and pointed at the closed observatory shutter. The entire interior of the dome was wood-lined.

As Roe passed the telescope, he gave it a friendly pat. "This old instrument dates back to 1935. A decade before I was born." He pointed at his feet. "Right in a room down there."

Seichan stiffened. "Are you saying you were born *here*? In the palace?"

Roe grinned back at her. "In fact, I'm one of the pope's children."

Clearly taken aback by this admission, Gray stopped the monsignor. "What are you talking about?"

Roe's smile widened. "During World War Two, the pope opened the summer palace to refugees from the Nazi occupation. Both Catholics and Jews. Over twelve thousand people crowded in here. Including pregnant women. The pope's bedroom became a makeshift birthing room. Some fifty children were born in His Holiness's bed."

"Ah, I get it," Gray said, "making them the pope's *children*."

Roe shrugged and continued across the dome. "Is it any wonder then that I still make this my home?"

As they reached the far side of the dome, the monsignor stopped at a blank mahogany panel in the wall. He removed a glossy metallic black keycard from a pocket. Each side of the card was embossed with a silver symbol of a crown surmounting two crossed keys.

The papal coat of arms.

While both sides looked identical, they were not. One had the darker key pointing to the left, the other to the right. They were *mirror* images of each other.

Seichan shared a glance with Gray, who also noticed. Both knew their meaning. The twin symbols represented a secretive sect within the Catholic faith, known as the Thomas Church. Father Bailey was a card-carrying member of this group, too, as had been Monsignor Vigor Verona in the past. These select few followed the dictates of a gnostic gospel never included in the Bible, the Gospel of Thomas, which followed the basic tenet: *Seek and ye shall find.* They believed the core of Christ's teachings was to never stop looking for God in the world—and oneself.

Seichan was not surprised by this revelation. *Who else is better suited to be the prefect of a secret Vatican library than a member of its secret church?*

Roe slipped the card into a hidden slot, and the mahogany panel slid aside, revealing an elevator, lined in the same wood. "After you," he said, waving the group inside.

For once, Major Brossard did not follow.

Apparently, this was a bridge he wasn't allowed to cross.

Once they were all inside, the monsignor waved his keycard over a reader. The doors closed and the cage began to descend.

"Where does this elevator go?" Gray asked Roe.

"To a set of ancient vaults. The oldest part of the palace dates back to the thirteenth century. But you might have noticed the ancient Roman amphitheater in the woods on these grounds. It was part of a larger complex, the villa of Emperor Domitian. The palace is built atop its ruins. We're headed down to the villa's old water cisterns and wells."

"Exactly how old are these ruins?" Maria asked.

"Parts date back two thousand years."

"In other words, *to the founding of Christendom*," Gray said, quoting Roe's earlier description of the contents of this secret library.

Roe smiled. "It only seemed appropriate to place the Holy Scrinium here."

The elevator bumped to a stop and the doors opened.

They all exited into a great bricked vault. Its walls spread out in a circle thirty yards wide. The dome of the roof was supported by thick stone arches lined by caged lights. Seichan had seen such architectural handi-work in Rome's ancient Forum, but she also recognized the size and shape from a moment ago.

Maria did, too, as she gaped around. "It looks to be the same size and shape of the observatory dome above us. Only made of stone here."

"As above, so below," Roe intoned with a hint of a smile.

Gray glanced at the man. "That's a quote from the Emerald Tablet of Hermes Trismegistus."

"*Esatto.* It only seemed appropriate, considering what I'm about to show you. Hermes was a Greek god gifted with forbidden knowledge of the universe." Roe set off across the space. "Come. Let me show you."

As the group followed him, Seichan noted three hallways branching off in different directions. Down the closest, massive steel doors lined the passageway. Electronic locks glowed crimson on the walls next to them, likely securing millennia-old treasures inside.

But the monsignor led them instead under an archway to a medieval-looking mahogany door banded and studded in black iron. He yanked on a huge ring and pulled it open. Firelight greeted them, along with a wash of warm air.

Beyond the threshold, tapestries draped a small reading room. Long desks abutted the walls, with dark lamps on them. Four wing-backed chairs circled a tilted wooden bookstand, which held aloft a large silk-draped volume. Past the stand, a small fireplace crackled and snapped.

The room was also occupied.

Father Bailey stood up from one of the chairs. He had left the group earlier, obviously to collect someone else to bring to this gathering deep under the palace.

Maria hurried forward. "Mac . . ."

The bearded climatologist remained seated, his arm in a sling, his shoulder bandaged. "About time you all got down here."

Maria fussed over him, but the man assured her he was feeling better. "They topped me off," he said, tapping his arm where he must have been transfused. "Feel good as new."

Seichan had been shot too many times to know that was not true. The wince as the man sat straighter also gave him away.

"I wasn't about to miss this show-and-tell," he added.

Bailey frowned. "Dr. MacNab was the only one here who actually saw the map aboard the Arab ship. We needed his confirmation."

Gray shifted closer, drawing the others with him. "Confirmation of what?"

Bailey turned and removed the silk drape from the book on the stand—only it wasn't a book. The light reflected off a large gold map inside a bronze case. It showed a topographic representation of the Mediterranean Sea and its surrounding lands.

Mac gasped from his seat. Shock drew him to his feet, his pain clearly forgotten. "That's what we found aboard the ship." He calmed himself enough to turn. "But it's obviously not the same one. It's in much better shape. And the astrolabe is missing."

Gray's face darkened, clearly tired of these secrets. "Where did it come from? Who made this?"

Bailey answered, "It was crafted by a great scientist and artist."

Roe moved protectively forward and turned to them. "It's the work of Leonardo da Vinci."

14

Amazing . . .

Gray listened as Monsignor Roe recounted the story of a secret meet-ing between Pope Leo X and Da Vinci in Rome, of the discovery of the design for a mechanical map tucked into an ancient volume of Arabic engineering from the ninth century. But Gray's eyes remained fixed on the artifact, studying the intricate detail of each golden coastline, mountain range, and island. He guessed the blue gemstone of the Mediterranean Sea was lapis lazuli. Forests were depicted in emeralds. The calderas of volca-nos were topped by fiery rubies.

Gray leaned closer, mesmerized by its beauty and artistry.

Regardless of its origin and inestimable value, he understood that this map's true worth lay in its historical and artistic importance. While Da Vinci's paintings, sketches, and notebooks graced museums around the world, *none* of the man's mechanical designs survived, not even his sculptures.

Still, Gray could not comprehend *why* such a masterpiece had been hidden for centuries. Its importance was beyond measure. He finally tore his gaze away and stared accusingly at Roe.

"What is this doing here?" he asked. "Buried and hidden all this time?"

Roe lifted a hand. *"Abbi pazienza.* I will explain."

Gray had little patience left. Men had already died over this mystery, and without answers, many more would likely suffer the same fate. Still, he bit back an angry response and gave the old priest some latitude to continue.

"Pope Leo commissioned Da Vinci to replicate the map found on those Arabic pages. According to its description, the map—when operational— would lead to the gates of Hell."

"To Tartarus," Gray said, remembering his earlier discussion with Painter.

Roe nodded. *"Esattamente.* The Greek version of Hell. Because *all* of this involves a dark period in Greek history."

"What do you mean?"

"Included with the design of the map was a chapter from Homer's *Odyssey.* The Greek story which tells the tale of the hero Odysseus's difficult journey home after the Trojan War. The chapter found was the one detailing Odysseus's voyage to the Underworld."

Gray opened his mouth, ready for another question, but Roe frowned at him like a scolding teacher.

"The map's designers were a trio of brilliant scholars, all brothers, who called themselves the *Banū Mūsā,* or the Sons of Moses. They studied at the House of Wisdom in Baghdad during the ninth century and went on to produce nearly two dozen volumes of scientific works and innumerable mechanical constructs. The basis for their work came from books that they had collected after the fall of Rome, important scientific treatises from across Italy and Greece. To gather that collection, they crossed back and forth across the Mediterranean, proving themselves also to be great sailors and navigators."

Gray pictured the large double-masted dhow locked in ice.

Was that their ship?

"Their goal was to search the darkest places of history and to preserve what they could find. The brothers became fixated on a particular period when all knowledge came close to being destroyed, a blank spot in the history books, one that to this day remains a mystery."

"When was that?" Maria asked.

"It was the period recounted in Homer's *Iliad* and the *Odyssey*. Because of that, some call it the Homeric Age. But its more apt name is the Greek Dark Ages. It spanned two centuries—from 1100 B.C. to 900 B.C.—and started with a huge war that swept the Mediterranean. The first true world war. By the end of it, three civilizations on three continents fell into ruin."

Gray knew enough history to fill in those blanks. "The *Greek Mycenaeans* in Europe. The *Hittite Empire* of western Asia. And the *Egyptians* of north Africa."

Roe nodded. "They all collapsed at the same time. Leading to two centuries of chaos and barbarism. Erasing nearly all gains in civilization's development. So, is it any wonder the Banū Mūsā brothers, these plunderers of fallen civilizations, took an interest in this era?"

"What did they do?" Maria asked.

"Here I can only imagine. But they were explorers, gatherers of clues. According to notes in the margin of their design, they came to believe that there was a *fourth* civilization involved in this world war. Even today, scholars are reaching the same conclusion after unearthing new records of that dark time."

Gray grew more intrigued. "But who were these unknown conquerors?"

"That's what the Banū Mūsā wanted to know. They scoured the region, searching for clues about this lost civilization, one that defeated everyone else, bringing about the dark ages—and then vanished. The brothers believed that Homer's stories were an important account. That these fanciful tales were more than myth, but recounted true events."

Gray knew modern scholars had come to the same realization, accepting that the fictional lands of Homer's story could be real places. Not just Troy, but many other sites, too. Again, the Banū Mūsā had beaten everyone to this conclusion.

And maybe to much more.

"You think they found it," Gray said. "They found this lost civilization."

"The brothers certainly believed so. And either from the description in the *Odyssey* or from what they discovered at some unknown site, they believed it was Tartarus, the Greek version of Hell."

Gray glanced to Mac, who wore a haunted look, likely remembering what had been freed from that ancient dhow's hold. The man would likely agree with that assessment.

"And it wasn't just those brothers who believed it was the entrance to Hell," Roe continued. "Pope Leo did, too. That was why he added this map to his Holy Scrinium, deeming it too dangerous, too heretical. Other popes either respected his choice or came to the same conclusion. So, here it has remained."

Gray struggled to piece things together in his head. "After finding this civilization, these brilliant engineering brothers encrypted its location into this map. But how did their version end up in Greenland?"

"That remains a mystery," Bailey admitted. "Maybe the ship got trapped unexpectedly in the ice. Or maybe the vessel was purposely wrecked." He pointed to the device. "Either way, no other trace remains of their discovery. Even this rendition was based on a *partial* schematic. Da Vinci had to improvise sections to achieve this copy."

"But it was not just details that were missing," Roe added. "The Banū Mūsā also employed an unknown fuel to power their map. They called it Medea's Oil. Named after the witch Medea, niece to the sorceress Circe, who turned Odysseus's men into pigs. The oil was said to be an emerald liquid, stored in airless pots, and capable of producing an unquenchable flame."

Mac sank back into his chair, his face pained. His eyes seemed to stare off into the past. Gray could almost see the flames burning there with the memory of the horrors aboard the ancient dhow.

"That sounds like what I witnessed," Mac said. "It seemed to even set water on fire."

Roe nodded. "I believe the compound was a version of Greek Fire—a volatile naphtha and quicklime mixture that even water could not douse—but in this case, from what Dr. MacNab reported, I suspect this oil was refined and made even more potent."

Maybe with a radioactive isotope, Gray thought to himself, remembering the radiation detected emanating from the map.

Bailey stepped around the bookstand. "Again, without access to this fuel, Da Vinci had to improvise, so he simply added this." The priest touched a manual crank on the side of the bronze box. "It seems to work well enough. Except for one important detail."

"What's that?" Maria asked.

"Like I said, the schematics were incomplete. In fact, the page illustrating the design of the astrolabe, the key to the map, had been partially torn away."

Torn away?

Gray considered this implication. "Do you think the plans could've been purposely damaged?"

Maria glanced to him. "If you're right, that would make it more likely that the ship in Greenland had been wrecked on purpose, too."

Gray nodded. "Like someone was making every effort to keep what was found hidden forever."

The two priests shared a look, both now wondering the same.

Bailey finally frowned. "But that's all changed now."

The priest crossed to another chair and opened a box sitting there. He turned back around, holding aloft what had cost lives and put Kowalski in jeopardy. The silver astrolabe reflected the firelight, making it look as golden as the map. Bailey stepped to the stand and seated the astrolabe with great care into the map's cradle.

"Or I should say *somewhat* changed." He reached to the crank. "Watch."

As he wound the device, everyone gathered closer. A tiny silver ship docked along the Turkish coast sailed out to sea. Likely pulled via magnets hidden beneath the sea's thin shell of lapis lazuli. Gray held his breath. Then the ship stopped and began to spin in place, as if lost.

"It is as I feared," Roe said. "Especially upon studying the photos sent by Dr. MacNab after recovering the astrolabe."

"What's wrong?" Mac asked. "Is it broken?"

"No," Roe said. "It seems we are still missing key pieces to this puzzle."

Gray remembered the video call with Father Bailey in Painter's office. The priest had used those same words. *Missing pieces.* "What do you mean?" he asked.

Roe answered, "If you remember our conversation about astrolabes, there is a distinct difference between the earlier *flat* ones and the *spherical* designs that came much later. For a flat astrolabe to function, it has to be built with a fixed *latitude* set to the builder's location."

Bailey elaborated, "For a flat astrolabe to work in Baghdad, you have to build it with that city's latitude fixed into it. After that, it would *only* function at that latitude. If you moved it to Paris, none of its amazing calculations and guidance would work."

"But a *spherical* astrolabe is universal in design. That's what makes them unique and rare." Roe waved Gray closer. "If you look, you can see holes across its surface."

Gray squinted and made out tiny perforations across the globe's inner shell. At least two dozen of them. Each marked with a tiny symbol. He imagined there must be the same number of holes on the underside of the cradled artifact.

"When you insert rods into specific holes, you can change the astrolabe's set latitude. Move the rods, and you can reset it to a new location. Over and over again." Roe faced them. "But without those rods, it's a blank, directionless slate."

Gray pictured that tiny spinning ship.

Bailey added even worse news. "And we don't know the right *number* of rods for this particular astrolabe or *where* to place them. The possible combinations are nearly infinite."

Gray now understood why Bailey had summoned him here. "In other words, this astrolabe might be the key to the map, but the *rods* are the key to the astrolabe. To activate the map and have it point to the correct location, we need to put the right combination into the astrolabe."

Bailey shrugged. "And without the rods and knowing where to place them . . ."

We're no closer to an answer.

Mac looked aghast. "Back in Greenland. When we activated the map, the little ship traveled a bit farther out to the sea. Which makes me think at least some of the rods had been in place. But they must've dropped out when the astrolabe fell, or maybe when I caught it."

"Then they're gone for good," Gray said. "Trying to find them in that glacier would be like searching for an unknown number of needles in the world's largest frozen haystack."

"What can we do?" Maria asked.

Roe stared at him, too, clearly wanting his help to solve this.

Gray shook his head, struggling for any answers. "Without those needles, there's nothing we can do."

Roe patted his shoulder and turned away. "I feared as much."

Still, Gray spent the next ten minutes examining the device from every angle. He refused to believe it was hopeless. His mind spun with possibilities. *If the rods had been in place, maybe by analyzing each of the holes—by looking for microabrasions or missing tarnish—we could identify the correct holes where they'd been seated. If we could fabricate new rods, then maybe—*

A huge boom shook through the vaults.

Then another and another in rapid succession.

With the last one, the ground jolted hard, throwing them all down. The mosaic tile floor fractured beneath them. A burning log was bumped out of the fireplace as the hearth's iron grate crashed down. It rolled against one of the tapestries and set it on fire.

Gray gained his feet and rushed to the door. "Stay here!" he yelled.

He skidded into the bricked dome. Seichan slid next to him, ignoring his warning. Across the space, the elevator doors were still open. Movement inside the cage drew his gaze. A figure dropped from above and landed in a crouch.

Gray tensed.

Seichan had a dagger in hand, somehow having managed to get the blade through the layers of security.

Out of the elevator, Major Bossard burst into view. As he ran, he carried his suit jacket bundled in his hands, then tossed it aside. He must have slid down the elevator cable using his jacket as insulation. His H&K submachine gun, still slung to his shoulder, bounced at his hip.

"Run!" he screamed.

Overhead, another thunderous blast. Behind him, the elevator cage blew out of its shaft in an explosion of rock, dust, and smoke. The brick dome shattered on the far side, huge sections crashed to the floor—then it all began to implode.

Bossard reached them. "Jets," he gasped out. "Missile attack."

More booms—some close, some far.

Bossard rushed them back toward the reading room as more of the dome collapsed behind them. The air choked with rock dust. "Bombarding the whole place," the major coughed out. "Concentrating here."

No doubt.

Gray knew the reason why.

After failing to secure the astrolabe, the enemy wasn't taking any chances with it.

If they couldn't have it, they were making damned sure no one else could.

Gray rejoined the others and got them moving. "Grab the map, anything else you can think of." He pointed toward the tunnel farthest from the dome collapse. "We need to get as deep into this bunker as we can."

Everyone moved. Following the monsignor's instructions, Bossard dropped the lid over the gold map. He then lifted it in both arms, demonstrating his considerable strength. Off to the side, Bailey gathered sheaves of papers from a desk, while Maria grabbed books. Mac, with his arm in a sling, tried to stay out of everyone's way.

More of the dome collapsed, washing a thick cloud of dust into the room.

Too close.

"That's it!" Gray ordered. "Everyone out!"

They fled the room, turned a corner, and ran down the neighboring tunnel. Their way was lit by the red glow of electronic locks sealing off storage chambers. The chain of crimson lights ran down the dark throat of the passageway. After seventy yards or so, the tunnel ended at a stone wall that blocked the way.

Gray reached out and put a palm against the cold volcanic stone.

Dead end.

He turned to face the others. Behind them, one by one, the red glows of the vaults blinked out. As darkness fell over the group, the collapse of the vault continued, closing relentlessly toward them.

"Is there any way out of here?" Gray asked.

Monsignor Roe's answer was a moan. "No . . ."

15

I have to risk it . . .

Elena crossed to the wood-framed cot in her stone cell. As she knelt beside it, she glanced to the roof, as if in prayer. Instead, while reaching under the thin mattress, she noted the old chisel marks across the ceiling. Fat candles flickered in niches hacked into the rock walls, while thick layers of accumulated wax—likely decades, if not centuries old—dripped down the walls.

She estimated she was a dozen stories underground—in one of the many ancient subterranean cities dug out of the rock in Turkey. She pictured those long-dead builders, using Bronze Age tools to excavate these multilevel metropolises. As an archaeologist in this region, she knew that more than two hundred such troglodyte-cave cities had been discovered throughout Turkey, mostly in the Cappadocia region to the east, but also here near the coast.

The most famous was discovered in the sixties, the Derinkuyu Underground City. She had toured that complex. It had its own rivers, bridges, and thousands of ventilation shafts that carried air down to its deepest levels, some of which were dug three hundred feet into the earth. The massive city had once housed over twenty thousand people. It had barns, churches, kitchens, storage cellars, even its own winery. Some of these ancient cities, like Derinkuyu, had been turned into tourist attractions, while others were still used to stable animals or kept as secret hideouts for unsavory elements.

Which was clearly the purpose of *this* cave-city.

Yesterday, the private jet that had flown Elena from the Arctic landed at a small airfield in the middle of the Turkish hills. After that, she had been driven by her captors to the outskirts of a small village, where in the cellar of a farmhouse, a door had led into this hidden complex.

She had been marched down stone stairs and along passageways strung with electric lights. In the upper levels, she passed rooms full of sleek gym equipment, free weights, and mat-lined rings. Another held shelves and racks of assault rifles and boxes of ammunition. Throughout the tunnels, they passed several hard-eyed men and women, all in red or black. From the subservience of those in red, she guessed them to be recruits in training. No one made eye contact with her as their group was led by the woman who called herself the Daughter of Moses. Even those in black gave slight bows of their heads as the woman passed. Clearly, she was high up in this group's hierarchy.

Elena could also guess the purpose of this subterranean complex.

A terrorist training camp.

Certainty grew the deeper she went. Stiff-backed gunmen guarded the entrances to each level. They stood posted before giant disk-shaped stones, as ancient as the city itself. To distract herself from her trepidation, she concentrated on the archaeological significance of her surroundings. To escape waves of raids and attacks, people over the centuries had retreated into these underground cities. They rolled those circular stone slabs to seal off each level. Battles had been fought across these lands going back millennia. The Derinkuyu complex dated back to the eighth century B.C., while others were even older. But most had been built during the depths of the Greek Dark Ages, when the entire Mediterranean was embroiled in a great war.

While being escorted down, she had run her fingertips along the walls, imagining the effort to dig out this city, and the hundreds like it. While the rock here was relatively soft—made up of volcanic tuff that could be carved and sculpted into these subterranean cities—the sheer manpower needed and scope of the excavation seemed excessive.

Questions slowly arose: *Why were these cities so hastily built during those dark ages? What were they all hiding from? What had terrorized them to such an extent that they had felt the need to claw their way down into the rock to escape it?*

In the deeper levels of the complex, she passed dormitories smelling of grease and grilled meats, another that served as a storage facility, stacked with crates, barrels, and sacks of dry goods. She estimated there was enough foodstuffs to last years. Below that, they reached a section that seemed to be a whole warren of mazelike rooms crammed tightly with dark bookshelves and cabinets full of shadowy artifacts. Curiosity about this buried library had slowed her feet, but her captors forced her even deeper, to a region lit only by candles and finally into this cell where she had spent the night.

They had left her with a cold dinner and fed her breakfast again this morning.

But Elena knew something had changed overnight. This morning, she had heard yelling echoing down from above. She had tried to question the red-clad recruit—a young woman, barely older than a teenager—who delivered her breakfast tray. When Elena asked about the commotion, the server's eyes had flashed with worry.

All Elena got was a terse warning from the recruit: *Do what they say. Tell them what you know.*

After that, Elena had paced her cell, plagued by a question.

What do they expect me to know?

Her hands finally found what she had hidden under her mattress. She withdrew the two small books—a copy of Homer's *Odyssey* and the journal of the dead captain—the contents of the package guarded over by the frozen corpse. With the books secretly tucked into the back of her trousers for the flight here, her body heat had thawed the frozen volumes. The leather covers were now pliant, the cords binding them pliable.

Whatever her captors wanted from her had to involve that ship and its history. Why else kidnap an expert on nautical archaeology, one who specialized in the Mediterranean? She knew her life depended on her continuing usefulness. She also knew her father would shake the very foundations of the world to find her, but until then—

I must survive.

To that end, she needed to be armed with as much information as possible.

No matter the risk.

She took the books to the crude table where her breakfast sat untouched. She had no fear of being watched, of hidden cameras spying upon her. Every surface of her cell, except for the stout wooden door, was solid rock. In fact, this entire dungeon was only lit by candles or flickering torches.

With no electricity and the stone too thick to allow even a wireless device to transmit, she felt secure enough to place the books on the table and cautiously peel back the cover of the one entitled *The Testament of the Fourth Son of Moses*. Originally wrapped in sealskin and sealed in wax, the pages had been kept dry over the centuries, the ink preserved. Though they were brittle with age, she could still turn the vellum pages if she was careful.

She began reading an account of its author, Hunayn ibn Mūsā ibn Shākir, the fourth son of a man named *Mūsā*—or *Moses*. She skimmed through the initial pages, which related to handwritten details of the ship's preparation, the picking of a trusted crew, followed by the first week of travel. It also held the captain's ruminations about Homer's work, including translated sections from the ancient Greek text *Geographica,* written by Strabo, a Greek historian from the first century who believed Homer's epics recounted historical events.

According to the journal, the ship reached an island described by the captain as *"the forge of Hephaestus"*—then the story suddenly stopped. A large section of pages in the middle had been sliced out.

Likely deliberately destroyed.

She frowned with disappointment at the missing pages—though in truth, she was more interested in the *last* section, which remained intact. She wanted to know what befell the ship, how it ended up in Greenland. The story picked up again with a huge storm and a hard voyage to what sounded like Iceland ("*an island of fire and ice, of steaming ground, and vast white forests*"), then from there to the coast of Greenland ("*to an ice-shrouded land beyond the rim of the world, haunted by ghostly bears furred in snow*").

Her heart pounded harder as she reached the final journal entry.

She read the date at the top: *Jumada Al-Thani 22, 248.*

The year—248—had to be based on the Arabic calendar, known as the *Hijiri* calendar. She converted it in her head to modern numbering and came up with 862.

In the ninth century.

And the time of the year: *late August.*

Her brows bunched.

It should have been too warm for those sailors to be trapped by winter's ice. So what happened?

She held her breath as she read the final entry from Hunayn ibn Mūsā ibn Shākir, the fourth son of Moses:

My dearest brothers—Muhammed, Ahmad, and al-Hasan—

forgive me for my betrayal, for defying the esteemed of the House of Wisdom during a time when our enemies grow emboldened and what I found could turn the tides of fate in our favor.

But know I had no choice. I write this as my last testament both as absolution and to serve as a warning.

As I scratch cold ink into vellum, the screams behind me have finally ended. For most of the night, I have crouched in my cabin with my palms clamped over my ears. It offered no relief. Even my prayers to Allah failed to shut out the screaming of my men, the pounding of their fists on the barred door, their pleading cries. Though their suffering and terror cut down to my marrow, I dared not relent.

Even now, I can picture the shayāṭīn—those fiery demons of Tartarus—mercilessly tearing into my men, a crew who had faithfully sailed at my side for two years. But as this tale will prove, the terror of a slow death can turn even an honorable man into an ignoble savage.

Five days ago, I brought this ship to these desolate shores. After learning the ungodly truth, I dared not sail this vessel into any port. Instead, I had ordered the crew to this lonely shelter along these frozen shores after a savage storm blew us beyond the rim of the world. I lied to them about the need for fresh water and salted meat for the long voyage home.

Instead, in the dead of night, I scuttled the ship—axing through the twin masts and shredding the sails. Upon learning of my sabotage, the crew argued and pleaded, even threatened, to be allowed to make repairs. When I refused, I read the stony determination in some of their faces, the wild terror in others.

Being one man against a dozen angry mutineers, I wielded the only weapon capable of ensuring this broken ship never left this frozen berth. In the dark of night, as all were asleep, I freed a hammer and broke one of Pandora's pots. I woke the legion inside, unleashing the shayāṭīn horde upon my own crew.

It was a necessary cruelty—for what is hidden here must never be found. And if it is found, may the horrors preserved inside this ship serve as a fiery admonition against looking any farther, of searching for Tartarus.

Even as I write this, with the screaming ended, I can hear the claws of the demons against the wood. I will wait for the horde to quiet once again. Then will begin my long vigil. I will bide the cold, set my traps against the unworthy, and wait for the bitter end. It will serve as my final atonement.

Until then, I beg Allah's forgiveness—for the bloodshed now, for my trespasses in the past. Still, I take comfort that the greater world has been kept safe—but for how long?

As I sit here, I can hear the ticking inside the Storm Atlas beside me, marking time with my heartbeat, counting down to certain doom. I should smash the infernal mechanism, but I cannot bring myself to do so. It is my last connection to you, my three brothers. I remember crafting this with you, a time full of laughter, excitement, and hope. Together we created the greatest of all navigational tools, like none engineered before, encrypted so only I can use it, and fueled by Promethean fire.

As I write these last words, I am reminded that it was the Titan, Prometheus, who stole fire from Zeus and gave it to mankind and was punished for his theft by an eternity of torment. So, too, I stole fire from Tartarus and brought it home—and now must be punished as well.

How I wish I had never followed those clues found in Homer's Odyssey *and discovered the entrance to Tartarus, where hid the Great Enemy of the poet's time, the blight that brought three kingdoms to fiery ruin. But I did find it, and in my excitement to return home, I brought back a barrel of what we believed to be Medea's Oil, as fiery proof of my discovery. But at that time, I had not dared to venture any deeper than the threshold into Tartarus, as I had too few men and my supplies were running low.*

Upon returning home, I told my tale, and we four brothers constructed the Storm Atlas, fueled it with Medea's Oil, and protected it with the Key of Daedalus. But only I was allowed to possess the beams of the Ship-Star, the three tools necessary to unlock the one true course amidst the map's many false paths. It was you, my brother Ahmad, who rightfully warned that only I should know the location of Tartarus, lest our enemies torture it out of those who stayed behind at the House of Wisdom.

Praise be to Allah for whispering such wisdom into Ahmad's ear.

Ten mighty dhows left our shores a year ago, ready to reap what could be found—but only one of those ships ever escaped Tartarus, and it will be my grave. I will keep this vigil beside the Storm Atlas until my last breath. For there is another reason I fear to take hammer to our greatest achievement. If what resides in the deepest bowels of Tartarus—those monstrous Titans—ever escape, the Storm Atlas may hold the only hope for the world. To that end, I will hold the keys to that salvation closest to my heart.

Still, a question plagues me: How long will the world be safe?

That unknown terrifies me more than any fiery demon.

Elena read through the last several pages, which were predominantly an expression of affection for the brothers who had been left behind, along with a litany of regret. She began to skim through the rest, but before she could reach the end, voices rose from behind the door. Lost in the story, she had not heard anyone approach her cell.

Gasping, she grabbed both books from the table and struggled to tuck them into her pants. As she did so, something fell out of the spine of Hunayn's journal. The objects struck and clinked against the stone floor. She dropped to a knee and discovered a trio of four-inch-long nails made of bronze. One end of each bore a tiny flag inscribed with a letter in Arabic.

What are these—

The bar on the door scraped behind her.

With her heart pounding harder, she snatched the bronze nails from the floor and pocketed them as she stood.

The door opened behind her with a complaint of old hinges. A familiar figure strode in. From the dark shade of the Daughter of Moses's features and the flash in her eyes, Elena could tell that something must have gone wrong overnight. The woman waved Elena brusquely forward, then immediately turned on her heels and headed back out.

"*Eajluu,*" she ordered in Arabic. "Come with me."

Elena hurried after her, drawing two armed men in her wake. "Where are we going?"

The woman refused to look at her. "To teach you the first of many lessons."

From her captor's hard tone, she was not marching Elena to some classroom or even to the dark library upstairs. In fact, they remained on this dungeon level.

As they crossed down a cavernous hall, Elena kept one hand in her pocket. She palmed the ancient bronze trinkets, keeping them from tapping against one another, fearing they would be heard.

Then out of the darkness ahead, a scream echoed.

She froze, but one of the guards prodded her with the muzzle of his rifle. She stumbled along, fearing the worst.

They're going to torture me.

At the end of the hall, they reached a double set of doors flanked by fresh torches, the flames dancing high. The Daughter of Moses pounded a fist, and the door was promptly opened.

The woman forced Elena inside. More fiery brands lit the stone chamber ahead. The heat was intense, the air smoky. To one side stood a bronze brazier atop a tripod, its basin aglow with ruddy coals from which the leather handles of branding irons protruded.

The heavy-browed giant who had accompanied them from Greenland returned to the brazier with a glowing iron and shoved its hot tip back into the coals.

Elena cringed as she identified the source of the earlier scream.

A huge man lay strapped to a wood table in the room's center. He'd been stripped to his boxers, his sweating, muscular bulk stretched across the planks. His arms were tied above his head. Thick leather straps secured his torso and legs to the tabletop. A blackened, blistering wound marred his upper left thigh, the flesh still smoking from the press of a hot brand.

The Daughter of Moses grabbed Elena's arm and dragged her closer. Once at the foot of the table, her captor patted its surface. "The Daesh jihadis invented this simple but effective device. They call it the Flying Carpet."

Elena girded herself, knowing the Daesh were better known in the West as ISIS.

The Daughter drew her to the side and nodded to the giant. "Kadir, a demonstration, please."

Kadir lumbered past them and stepped alongside the center of the table. He reached to a large steel wheel there and slowly turned it.

The table started to bend. The hinged middle rose up, while the ends dropped down. The man strapped and sprawled across its length groaned as his spine was bent backward. Each crank brought his vertebrae closer to breaking.

The Daughter lifted a hand. "For now, only a *small* demonstration, Kadir."

The giant stopped turning the wheel and straightened. "*Özür dilerim,*

Nehir," he mumbled apologetically, then quickly bowed his head and corrected himself. "*Ana asfa, Bint Mūsā.*"

Elena eyed her female captor, whose face went even darker. Kadir's first apology had been in *Turkish,* then repeated in *Arabic.* Elena studied both of them as the realization struck her.

Could they be Turks . . . either masquerading as Arabs or using their language for some reason? Elena also learned one other detail from Kadir's slip of the tongue: the true name of her captor.

The Daughter of Moses's real name must be *Nehir.*

Clearly irritated, the woman dragged Elena onto the top of the table and brusquely shoved her toward the tortured man. "Either help us, or this American will suffer in your stead."

Elena turned to the figure on the table. Horrified by all that had happened, she had failed to get a good look at him. Sweat dripped from his strained brow. Dried blood caked his swollen nose. She had not expected to recognize the man—but she did.

It was the man Maria Crandall had been seeing for two years. Though Elena had never met him, Maria had sent her pictures, posting even more on Instagram. Elena remembered the two of them had been planning to meet her in Greenland. She stared down at the man, shocked and confused.

What is he doing here? Where's Maria?

"Joe . . ." she whispered at last.

"Don't help them," he croaked back at her.

His words set off the already angry Nehir. She cursed, and from the way she glared at the man, Elena suspected Joe might be the source of her dark mood this morning.

But what did he do?

Nehir waved to Kadir. The giant swung back to the crank and began to slowly turn the wheel. The table bent more—as did Joe's spine. His neck stretched in agony; fresh blood flowed from his nostrils.

"Stop!" Elena yelled, fearing Nehir might shatter the man's spine before her fury could be reined in. To appease the woman and focus her attention elsewhere, Elena reached to the back of her pants. "Here . . . I found these aboard the ship in Greenland."

Elena pulled out the two weathered books and shoved them at Nehir.

The woman took them. She quickly noted their titles, and her eyes grew wide. She barked to Kadir, who then rewound the crank, drawing the table flat again. Nehir promptly headed to the door and hurried out with her newly acquired treasures. But not before ordering the armed guards to return Elena to her cell.

As Elena was prodded at gunpoint toward the exit, Joe frowned at her, looking angry at her capitulation. She turned away, knowing the truth, hearing it clink in her pocket.

Don't worry, Joe. I haven't given them everything.

At the room's threshold, she turned back to the table, plagued by one immediate question.

"Where's Maria?" she called out.

He let his head drop to the table and sighed. "Safe . . . she's safe."

Relieved, Elena allowed herself to be led away.

Finally, a bit of good news.

16

This is bad . . . and only getting worse.

Maria listened as a hush fell over the subterranean vault hidden beneath the Pontifical Palace. The barrage had ended a few minutes ago. The bombing had been brief, but brutal. Even now, rocks continued to fall with muffled crashes deeper down the tunnel in which they were trapped.

This little fragile pocket is not going to last much longer.

And they all might run out of air before that.

The group pressed cloths over their noses and mouths, trying their best to filter out the rock dust choking the space.

The bobbling beam of a flashlight approached as Gray returned with Major Bossard. The two men had gone to inspect the rockfall that blocked the tunnel a short distance down. They passed Seichan, who inspected one of the darkened vault doors with another flashlight.

"No way through," Gray reported as he joined the group huddled at the tunnel's end. "I also tried my sat phone over there. Still no signal."

No surprise on either count.

"Bastards are nothing if not consistent," Mac said as he sat with his back against the wall, his slung arm cradled to his chest. "Second time in two days those jackasses sealed me up in a tomb. First one made of ice, now rock."

Something he said gave Maria pause, but she couldn't put her finger on it.

Father Bailey cast a chagrined look at the climatologist. "I'm sorry I brought you down here."

"Hey, I'm not complaining. If you'd left me up in the medical ward, I'd likely be dead by now. Sounded like they bombed the crap out of everything up there. So even if this ends up being my tomb, you bought me a little more time."

Maria straightened.

That's it.

"But this isn't a *tomb,*" she said and swung to Monsignor Roe, who knelt beside the map box, as if intending to protect the Da Vinci treasure with his last breath. "Didn't you say that the Holy Scrinium had been installed in the cellars of an old Roman house?"

Roe lowered the fistful of cloth from his mouth. "*Si*, the villa of Emperor Domitian."

"And it's down here where the Romans dug out the villa's water cisterns?"

"That's right."

"But *where* did the water come from to fill those cisterns? Do you know if they were drawing water from Lake Albano?"

"I . . . I believe I read about that." Roe nodded. "The Romans excavated these cisterns to be *below* lake level and angled aqueducts up to the lake, so gravity would bring fresh water down here."

Gray joined her, giving her a nod of approval. "Could those aqueducts still be there?"

"I don't know," Roe admitted. "But I do know that the Holy Scrinium doesn't occupy the villa's entire foundations. The library complex was walled off from those older sections centuries ago."

"Do you know where?" Maria asked.

"*Sì, certo,*" Roe said, but he looked sickened as he pointed. "It's at the end of the other tunnel. The one to our south."

Mac groaned. "Sounds like we picked the wrong rabbit hole to run into. No way we're burrowing our way over there."

"There might be another way," Roe said. "Let me show you."

They gathered around the monsignor as he used a finger to draw in the dust on the floor. He inscribed three radiating lines, then connected them with concentric arcs.

"All three main tunnels are connected to one another by the library vaults, which curve from one tunnel to the other," he explained. "If we could get through one of these doors in this tunnel, we could cross through its library vault and over to the next tunnel."

"But there's no power," Maria said. "And the doors are still locked. We can't—"

"I can," Seichan said. She stood up from her inspection of the only door not buried under tons of rock and pointed a steel dagger at its electronic lock. "But we'll have to be quick. And we'll only have one chance."

7:14 A.M.

Sometimes it's good to be bad.

Gray silently thanked the heavens for Seichan's illicit past. "Didn't know breaking into bank vaults was part of your Guild training," he said as he watched her work.

She shrugged. "I learned this trick long before the Guild. It's not much different than hot-wiring a car. Back when I used to joyride through the backstreets of Seoul as a kid."

Gray tried to imagine a carefree version of this woman, a wild-eyed girl running roughshod through the streets of Southeast Asia. Even now, there remained large swaths of her past that were unknown to him. He prayed he would have the chance to fill in those gaps.

"Quit wiggling the light," she scolded him.

He refocused his flashlight. She had already used her blade to pry open the electronic lock's front plate. She squinted as she wired the open back of his satellite phone to the guts of the lock.

She turned to Monsignor Roe, who stood next to her. "If this works, we'll only have seconds for you to swipe your card and for the locking mechanism to release. After that, the circuitry will be toast. Are you ready?"

He nodded and held aloft his glossy black keycard.

"On my mark." She touched the final wire to the lead on phone's lithium-ion battery. "Go."

The crimson light on the lock briefly flickered. Roe hurriedly swiped his card across the reader. The lamp switched to green. A rumble of gears sounded—then a bright spark snapped across the exposed circuitry, and the light went dark.

Seichan stood up, tugged on the door handle, and swore when it didn't budge. The lock had failed to complete its cycle.

They'd been so close . . .

Clearly frustrated, Seichan stepped back and kicked the vault. The impact shook the frame, and something loud clicked and tumbled inside the door. Everyone looked at each other and held their breaths.

Seichan reached again and pulled on the handle.

The door swung open this time—to the cheers of those gathered behind her.

Gray drew her into a hug. "My beautiful bank robber."

"We're not out of here yet," she reminded him.

Her words were punctuated by the loud crash of a boulder down the tunnel.

Gray got everyone moving through the door and along a dark, curved hallway, both sides lined by hermetically sealed glass doors. He caught glimpses of bookshelves and cases holding shadowy treasures, some glinting gold or silver in the meager light. But they had no time for sightseeing in this forbidden library.

They quickly reached the far door. It had a manual lever on its inside, meant to facilitate the escape of anyone trapped in the vault.

Like us.

Gray pulled the lever down and pushed the door into the next tunnel. He flashed his beam around. The next passageway was blocked on the right by a pile of rock and debris. But on the left, it ended at a brick wall.

He led the others to it.

"What now?" Maria asked as she ran a palm over the bricks. "How are we getting through there?"

Major Bossard pushed to the front and lifted his H&K submachine gun. "I may know a way."

Gray got everyone back into the shelter of the vault as the Swiss soldier unloaded his entire magazine at the wall, concentrating on a pair of bricks that looked the most fragile. By the time his deafening barrage ended, he had pulverized those two to dust and knocked out several bricks around the opening.

Gray followed Bossard back to the wall to inspect his handiwork. The major shoved and kicked the opening larger. Gray then leaned his head and an arm through the hole and shone his flashlight into the next space. It was cavernous, excavated from the volcanic rock, and at the bottom, his light reflected off a black mirror.

Water.

He sighed with relief.

In short order, they knocked down more of the wall and climbed down a series of carved steps into the next room. In the center, a square pool thirty feet across was full of water. Gray circled its edge, probing its depths. On one side, he discovered an arched opening of a tunnel—the mouth of an old Roman aqueduct—a yard or so below the surface.

The others gathered around him.

"I'll swim down there," Gray said. "See if it's passable all the way to the lake."

Seichan stepped in front of him. She had already shed her jacket and blouse and now kicked off her boots. "I'm the faster swimmer." She poked his midsection. "And there's the matter of this."

Gray wanted to object, but he knew she was right—maybe not about his gut, but she was definitely part fish, if not full mermaid. If anyone could make it to the lake, it was her.

"All yours," he said.

She doffed her trousers and picked her flashlight up off the ground. As she straightened, her eyes glinted in the light.

Her excitement set his own heart to pounding. "Be caref—"

She dove smoothly into the water and, with barely a ripple, vanished into the black depths.

Mac joined Gray. "You're a lucky, lucky man."

Don't I know it.

7:27 A.M.

Seichan thumbed on her flashlight as she kicked into the dark tunnel. The passageway was barely wider than her shoulders, which hindered her kicks, but the closeness of the walls allowed her to push against the stone and propel herself forward.

She led with the flashlight extended in her other hand.

She didn't know how far she was from the lake, so she conserved her energy, moving with speed, but wasting no effort. Each stroke and kick was controlled, meant to propel her forward with an economy of movement. She kept her lips pressed closed; her chest relaxed.

She let the occasional bubble escape her nose, tricking her body into thinking she was close to taking a new breath, which eased the strain and lessened the instinct for her body to rebel.

Keep going . . .

She fluttered her legs and pawed at the wall with her free palm.

Then the reach of her flashlight's beam struck an obstruction in the tunnel ahead. She swam up to it. A boulder blocked the aqueduct. The passage around it was too narrow for her to get through.

Inwardly cursing, she probed the rock and found it to be more of a slab, jammed crookedly in the tunnel.

Maybe . . .

She grabbed the upper edge and braced her feet against the walls. She tugged, pulled, and rocked the slab until it finally fell flat on the bottom, opening a wider gap above it. She shoved her head, and one arm through, then wiggled and contorted her torso. Her toes scrabbled at the stone behind her as she fought to jam her way past the obstruction.

Then she got stuck.

She knew it in an instant. While Gray might enjoy the heft and weight of her hormonally enlarged breasts—and Jack, too, for that matter—it proved problematic now. She tried reversing back out, prepared to return to the cistern and admit defeat.

But the effort only jammed her tighter.

Can't get through—or back.

An edge of panic threaded through her. Her lungs grew strained, and not just from resisting the pressure of the rock walls. Images of Jack flashed through her: gurgling happily in the bath, fussing over a nipple, sucking his little thumb. Even now, doubts plagued her. A part of her still wondered if Jack wouldn't be better without her. And even deeper—

Am I better without him?

Before guilt sapped her strength and will, she ground her teeth. She didn't know which was the right course with Jack, but she knew one thing for certain.

I'll be the one to make that decision.

She wasn't about to die down here and have that choice taken from her. So she exhaled all her breath, emptying her lungs completely. Life-giving air bubbled over her face, billowed through her hair.

With her chest collapsed, she gained a fraction of extra space, enough to free herself. She hung there for a heartbeat. She still had enough oxygen to get back, but what good would that do? How would that bring her any closer to Jack's side, if that was her decision?

Screw it.

She kicked with her legs and sailed past the obstruction.

Following her light, she sped along the aqueduct, quickly passing the point of no return. Her diaphragm cramped below her lungs, trying to force her to take a breath. Her vision squeezed. Her motions became more frantic.

Still, the spear of her light only found more darkness ahead.

Her vision narrowed toward a pinpoint.

Not going to make it.

7:44 A.M.

Gray paced the edge of the cistern's black pool. He checked his watch for the hundredth time. Sweat pebbled his brow, and his breath heaved in and out.

"She's been gone over ten minutes," he said to no one but himself. "She should be back by now."

Maria tried to calm him. "She could be looking for help."

"Or just catching her breath for the swim back," Mac offered.

Gray shook his head. He had already stripped to his boxers, needing to do something, to be proactive while he waited. He stepped to the pool's edge.

"Give her another minute," Maria warned.

Father Bailey offered a grimmer insight. "It'll do no good to go after her. If she got into trouble, it's already too late. No one could hold their breath for ten minutes. You'll only endanger your life, too."

Gray balled a fist, ready to punch the priest. Instead, those words goaded Gray to the water's edge.

I can't wait any longer.

As he leaned to dive in, the black water grew brighter below him. He stumbled back as the glow became a bright light. A head popped out of the water, the face obscured by a mask and the mouthpiece of a scuba regulator. But Gray recognized her.

"Seichan . . ."

Before she could respond, another figure, then another, surfaced behind her. The strangers wore masks, wetsuits, and scuba gear.

Gray was momentarily baffled. Who were these men? How did Seichan raise a rescue team in scuba gear so quickly? Then he knew the answer. He glanced over to Maria, remembering there had been a crew already in the lake, searching for Kowalski's body. Seichan must have eventually escaped the aqueduct and reached the open lake, where she hailed the search crew and recruited them for this rescue.

Seichan spat out her mouthpiece and shifted her mask up. "Ready to get out of here?" she called to him.

Hell, yeah.

Over the next half hour, the search-and-rescue team ferried everyone through the aqueduct and out to the banks of Lake Albano. While their group should have been jubilant at surviving, no one celebrated.

Sirens echoed all around. Helicopters chased across the sky as the morning sun crested the caldera's edge. Gray stood beside the lake with his satellite phone pressed to his ear. He stared up at the smoking ruins of the Pontifical Palace. A thick black pall churned skyward, while fires smoldered at its heart. From what could be seen, that entire section of the volcanic rim had been blasted into a cratered pile of rubble.

Gray barely heard Painter on the phone. "The jets had proper military clearance and call signs," the director explained. "They might even have been Italian Air Force jets. We don't know yet. Reports are that the pilots ditched the two aircraft into the Mediterranean after jettisoning from the planes. Search crews are scouring the seas."

Gray tore his gaze from the destruction above to the reason behind it. Monsignor Roe and Major Bossard, both wrapped in blankets, stood guard over a tarp-wrapped treasure, the Da Vinci map.

How many had died over that damned thing?

He remembered the monsignor's story of a summer school under way on the papal grounds. The new observatory was a mile from the palace, but was it far enough away? His grip tightened on the phone. He intended to make sure the deaths here were not in vain and that those responsible were held accountable.

Gray spoke sternly: "We may not know *who* orchestrated this attack, but from their tactics and hardware—the jets, the submarine up in the Arctic—these are not lone-wolf terrorists."

Painter agreed. "Whoever they are, they must be state-sponsored. Some hostile country or countries is backing them. Kat also believes it's why they seem to know our every move. Too many intelligence agencies are involved. We don't know where our intel is leaking, but until we plug it—"

"We need to go dark over here."

"I suggest pitch black."

Gray stared at the small group huddled on the shore. They needed to get moving, get out of sight ASAP. But what then? Two questions were the most pressing.

Where do we go next?

And more important . . .

Who is our enemy?

17

At last, the world will soon burn.

With glory shining bright in her breast, Nehir Saat descended into the depths of the buried city. She had been summoned from the neighboring village of Kumkale, where in a small tea shop she had borne witness to the first harbinger of Armageddon. On a television there, she and other Sons and Daughters had watched the cacophony of news coming from Italy, the footage of a palace burning, of bodies in the streets.

Only the sheeted forms of children finally made her look away.

Innocents turned into martyrs, she had to remind herself, but it failed to quell the grief, even guilt over their deaths. She prayed they had not suffered and had found their way to paradise—where they would not have long to wait. She took solace in the fact that when the gates of Hell fell, paradise would eventually return to earth.

Bringing with it all those children.

Including her own.

Both of them.

She paused on a stair and closed her eyes, momentarily overwhelmed by grief. When she was a child, her father had sold her and her brother into prostitution. She was eight, Kadir ten. She had been raped repeatedly and carried scars both physical and emotional.

Eventually, when they were not earning enough for their father, he sold them to a monster in Istanbul. She was forced into a temporary marriage—known as a *mut'a*—which contracts the union for a set period of time, from one hour to ninety-nine years. During that contract, she bore two children, a boy and a girl, both unwanted by her provisional husband. The babies were slaughtered after their births. She had tried to protect the last child, the girl whom Nehir had silently named Huri, which meant *angel*. As punishment, her husband cut the ragged line down Nehir's chin and throat. Kadir, only fourteen at the time, but already large, became enraged and broke the man's neck. She and her brother had fled afterward, but Kadir remained her protector always.

Eventually they drew the attention of the Sons and Daughters.

She suspected it was Kadir—whose reputation in the slums of Istanbul grew with his size—was the one whom they truly wanted to recruit. But her brother would never leave her side, so they were taken together. Little did they know that Nehir would prove to be the true warrior of the pair. Kadir was too slow, both in mind and body, and in many ways, his heart was too easily wounded. But he did as he was told.

Nehir, on the other hand, was swift with her knives, flawless with her marksmanship. But it was her sharp intelligence that allowed her to rise quickly in the ranks and eventually become the First Daughter of Mūsā.

Determination had driven her back then—and now.

She intended to live long enough to see this world burned away and replaced with a new paradise—a paradise where those who had died in Allah's good graces would be returned to their loved ones. Including her lost children.

And now I am so near to seeing it happen.

With a lighter spirit, she continued down the stairs, summoned by Mūsā to the heart of *Bayt al-Hikma*, the House of Wisdom. This level of the buried city housed countless texts, some dating back to 1258, to the Fall of Baghdad, when Mongol hordes led by Genghis Khan's grandson invaded the city, setting fire to mosques and homes, slaughtering its inhabitants. But the worst atrocity of all was the destruction of the city's centuries-old academy of higher learning, the true flower of the Islamic Golden Age: the House of Wisdom. The Mongols had plundered the school, tossing its books into the Tigris River. It was said those waters ran *black* for days from all the ink—then later *red* with the blood of murdered scholars.

It was why, even today, the Sons and Daughters wore those colors.

But before the siege could be fully set, a scholar named Nasir al-Din al-Tusi—the first who would bear the title of Mūsā—rescued four hundred thousand books, stealing them away under the cover of darkness. It was those texts that became the foundation for the new House of Wisdom, one hidden from the world. To protect this secret, Nasir gathered the first Sons and Daughters, training them harshly and completely to be its warrior-scholars, guaranteeing that such an atrocity never happened again.

And it hadn't.

The current Mūsā was the forty-eighth to rule the House of Wisdom.

And he will carry it to its greatest glory.

With utmost humility and respect, Nehir bowed and entered into the sprawling warren of rooms that made up the library. It spread over forty acres and now housed tenfold what Nasir had rescued.

She found her leader in a small chamber lined by rows of long desks. Mūsā stood behind one, flanked by two elder Sons, who served the library.

She paused at the chamber's threshold.

Mūsā noted her presence and waved her forward. She crossed to the table, keeping her head bowed, her eyes cast down.

"My dear Daughter," Mūsā said warmly, "Allah truly smiles upon you."

"Thank you," she muttered, feeling awkward at such praise.

"The two books you secured from Dr. Cargill have proven fortuitous. Monumentally so."

He nodded toward the table's surface, where the old volumes were spread open, with more books piled to either side, likely gathered for research into the revelations found within the texts recovered from the dhow in Greenland.

Mūsā touched one of them. "Herein lie the treacherous last words of the traitorous fourth brother to the Banū Mūsā. While his story is incomplete, we've discerned much in a short time, offering us hope to pick up the lost trail to Tartarus."

Her heart pounded. She had hoped as much when she had been handed those old volumes and delivered them here.

At long last.

Mūsā straightened and stared at her. "I will pray that Allah continues to smile on you, though I already have faith that this will happen. For I have an important task for you."

"Whatever you command."

"You and your brother Kadir must go and search for that lost trail. I will send you with a cadre of Sons and Daughters, along with the two prisoners. Use one against the other to enlist their cooperation to help you find those threads. You will also take the Storm Atlas, as I believe it will still be of value in discovering the true path to Tartarus."

She bowed deeper, honored by the responsibility. "I will not fail you."

"Of this, I also have faith."

She straightened, accepting his praise, feeling even worthy of it. "But where do we go? Where might we pick up this lost trail?"

He motioned her to his side. When she joined him, he pointed to the open journal written by Hunayn ibn Mūsā. His fingertip ran along a scrawled line on one page. "The log of the voyage is interrupted after this, but the traitor named his ship's last port before continuing to Tartarus. It is *there* where you will seek his trail."

She leaned down and read what was written.

صياغة هيفايستوس

Her blood chilled with the implication as she translated it.

The Forge of Hephaestus.

"It is no easy task I've set for you." Mūsā stared hard at her, as if sensing her trepidation. "For you must travel to where even angels fear to tread."

THIRD

THE FORGE OF HEPHAESTUS

Sing, clear-voiced Muse, of Hephaestus famed for inventions. With bright-eyed Athena he taught men glorious crafts throughout the world—men who before used to dwell in caves in the mountains like wild beasts.

—HOMERIC HYMN 20 (TRANSLATION BY HUGH G. EVELYN-WHITE. *HESIOD, THE HOMERIC HYMNS AND HOMERICA.* CAMBRIDGE, MASS., HARVARD UNIVERSITY PRESS; LONDON, WILLIAM HEINEMANN, 1914)

18

These bastards do know how to travel in style.

From the view out of the window, Kowalski took in the breadth of the superyacht stretching out around of him. He and Elena had landed aboard the yacht five hours ago. They'd been flown from the coast of Turkey to a small island, where a helicopter had ferried them to the middle of the Tyrrhenian Sea for a rendezvous with this sleek ship.

And what a beaut it is.

The silver yacht was more than three hundred feet long and rose from a deep draft to a superstructure of four levels. He was currently imprisoned on its top floor, in a wide lounge with panoramic views toward the bow and both sides. Behind him, Elena sat at a desk buried in books and scratched notes on a yellow legal pad. She had already filled one and was onto her second. He didn't interrupt her or begrudge her focus.

In fact, he was counting on it.

He used the time to study his floating prison, judging it with the critical eyes of a former seaman. As they shackled him into leg irons, he had listened to the engines belowdecks. *Sounded like twin diesels, maybe hybrids, definitely powering a water-jet propulsion drive.* Once he and Elena had been taken aboard, the ship had ramped its engines and swept north-west over the sea, running close to thirty knots, an impressive speed for a yacht this size.

And that was not all that impressed.

The yacht didn't have just one helipad, but two: one at the bow, and another directly over his head. In addition, he had been marched through a garage space that housed a line of black jet-skis with their noses pointed toward the closed door to the sea—along with what appeared to be a four-man submersible equipped with dual launchers for mini-torpedoes.

The latter was a firm reminder. Though the ship's sleek profile might look like a party boat on the outside, inside it was all business. The crew—easily several dozen—all carried weapons, which they concealed when on deck, but showed more brazenly when inside.

He tapped a knuckle against the window. Even this glass looked extra thick, likely bulletproof, probably able to withstand a blast.

With a sigh, he stared out at the view beyond the bow. The sun sat on the horizon, perched just above the dark volcanic cones of an island, setting their cinder edges on fire. The lower slopes were dark, ominous, falling away to shadowy forests and small lighted hamlets along the coast.

"Whoever named this place had no imagination," Kowalski mumbled. "You got an island covered in volcanos, so you name it Volcano."

"Vulcano," Elena corrected, stretching back from the desk. She removed a set of petite reading glasses, tossed them on a legal pad, and rubbed red-rimmed eyes. "The place was not named for the volcanos, but for the Roman god of fire, Vulcan. The same god who the Greeks called Hephaestus."

Kowalski turned from the window with a jangle of his leg irons. "Then I guess calling it Vulcano is better than naming it Hephaestos or something."

"Actually, it was once called that, too."

He'd meant it as a joke, but she took him seriously.

Women just don't get me.

"The ancient Greeks named this island *Thérmessa,* which means 'land of heat.'" She nudged a thick book on her table. "But here a Greek historian calls it *Hiera of Hephaestus* or 'the Sacred Place of Hephaestus.' Which could also be translated as 'Sacred Fire,' depending on the context."

Kowalski turned back to the view. The sun had dropped lower, further igniting those crystalline cinder cones. "It does look like it's on fire."

Elena stood up and joined him at the window. "Maybe that's why the Greeks thought Hephaestus was still working here. They believed this place was where he crafted weapons for Ares, the god of war. Deep beneath the island, Hephaestus would hammer and stoke his fires. The Greeks believed the periodic explosions of smoke and ash from the island's volcanos were due to the mighty blacksmith clearing out his chimneys. But really all the volcanic activity here is just the African tectonic plate jamming itself northward into the Eurasian plate."

"Not quite as romantic," Kowalski said.

"No, it's not," she admitted.

As they watched, the sun finally sank away and winked out.

Kowalski shared a worried look with her. "Sun's down," he said. "You know what that means."

She nodded and hurried back to her desk.

He followed her, clanking his chains. "I don't think any last-minute cramming is going to help."

After they had boarded the yacht, their captor—the cold-eyed woman named Nehir—had marched them up to this lounge, where several of her crew dumped boxes of books. She had then locked them both in here, with a simple instruction: *Impress me by sundown or he'll suffer.*

It was clearly a test.

And I'm the whipping boy.

Though they weren't exactly planning to *whip* him.

While being put into chains, he had noted a crate being opened. The hulking brute, Kadir, removed a brazier, a tripod, and a heavy sheaf of branding irons. As he did so, the giant never took his dead eyes off Kowalski.

Even now, as Kowalski reached Elena's desk, his left thigh throbbed from the red-hot poker burned into him this morning. The bastards, at least, had done him the courtesy of bandaging the wound. Not out of kindness, he figured, but more out of a concern that their whipping boy might die prematurely of blood poisoning. They certainly didn't bother to set his broken nose, only taped it. Nor did they address the giant bruise across his lower back after almost breaking his spine.

I mean, how much can a few goddamn ibuprofens cost?

The double doors to the lounge swung open behind Elena. She turned with a slight flinch. Armed guards could be seen posted out in the hall, along with the shadowy mountainous threat of Kadir, who stood with his thick arms crossed.

Nehir swept into the room, all in black, even the scarf over her hair. She was accompanied by two men with stubby assault rifles in their hands. They were taking no chances with Kowalski.

Nehir's dark eyes took in the room, lingering on the sprawl of books and papers on the desk. "I see you've been busy."

Elena turned back to Kowalski, her eyes bright with fear as she looked up at him. They both knew what came next.

Test time.

9:06 P.M.

I'm not ready.

Elena looked aghast at the piles of books. She knew they must have come from the subterranean library back in Turkey. The collection had been brought to her without any preamble or explanation. There were works by Greek, Roman, and Persian scholars. Hundreds of books. She barely had time to sort them, let alone digest them.

In the crates, she found Plato's *Timaeus* and *Critias*, which dealt with his theories on Atlantis. Then there was Aeschylus's *Agamemnon*, which offered another view of the Trojan War. Then *Medea* by Euripides, the tragic story of a witch who fell in love with the mythic warrior Jason.

Elena barely had time to skim through the two fat books of *Histories* by Herodotus.

And that was just the Greeks.

Still, she knew what was expected of her without being told.

Nehir voiced it with her first question, as she waved out to sea. "Do you know why we're here?"

Elena licked her lips and stood, feeling better without this woman looming over her. "That's Vulcano, home to the mythic foundry of the god Hephaestus."

A nod.

Elena stared down at the three works she had decided were the most important. The first two were obvious. Nehir had given her photocopies of the two books found aboard the ancient dhow. Elena added another: a two-thousand-page treatise by the Greek historian Strabo, titled *Geographica*.

She reached down and placed a palm on the copy of the captain's journal. "Hunayn's account stops shortly after it starts, but where it left off, he admits to reaching what he calls the *Forge of Hephaestus*." She looked over to Nehir. "Which must be this island."

"As our Mūsā had also devised."

"And I must be here to help you pick up the trail that vanished into history, to find out where Hunayn went next."

"Precisely." She waved across the stacked books and scribbled notepads. "So, what have you determined?"

Joe scoffed loudly. "Really? You expect her to solve a mystery in five hours that you all couldn't figure out after five centuries."

"Eleven centuries, actually." Nehir seemed unfazed by his outburst and kept her focus on Elena. "But I do expect Dr. Cargill to have figured out *why* the traitorous Hunayn chose to come here. Why did he seek out the Forge of Hephaestus?"

Elena did her best to answer. She shifted her hand over to the thick volume of Strabo's *Geographica*. "According to what the captain wrote, he put great faith in Strabo. The historian not only admired Homer for his poetry, but he also believed—like Hunayn—that the *Iliad* and the *Odyssey* were based on real events. Strabo vehemently advocated his position and sought proof, which he gathered and put into this book. Knowing this, the captain picked apart Strabo's work, looking for clues on where to go next."

"And what specifically drew Hunayn to these shores?"

Elena moved her palm again, this time coming to rest on the Arabic copy of Homer's *Odyssey*. "Hunayn marked up his volume of Homer's epic. Underlining sections and making notes. But he seemed especially intrigued by the *creations* of Hephaestus." She turned to pages she had dog-eared. She translated one of those sections aloud. "*'On either side there stood gold and silver mastiffs which Hephaestus, with his consummate skill, had fashioned expressly to keep watch over the palace of King Alcinous; so they were immortal and could never grow old.'*"

"Immortal dogs?" Joe asked.

"Made of precious metals," Elena added. "Gold and silver. Homer is describing metal dogs that could move on their own. Plainly it was a topic that caught Hunayn's imagination and interest. Especially as he and his three brothers—the Banū Mūsā —had written multiple books about crafting mechanical tools."

Nehir nodded. "Like *The Book of Ingenious Devices*."

"Exactly. So, of course, Hunayn's attention focused on what Hephaestus had crafted. In the margin of that section I just read, Hunayn also copied passages from Homer's *Iliad*, where it states that Hephaestus's forge had little wheeled tripods that ran about on their own, doing his bidding, while the god was also served by *'golden handmaids who bustled about their master like living women.'* Again, Homer is describing automatons, including mechanical women who did whatever he asked."

"Gotta admit it," Joe said. "I wouldn't mind a couple of those."

Elena ignored him. "It's clear that Hunayn was obsessed with this subject. He made a few more notes in the margins about other references to such wonders. Bronze horses that could pull chariots. A metal-winged eagle that Zeus sent to torture Prometheus for stealing fire. And if Hunayn believed, like Strabo, that Homer's stories were true—then why not these creations of Hephaestus?"

"So, you're thinking he went looking for them," Joe said.

She nodded. "While I don't know *where* he went to look, I do know *who* he was searching for."

Nehir frowned with disbelief. "Truly?"

Elena flipped to another marked section of the captain's copy of the *Odyssey*. "Shortly after Odysseus left the Underworld, he ended up in a strange lost kingdom, one that is *'the farthermost of men, and no other mortals are conversant with them.'* These people—the Phaeacians—were also mysteriously advanced technologically. Their ships are described as fast as *'falcons, swiftest of birds'* and capable of sailing by themselves. You plug in a course, and the ship takes you there. In fact, it's how Odysseus finally makes it back home, aboard a Phaeacian ship."

Nehir dismissed this account with a wave. "I see now. You believe it is these *Phaeacians* who the traitor Hunayn was trying to find. Why?"

"Remember those gold and silver dogs that Hephaestus created. The *Odyssey* states the god gave them to a king—King Alcinous. *He* was the ruler of the Phaeacians."

Nehir's brows furrowed.

"Here was a god who gave gifts to an unknown people. Maybe supplied them with a whole lot more. It had to intrigue Hunayn. He and his brothers were always scavenging for knowledge lost by other kingdoms. Hunayn's whole voyage started because he was tasked with finding more about the people who he names in his journal as the *'Great Enemy of Homer's time,'* a people who wiped out three kingdoms in one fell swoop. Who could possibly have the strength and technology to accomplish that?"

Nehir met her gaze. "The Phaeacians."

"Considering Hunayn's mind-set and obsession, I see him coming to that conclusion." Elena faced her adversary. "Hunayn left here looking for the Phaeacians. And if I'm right, I think it might give us some guidance on where to go next."

As Nehir remained quiet, Elena sank back to her seat and bit her lip, hoping it had been enough. Finally, the woman turned and barked at the door, summoning Kadir.

Oh, no . . .

The giant barged into the room, ducking his head to enter. As he marched inside, Elena cast an apologetic look at Joe.

I'm sorry.

Kadir crossed to the desk, carrying a large cloth-bound bundle under one arm. She imagined it was some new device to torture Joe, to punish her for failing this test. Instead the giant swung the object up, and with surprising gentleness, placed it on top of her notes, then stepped back.

"That is your next challenge," Nehir said and waved for Elena to open it.

She stood up and unfolded the bundle. She gasped as she recognized the age-tarnished bronze box from the frozen dhow. Her hands trembled over its surface—not at the fear of its low-level radiation, but at the treasure inside.

She stared over at Nehir. "What do you want me—?"

The woman turned away, motioned Kadir to follow, and said, "By noon tomorrow, I expect new insight into the map of the Banū Mūsā." She cast a look back at Elena—then Joe. "Or else Kadir will be teaching you both a much harder lesson."

Elena stepped after the woman. "I can't possibly do that. You know parts are missing." She pictured the astrolabe tumbling out of its cradle in the map.

Nehir ignored her and left with the other men.

Elena returned to her desk and stared down at the centuries-old artifact.

Joe joined her. "Pick up your pencils, kids," he said. "Time for part two of the test."

Elena reached down and lifted the lid, revealing the map. Again, its gold and precious jewels reflected the light, gleaming with a fiery magnificence. She gasped again and almost dropped the lid back down.

How could this be?

Inside the box, nestled in that golden glow, shone a brilliant silvery sphere, inscribed with constellations and symbols and encircled by the arms of decorated compasses.

It was the missing astrolabe—the Daedalus Key returned again to its cradle.

Joe groaned. "This can't be good."

19

This had better be worth it.

Gray strode up the steep street in the heart of Cagliari's old town, the seaside capital of the island of Sardinia. Ahead, the narrow avenue passed under a huge stone arch, flanked by Doric pillars and topped by an entablature of a crown and shield with the title REGIO ARSENALE beneath it. This corner of the old city, known as the Arsenal, once housed the city's military barracks and prison.

But no longer.

Outside the arched gate, a long black banner hung with the silver words MUSEO ARCHEOLOGICO NAZIONALE DI CAGLIARI emblazoned on it. The former military square beyond the archway now served as Cagliari's museum district.

Monsignor Roe led Gray under the stone arch, talking nonstop, sharing Sardinia's history. It seemed the Mediterranean's second-largest island had a rich military history. Gray barely heard any of it, knowing the priest was nervous, anxious after all that had happened.

He wasn't the only one.

Seichan trailed a few steps to the side. Her gaze swept every inch of the sunbaked plaza as they entered it.

Piazza Arsenale already bustled with locals going about their morning, along with clutches of excited tourists gathered around guides holding up flags or umbrellas, likely groups from the three massive cruise ships docked at the city's port. Overhead, seagulls screamed and swooped, while underfoot, clutches of pigeons danced about people's legs.

At least the crowds and noise offered some cover.

Yesterday, after the attack on Castel Gandolfo, Gray had wanted somewhere to get out of sight, both to regroup and to hide the fact they had survived the bombardment. Monsignor Roe had recommended coming here, sailing two hundred miles to the island of Sardinia. They had traveled sixteen hours aboard a fishing trawler, captained by an old family friend of the priest, coming to port after two in the morning.

The others were still ensconced at a small seaside hotel. Gray had left Maria and Mac, both bleary-eyed and still shell-shocked, nursing mugs of coffee. Father Bailey had returned to his study of the treasured Da Vinci map. All of them were guarded over by Major Bossard.

Without knowing whom to trust or which agencies had been leaking intel to the enemy, Gray had needed his group to stay lost. He had even removed the batteries from his encrypted satellite phone. Instead, he had bought two burner phones this morning from a kiosk outside the cruise terminal by their hotel; he'd left one phone with Maria and carried the other in his pocket. It was the best he could manage.

For now, they had to remain ghosts.

As he and the others reached the steps leading up to the museum, Gray finally stopped their guide. "Monsignor Roe, why did you want to come here?"

And Gray didn't just mean this museum. The priest clearly had some reason to suggest traveling to Sardinia. Gray hadn't pressed the matter. The island was as good as anywhere to vanish from the world. Plus, the monsignor was obviously exhausted and haunted after seeing his home— where he'd been born—destroyed. He had also lost an untold number of friends and colleagues. Even his life's work—the Holy Scrinium—was likely beyond salvaging.

So, Gray had given the old man some latitude, but now he wanted answers, sensing some intent behind the priest's recommendation to come here.

Roe shaded his eyes, staring at the museum entrance, then nodded. "*Sì*. I have a friend here, someone I've known for decades and trust with my life. If you would know your enemy, he will help."

"What do you mean by *know your enemy*? How could anyone here know about who attacked us yesterday?"

"No, you misunderstand. He will not help us with that. Though I've given that question much thought while we sailed here. I had a hard time sleeping aboard the boat, with all its rocking and jostling."

Gray imagined it wasn't the trawler's lack of stability that had kept the old priest awake.

"After all that thinking, I may have some insight," Roe admitted, looking a little sheepish. "Maybe not insight. *Hunch* might be the better word."

Seichan sidled next to them but kept her eyes on the square. "I'll take even a hunch if it'll help us find those monsters."

Roe patted her arm, as if she were the one who needed consoling. "Last night, I went over and over again in my head what you told me. About Dr. MacNab's story in Greenland. About the horrors he saw. It struck me as strange that the enemy would so readily leave that place without the astrolabe, what they called the Daedalus Key. All that effort, only to recover part of the map device."

"As I understand it, things went south quickly," Gray said. "The assault team lost most of its men."

"You may be right, but you mentioned that they spoke Arabic, and that they seemed to know far more about all of this."

"What are you getting at?" Seichan asked.

"Do you remember the pictures I showed you of the only surviving spherical astrolabe? It was also made in Arabia. Signed by its maker, a man named Mūsā. It looks very much like what Dr. MacNab recovered from that ship. It made me wonder last night if what is sitting in the Oxford museum was someone's attempt to replicate the Daedalus Key. If you remember, the schematics that Da Vinci used to craft his version of the map were missing the plans for the astrolabe. That page had been torn away."

Gray considered the implication. "You're thinking someone still has that missing page—at least part of it—and tried to replicate it."

"And maybe they succeeded, maybe they created their own Daedalus Key."

If the monsignor was correct, then the enemy could already have both pieces to the puzzle: the original Banū Mūsā map and a replicated astrolabe.

Roe shrugged. "But like I said, it's a *hunch*. Or maybe just the fevered imagination of a tired priest. Either way, that surviving astrolabe in Oxford had the Arabic date of 885 inscribed on it, which is 1480 in the Gregorian calendar. If someone had been trying to re-create the Daedalus Key, they must have been attempting to do so for centuries. If I'm right, then someone has preserved that knowledge all this time, perhaps a secret society. Maybe our unknown enemy is part of that same group. Like you said, they certainly *do* seem to know more about all of this than anyone else."

"You could be right," Gray admitted.

He stared at Roe, struck again by the monsignor's resemblance to his old friend Vigor Verona. But it was no longer just the man's outward appearance. This tired old priest was just as brilliant.

Seichan waved at the museum. "That's all fine and good, but who are we meeting here, and what did you mean about knowing our enemy if it wasn't those who attacked us?"

Roe squinted at the sky. "It is getting hot already. Let's find those answers inside. Where it'll be much cooler."

Gray swiped his sweaty brow, appreciating this suggestion.

Definitely a brilliant man.

10:22 A.M.

Seichan waited in the cool lobby of the museum. While she enjoyed the air-conditioning, she wondered what they were doing here. One foot would not stop tapping. She wanted to blame her impatience on nerves stretched taut by the adrenaline rush from yesterday's attack, but she could not fool herself into believing that.

Before leaving the Italian mainland, with all their gear abandoned, she had been forced to buy a new breast pump, but in their haste to leave, she had to settle for a hand pump. In the privacy of the trawler's cabin, Gray had assisted her, which was in no way erotic, even with his stimulation to help her. It was, in a word, humiliating.

Like milking a cow.

But her shame rose not out of pride. Gray had been kind and patient, even under the circumstances. His touch had been gentle, his words encouraging. Instead, her mortification came from knowing *who* she had been in the past. She had been honed into the sharpest dagger by her former masters. She could move silently, swiftly, believing herself in those moments to be more shadow than substance. In the heat of those moments, she sensed every fiber of muscle, every nerve ending in her skin.

And now what am I?

Even here, in the middle of a mission, her body rebelled, trying to force her back into a role she wasn't sure she wanted to resume. It would not let her settle into herself, to become that *shadow*. Instead, the *substance* of herself refused to be ignored.

She shook her arms, trying to dispel the tension.

But deep down, she knew this wasn't the real issue.

Unbidden, she pictured Jack's mop of dark hair after a bath, still tangled with soapy bubbles. The sense memory swelled through her, of baby shampoo, of his milk breath. Though thousands of miles away, he was still with her, inescapable.

She closed her eyes.

She knew this was the true source of her nerve-jangling anxiety. Forced to go dark, she had been unable to call Kat, to check on Jack, to make sure he was doing well. She hadn't expected it to choke her up so much.

Gray touched her arm. "Are you okay?"

She flinched but nodded.

"It looks like Monsignor Roe is heading back," Gray said.

Across the lobby, the old priest pushed through the crowd, accompanied by another. The bespectacled man with salt-and-pepper gray hair looked to be in his sixties, wearing a white museum smock and a welcoming smile.

Monsignor Roe made a surprising introduction. "This is Rabbi Fine."

The newcomer shook both their hands. "Please call me Howard. I think we can forgo any rabbinical formalities. Especially as Sebastian tells me you need to consult me on matters archaeological." He motioned to the museum. "Well, you've certainly come to the right place."

The monsignor smiled. "Howard and I studied together, back in our university days. We also worked a joint project to preserve the remains of the old Jewish catacomb in Rome."

"Back when I was an archaeologist for the Israel Antiquities Authority. After that, we went our separate ways. Sebastian into service with the Vatican, and I into rabbinical studies. But we both remain lovers of history at heart. In fact, I oversee several dig sites here in Sardinia, of the local Nuragic tribes, a Bronze Age people that occupied this island for sixteen centuries, until they vanished."

"Not only is Howard a rabbi," Roe explained, "but he has degrees in archaeology and anthropology. So, I'll let him guide this tour."

Gray frowned. "What is he going to—?"

Howard turned and headed for a wide set of stairs. "If I understand what Sebastian wanted me to share, I think we should start on the second floor."

As the rabbi set off, Roe whispered back to them. "I just told him about an ancient enemy that we wanted more information about. Don't worry. I was discreet."

Seichan shared a look with Gray.

That had better be true—for all their sakes.

Gray kept close to the monsignor. "What ancient enemy?"

Roe hung back long enough to say, "The ones mentioned in the old schematics that Da Vinci used to construct his gold map. The enemy who the Banū Mūsā brothers believed resided in Tartarus and who waged war on three civilizations, destroying them all and leading to the Greek Dark Ages."

"What does any of that have to do with Sardinia?" Seichan asked.

"Because I think the enemy came *here* first." Roe left them, hurrying to catch up with his friend. "I'll let Howard explain."

Seichan stared at the two men.

One a Catholic, the other a Jew.

And we're being hunted by Arabs, likely Muslims.

At least, all the major religions of this area were represented.

The rabbi took them to the second floor and drew them to a stop before a five-foot-tall stone slab, inscribed deeply by an angular script. "This is the Noro Stone," Howard explained. "A treasure of our museum. It dates back to the eighth or ninth century B.C."

Roe lifted an eyebrow. "In other words, to the middle of the Homeric Age, the Greek Dark Ages."

Howard faced the rock. "The inscription here is one of the oldest examples of Phoenician writing. It is incomplete, but the best translation tells of a great war fought on these shores by the Nuragic people against a powerful enemy, one that led to great ruin."

Seichan glanced over to Roe, who looked all too happy with himself. "Who were they fighting?"

Howard smiled. "Ah, an age-old mystery, one that I've been trying to solve."

You and a bunch of murderous bastards.

"One of the reasons I'm here at the museum is that I'm overseeing the installation of an exhibit on that very subject matter." The rabbi waved them over to a nearby room that was roped off and separated by hanging sheets of plastic, the exhibit plainly still under construction. "It's all about the Sea People."

Seichan frowned as she followed the man through the plastic sheets to the small space inside. In the center stood two rows of mostly empty display cases. A few held bronze weapons and tiny statues. But their guide led them to the back wall, where pictures had started to be hung.

"Like much of the history of the Homeric Age, little is truly known about the Sea People," Howard explained, "so even putting this installation together is proving to be a challenge. All we really know is that they were a seafaring confederation, likely rising out of the western Mediterranean. But whoever they were, once they burst into the eastern half of the Mediterranean, they laid waste to civilization after civilization, leading to centuries of darkness."

"The Greek Dark Ages," Gray said.

"Correct." Howard drew them to a wall display. "Here's a map that lays out those conquests, so you can get a general scope of the Sea People's assault."

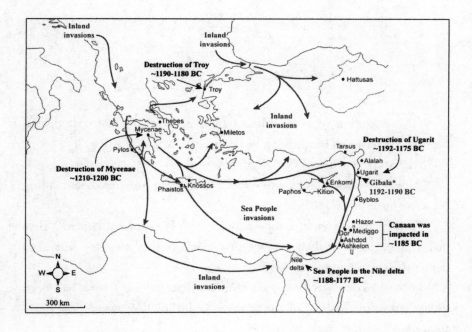

Seichan leaned closer next to Gray. She noted the sweep of arrows showing the attacks upon Greece, upon the Middle East, and down to Egypt. If the dates on the map were correct, every kingdom around the Mediterranean fell in less than twenty years. It appeared to be an all-out assault—*all rising out of the west.*

Howard continued, "The best accounts of this war—as scant as they are—come from the Egyptians, who were soundly defeated. And while details are scarce, the overlying gist of those stories was one of abject terror. Come see."

Howard moved down the wall to another display. This one appeared to be a rubbing taken from an Egyptian site. It showed a chaotic, insane battle, on land and sea, with Egyptian soldiers in the throes of battle, dying by the hundreds.

"This depiction was found in a temple near Luxor. Not only does it capture the terror so beautifully, but do you see what's missing?"

Seichan frowned, but Gray figured it out.

"Nowhere does it show *who* is attacking them, only soldiers fending off some force just out of view."

"The Egyptians were a superstitious lot," Howard explained. "They placed much faith in their iconography. I believe they were too fearful to depict the enemy, to reveal them."

Seichan remembered Mac and Maria's description of what had been unleashed from the hold of the shipwrecked dhow. *No wonder the Egyptians didn't want to draw them.*

Monsignor Roe spoke. "But maybe *someone* else tried to reveal them."

His words seemed to surprise even Howard.

Roe pointed up. "Show them the Giants."

10:38 A.M.

Holy mother . . .

Gray gaped at what stood before him. He would've sworn out loud if not for the presence of the priest and the rabbi. The installation consumed most of the third floor of the archaeological museum. The hall held tall cases and wide pedestals to accommodate the statuary housed within.

Howard introduced the collection with a bit of drama, which was not unwarranted. "Welcome to the presence of the *Kolossoi,*" he said with a wave of an arm. "The Giants of Mont'e Prama."

Gray glanced over to Seichan, then to Monsignor Roe. He now understood why the priest had dragged them all to this island, why he had kept silent.

This needs to be seen in person.

Howard led them around. "These massive sandstone warriors were discovered broken and buried on a farm on the west coast of Sardinia, along the Sinis peninsula. We estimate there were once forty-four giants, though we've only restored a little over half of them."

Gray stepped up to one of them. It stood twice his height. It appeared to represent an archer, prepared for battle. Nearby was another with a sword, and one with the huge fists of a boxer.

"There remains some question as to their age," Howard admitted. "But it's generally accepted that the Nuragic people carved these statues during the Greek Dark Ages, roughly right after the Sea People would have swept through here."

"What were the Giants' purpose?" Seichan asked.

"To act as sacred guardians," Howard said. "They were dug up amid the ruins of a sprawling necropolis on the slopes of Mont'e Prama. It is believed they stood guard over the dead, possibly the bodies of men and women slain by the Sea People."

Roe nodded. "Prama overlooks the *western* sea, as if the Giants were watching for those invaders to return, ready to do battle."

Gray understood the monsignor's implication. It would support the idea that the enemy had come from that direction, from the west.

"Rumors and myths abound about these massive figures," Howard continued. "It is written that these statues would come to life if Sardinia were ever attacked. That they would shed their stone, revealing bronze armor beneath, then cast boulders down at any invaders from atop Mont'e Prama's heights."

Gray pictured bronze versions of these statues and felt a shiver of dread—not that they might come to life, but at what that story implied, especially considering the Giants' odd appearance. He remembered Mac's story of the lumbering, bronze beast shattering through the hull of the dhow.

Roe stoked his growing trepidation. "The other myth written about them is that they were carved in this way to mimic the look of their attackers. Sculpted to make the enemy think its own people were already here and skip past this island."

Seichan looked as ill as Gray felt.

He stared up at the giant head in the display cabinet. The face was flat planes, with slits for a mouth and nose. The head was domed unnaturally high, surmounted by a knoblike top piece. But it was the eyes that made him shudder: perfect concentric rings that stared dully forward. He pictured bronze versions of these statues.

If this was the true face of the enemy . . . or at least, a representation of their bronze constructs . . .

Monsignor Roe continued: "All of this implies that the Nuragic tribes believed the enemy was still out there, ready to return at any time."

Gray again remembered Mac's story.

Something certainly was still out there.

"But that's not the only reason I asked you all to come to Sardinia," Roe said, drawing back Gray's attention. "The other reason concerns the thousands of structures dotting this island, the mysterious *nuraghe*."

"Which are what?" Seichan asked.

Howard answered, "They're stone fortresses built by the Nuragic tribes. Several thousand still exist on the island, going back four thousand years. Many still stand because they are masterworks of engineering and design, far superior to what one would expect from a Bronze Age people."

In other words, Gray thought, *tech too advanced for the people living here.*

Roe stepped closer to him. "But you should know the ancient Greeks had a different name for the *nuraghe* fortresses. They called them *daidaleia*."

Gray looked harder at the monsignor.

"For Daedalus," Howard confirmed. "The mythic master craftsman of the Greeks, the man who devised the Labyrinth that housed the minotaur, who was the father of Icarus, the boy who died when he flew too close to the sun."

Also the man whom the key to the golden map had been named after.

"I don't understand," Seichan said. "Why were those ancient fortresses named after Daedalus?"

Roe answered, "Because Sardinia was his home."

20

I'm not going to make it.

Elena checked the lounge's wall clock for the hundredth time. The glare of the midday sun reflected off the surrounding seas, sharpening her headache. The noon deadline set by Nehir weighed on her. She had been up all night, only catnapping on the sofa when she couldn't keep her eyes open any longer.

Joe had mostly kept her company, but when his conversation turned into riotous snoring last night, she had chased him below, all but shoving him at the guards out in the hall. She had needed to concentrate.

Then a couple of hours ago, Joe had returned, along with breakfast.

By that time, her sprawl of books had spread to twice its size.

Joe slowly paced the lounge, skirting her piles of books. His leg irons clanked with each step. He winced and groaned occasionally, clearly pained by the brand burned into his thigh.

Guilt ate at her.

If I don't solve this, he'll suffer worse.

He continued his clanking and groaning until she couldn't take it any longer.

"Can you please quit that?" she begged.

Joe cringed. "Sorry." He tried to slink quietly to the sofa, but it only made the chains clink louder. He finally reached the leather seat and sat down. "How're you doing?" he asked.

As an answer, she placed her head in her hands.

"Maybe if you talked it through," he said. "Gray always likes to do that."

She didn't know who *Gray* was, but maybe Joe was right. She glanced out to the three towering calderas of Vulcano. She had spent most of the night reading about Hephaestus, the god of the forge. She had searched for every reference to the blacksmith's creations—which were numerous.

The god had crafted special arrows for the huntress Artemis, magical shafts that never missed their mark. He fashioned armor for countless heroes, including Achilles from the *Iliad*. But it was his autonomous creations that she had concentrated on.

Even here, Hephaestus had been busy. He built a temple to Apollo, the god of music, and adorned it with the *Keledones Chryseai*, six golden statues of women who would sing on command. For King Minos, the blacksmith built a bronze hunting hound named Laelaps. According to Apollonius's *Argonautica*, Hephaestus had created an army of bronze warriors that once awoken would keep on killing until destroyed.

But there were two creations she found the most intriguing, remembering the stories Joe had related to her, about Mac's encounters with bronze killing machines.

"Let me read you something," Elena said and drew out the pages of *Argonautica* again from the piles on the desk. She skipped to a passage she had flagged and translated it aloud. " '*The craftsman-god Hephaestus had fashioned for the palace of Aeetes a pair of bulls with feet of bronze, and their mouths were of bronze, and from them they breathed out a terrible flame of fire.*' "

Joe sat up straighter. "That sounds like what Mac and Maria saw in that cave, what tried to attack them."

Elena believed she had caught a glimpse of it, too, before being taken away. She remembered seeing a horned, fiery figure emerge from the smoke of the burning dhow. "They were called the *Khalkotauroi*," she said. "Also known as the Colchis Bulls. Terrifying creatures, with bodies of bronze, horns of silver, and eyes of rubies. They were eventually subdued by Jason of the Argonauts, who doused their flames with a black potion given to him by the witch Medea, '*a powerful pharmaka called Promethean Blood.*'"

Joe looked at her, not getting what she was implying.

She sighed. "Mac said the fiery crabs were preserved in black oil in giant storage pots. And when he splashed the same oil on one of them, it killed the fires fueling the creature."

Joe slowly nodded.

"And then there's the story of Talos, a giant bronze guardian of the island of Crete. It was also built by Hephaestus. The Greek poet Simonides of Ceos described Talos as a *phylax empsychos*, an 'animated guardian.' Talos would run around the island throwing boulders down on anyone who threatened Crete."

"I'd say that's animated, all right," Joe admitted.

"But there's two details about him that I think are important. First, another way Talos killed people was to run up and hug them against his red-hot bronze form, burning them alive with the fires inside his body."

"Sounds sorta like what those flaming crabs were trying to do."

She nodded. "It was also written that Talos was powered by a golden ichor, an oily fluid that burned with fire and could not be put out. Which again matches Mac's description of what seemed to fuel those fiery crabs."

"If you're right, then Mac wasn't the only one who had encounters with these creatures." Joe stood up and clanked over to her side. "Way in the past, others must've run into something like them, too."

"And built mythologies around them."

As an archaeologist, she knew many myths were based on kernels of truth.

"But how does any of this help us right now?" Joe asked, turning to the wall clock.

"It doesn't," she admitted.

Nehir had ordered her to glean some insight about the golden map, to help guide her team to where Captain Hunayn had traveled after leaving the island of Vulcano.

She stood up and shifted over to the map box and lifted its lid. The golden coastlines gleamed around the rich blue of the lapis lazuli sea. But her gaze focused on the silver astrolabe resting in its cradle. She knew now it wasn't the same sphere from the ancient dhow. It was clearly too new.

Someone made a facsimile.

Last night, she and Joe had risked flipping the lever on the map's side. They retreated a few steps, remembering the radiation given off by it. They had listened as gears turned, the box hummed, and once again, the tiny silver ship—likely representing Odysseus's boat—left its port in Troy. It sailed out a few inches into the representation of the Aegean Sea, then stopped and spun in place.

They had tried it again a few times during the night, but only achieved the same result. She had gained no new insight and finally stopped trying, fearing they were irradiating themselves for no reason.

Still . . .

She reached down with both hands and gently lifted the silver astrolabe out of the map. She had not dared try this before, but desperation now made her risk it.

"If you break that . . ." Joe warned.

"Hush."

She sensed something important about the astrolabe, something she was missing, something her sleep-deprived mind couldn't grasp. She lifted it closer and rotated the sphere in her hand. She noted the tiny pinprick holes drilled throughout the inner shell. Likely serving as ventilation holes for the clockwork mechanism inside.

Wait . . .

She shifted the astrolabe to one hand and reached to her desk. She moved the photocopy of Hunayn's journal closer and turned to the last few pages and read a line there: " '*Only I was allowed to possess the beams of the Ship-Star, the three tools necessary to unlock the one true course amidst the map's many false paths.' "*

She straightened with a start. "I've been such a fool." She held out the astrolabe toward Joe. "Hold this."

He did so with a sick expression, as if she'd just passed him a coiled rattlesnake.

She reached into her pocket and removed the three bronze pins that had fallen from Hunayn's journal. The captain had been protecting far more than just those old books.

"What are those?" Joe asked as she approached him with the bronze rods.

" *'The beams of the Ship-Star,'* " she said, quoting the journal. "As a *nautical* archaeologist, I should've already figured this out. The Ship-Star is one of the old names for the North Star, a shining beacon for sailors going back millennia."

"And that's important, why?"

She ignored his question and examined the tiny flags at the tip of each pin. A tiny Arabic symbol was inscribed on each. As Joe held the astrolabe, she searched its surface, looking for the corresponding mark.

"There you are," she whispered as she found the right one.

She carefully inserted the pin with the matching flag into the little hole next to it. Then after some furtive squinting, she found the second and pushed its rod into place

She explained as she looked for the last symbol, "Astrolabes have to be constructed to the latitude of the user, fixing the North Star at its center." She tapped the silver artifact. "But not *spherical* astrolabes. They're universal tools. One can set them over and over again, almost like programming them, by recalibrating the astrolabe to each location you go."

"How?"

She found the last symbol and seated the final pin. "Like this. Depending on where and how many pins you use to lock it down, you can reset it."

To unlock the one true course.

She took the astrolabe and seated it back into its cradle. She swallowed and glanced to Joe, passing on a silent questioning look.

Do we try this?

He nodded.

She reached to the side of the box.

"Stand back," she warned and flipped the lever.

11:34 A.M.

Here we go . . .

Kowalski held his breath and retreated two steps with Elena. He worried that the entire contraption might blow up in their faces. He found himself holding Elena's hand. He felt her tremble—but was it from fear or anticipation?

Ahead of them, the map box hummed, and the astrolabe turned in its cradle, spinning one way, then another. Its inscribed arms swung over its surface in a complicated dance.

"Look at the silver ship," Elena exhaled in wonder. "I think it's working."

The tiny boat glided over the shiny blue gemstone. It sped across the Aegean Sea, briefly pausing at various tiny islands, then onward again.

"I wager those are ports that Hunayn believed Odysseus stopped at. Maybe that last one was the island of the Cyclops, or perhaps the sorceress Circe's home. . . ."

Kowalski watched as the ship left the Aegean and sailed around the southern tip of Greece. It then spun wildly as it crossed the Ionian Sea.

Elena pointed. "I think that represents when Odysseus's crew opened a bag of winds given to them by King Aeolus, thinking there was gold inside. The released winds drove the ship away from Odysseus's homeland in Greece."

Finally, the silver ship stabilized as it rounded the end of Italy's boot and passed the island of Sicily. From there it crossed over to a row of tiny golden islands topped by tiny rubies.

Volcanos.

They both glanced out the yacht's windows to the sunlit calderas of Vulcano. Kowalski almost expected to see a great silver ship glide past the yacht and head to that island.

"Looks like they definitely came here," Kowalski said and returned his attention to the map.

After the tiny ship reached the chain of volcanic islands, it stopped again.

Elena squeezed his hand.

They both held their breath.

Where will it go next?

But the silver ship remained alongside those islands—and stayed there.

Kowalski finally exhaled in defeat, no longer able to hold his breath. "Maybe it's broken."

She shook her head, apparently refusing to believe it.

"Then maybe you have to put in new coordinates. Move those rods around to—"

The map box quaked on the table, making them both jump back. The humming intensified to the whistle of a kettle—then the entire gemlike surface of the Mediterranean broke apart, shattering outward from the volcanic islands into a spiderweb of cracks. The fragmented seams released a sulfurous steam.

Kowalski drew Elena back by the hand. "It's gonna blow."

"No." She freed herself and stepped closer to the map. Her gaze visibly ran along the maze of steaming lines, crisscrossing and bisecting each other across the sea. "It's like Hunayn wrote. *The map's many false paths.*"

Curious, Kowalski risked joining her.

As they watched, all the cracks sealed back up, erasing those false paths, so perfectly that the lapis lazuli looked as pristine as before, like one big piece of the gem.

Except one seam remained—and widened.

Steam from that crack hissed away, replaced with golden fire, the flames rising from the fuel inside the map. They formed a fiery river flowing west from the shores of Vulcano, across the Tyrrhenian Sea to the southern tip of Sardinia, then due south until it reached and traced the northern coast of Africa, heading west.

Elena leaned even closer, risking the heat, the radiation. "All this drama almost looks like some fiery representation of plate tectonics. Look at how—"

"Ship's moving again," Kowalski warned her, drawing her straighter again.

Back at the ruby-tipped representation of Vulcano, the tiny ship finally set sail again, diving into that golden river of fire. The flames masked most of its path, but the silver ship flashed out of the gold fire as it paused at Sardinia, then turned and headed south toward Africa.

Kowalski followed that fiery stream along the continent's coast until it passed through the Strait of Gibraltar.

Where is it—?

A loud voice rose from beyond the lounge's double doors.

Uh-oh.

Kowalski rushed to the map, while checking the wall clock.

She's early.

He flipped the switch on the side of the bronze box and closed its lid. He kept a palm there, feeling the vibrations inside slowly subside. The humming also grew quieter.

"C'mon . . ." He willed the device to fully shut down. To Elena, he warned, "Don't say a word. They can't know what just happened."

Elena's eyes widened, the wonder shining there turning to fear. "But you'll be—" She waved to his leg.

"I can take it."

He turned to the doors as they crashed open. Nehir stalked into the lounge, followed by the brute Kadir.

At least, I hope I can.

11:58 A.M.

Elena shivered as Nehir approached, leaving the giant at the door. She fought to keep from looking at the map box. She glanced guiltily at Joe.

What am I going to do?

The fiery triumph from a moment ago died to cold embers. She knew that if she stayed silent about what they had just learned, Joe would suffer.

That's if we can even keep this secret.

As Nehir crossed toward the desk, the woman's nose crinkled. "What's that burning smell?"

Elena stiffened. Moments ago, struck by realization about the astrolabe and the bronze pins, she had been too excited not to try operating the map. Up until then, she had gotten no sense that she and Joe were being watched, of hidden cameras. And from Nehir's question now, the enemy had clearly not been eavesdropping, likely overconfident that they had the upper hand.

But what now? Had she and Joe been caught red-handed?

She swallowed, struggling with what to say.

Joe took the lead and marched forward, stepping in front of the woman, momentarily blocking Nehir's view to the map box. "If you don't like the smell of burnt flesh, then quit shoving red-hot pokers into me."

He turned slightly to rub his leg, while casting a worried look at Elena.

Nehir rounded past him awkwardly. "That'll depend on how productive Dr. Cargill has been this morning."

Elena hid her relief, but they were not out of the woods. She nervously opened and closed a fist. "If I had more time—"

"Ah, but you don't." Nehir waved back to Kadir. "My brother has no patience, I'm afraid. If you can't entertain us, I may have to find another distraction for him. You will be allowed to watch, of course."

Elena felt the blood drain from her face—even more so, when Nehir elbowed her aside and reached to the map box.

"As I warned you last night," Nehir said, "we need your valuable insight into the Banū Mūsā map. To tell us where to go next."

"I don't know if I'll be able to—"

Nehir touched the side of the box, then placed her palm against it. "Why is this hot?"

Elena cleared her throat, searching for a lie. "We . . . we tried running it multiple times this morning. To see if it would help me figure anything out."

Nehir nodded at this explanation. "And?"

Elena couldn't speak, striving to think of something to keep the woman from opening the box. She failed.

Nehir shifted her hand and lifted the box's lid, exposing the map.

Cringing, Elena tilted up on her toes to get a better look, fearing the worst, expecting flames and defeat. Instead, the expanse of the Mediterranean looked intact, the lapis lazuli as flawless as it had been for centuries. Even the tiny silver ship of Odysseus had returned to its port along the Turkish coast.

Elena exhaled too loudly, drawing Nehir's attention, which at least kept the woman from noting the tiny bronze pins in the astrolabe.

"Well?" Nehir asked. "Where do we go? And why?"

Elena knew the answer to the first question, remembering where the tiny ship had stopped at briefly after leaving Vulcano—but she dared not share with Nehir *how* she had come by that information.

I need another explanation that she'll buy.

Elena stared across the piles of books. Maybe it was panic, maybe it was desperation, but suddenly she knew what had been escaping her all morning. It struck her like a hammer between the eyes. She might have missed it still, except for the tiny ship stopping along the coast of Sardinia.

"If you can't help us," Nehir threatened, "then I may need to inspire you."

Elena rubbed her temples. She remembered holding the astrolabe a moment ago, sensing its significance, but she got too distracted by all that followed.

"It's the Daedalus Key," Elena said.

"What about it?" Nehir pressed.

"Hunayn and his brothers picked that name for a reason. I imagine the Storm Atlas got its name because Odysseus's ship was tossed about repeatedly by god-driven tempests. But why did the brothers choose *Daedalus*—out of all the mythic characters' names—to christen their astrolabe?"

"Intriguing," Nehir admitted. "But what of it?"

Elena drew upon her night-long research. "Daedalus was a master craftsman, like Hephaestus. Only he was a man, not a god. Still, he invented all manner of *ingenious devices*." She stressed the last to reference the Banū Mūsā brothers and their most famous book. "Daedalus fashioned the confounding Labyrinth where the monstrous Minotaur was kept. He crafted Icarus's wings."

She waved toward the books. "According to both Sophocles and Aristophanes, he also built animated lifelike statues. So deft of foot, that they had to be tied down or they'd escape. His reputation was such that the word *daedala* was coined to describe moving statues that were so perfect in form that they seemed beyond anything humans could create."

Nehir folded her arms, trying unsuccessfully to hide her interest.

Elena continued. "Is it any wonder then that Hunayn—who came here because of Hephaestus's reputation—would not seek out the trail of Daedalus just as ardently?"

"And where would that lead him?"

"According to myths, Daedalus was forced to flee Crete after he betrayed King Minos by revealing the path through the Labyrinth. On the run, he first fled to Sicily, then over to nearby Sardinia, where he made his home. That's where we need to go next."

Elena hated to give away the next port on Hunayn's journey, but if it helped keep her secret about the map—and keep Joe from the tortures at the hand of Kadir—so be it. It was not like that information would prove all that useful. It was but one stop among many.

Nehir's firm frown suggested the woman doubted the value of this information. Elena knew she had to drive this home for any hope of saving Joe.

"Two other details," she said. "We know Hunayn was following what he believed to be Odysseus's trail, hoping to find the mysteriously advanced Phaeacians, the people he likely believed were the destroyers of civilizations."

Nehir uncrossed her arms long enough to wave at Elena to continue, plainly accepting this.

Good.

"One of the places where Odysseus tried to dock was at the island of the Laestrygonians. It was the home of man-eating giants who cast giant boulders at Odysseus's ships, destroying all but the hero's boat."

"And what does this have to do with Sardinia?" Nehir asked.

"Because of a first-century Roman geographer, Ptolemy. Like Strabo, this scholar wrote a book titled *Geographica*. Surely Hunayn would've read this text, too." She pointed to a scatter of books. "I certainly did, at least the parts pertaining to Homer's *Odyssey*."

"So?"

"In that book, Ptolemy mentions a tribe occupying northwest Sardinia. He called them the Lestrigoni—which sounds an awful lot like Laestrygonia. Upon reading that, how could Hunayn not go there? Plus, the western side of Sardinia has ancient giant statues that were said to protect the island by hurling boulders at ships. Again, just like the Laestrygonians."

Nehir nodded, her gaze introspective.

Even Elena was now wondering if her reasoning was the same used by Hunayn to voyage to Sardinia during his first search for Tartarus. Still, she knew she needed to continue talking and not give Nehir a chance to pick apart her logic.

Elena pointed to the map. "Which brings us back to Daedalus. The namesake of the astrolabe. A man as ingenious as Hephaestus. But keep in mind, Daedalus was a *man*. Not a god. Even modern scholars believe Daedalus might have been a real person. Either way, here was a man who could build and craft incredible creations, nearly superhuman in design and function, certainly in advance of his time. What does that description remind you of?"

Nehir frowned and shook her head.

Elena posed another question. "Who was Hunayn searching for? What mysterious civilization did he believe brought the three mightiest Mediterranean kingdoms to ruin?"

Nehir straightened. "The Phaeacians." The woman locked gazes with

Elena, clearly understanding her final point. "You think Daedalus was a member of that group. That he was Phaeacian."

"I think Hunayn believed that—and it drove him to Sardinia to find out." She crossed her arms. "I know that's where he went next."

Elena actually did—though not necessarily for the reasons she'd given. But she hoped it had been enough to spare Joe.

Nehir nodded. "Very good, Dr. Cargill. Then that's where we'll head next."

Elena sighed with relief.

Nehir turned away, but not before making a last cryptic statement. "Luckily we already have people there. Cleaning up a few loose ends."

21

Maria stood on the hotel room balcony, enjoying the last few minutes of sunlight. The day had been steamy, made all the more stifling by being cooped up in the hotel. The confinement also heightened her anxiety. When she was moving, it had been easier to distract herself from her fears about Joe.

Now she had too much time to think, to dwell on it.

Where is he? Is he even alive?

Her fingers tightened on the wrought-iron balcony rail.

Gray had ordered them not to leave the premises, while he got to traipse around the island with Seichan and Monsignor Roe. He had called forty minutes ago to report that they were on their way back after surveying the ruins of a necropolis on the western side of the island, trying to glean information about the conquering horde that had swept through the Mediterranean in ancient times.

The Sea People.

Imagining those seafaring tribes, she closed her eyes and took deep breaths of the salt air—but with it came a strong hint of diesel. She opened her eyes and scowled at the three behemoths docked at Cagliari's cruise port three hundred yards down the street. The massive ships clashed with the city's tangle of narrow cobblestone avenues and quaint shops and wine bars. Three stories below, the main drag was abuzz with tourists, packed even tighter down by the entrance to the city's two giant docks. As sunset approached, passengers were returning to their ships after invading the tiny town.

Seems Sardinia is still being plagued by Sea People.

She began to turn away—when the staccato pops of gunfire drove her down to her knees, ducking her head. She gasped, her heart in her throat.

They found us.

Then she heard laughter rising from below.

Past the open slider, Mac noted her panic from inside the room. He came out onto the balcony and helped her up with his one good arm. "Just firecrackers," he assured her.

She had already figured out that much. She returned to the balcony rail with Mac, hiding her flushed face, feeling stupid.

"I heard from the hotel staff that there'll be fireworks tonight," Mac said. "They'll be shooting them over the water. Probably as entertainment for the departing cruise ships."

"No," Father Bailey said, joining them. "That's not why."

The priest stretched a kink out of his back from his daylong study of the Da Vinci map. He had finally given up and repackaged the box into a hard-sided roller bag that they'd purchased dockside in Italy. The treasure was guarded over by Major Bossard, who maintained a post by the door, armed with a pair of SIG P320 pistols, one held in his hand, the other holstered under his jacket.

Maria waved out to sea. "Okay, then why are fireworks scheduled for this evening?"

"Because tonight is the Festival of San Giovanni," Bailey explained, "honoring the feast day of John the Baptist. It's celebrated across Europe in various fashions."

Maria looked askance at the priest. "Which means fireworks here? Doesn't feel exactly pious and religious."

"Ah, the tradition in Sardinia has its roots in more pagan celebrations. June twenty-fourth was considered by the ancients to be the summer solstice, a particularly magical time, when the sun and moon unite, represented by fire and water."

Maria looked out to sea. "Thus, the fireworks over the bay."

"And beach bonfires," Bailey added. "It's traditional here to make a wish and jump over the flames to make them come true."

"I'll settle for birthday cake and candles," Mac said.

As the sun set, more people gathered below. They lined the streets, spilling out onto the cobblestones. More were packed under the awnings of seaside cafés, including directly below where rowdy songs echoed up, along with laughter and drunken shouts. Across the bay, a handful of bonfires were ignited, the flames bright in the growing darkness. To either side, other hotel guests followed their group's example and emerged onto their own balconies for the night's viewing.

Mac searched the crowds below. "If Gray and the others don't get here soon, they'll miss the fireworks."

A loud boom made Maria jump—but it wasn't the beginning of the festivities. She twisted around as the room's door swung open on its own, the knob and lock blasted away. A trio of fist-size black objects were tossed inside and bounced across the floor. Bossard was already in motion, rolling from his chair to the side, but it proved too late.

The first grenade blast tossed him high against a nearby wall.

Mac tackled Maria to the side as the other two grenades bounced toward the open balcony. They blew, but rather than bursting into shredding shrapnel, the pair exploded with thick clouds of black acrid smoke.

Father Bailey dove low into the pall, clearly going for the map inside.

Maria had caught a glimpse of the case flying toward them as the blast blew the table away from the door. Bailey must've seen it, too. The case had landed near the balcony slider.

She cursed the priest's recklessness but crawled after him nonetheless, ready to help.

"Get down," Mac warned her.

A strafe of gunfire shredded the smoke, shattering glass. But the shooter fired blindly and high into the room, missing both Maria and Bailey. The priest grabbed the roller bag handle and scooted backward.

From her low vantage, Maria noted the smoke swirl near the door as men rushed in. Then sharp pops from the left. *Bossard . . .* Muffled cries, and a body near the door crashed in the smoke. A chatter of return fire blasted toward Bossard.

Bailey dragged the roller bag past her.

She started to follow—when something skittered across the floor. A black SIG pistol spun up to her. Bossard's second weapon. A drape of smoke lifted enough to reveal the major sprawled and bloody on the floor. His arm was outstretched toward her, his eyes staring, but blind.

She snatched up the weapon and fired into the smoke as she retreated after Bailey. She emptied the entire magazine, then ducked to the side of the open door. Bailey swung the heavy case over to the railing's edge and dropped it down the gap between their balcony and the next.

"Go, go, go," Mac urged. He had ripped off his sling and helped Maria over the rail, all but tossing her. They were sticking to a preplanned evacuation route.

She dropped the twenty feet to the awning over the hotel's patio restaurant, just missing the case sitting there. She used the bounce in the taut fabric to roll to the side. Bailey and Mac crashed together next to her.

She understood their haste.

Gunfire peppered from above, tearing through the fabric. Screams erupted from the restaurant below. Maria and the two men scrambled for cover, getting directly under the balcony, spoiling any direct shots from above.

Bailey tried to tug the case after them, but one of the wheels had perforated the fabric and trapped it.

"No time!" Mac yelled.

He's right . . .

They needed to get lost in the crowd, where confusion reigned. Panic had begun to spread from the hotel. Still, farther out, the music, the festivities, the partying had masked most of the firefight and blasts.

The three of them scooted to the awning's edge and dropped into the chaos of the patio restaurant. Tables and chairs were overturned. Patrons jostled and fled in all directions. Maria caught a glimpse of a woman sitting on the ground, crying, her shoulder bloody.

Guilt stabbed at Maria, but she turned and rushed with Mac and Bailey into the spreading panic. They pushed and shoved into the masses now spilling out and filling the streets. They followed the tide, rather than fighting it.

Bailey kept looking back. She knew what they'd lost, but there was nothing to be done about it. They had a more immediate concern.

Maria searched around.

Where can we go?

9:24 P.M.

Three blocks away, stalled in festival traffic, Gray immediately spotted the plume of black smoke billowing from the hotel's third floor. He caught a glimpse of bodies leaping to the awning below.

He leaned forward. From the sedan's backseat, he growled to Rabbi Fine and Monsignor Roe. "Stay here."

The group had just returned from an excursion to the Mont'e Prama necropolis, where the giant statues had been found—not that they had learned anything new, which clearly disappointed the monsignor and the rabbi.

Gray turned to Seichan. "Let's go."

He bailed out one side, Seichan the other. They both ran along the edge of the street, dodging people fleeing in the opposite direction.

Seichan kept up with him. "How did they find us?"

He shook his head, his heart pounding. It was a question that could wait. He nodded ahead to a figure rounding out of an alley between the hotel and the next establishment. The guy carried an assault rifle, trying his best to conceal it next to his thigh.

Gray rushed up behind him, hooked an arm around his throat, and flung him around. He smashed the gunman's head into the corner of the building. Bone cracked and the body went limp.

Seichan caught the rifle as it dropped and passed it to Gray. She continued ahead, a dagger in her hand. She pointed its tip to another two figures holding pistols cradled at their waists. They stood at the edge of the now-empty patio restaurant and stared up at something sitting atop the awning, heavy enough to sag the fabric.

The team's roller bag.

Gray and Seichan closed the distance.

One target must have heard something and turned. Gray lifted his rifle's muzzle and squeezed a three-round burst into the man's chest. The impact at such close range knocked the man off his feet and across a table. Seichan slashed out as the other spun around. Blood flew from a clean slice across his neck.

As the man fell with a gurgling cry, shots were fired at them from inside the hotel. Gray dropped to a knee and laid down sporadic bursts through the door to hold back those inside. More rounds fired from above, pelting through the awning and ricocheting off the stones. Gray didn't move, knowing his position was shielded under the canopy from the view above.

To the side, Seichan danced through the gunshots.

She reached the sag in the awning, leaped to a one-legged balance atop a chair, and slashed high with her blade. She continued onward as the slice in the fabric overhead tore further. The roller bag toppled out of the hole and crashed to the table behind her.

Gray emptied the last of his stolen rifle's magazine, tossed the weapon aside, and lunged for the case. He yanked it to him, as an assailant burst out of the door, taking advantage of the sudden halt in Gray's suppressive fire—only to be met by Seichan's knife as she whipped the blade, letting it fly from her fingertips. It struck his right eye hard enough to snap his head back.

Gray hauled the bag up in one arm and hugged it to his chest.

Seichan joined him, her eyes flashing brightly. Together they ran under the awning and burst out into the crowd. They followed the flow away from the hotel and back to the sedan.

Gray reached it first.

The front seat was empty. Seichan touched a crisp bullet hole through the driver's-side window. Gray spotted blood splatters across the leather headrest. He cursed himself for abandoning the two men. He prayed they were still alive, perhaps captured, not bleeding out in some alley.

He shared a guilty look with Seichan.

But there was nothing to be done about it right now. Knowing their attackers could still be near, they retreated into the crowd. He looked back. Maria and the others had fled in the opposite direction. He plotted how to regroup with them and get somewhere safe.

Then a thunderous boom echoed over the water, loud enough to be felt in the chest. Gray froze, as did many of those around him. Faces turned upward. Overhead a huge flower of fire burst across the night sky, blazing in crimson and gold.

The fireworks show had begun.

9:44 P.M.

Mac stood with the others in a shadowy corner of the dockside plaza. He cradled his left arm. Each blast in the sky made his shoulder throb. His gaze searched the packed festivalgoers filling the square for any new sign of threat.

Half a mile away, emergency lights glowed and spun over by the hotel, but out here by the cruise dock, few paid any attention. Gazes were fixed to the skies. Music blared all around, fireworks boomed over the water, and the sound of merriment abounded.

Such was human nature.

As he and the others fled from the hotel earlier, the panic around them had bled away, diluted by the press of the crowd and weakened by the growing distance. The firefight had only been witnessed by those closest. Farther away, few gave the commotion any notice, likely attributing it to partying that had gotten out of hand. Even those who had fled alongside them had eventually slowed, stopping and looking back, feeling safe enough to go from potential victim to gawking bystander.

Then the fireworks had started, and all was seemingly forgotten.

Though maybe not entirely.

He sensed a tension in the crowd, a herd of cattle on edge. In between the booming blasts of the fireworks, the sharper cry of sirens cut through the crowd. The noise drew eyes toward the twirling lights. Many others whispered in ears and pointed that way, too. The news of what had happened was spreading through the crowd, likely amplified with each telling.

Mac shook his head, missing the quiet and isolation of Greenland's glaciers.

Next to him, Maria lowered her burner phone, flinching at another boom from above. She waved for Mac and Father Bailey to lean closer. "Gray and Seichan will be here in a few minutes. We need to be ready."

Gray had already called once, updating them on what had transpired at the hotel. While the two had managed to grab the Da Vinci map, it seemed Monsignor Roe and the rabbi had been captured, if not killed.

With the same fate hanging over them all, Maria had suggested a refuge, a place where even the enemy would have a hard time reaching them, while offering a way off this damned island.

That's if we can get there.

"They had better hurry," Father Bailey said dourly, stricken by the news of his friend. "That's the last cruise ship still docked."

Mac stared across the plaza to the port entrance. A gateway blocked access to the massive dock. Two other cruise ships had already departed when the fireworks had started, sailing out to sea under that booming farewell. The last was a smaller liner from the Regent Seven Seas group— though *small* was a relative term. The ship still towered more than a dozen levels above the sea. Even from here, a band could be heard playing up top, preparing its passengers for the upcoming departure.

Moments ago, the ship's passenger gangways had been pulled in. The only access point now was a crew gangplank and a lower loading dock where handcarts were still being rolled in, stacked high with crates to resupply the ship.

Mac and the others all kept watch—on the crowds, on the final preparations dockside, even on the sky as fiery blossoms lit the night.

Finally, a rumble of tiny wheels over cobblestones drew Mac's attention behind him. Gray crossed through the packed plaza, dragging the case, while Seichan's gaze swept the crowd. The pair hurried over to them.

"Are you ready?" Gray asked, his face both angry and determined.

He got confirmations all around.

"Then let's go." He glanced over their group. "Who's got—"

"I do," Mac said.

Gray nodded and led them toward the port entrance. It was minimally protected, just a wooden drop gate to stop traffic and a narrow sidewalk guarded by a gatehouse. Once halfway across the crowded plaza, Gray signaled Mac.

Time to get the herd moving.

He lit the fuse on the fistful of firecrackers in his hand. Earlier, he had bought three packages from a little fireworks stand at the edge of the plaza. He had unboxed them and twisted their cords into one big bundle. Once the fuse was sparking, he dropped the load to the pavement and kept going.

After four long strides, a loud popping erupted behind him, the firecrackers snapping and dancing on the cobbles.

Mac cupped his mouth and yelled. *"He's got a gun! Run!"*

Father Bailey repeated the same in Italian.

Gray in Spanish.

Maria simply screamed, spinning around, clutching her shoulder.

As the firecrackers continued to blast away, the already tense crowd reacted immediately. They bolted away from the noise, spreading the panic. More cries rose as people were jostled or trampled. The crowd rushed the wooden gates, pouring around it. More fled past the guard station by the sidewalk, cramming their way through, bottlenecking for a moment, then surging across, determined to reach the stretch of open dock to get away from the shooter.

Someone at the barrier tried to quell the crowd with a bullhorn, issuing orders in crisp Italian, full of authority. Not only was he ignored, but it only served to ramp up the panic.

Mac and the others followed the flow, sticking together, elbowing their way forward. Once past the gates, they kept to the stream of people running alongside the docked cruise ship. When they reached the loading area, they slowed. The first wave of the panicked crowd had cleared a path, knocking over handcarts, toppling stacks of boxes, driving the laborers away.

Overhead, the fireworks show reached its crescendo, blasting missile after missile into the air, to a deafening climax. The dock's planks shook with their reverberations. The sky blazed with fire.

As night turned into day, Gray searched for the right moment—then waved to their group. "Let's move!"

They quickly pounded up the short wooden gangway and through an open hatch in the ship. A couple of dockworkers spotted them and yelled after them. But the pair were probably too addled by all the chaos to offer much protest.

Bailey called back calmly in Italian, exposing the Roman collar of his priesthood. Whatever he said—or maybe priests just had that much authority here in Italy—the workers didn't pursue them, likely leaving it to their superiors on the upper decks to sort things out.

Their group hurried away before that sentiment changed. They followed signs, climbed stairs, and eventually ducked through a doorway.

They stepped from the ship's cold, utilitarian spaces of whitewashed metal walls into a warm hallway of polished teak and carpeted floors. The tinkle of a piano in the distance welcomed them. It was like crossing from the drab cornfields of Kansas into a technicolor Oz.

Before they could take more than a few steps, a waitress swept down the hall toward them, holding aloft a tray full of fluorescent drinks, several with umbrellas. She slowed when she came upon their disheveled group.

"*Buonasera*," she said with a smile, then seemed to get a read on the room and switched to English. "Did you enjoy the fireworks?"

No one said anything, only gave her stunned looks.

Her smile stiffened but didn't fade. "You should know the sail-a-way party is under way on the Cleopatra deck. Next stop—Majorca!"

She slid past them and whisked happily down the hall.

After the waitress was out of earshot, Maria turned to Gray. "What now?"

Mac answered, adding his contribution to the night's plan, "I say we pay Cleopatra a visit. I could damned well use a drink." He glanced to Father Bailey. "Excuse my French, Padre."

Bailey absolved him with a raised palm. "I could also use a damned drink."

22

This is fuckin' embarrassing.

Belowdecks, Kowalski stood in his cabin's tiny bathroom, which consisted of a steel toilet with a sink built into its back tank and a showerhead sticking out of the ceiling. The floor had a drain in it. Apparently, one was supposed to close the cubicle's door, and the entire bathroom became a shower stall.

Maybe if you were a mouse with anorexia.

The rest of his cabin was hardly any larger. It had an upper and lower bunk that folded up against the wall, like the sleeper car on a train—only smaller. But the bathroom was his nemesis. Every time Kowalski moved, his elbows struck the walls. And the rocking of the yacht made everything extra challenging. Case in point: taking a leak. He stared down at the drenched left leg of his pants.

"Doesn't this just take the cake."

He zipped up and cursed under his breath. Brushing past the bunk, he shuffled to the door with a jangle of his chains. He pounded his fist. "Hey! Need a little help in here."

The yacht rocked again, throwing him sideways. They were anchored off Sardinia, where the sea was choppy. It had taken them eight long hours to cross the Tyrrhenian Sea from Vulcano to reach this port. He had managed a brief view of the place as they motored toward it just after sunset. The lights of a big city lit up the coastline. Fireworks splattered the sky above it, but from a mile out, the display appeared anemic, just little puffs of fire.

Still, he could not stop staring. The shoreline had been tantalizingly close, and the city large enough for a guy to get lost in—or a guy and a girl.

He pounded again. "Hey!"

A muffled call came from the next room. "Are you all right?" Elena asked.

He stared down at his wet leg.

We'll see.

He hammered nonstop, until someone finally swore and the locking bolt scraped. A stocky man yanked the door open. He pointed a compact MAC-10 machine pistol at Kowalski's chest. Another guard backed him up out in the narrow hallway with the same style of weapon, only holding his firmly with both hands.

"What you want?" the lead man barked in broken English.

Kowalski backed up a step. Standing shirtless and in his socks, he could not look like much of a threat. Still, he lifted both palms.

"I don't want any trouble. Just need a hand cleaning up." Keeping his arms high, he jabbed a finger down at his leg. "I don't want to sleep like this all night."

The guard looked down, squinted, then his eyes widened. He turned to his buddy in the hall and said something in Arabic. They both laughed themselves close to tears.

"Yeah, real funny, Chuckles. I need to get out of these, and I can't do that in these chains." He shrugged. "Or you can help me cut these pants off and go ask Kadir if I could borrow a pair of his sweatpants. Probably be too baggy but I'll manage."

The mention of the hulking brute sobered them up.

"Just unlock one of my ankles," Kowalski said, shaking his soiled leg. "I'll do the rest."

"No." Chuckles nodded toward the bathroom. "You clean while wearing on."

"And sleep in wet pants all night?"

Chuckles waved dismissively. "Then sleep like this. In piss pants."

Kowalski took an angry step toward the guy. "Listen, bub!"

The guard raised his weapon higher, cursing him in Arabic, and drove Kowalski deeper into the room—in fact, deep enough.

Okay, Chuckles, let's dance.

The yacht gave a gentle bobble, but Kowalski pretended like the boat had been struck by a rogue wave. He fell against the bunk beds, then shoved his arm up, slamming the foldable upper tier into Chuckles's chin. Metal met bone with a satisfying crack.

As the guard's head snapped back, Kowalski relieved the man of his weapon, spun it around, and fired a point-blank burst into his chest. As he hoped, two rounds blasted clean through and hit the second guard standing at the threshold. The impacts threw the man against the far wall. Still, the guard swung his weapon toward the door.

Oh no, you don't.

Kowalski had Chuckles's shirt balled in his fist and was already moving. He carried the dead man like a battering ram and lunged out the door. Still firing through the body, he slammed into the second assailant, pinning him there while continuing to squeeze the trigger. He only stopped when the man slumped, his head falling crookedly.

He let both bodies drop and rushed to the next door. He slid aside the locking bolt and pulled it open. Inside, Elena gawked at him, then collected herself and rushed toward him.

"So, it worked," she said breathlessly.

He crossed back to the bodies and retrieved the second machine pistol. He straightened with one clutched in each hand now. "Tried to get them to free an ankle. But no go. Probably didn't even have the keys."

"Where do we—?"

"This way."

Kowalski led her toward the ship's stern. They needed to get down another level. He prayed no one heard the spate of gunfire. By keeping the muzzle pressed against solid flesh, he had done his best to muffle the shots.

Their escape was risky, but he knew they had to take the chance.

It was now or never.

Earlier, as the ship dropped anchor off of Sardinia, it was plain something had gone wrong with whatever those bastards had been planning on shore. Nehir had stormed into the lounge and ordered Kowalski and Elena to be taken below. Earlier in the day, Nehir had given Elena another deadline to come up with more information to help the bastards.

Midnight tonight.

So, Elena had spent the day poring over history texts, reading ancient poems, even studying geology books. But all of Elena's work and Nehir's timetable had been set aside as the situation had suddenly changed.

While being led belowdecks, Kowalski had heard Nehir yelling, dressing someone down. More of her crew passed them, running up to the lounge. Apparently she was demanding all hands on deck.

Either way, Kowalski knew this opportunity might be their one chance. With most of the crew above and land so close, they had to risk it. During the long voyage here, they had sketchily outlined a plan, whispering in secret, though neither of them really thought it would ever play out. It was more to buoy their spirits.

But the Fates must have been listening.

On the way down here, Kowalski had warned Elena to be ready. Still, it had required some last-minute improvisation on his part. His soaked leg was not part of that original plan—and sure, maybe it wasn't the most brilliant ad-libbing, but it had gotten the job done.

They quickly reached a set of stairs down to the bottom deck.

He led with both pistols raised and did his best to move quietly with his chains. He held his breath the entire way down. He checked the lower hall and pointed a gun to the right.

"The yacht's garage is down that way," he whispered. "Through the double doors. But we'll have to move fast."

Her eyes were huge and shiny with fear, but she nodded.

"Okay," he said. "Let's do this."

10:22 P.M.

Elena kept close to Joe as he stayed low and rushed down the narrow hallway. She cringed with every clink and clank of his chains. But they reached the double doors safely.

Joe exhaled in relief, likely as surprised as she was that they'd made it this far. He grabbed the U-shaped handle and tugged on it—then tried pushing it. He closed his eyes and leaned his forehead against the door's polished teak surface.

Locked.

"What about sneaking up top?" Elena whispered. "We could dive overboard and swim for shore."

"Even if we could get all the way up there without being seen . . ." Joe looked down at his leg irons. "It's a mile or more to shore."

She understood. He'd never make it, not with his legs weighted down.

He turned to her. "But *you* could do it." He lifted both pistols. "I might be able to blast our way to an outside rail, and you could jump."

"They'd kill you."

"Probably, but no plan's perfect."

She shook her head. "No. We do this together."

Joe nodded and pushed her back. "In that case, we'll have to ring the dinner bell."

He aimed both machine pistols at the teak door and fired at the lock. The noise of the twin guns in the narrow hall was deafening. She clamped her palms over her ears, but it did little to muffle the sound of that barrage.

Finally, he stopped firing. He tossed aside the pistol he'd just emptied, but he kept the other.

His machine pistol had chewed a ragged fist-sized hole through the thick wood, taking the lock with it. Joe stepped forward and kicked the door open. Over the ringing in her ears, she heard shouts from the decks above, along with the pounding of boots.

Joe turned and reached for her hand—when a wave rocked the ship, throwing her against the opposite wall. But it wasn't a wall. A door opened behind her. She fell backward through it. Strong arms caught her, one hooked around her waist, while a hand grabbed the base of her ponytail. She was yanked to her tiptoes.

She caught the briefest glimpse of the giant Kadir.

Joe swung around and pointed his pistol. His face was beet-red, his expression angry. It quickly turned pained as he saw he had no shot without risking her.

Elena realized it, too.

As the giant dragged her deeper into his cabin, shouts grew louder, echoing down the passageway. Boots hammered toward them.

She met Joe's eyes.

"Go," she said.

10:26 P.M.

Across the hallway, Kowalski had one second to make his choice—but knew he had none. To hold his ground would only get him killed, and likely Elena, too. The best hope for both of them was to turn tail and run.

He locked eyes with Kadir.

This ain't over, bastard.

Kowalski backed into the garage. With a curse, he slammed the door and searched the area around him. A fire ax hung on the wall next to the door. He yanked it free and jammed its handle between the two U-shaped door handles on this side.

The brace would not last long.

But hopefully long enough.

He hooked his pistol's strap over a shoulder and shuffled down the three steps to the main floor of the garage. Yesterday, while boarding the yacht, he had gotten a good view of the space. Six black jet-skis, three to a side, sat on wheeled rails tilted toward the closed stern door. Between them stood a four-man submersible, armed with mini-torpedo launchers.

As he squeezed past the sub toward the stern's garage door, he imagined using the vessel's weaponry to sink the damned boat.

Fat chance.

Instead, he did what he could. He reached the large red button next to the garage door and punched it. A motor sounded, and the metal door began to rise. A stiff wind blew in, smelling of salt and hope.

As he turned, something heavy slammed into the double doors behind him.

Kowalski cringed, but the ax held. He shuffled to a rack of vests with dangling keys. He snatched one, praying the jet-skis were all keyed the same.

Need a little luck here.

Gunfire erupted at the door. Rounds tore through the thick teak.

Kowalski ducked and did his best to hobble over to the closest watercraft on its rails. By now, the garage door had risen halfway, revealing a black sea rocking with waves. The opening was still not high enough for the jet-ski to pass through.

He used the time to toss the vest onto the watercraft, then kicked and clawed himself up onto its raised seat. He finally got his belly over it, hanging like a saddlebag over the back of a horse.

A loud CRACK cut through the rattle of gunfire. The two halves of the ax flew across the space as the doors burst open.

Crap.

He snatched the machine pistol and fired awkwardly toward the door as the first men tried to enter. It was enough to drive them back into the hallway. Then his weapon clicked, and the trigger froze.

Cursing, Kowalski tossed the empty weapon and grabbed the upright crank next to the rails. He yanked it hard. The tracks snapped forward with a spring-loaded jolt, extending beyond the yacht's stern.

Jarred, the ski shot down the wheeled rails—and sailed high over the water.

He held his breath as it flew, then gasped when it crashed into the waves. The impact almost tossed him overboard. Clinging tight, he fought his legs to the back and gripped the sides of the seat with his knees. It was the best he could manage with his ankles still bound. He fumbled the key in place, thumbed the red ignition button, and the jet motor growled.

That'll do.

Staying low, he reached to the handlebars and squeezed the throttle. The ski nosed up and shot across the dark sea—and not a second too soon.

The waves behind him shredded with gunfire.

A bright searchlight ignited from the stern deck and chased after him. He scooted up, sitting on his bound ankles, squeezing with his knees. The loose flotation vest flew away, flapping in the wind, threatening to tug out the imbedded key, which would conk out the engine.

No, you don't.

He snatched the vest back and stuffed it under his butt.

By then, the bright beam found him, blinding him. He leaned and yanked the handlebars to the one side and darted back into darkness. More gunfire peppered the water. A few pinged off the back of the ski.

Behind him, a loud whine cut through the chatter.

Then another.

And another.

More jet-skis in pursuit.

Kowalski ducked lower, intending to keep his lead. He raced toward the shore, now a half mile off. He spotted bonfires burning along a beach. Closer at hand, a buoy field was crowded with moored boats, several with lights.

I can make it.

Then the engine coughed, caught again—and died.

He stared at the illuminated display, where the icon of a tiny fuel pump blinked.

He groaned at his luck, realizing he'd picked a ski with a near-empty tank.

Out of gas.

10:32 P.M.

Elena stood teary-eyed on the stern deck of the yacht. Kadir had a fist still snarled at the base of her ponytail. He had never released his grip after capturing her, dragging her along like a toy doll up from the lower decks. The back of her scalp burned—but the tears that threatened were not due to the pain.

She stared out to the dark sea.

A searchlight swept the waters. But at least the trio of men with assault rifles had stopped firing into the waves. Kowalski must've made it beyond the range of their weapons. Still, he was far from safe. The scream of pursuit echoed over the water, ready to run him down.

Her eyes strained to pierce the darkness, to know what was happening. She prayed he reached shore.

Godspeed, Joe.

10:33 P.M.

Kowalski perched at the back of the ski's seat. He used his considerable bulk and heavy chains to weigh down the craft's stern. He stared over toward the field of buoys and boats, so tantalizingly close.

Behind him, the whine of skis trebled in volume. It sounded like they were coming from everywhere, spreading a wide net in the darkness.

Running out of time . . .

He fought the waves, doing his best to keep the stern low and the nose high. Balanced in the back, he reached a long arm to the ignition button. He prayed there was a little gas left in the tank. By weighting down the back of the ski, he hoped to shift the remaining gas to the fuel line at the rear of the gas tank.

Is that asking too much?

He grimaced and pushed the ignition.

The engine sputtered—then caught with a growl.

He heaved out a breath and squeezed the throttle. The jet-ski bolted forward again. As it cut through the waves, he struggled to keep the bow high. If he let it fall, the last dregs of gas would slosh away from the fuel line, and he'd be dead in the water again.

Unfortunately, that meant going slow, judging the best course through the chop.

He tried to ignore the scream of the engines behind him. He clenched his jaws, focusing on his goal. Ahead, the lights of the buoy field grew. But it now sounded like the hunters were at his heels. The spread of their whines had narrowed to an arrow pointed at him.

Or maybe it was just his paranoia.

Still, he reached the edge of the buoys and entered the field of boats. He angled into them, trying his best to keep out of sight. He shied away from any vessels with mooring lights and kept to the darkest path.

Just need to get through here.

The beach and its line of bonfires was only fifty yards past the last row of buoys.

But halfway across the field, the ski's engine coughed and died.

He swore.

So close.

The momentum of the ski drifted him against the side of a dark schooner, its sails all tied down for the night.

He stared up and reached for the boat's rail.

Maybe.

10:34 p.m.

Elena maintained her post on the deck, not that she had any choice. Kadir loomed next to her, but at least the giant had shifted his grip to her arm. He had finally let go of her ponytail, but only because Nehir had ordered it. Still, his fingers squeezed hard, bruising down to the bone.

Nehir stood at the rail with a radio gripped in one hand. With her other, she held binoculars up to her eyes.

A tiny voice, speaking Arabic, rose from her radio. *"Found the water-craft floating among the boats. Abandoned. The flotation vest's still hanging by its lanyard."*

Without lowering her binoculars, Nehir lifted the radio to her lips. "Search the nearest boats, sweep wider if you have to. Also watch the waters in case he tries to swim for shore."

Elena knew Joe could never swim all the way to the beach, not weighted down with those chains.

Even Nehir must have realized it. "Be thorough. Turn over everything. Break into cabins, if you have to. Don't leave anything to chance."

Elena stared at the scatter of lights on the water. She hoped Joe was smart enough to find a good hiding place and stay out of sight. The hunters couldn't search forever. Eventually they'd have to give up.

She sent a silent message to Joe.

Don't do anything stupid.

10:35 P.M.

Kowalski had no confidence in his plan, relying on his usual bullheaded stubbornness to keep moving. He knew Gray would've come up with something clever. Find some way to ambush the hunters or hot-wire a speedboat.

Instead, Kowalski paddled one-armed through the dark water. His other limb remained hooked through the ring of a life preserver. He had stolen it from the dark sailboat he had bumped against. As he paddled, his legs hung straight down, the chains now anchors.

He strained his ears, listening for any threat. So far, it sounded like the hunters were over by where he'd abandoned the jet-ski. He assumed they were searching nearby boats.

Keep looking, assholes.

He moved as silently as he could, trying not to splash, keeping low in the water. He edged row by row toward shore. A jet-ski suddenly revved louder. He heard it speed away—then come back round again.

Back and forth.

In a search pattern.

Uh-oh.

Knowing he didn't have long, Kowalski paddled harder, even tried to dolphin kick. He rounded the second-to-last row of boats and struggled across the gap toward the rocking hull of a large Cobalt cruiser tied to the final line of buoys.

As he reached its shadow, the hunter came into view with a screaming whine.

Kowalski took a deep breath and let go of the life preserver. The anchor around his ankles dragged him into the depths. He plummeted meter after meter. Overhead, the wake of the jet-ski swept past without slowing. At least, he hadn't been spotted.

Finally, his feet hit sand.

Standing there, he fought to get his bearings. The dark bulk of the Cobalt hung overhead, faintly illuminated by a fiery glow.

Kowalski turned toward the source of that fire.

Looks like I'm walking from here.

He set out, holding his breath, the salt stinging his eyes. He dragged one weighted foot, then another. Step by step. He waved his arms to help him along, not that it did much good.

Slowly the diffuse glow ahead separated into distinct pools.

But too slowly.

His chest burned with the effort to hold his breath. Still, he plodded on, doggedly determined. Eventually, waves began to jostle his upper body. A few more steps and he got his nose above the water. He blew out a lungful of stale air and drew in a fresh batch, taking in some seawater with it as a wave crashed over him. Choking, he fought forward again, until he could get his head fully above water.

Gasping, he turned to check the buoy field.

The whining continued to echo from there.

Good enough.

To play it safe, he ducked down and crossed the final distance under-water. He reached a bevy of swimmers, their legs kicking, arms splashing. He heard the thump-thump of loud music, muffled by the water.

At last, he crawled on his hands and knees out of the sea and onto shore, dragging his chains through the sand. He headed toward the nearest bonfire, just as a young man leaped over it. The partier landed in front of him.

Kowalski looked up.

The youth babbled in Italian at him.

Whatever, dude.

Waving a weak arm, Kowalski rolled onto his back, sure he looked like some long-dead sailor rising from the accursed depths.

He lifted a hand.

"Who has a goddamned cell phone?"

23

From the stern of a large hydrofoil, Elena gripped a rail as the craft accelerated over the water. It slowly rose on twin wings and sped even faster. Behind the ship, a tiny fireball burst in the darkness and rolled into the night sky. The brightness briefly illuminated the blasted, smoking remains of the other yacht.

She felt a surge of hope at the sight.

If she had any doubts that Joe had escaped, the destruction of the yacht helped dispel them. An hour ago, the search had been suddenly called off. The yacht had raised anchor and sped away from Sardinia. It rendezvoused with the sleek hydrofoil, which flew like a silver bird up to them, then lowered alongside the ship. The transfer of gear and personnel had been swift, including the research library, which suggested Elena's work here was not done.

The chains that now bound her ankles seemed to confirm this. She had expected worse punishment, but apparently Nehir still needed her.

Unfortunately, Elena had also gained a new shadow.

Kadir stood grimly behind her.

She ignored him and stared out to sea. It had fallen dark again, but her hope remained. Clearly her captors considered the yacht compromised, which would only happen if they believed Joe had survived.

Footsteps sounded behind her.

She turned as Nehir strode up to her.

"Kadir, take her below and keep her there until we reach the *Morning Star.*"

He nodded with a grunt and grabbed Elena's arm. As he hauled her away, Nehir grabbed her other arm and stopped them. The woman's eyes shone with a fury that scorched. Elena felt the waves of loathing emanating from her. It burned away Elena's momentary glimmer of hope.

"You are lucky," Nehir spat darkly. "But even luck runs out."

Nehir let her go, waving Elena out of her sight.

Kadir dragged her off the deck and down to a small kitchen. He pushed her into a chair. She didn't fight him, not that she could. She felt drained, despair sinking in. From Nehir's words, they must be ferrying her to another ship, the *Morning Star.*

If true, how would anyone ever find her?

Despite the terror and anxiety, she soon found her head resting on the table, cradled in her arms, as hour after hour passed. She fell asleep at one point, only to be awoken by the blast of a ship's horn.

She sat up abruptly, momentarily lost as to where she was. But a glance revealed Kadir's solid presence, grounding her back to the danger. It looked like he hadn't even moved.

Nehir clambered down and barked to her brother.

Elena stood on her own, knowing what was expected. Still, Kadir grabbed her arm and marched her out onto the deck. The seas had quieted to an eerie calmness, as if the world were holding its breath. The full span of the Milky Way arched overhead, reflected again in the black waters.

A large ship hung between, as if floating in space.

It was silvery white, ghostly in countenance, easily dwarfing the hydrofoil. It was twice the length of the previous yacht, stretching more than five hundred feet, a veritable floating city, with its superstructure climbing five stories above the main deck. But there was no bulkiness to its shape; it was sleek, with a palpable air of danger, like a dagger waiting to be used.

Elena swallowed, overwhelmed by the sheer size of it.

"The *Morning Star*," Nehir whispered with awe.

The hydrofoil closed the last of the distance. Gangplanks were extended from the hydrofoil's deck to hatches halfway up the hull of the superyacht.

"Come," Nehir ordered.

The woman led her to the forward gangway. As Elena jangled across it, a thumping rose overhead. She stared up. The bright lights of a helicopter swept across the sea toward the ship.

Who's coming?

Kadir shoved her from behind.

Elena stumbled forward, grabbing for the handrails to keep upright. She hurried after Nehir and ducked through the hatch into the other ship. Once inside, Nehir spoke to someone, who guided them to a stairwell. Elena climbed around and around, struggling under the weight of her chains, breathless by the time she reached the top.

A strong wind gusted through a nearby hatch, which led to the open bow. The source of the gale landed on a helipad out there. As the helicopter touched down, Elena was forced out onto the deck. She lifted an arm against the blast of rotor wash.

A two-man team ran forward, ducked under the blades, and set about fastening tie-downs to the helicopter's skids. As they worked, a side door opened in the aircraft.

Nehir marched Elena closer, then made her halt. The woman leaned to her ear. "With your friend gone, we found *two* to replace him. To keep you motivated. A pair that I believe will be far more helpful than the other."

From the aircraft's cabin, two older men were led out in shackles. One looked like a frail monk with a fringe of gray hair. The other had a bandage binding a thick cotton wad to one ear. Even from yards away, Elena saw it was soaked in blood.

The pair were marched past her.

She twisted with a frown.

Who are—?

Nehir suddenly dropped to one knee next to Elena, drawing back her attention. Kadir did the same on the other side.

A tall, hard-faced man in a trim tan suit climbed down from the helicopter. His hair was light gray, his eyes as dark as coal pits, his complexion a dark honey.

Nehir bowed her head. "Mūsā, we welcome you."

The man showed no reaction, only a barest nod of acknowledgment. From the title and obeisance shown him, Elena realized he must be their group's leader.

But there was one last passenger aboard. A dark-suited figure hopped deftly to the deck, ducking under the spin of the rotors. Once clear, he straightened, combing fingers through the slight curl of his dark blond hair. He wore a smile of greeting as he stepped forward.

Then he stopped, studied Elena up and down with a frown, and turned to Mūsā. "Ambassador Firat, are the chains really necessary?"

Struck dumb, Elena struggled to make sense—of his presence, of her world upended. She finally eked out one word.

"Daddy?"

FOURTH

THE PILLARS OF HERCULES

Tardy with age were I and my companions, when we came to the strait pass, that Hercules ordain'd were boundaries not to be overstepped by man.

—THE WARNING BY ULYSSES/ODYSSEUS TO VIRGIL IN DANTE'S *INFERNO*

24

Gray stood naked on the suite's private balcony overlooking the bow of the *Seven Seas Explorer*. The bright morning sun blazed down upon the Mediterranean, polishing it to an unreal sapphire blue. Warm salty breezes washed over him, drying his skin after soaking in the outdoor spa. Down below, flags at the tip of the bow snapped and flapped.

Ahead, the coastline of Majorca grew larger before him as the cruise liner neared its next destination.

From one island to another . . .

Gray felt like Odysseus, tossed about by the gods with little control over his fate. Of course, Homer's hero had not sailed the seas in such style as this. Gray stood outside the master bedroom of the *Explorer*'s Regent Suite, which stretched the beam of the ship's forward deck on the fourteenth floor. On the opposite side, a second bedroom connected to a common space, which consisted of a dining room and lounge, centered around an onyx bar.

The suite had been a small perk for breaking radio silence.

After stowing away aboard the ship last night, Gray had returned the battery to his encrypted satellite phone and called Sigma command. He saw little reason not to. Going dark for the prior two days had done his team little good. They'd still been hunted down and ambushed.

His grip tightened on the balcony rail.

Ahead, the Majorcan city of Palma—the capital of the Balearic Islands, an archipelago belonging to Spain—stretched across the bay. Even from this distance, the city's most prominent landmark stood out. The Gothic façade and spires of the Cathedral of Santa Maria towered over the tumble of the sunbaked city.

Its massive presence reminded him of all he'd lost. The whereabouts and fate of Monsignor Roe and Rabbi Fine remained unknown. The body of Major Bossard, who had served two popes, lay in a morgue.

Gray had updated Painter on all that had happened, trusting the director to shut down Cagliari and scour the city for the two missing clerics. But Painter had pulled other strings, too. At midnight, shortly after Gray's call, the ship's purser had approached their group at a poolside bar, carrying a set of keys on a tray. He took their party to deck fourteen—and opened double doors to the luxury two-bedroom suite.

Apparently, the steep price for this grand accommodation had kept it vacant.

No one in their group complained.

Exhausted, they had all collapsed, spreading out across the cabin.

The suite came equipped with cameras that kept watch on the hall. In addition, two of the ship's security guards were posted outside the doors. Still, Gray rotated with Seichan to keep watch during the night.

During his shifts, Gray received ongoing updates from Painter.

At least there was some good news.

Impossibly, Kowalski had washed up on a beach near Cagliari, arriving there only an hour after Gray's group had departed. He came with his own harrowing tale, but also word that Dr. Elena Cargill was still alive, held aboard a yacht by those who had kidnapped her in Greenland. Unfortunately, by the time authorities could be roused, the yacht had vanished.

A search continued for it.

Sounds of splashing water drew Gray's attention. Seichan climbed from the spa behind him. His breath caught as she stepped out and arched her back. She shook loose a drape of black hair. Rivulets of steaming water traced her curves and ran down her flat stomach. With little else to do while the *Explorer* headed to port, the two had enjoyed what the suite had to offer, including the gold-plated master bath with its two heated stone lounges and its own sauna.

Still, it all paled to the stunning beauty standing before him.

He crossed over and drew her close. His hands slid down her backside. She smelled of jasmine blossoms from the bath salts and a spicy musk that was all her. After Jack had been born, they'd little time for intimacy that wasn't furtive and quick.

"We have an hour before we reach port," he said huskily in her ear.

"Then I should pump again."

"Hmm . . ." He glided one palm farther down, gripped the back of her thigh, and lifted her leg to his waist. "I think that could wait."

"Do you?" With a grace that defied gravity, she raised her other leg and wrapped it fully around him. "Are you sure?"

He rolled her against the wall and let her feel how firm he was on the matter.

She knotted her fingers in his hair and pulled him to her lips.

The next hour went by too fast. A ship's announcement finally roused them from the tangle of sheets on the bed. They quickly showered, dressed, and reluctantly abandoned the temporary refuge.

Before opening the door, Seichan stepped in front of him, blocking the way. "We should do this again."

He stayed close to her, cocking an eyebrow. "I don't think we have time, but I'm willing to try."

She placed both palms on his chest, something she only did when she was serious. "I mean this. Us together. We need more of this."

He stared into her eyes. "I miss this, too. But Jack—"

"I can't just be a mother," she blurted out.

In that moment, he saw what she had been trying to hide for weeks, maybe months. The guilt, the sadness, the confusion inside her. He leaned his forehead against hers. "I never want you to be just a mother. I love Jack with all my heart, but you *are* my heart. And if we're not our truest selves—with him, with each other—then we're no good to our son."

She sighed and glanced down. The guilt had softened in her eyes, but he feared it was not gone. He could tell she remained unresolved, and it set his heart to pounding harder, worried.

The cruise director's voice came over the ship-wide intercom, announcing that they'd reached port and that disembarkation was available for tour groups and individuals.

Seichan patted her palms on his chest, as if tabling the matter. "Let's go."

They headed out of the bedroom into the common areas, greeted by the music of Tchaikovsky from the suite's Steinway piano. Gray had heard the muffled bits of various classical pieces and assumed it was the self-playing feature on the instrument. But Father Bailey was sitting at the keyboard and playing the final chords.

Mac stood next to the piano, his arm back in its sling. He cradled a mug of coffee and nodded to the table. "The butler brought in lunch and a tea service."

Seichan crossed over to the tower of little cakes and finger sandwiches.

Gray joined Mac and Bailey as the priest stood up, massaging his hands and wrists.

"A bit rusty," Bailey said. "But it helps me think."

Gray knew what puzzled the man. It sat on the lounge's coffee table. The lid of the bronze box stood open. The gold map and silver astrolabe shone brightly in the streaming sunlight. He also noted Maria out on the cabin's public deck, staring toward the bustle of Palma's port. Gray knew she wasn't appreciating the sights, but keeping watch.

"Still, haven't learned anything new," Bailey admitted, frowning at the map. "And without Monsignor Roe to help offer guidance . . ."

They had reached a dead end.

Gray knew this, too. Even the bright sunlight could not dispel his growing gloom. As he stared down at the map, he again felt that sense of being lost at sea, with no compass to guide him safely home.

A knock drew all their eyes to the foyer, to the cabin door.

Someone else heard it, too.

12:10 P.M.

Oh, thank god . . .

A few minutes ago, Maria had thought she'd spotted a familiar large bulk climbing the gangway by the dock, but she couldn't be sure. So she was already in motion before the second polite rap on the door. She burst from the balcony and rushed across the breadth of the suite, past the others in the lounge.

She headed straight to the door.

Gray called after her. "Check the security cam before—"

Don't need to.

She knew who it was. With every step, she felt the pressure inside her easing, the weight on her shoulders growing lighter. Unable to stop herself, she grabbed the handle and yanked the door open.

Startled, the room steward at the threshold stepped back.

She shouldered past him and leaped at the guest next to him.

Joe dropped a large duffel bag and caught her in his arms with a loud *oof.*

She clung hard to him, trying to squeeze away her guilt. "I'm so sorry, Joe."

"Sheesh, for what?"

She tried to answer, to explain about leading him astray back at Castel Gandolfo, for sending him off with any empty case. But she knew that wasn't the true source of her remorse. She knew it in this moment, in his arms. Her shame and guilt rose from the doubts she had harbored, that she had let build—for him, maybe even for herself—about their relationship, about their future.

Fear of losing him had burned that all away.

Her love for him ached inside her.

I don't ever want to lose you.

Unable to put this into words, she buried her face in his chest, inhaling his sweaty aroma, feeling the train-engine heat of his body. The arm around her was an iron strap.

How could I have ever doubted this?

Joe carried her inside before finally setting her down, somewhat roughly. She kept hold of his hand. His other palm rubbed his lower back, his expression pained.

"I'd carry you to the ends of the earth, babe. You know that. But maybe not right now. Not after someone tried to break my spine."

"Sorry," she said again lamely.

She stared up, noting his taped nose, the nostrils stuffed with cotton. She had heard all that he'd gone through, the tortures endured. And as much as she was beyond happy to have him back, his injuries tempered her jubilation, reminding her that Elena was still in the hands of those same people.

If she was even still alive.

This thought sobered her up.

Joe nodded as Gray carried the large duffel. He needed both arms to haul it over to the lounge. "Gifts from Painter," Joe explained. "Found the bag waiting dockside. Hope it's everything you asked for."

Gray knelt down, unzipped it, and took a brief inventory. Maria spotted a stack of black polymer cases, the topmost stamped with SIG SAUER. There was also a stubby rifle of some sort, sitting atop boxes of ammunition.

Gray ignored the armaments and pulled out a ten-inch e-tablet. "For now, we're going to leave the search for Dr. Cargill to Painter and Kat. They're also following up Kowalski's lead about that underground encampment where he and Elena had been held, somewhere near the Turkish coast."

Gray stood up with the e-tablet and turned to the group. "As for us, we still don't know *who* the enemy is, but we know *what* they're after. The cruise ship will be overnighting here, so we have less than a day to figure out where to go next." Gray turned to Joe. "To help with that, I want to hear every detail about what happened aboard that yacht, everything Dr. Cargill told you, or hinted at, or even muttered under her breath."

Joe ignored him and stepped over to the coffee table. "You have one of these, too." With his fists on his hips, he studied the map and astrolabe with a frown. "Where did you get it?"

Father Bailey explained about the Holy Scrinium, about Leonardo da Vinci.

Joe waved the history lesson aside. "Yeah, fine, but did you get it to work?"

"Well, no," Bailey admitted.

Joe sighed in exasperation, unbuckled his belt, and dropped his trousers to his ankles. Luckily, he was wearing boxers. He reached to a thick bandage around his thigh. Maria had heard about him being burned by branding irons.

Joe fiddled with the wraps, then unsheathed a trio of thin bronze rods that were pinned and secured under his bandage. "Elena found these. Gave them to me for safekeeping. She didn't want those bastards finding 'em. Maybe feared she might give them up under torture or something."

"What are they?" Maria asked.

"Elena called them 'the Beams of the Death Star' . . . or something like that." Joe pointed to the astrolabe. "You stick 'em in there to make the map work."

Gray took and inspected the rods.

Bailey looked over his shoulder, his words breathless. "They're the tools to unlock the Daedalus Key."

12:28 P.M.

Kowalski did his best to explain all that had happened with the other map. He paced in a circle around the coffee table. Gray and Father Bailey sat on their knees before the map. The two searched together to match the proper symbols to the flags on the bronze pins.

Everyone else hovered around them.

Kowalski finished his account, "Before the damn thing could complete its run, we were interrupted."

"So, you never saw where the ship ended up?" Gray asked as he inserted a second pin.

"Like I said, we were interrupted. Maybe Elena saw something that I missed. She was closer, willing to risk getting radiation poisoning." He shrugged. "I plan to have kids someday."

He gave Maria a quick glance.

Right?

She frowned and waved him back toward Gray.

Bailey rotated the astrolabe in one hand, then pointed to a spot on the inner sphere. "Here. That's the last symbol, isn't it?"

Gray squinted closer and nodded. "Hold it steady." With great care, he slid the third rod into place.

Bailey then twisted on his knees and gently lowered the astrolabe into its gold cradle. Bailey bit his lower lip and glanced at Gray.

Kowalski knew everything depended on what happened next. "Now you just have to flip the lever on the side," he said. "And stand back."

Bailey frowned at the map. "If only it were that easy. I'm afraid it'll take a little more elbow grease."

"I'll let you do the honors," Gray told the priest.

"Okay." Bailey shifted to the side and reached to a little wheeled crank. He began to slowly turn it and explained to Kowalski. "Without that fiery fuel source, we have to do this manually."

Still, Kowalski took a cautious step back.

He *did* want kids.

He ended up next to Maria and took her hand. They watched together as the priest wound and wound the crank. On the map, the tiny silver ship set sail from the golden coast of Turkey and over the azure gem of the Aegean Sea.

"It's working," Maria whispered, her fingers tightening.

The ship bounced around some islands, pausing here and there, then spun away from Greece and across the Ionian Sea. It then ducked under Italy's boot and slipped between the toe and the island of Sicily.

No one breathed, all eyes on the map.

"Next stop, Vulcano," Kowalski whispered.

"Hush," Maria scolded, as if he were spoiling the plot.

The boat rounded Sicily and stopped at the chain of islands with little rubies on top of them. Maria glanced at him.

He shrugged. *Told you so.*

Bailey continued to turn, but nothing happened. His brow furrowed. "I think something's wrong."

Kowalski waved for him to continue. "This next part takes a bit longer."

Nodding, trusting him, the priest wound the little crank. Finally, the map box jolted on the coffee table as some spring-loaded mechanism gave way inside.

Kowalski drew Maria back a step. "Don't get too close."

As before, the lapis lazuli of the Mediterranean split along invisible lines, shattering apart in a maze of cracks, spreading outward from the volcanic islands in a complex, byzantine pattern.

"The false paths," Kowalski explained.

Bailey slowed his cranking, his expression both pained and awed. "I wish Monsignor Roe were here to see this."

Gray warned him, "Keep going. Don't stop."

The priest sped up his turning. As he did so, the seams drew together and closed, returning a perfect surface to the sea. Only one crack remained and slowly widened and extended. It stretched from Vulcano, to southern Sardinia, then down to northern Africa. The tiny ship set off, dipping into the seam, carried by a tiny rod, maybe magnetized to some bit of iron hidden in the keel of the silver ship.

"That's disappointing," Kowalski mumbled.

"What?" Maria asked.

"Where's all the steam? The fire?"

"No fuel," she reminded him.

He harrumphed, dissatisfied.

The ship ran along the exposed crack, sailing west across the coast of Africa, catching up with the extending seam at the Strait of Gibraltar.

"That's where it went before," Kowalski commented. "From there, I don't know where—"

Bailey cranked and something metallic popped loudly from inside the map. The box jolted again, hard enough to fracture the Mediterranean Sea. Pieces flew out. The rest of the lapis lazuli jigsaw puzzle collapsed in on itself, leaving a few blue shards still hanging askew. Bronze gears and wires shone from inside, revealing the trick behind the magic.

Mac shook his head. "Maybe it's best Monsignor Roe wasn't here to see this."

The priest looked sickened, continuing to wind the wheel. "There's no more tension."

Gray simply admitted what they all knew. "It's broken."

Proving this, the tiny silver ship tipped from its magnetic perch and toppled into the clockwork mechanism and vanished.

"There goes Odysseus," Kowalski mumbled.

Bailey sagged. "Maybe we damaged it bringing it here."

Seichan put a hand on the priest's shoulder. "Or maybe it was never complete. Didn't you say Da Vinci was working from partial plans? That he had to improvise sections?"

Bailey just sighed.

"No matter." Gray stood up. "There's nothing to be done about it. We go back to where we started."

He turned to Kowalski with a clear intent. Any hope from here depended on how much Kowalski could remember.

Great.

Kowalski glared at the ruins of the map.

Stupid Da Vinci.

25

Who can I trust here?

Elena sat at a desk in an opulent two-story library that stretched be-tween decks three and four of the *Morning Star*'s superstructure. The space was paneled in tigerwood and mahogany, the railings sculpted of wrought iron in an angular Moorish design. A wealth of books and curated arti-facts from Arabian navigational history were protected behind glass doors. A spiral staircase led up to the second level, where gilded ladders reached the tops of the tallest shelves.

She rubbed her sore eyes, ignoring her reading glasses sitting on a stack of books. She had not slept all night after boarding the yacht and being greeted by her father.

Why is he here? How could he be involved with these murderous people?

None of it made any sense. And her father had offered no explanation upon arriving, only giving her a hug and a promise to explain everything in the morning. Then he had vanished into the yacht with the man called Mūsā, his arm around the ambassador, as if they were the dearest friends.

Afterward, Nehir and Kadir had taken her to a sprawling stateroom, as richly appointed as this library. While being hauled there, Elena had noted the number of armed men and women in the halls. She had been marched through an entire level that doubled as a shipboard armory, seemingly equipped with enough firepower to take down a small nation. Clearly, beneath its skin, the *Morning Star* was an opulent war vessel.

Before locking her in the stateroom, Nehir had removed her ankle chains—though from the woman's silence and dark countenance, she had not been happy to obey these instructions from her father. Still, Kadir had remained posted at her door all night. Even now he stood outside the library, his arms crossed, his back to the set of glass double doors.

A low murmur drew her attention to the side. The only section of the library not lined by bookshelves was an area cantilevered out from the superstructure, hanging over the water. A curve of windows offered a panoramic view of the seas and the nearby Tunisian coast of North Africa.

Two men sat at a table across from each other, as if playing a game of chess, only their board was the golden map. Earlier, the pair had introduced themselves to her, and they had all shared their respective stories. The injured man, Rabbi Howard Fine, had been cared for overnight. The bloody wad of cotton bandaged over his ear had been replaced with a clean, tidy wrap. His eyes this morning remained glassy from pain relievers. The other new arrival was Monsignor Sebastian Roe.

It was the priest who had told her how he—along with colleagues of Joe—had been ambushed on Sardinia. She had also discerned why these two men hadn't been killed. Both were archaeologists, steeped in the line of mythology and history important to the task at hand. They were intended to serve as her research aides—and likely as hostages to be tortured if she failed to deliver.

Elena was under no misconception that the fundamentals of her situation had changed with the arrival of her father. While the accommodations were better, everything else was the same.

She stared in silence as the two whispered over the map. Monsignor Roe had told her about the Da Vinci replica of the device, of the original Daedalus Key joined to it. Apparently Joe's colleagues still possessed that.

Elena placed great hope in this information.

Joe, don't let me down.

Earlier, she had skipped over one part of her story—about what she and Joe had witnessed with the map after unlocking the astrolabe. While she sensed no malice or dissembling from these two, she had been too shaken up by her father's arrival.

Who can I truly trust? The safest answer. *Only myself.*

So she had stayed silent about the map's revelations.

Not that any of this relieved her of the obligations imposed on her. Nehir made sure of this over breakfast in the library. She had demanded to know where Elena believed Captain Hunayn had sailed to after leaving Daedalus's home in Sardinia.

She knew the answer. The map had already revealed it. She pictured the tiny silver ship of Odysseus sweeping south from Sardinia, in a river of tectonic fire, only to briefly come to port along the Tunisian coast. Again, Elena had needed some other excuse, a line of reasoning to point in that direction, to bury what she truly knew under a mountain of facts. She had wanted to balk, to refuse, but she had no fight left in her. She was too tired and too shaken by her father's arrival. And in the end, what would it matter if she gave up this next port?

Elena stared past the two men to the distant coast of North Africa. Yesterday—before her aborted escape attempt—she had searched through the stacks of ancient books, returning again to Strabo's *Geographica* to come up with the rationale to sail to Tunisia.

She had explained everything to Nehir over breakfast, relating scores of rumors about an island off the African coast. It was said to be the home of Homer's *Lotophagi*, the infamous Lotus-eaters who fed Odysseus's men a narcotic nectar and lulled them into sleep. Ancient writers—both Herodotus and Polybius—advocated that the Tunisian coast was where that island would be found.

Elena reinforced this by referencing Strabo, whose wisdom Hunayn had placed great stock in. Elena had shown Nehir the line in *Geographica* where Strabo stated the true location of the Lotus-eaters:

Λωτοφαγῖτις σύρτις *Lōtophagîtis sýrtis,* which translates as "Syrtis of the Lotus-eaters."

Elena got further support from an unexpected source. Monsignor Roe had interjected, confirming that Strabo's "Syrtis" was the ancient name for modern-day Djerba, an island along the Tunisian coast.

Nehir had accepted this rationale and left.

Shortly after that, the *Morning Star* had swung to the south and sailed three hours to reach the African coast.

But what now?

She held out one hope. If Joe and the others had a functional version of the map and the original Daedalus Key, maybe they could beat these bastards to the final destination.

She held tight to this thin lifeline.

But would it be enough?

1:40 P.M.

An hour later, voices drew Elena's attention to the library's glass doors. Nehir was back, speaking to Kadir. But she had not come alone.

Elena stiffened at the sight of her father. Despite her anger, his familiar face triggered a flush of warmth inside her, her body instinctively reacting to the man who had raised her, who had taught her right from wrong, forged her moral compass, who instilled in her a love for the sea, for nautical history.

The momentary flush turned cold. She had heard the term "heavy of heart," but only now did she realize that the phrase was not just metaphorical. Her heart felt like a leaden weight in her chest, each beat dull and listless. She rubbed a knuckle along her breastbone, trying to unknot the pain there, but failed.

Nehir unlocked the library door with an electronic keycard and ushered her father into the room. She followed behind, drawing Kadir in with her.

Her father opened his arms wide and crossed the library. "Elena, my dear."

She stood and icily accepted his hug, but she did not return it.

He seemed not to notice and finally broke the embrace. "I'm sorry it took me so long. There's an EU summit going on in Germany. It was already on my schedule as chair of the Senate's Committee on Foreign Relations. A bit of fortuitous timing, offering me the perfect excuse to fly here. Though, of course, I'm participating remotely after getting the word about, well—" He waved to encompass the breadth of the yacht.

Elena tightened her jaw, but it was actually good news. If word of her apparent survival had reached her father, it implied Joe had made it safely to those in authority.

"Luckily," her father continued, "the *Morning Star* is equipped with a sophisticated communications system, capable of bouncing signals all around—not only is it masking my location, but it's making it look as if I'm teleconferencing from my hotel room in Hamburg."

Elena finally found her voice. "Dad, what the hell are you doing here?"

"Ah, yes, that's why I came down here during a break at the summit." He lifted a hand to the table by the glass wall. "Come and I'll explain."

She wanted to tell him to fuck off, but she also wanted answers, so she followed him to the table. They took the remaining two seats, joining Monsignor Roe and Rabbi Fine.

Nehir came along and stood nearby.

As they settled to the table, her father glanced around and asked, "What do you know about the Apocalypti?"

Roe flinched, his eyes widening and staring hard at her father, but the priest remained quiet.

"I never heard the term," Elena admitted. "Unless it's plural for Apocalypse."

Her father smiled. It was the wry, boyish grin that had won him four terms in the Senate. "I suppose, in a way, that's true. I learned of the group during my second tour in the Middle East. During a combat mission, my infantry troop rooted out an Apocalypti cell in Baghdad. A prisoner was taken, along with a great number of texts. While guarding the man, I learned about who they were and what they were about. After talking with him, after reading the core texts of the Apocalypti, I was swayed. I recognized that we shared a common goal."

Elena glanced to Nehir, to Kadir. "Are . . . are you saying the prisoner secretly converted you to Islam?"

Her father gave a short laugh. "Of course not. I'm as devout in my belief as they are in theirs. I know they're wrong. And they know I am. But like I said, we both share a common goal."

"Which is what?" Elena asked.

"To bring about the Apocalypse by any means necessary."

Elena felt her heart drop even farther in her chest. She pictured the horrific weapons stored in Hunayn's dhow—and the radioactive hellfire that fueled them. The group here must be planning on using the dreadful power and the lost knowledge hidden in Tartarus to bring about a global war, to unleash Hell upon the world at large.

Her father continued. "After we bring about Armageddon, we'll let the chips fall where they will. Ambassador Firat believes he will become the legendary Mahdi of his faith, the twelfth imam who'll guide the world to its end. Whereas I follow the teachings of Christian scholars who view Armageddon's path and outcome very differently."

He shrugged. "But it is not only our two religions. The Apocalypti accept all who would see the world end according to their own beliefs. The Rapture and Tribulations of the evangelicals. The Hindus who await Kalki, the final incarnation of Visnu. Buddhists who watch for the appearance of the seven suns that will destroy the world. Even those of Jewish faith, who share some form of apocalyptic vision."

He waved to the rabbi. "I'm sure you're familiar with the prophetic books of Zechariah and Daniel."

Rabbi Fine frowned. "Indeed. They speak of a Messianic Age, when the Jewish diaspora would gather in Israel, and a great war would ensue, during which time the Jewish messiah would return, and a new world would be born out of that destruction."

Her father nodded, an exalted glow rising in his eyes. She knew her father was devoutly Catholic, discovering the depth of his faith after Elena's mother died of breast cancer two decades ago. It was one of the reasons many considered him to be the new JFK—only her father adhered to a far stricter code of moral ethics than Kennedy.

Or so I thought.

Elena challenged her father. "So, you're telling us the Apocalypti are a coalition of religious zealots that adhere to a shared apocalyptic viewpoint."

"Not to be a stickler, but your use of 'religious zealots' implies a level of blind faith. In fact, we are open to multiple viewpoints. We include many members in the scientific field. In fact, we have members who have *no* religious affiliation at all, strict atheists, who cling to their own versions of the Apocalypse. Whether it be something current like climate change or a global pandemic or something far in the future revolving around the end of the universe."

"That's an awfully large tent," Elena noted.

"But as I said, we share a common goal."

Roe leaned back with a slight moan. "To force the hand of God. To strive to trigger Armageddon."

"As they say, God helps those who help themselves." Her father grinned. "I don't know which of our groups will be proven correct when we open the gates of Hell and purge the world with fire. Will Ambassador Firat become the fabled Mahdi and help forge a new paradise out of the ashes? Or will I rise to fulfill *my* own destiny?"

Before Elena could ask her father what he meant by that, he waved to Elena, then Nehir. "Either way, it does seem like the hand of providence is guiding us. Look how events have united my dearest daughter with the First Daughter of Mūsā, who together will help us open those very gates?"

Elena wasn't ready to assign the Hand of God to such a union. She wasn't even willing to believe it was coincidence. Last night, unable to sleep, she had reevaluated her upended world. It had been her father who had encouraged her love of history, guided her into archaeology, even instilled in her a love of the sea. Had he been grooming her all along to serve his own ambitions? Had he guided her into a field where she would seek out lost knowledge, all to help him fulfill his destiny?

Which was what?

She swallowed hard. "If you're not going to be Mahdi, what do you think you're fated to become?"

The exalted glint grew to a fire in his eyes. He clearly had been wanting to tell her this for ages. "Jeremiah, chapter twenty-three, verse five."

Roe shook his head. The monsignor clearly understood. Even Rabbi Fine looked sickened.

"What?" Elena asked.

Her father quoted from the Book of Jeremiah. " *'For the time is coming, says the Lord, when I will raise up a righteous descendant from King David's line. He will be a King who rules with wisdom. He will do what is just and right throughout the land.'* "

Elena understood what her father was implying. Apparently he had greater ambitions than just being the president of the United States. She stared at her father, seeing the madness behind the exaltation, the ambition behind the bloodshed.

"You intend to be King David reborn."

2:01 P.M.

Such blasphemous kuffār . . .

Nehir scowled, deeming them all infidels for denying the blessing of God. She cast her dark gaze upon Elena Cargill. The woman's father had declared it divine providence that had brought them together. Nehir refused to believe this, to accept being bound to this weak woman—not by fate, certainly not by Allah.

Prior to heading to Greenland, Nehir had been told that her target was a senator's daughter, but Mūsā had never informed her that the woman's father was a high-ranking member of the Apocalypti. As First Daughter, she should have been privy to this knowledge. She had come close to killing the woman last night after she tried to escape. If Nehir had done that, she would have been hunted down and brutally punished, most likely tortured and killed.

Only at the last moment had Mūsā told Nehir the truth, more out of necessity than anything. Afterward, he had ordered her to bring the woman to the *Morning Star*—Mūsā's personal stronghold. It was normally considered an honor to walk these decks, but since setting foot here, Nehir had felt nothing but a hot anger burning in her gut, a heat that was all too familiar.

For her entire life, men had betrayed her, used their power to try to control her.

She had believed Mūsā to be different, placing her trust in him.

She clenched a fist and took a deep breath, trying to quell the flames inside her. She reminded herself that it was a minor treachery committed upon her by Mūsā, one she would strive to forgive—*must* forgive.

As she listened to Senator Cargill declare himself to be the heir to King David's throne, the gall of such a claim dampened some of her fury. She knew in her heart that Mūsā would be Mahdi, the prophesied "guided one" who would lead all the Sons and Daughters to greater glory.

And as First Daughter, I will sit at Mahdi's right hand.

Only that path—followed faithfully—would bring her dead children back to her. Still, she found it hard to stand in this room with these *kuffār*. Did not the holy Qur'an state clearly in Sura 8:58 that *unbelievers are one's sworn enemies*?

Long ago, Nehir had asked that same question of Mūsā. He had tried to calm her misgivings about the Apocalypti, explaining the practical necessity of this confederation with the infidels, teaching her how using an enemy's own resources to bring them low honored the Qur'an. Over time, she came to accept that the Apocalypti were more powerful together. Come Armageddon, all infidels would burn in a purifying fire. Only those of proper faith would emerge, made all the stronger by those flames, forged into an almighty sword to lead the righteous into a new world.

Until then . . .

We are stronger together.

As if hearing this—or perhaps moved by Allah—Senator Cargill expounded on this very idea to those seated at the table. His words reinforced what Mūsā had taught her, helping to douse the fire inside her. Or perhaps it was the looks of dismay around the table that softened her scowl.

"We are everywhere," the senator explained. "We have loyal followers in religions all around the world. In governments. In militaries. In universities. And even thousands more who do not know they *are* us, who unwittingly support our cause. In fact, if you simply believe the world will soon come to an end and do nothing to stop it, *you* are one of us."

The anguish in Elena Cargill's eyes brought Nehir great joy.

The woman's father continued: "Only those at the highest echelon of the Apocalypti have full knowledge of our global breadth. It is why you cannot move without us seeing you." He reached and gripped his daughter's hand. She pulled away, but he held tight. "For example, we know your friend Joseph Kowalski has joined his friends."

Elena gasped.

"So, to rid you of any hope that help will come," her father said, "I must teach you a hard lesson. From the Book of Ezekiel. Chapter thirty-three. Verse eleven."

Nehir smiled, feeling the last embers inside her smother to a cold satisfaction.

The Catholic priest explained, quoting that passage, " *'I take no pleasure in the death of the wicked.'*"

26

Kowalski rolled his eyes and paced before the ruins of the golden map. "I don't know how many times I can go over it. That's everything I remember." He pressed a palm to the sharp twinge in his lower spine. "And my back is killing me. I'd really like to try out that spa of yours."

"Not yet," Gray said as he and Father Bailey tried to put Humpty Dumpty back together again.

Kowalski knew it was a lost cause.

The two men knelt on either side of the Da Vinci map, doing their best to fish out the last lapis lazuli shards from the innards of the map mechanism. Maria, Seichan, and Mac sat to one side, collecting the blue pieces, slowly reconstructing the expanse of the Mediterranean Sea on the coffee table. The group had spent the last ninety minutes examining the remains of the broken map, searching for any clue to where the device wanted them to go.

Bailey sighed. "Half the gears and mechanisms were knocked awry when that mainspring blew. Maybe with time and by consulting the old designs that Da Vinci worked from, we might be able to figure something out."

"Doubtful," Gray said. "Even if we had the time, I suspect the map was engineered to obscure its ultimate intent. According to what Kowalski told us about the journal found aboard the dhow, only Captain Hunayn had the tools necessary to make the map unlock its secrets."

As Kowalski feared, Gray turned those icy eyes on him. "Tell us again everything you remember. Start from the beginning."

Kowalski groaned. *Not again.* But he knew everyone was counting on him; even Maria looked at him, her face hopeful, giving him a small nod of encouragement. So he started from when he had first met Elena. That memory alone awakened the burn in his thigh from the branding iron.

"They were using me to force Elena to cooperate," Kowalski started. He continued step by step, stopped often by Gray, who consulted his e-tablet to look up some reference that Elena had mentioned. There had been so very, very many.

He racked his brain for every detail, for every bit of conversation, but he harbored no hope that this line of inquiry would lead anywhere. Elena had certainly not figured out where they needed to go, so how could sharing what they'd talked about offer any clues?

"She was really obsessed with that Strabo guy's book, *Geographica*. It was huge, over two thousand pages. She read mostly in silence. If she learned anything more from it, she kept it to herself." He threw his hands high. "That's it. End of story."

Gray spent another ten minutes in silence, searching through his e-tablet. "I'm missing something."

Maybe a few screws, if you think you're going to solve this.

Gray turned to him.

Kowalski growled back. "If you ask me one more time . . ."

"No, that's fine. But I think Dr. Cargill was on to something." He pointed to his e-tablet. "I listed all the books you mentioned she used as references. By comparing the texts that she studied at the beginning to those she reviewed later, Elena had begun to make a notable change in her research."

"How so?" Bailey asked.

Gray kept his eyes on Kowalski. "You mentioned that Elena had started looking at geology books."

Kowalski shrugged. "So?"

"When you reached the island of Vulcano, you said she went on and on about the history of that island."

"Mostly about the god Hephaestus."

"But near the end, she made an offhand comment, mentioning how all of the volcanic activity that generated the mythology about Hephaestus was really due to tectonic activity."

Maria nodded. "The science behind the myths."

"But even then, Elena didn't seek out any geology texts," Gray said. "Only later, *after* the map was activated, carving a fiery line across the Mediterranean." He stared hard at Kowalski. "Tell me again what she said at the time, try to remember exactly, every word."

Kowalski closed his eyes. He pictured the blaze of the map, the golden flames. Elena had leaned closer to it, clearly awed by the display. "All I remember is her mumbling something about it being like a fiery version of tectonic plates banging together."

Gray nodded. "And after that, she started asking for geology texts?"

"I guess so."

Gray returned to his e-tablet. Kowalski stepped to look over his shoulder, to see what the guy was trying to figure out.

What difference did it make if Elena wanted to read geology books?

Kowalski watched Gray bring up a topographical map of the Mediterranean, very much like the golden version on the coffee table. He squinted at—

A thunderous blast jolted the entire length of the cruise ship. The liner's stern shoved up, tilted high and rising. They were all thrown toward the bow.

The Steinway broke from its perch, rolled, and crashed into the window, breaking out several panes. Bottles and glassware flew from the bar, shattering and rolling after the piano.

The gathered group tumbled toward the balcony doors, which had been left ajar. Maria went flying through, landing and skidding across the deck. Kowalski lunged forward, sprawling on his stomach, and caught her ankle with one hand and grabbed the jamb of the door with the other, stopping her.

She stared at him, her eyes wide with terror.

I got you.

He glanced back over his shoulder, pulling her with him. He watched the gold map, teetering on the edge of the coffee table—then it toppled over with a spill of crushed lapis lazuli.

"Hang on!" Gray yelled.

What d'ya think I'm doing?

Before Kowalski could catch his breath, the stern fell back into the sea, slamming hard with a great splintering crash into the edge of the dock. They were all tossed the other way. The piano rolled from the broken window and barreled into the onyx bar with a resounding gong of its jolted strings.

As the ship rocked back again, Gray gained his footing and ran through the balcony doors. He had his satellite phone already out and pressed to his lips.

"What's your status?" Gray yelled.

Kowalski frowned, not understanding. He helped Maria up and hurried after Gray. As Kowalski stepped out onto the balcony, the roar of engines deafened him. A huge plane swept low over the cruise ship. It sailed out over the bay and shot a line of objects from its undercarriage into the sea. A chain of muffled explosions followed, blasting huge fountains of water high into the air.

Depth charges.

Kowalski looked to the sky. The jet banked steeply over the bombardment and circled around for another run. He recognized the aircraft now, a Poseidon sub hunter. He could also guess who commanded it, picturing the same plane sitting on the tarmac of an Italian air base.

Out in the bay, a second volley of depth charges blasted the sea. Amid the roil and spray, a black steel whale lifted its tail high, then rolled and toppled sideways, sinking belly up into the sea.

Kowalski knew it had to be the same submarine that had carried Elena away from Greenland. Or another like it. Either way . . .

Kowalski stared upward.

Looks like Pullman finally caught his damned fish.

3:03 P.M.

"Say again!" Gray hollered into his sat-phone, trying to hear over the blasts and roar of the jet's engines.

Commander Pullman reported, *"Sorry for the late save. Target's running AIP engines."*

Gray understood. Submarines equipped with Air Independent Propulsion swam even stealthier than nuclear versions. Some had even slipped through antisubmarine defenses during U.S. Navy war games.

"Boat kept ghosting on us. Probably Russian Lada-*class. Only got a firm lock when it fired off the first torpedo."*

Gray felt the roll of the *Explorer* under him as it settled crookedly in the water. Luckily, the ship had only been hit by a single torpedo. The cruise ship continued to list as it took on more water. Prior to the attack, most of the *Explorer* had quietly been evacuated. With a majority of the cruise ship's passengers already on tours, it had been easy enough to get the remaining travelers offloaded, along with most of the crew, using a gas leak as an excuse.

Last night, well before dawn, Commander Pullman's plane had dropped a ring of sonobuoys around the port, prior to the cruise ship's arrival. Gray knew their tormentors would attempt another attack, especially after his team had broken radio silence. In addition to the air-and-sea support, a Spanish military team had been covertly stationed at the dock entrance in case of a land assault.

But Gray knew any attack would likely come from the sea.

He lifted his phone. "Hold off any more charges."

"Understood. You want survivors to question. Dive and rescue teams are en route."

Gray hoped there were survivors, but his main ambition had been to send the enemy a message. *You will not catch us by surprise again.*

As Gray headed back inside, the ship lurched and tilted even more to starboard.

"We need to get off this boat," Kowalski warned.

Gray doubted the *Explorer* would sink, but Kowalski was right. He crossed to the toppled gold map, knelt down, and with a grunt, flipped it right-side up. He then grabbed a section of the gold map, and with some tugging and effort, pried it away. He straightened with the piece in his hands.

"Let's go," he ordered the others.

Father Bailey looked down at the ruin of the Da Vinci treasure. "Shouldn't we take the rest?"

"I'll let the authorities know to secure it and get it returned to Italy. But we don't need it anymore."

Kowalski dogged his footsteps. "Why?"

Gray headed to the doors, hoping the enemy had gotten his message loud and clear, that it would make the bastards more cautious. He turned to Kowalski and explained why.

"Because I know where we need to go."

27

Who's teaching who a lesson?

Elena wanted to laugh out loud, but she bottled up her jubilation. She and the two old men had been marched from the library to the super-yacht's communications room. A line of monitors displayed live feeds from multiple cameras set up around Palma's port.

She had cringed when an underwater camera from a submerged submarine—likely the same one she had traveled aboard—showed a sleek torpedo sailing out into the water, then vanishing into the distance. Another monitor showed its impact into the stern of a docked cruise ship. The liner jolted hard, its stern bumped high by the blast.

Her heart clenched in her throat as she thought about Joe aboard that ship.

All around her, cheers rose from those gathered in the communication room. Fists were pumped in the air. Nehir stood next to Elena, wearing a savage grin.

Then everything changed.

The row of monitors showed different views of a jet flying past, then depth charges being dropped, followed by a cascade of blasts. The underwater view bobbled amid flashes of fire and huge explosive bubbles—then canted wildly until finally going dark.

A dead silence followed.

On Elena's other side, her father swore sharply.

So much for today's lesson, Dad.

Her father turned to Firat. "If they apprehend any of the crew, we risk being compromised."

The ambassador scowled. "Those aboard don't know enough to do lasting damage. A nuisance at best. And they are most loyal. They will not allow themselves to be taken alive."

These assurances did little to drain the flush from her father's face. He turned to Elena, his words stiff as if he had trouble unclenching his jaw. "It seems our timetable must be accelerated. You will cooperate fully to make sure that happens."

She gave the smallest shake of her head.

I'm done playing this game.

Her father must have noted her determination. "Sadly, as this lesson failed, clearly another is needed."

He snatched a pistol from the holster of the man next to him—then turned, lifted the weapon, and fired. With the deafening blast, the back of Rabbi Fine's skull exploded, splattering against the back wall. The man's body crumpled to a pile on the floor.

Elena screamed and stumbled back, only to have her shoulders grabbed by Kadir. Monsignor Roe covered his face and turned away. Even Ambassador Firat looked shocked by the cold-blooded murder.

Her father calmly passed the weapon back to the guard and wiped his palms together, as though he'd just finished drying the last of the dinner dishes. "Do I have your attention, young lady?"

She shook her head, then nodded, too shaken to make sense.

"I hope I've made my point clear," he said. "You will cooperate to your fullest." He glanced to the old priest. "Or the next death will not be so quick and merciful."

She collected herself enough to nod in agreement.

Her father turned to Nehir. "Please return my daughter and Monsignor Roe to the library." His gaze settled back to Elena. "You have one hour."

Numb with shock, Elena took no note of her surroundings as she was led away. Her stomach churned queasily. She found it hard to breathe. Tears blurred her vision. When she finally reached the library, Nehir pushed her across the threshold.

"One hour," the woman repeated before leaving.

Kadir remained outside.

Monsignor Roe stepped over and took her in his arms. She felt the thin limbs of the old priest shaking. Still, he did his best to console her. "He's with our Lord now," he whispered. "In eternal peace."

"How could my father do that?" she moaned into the man's chest. "Who is he?"

"I don't know." He sighed, the trembling in him calming. "Even at my age, I cannot comprehend the depths of some men's depravity. I was born in the middle of a world war—which followed on the heels of another, what was called 'the war to end all wars.' Such naivete. Look what we still do to one another."

She nodded against him, taking deep breaths.

He finally shifted and held her at arm's length so she could see his sincerity. "You do not have to help them."

"But—"

"No, my child. I've lived a long life. If I must die, so be it."

"They'll torture you."

"It is just flesh. They cannot touch my soul. All the saints throughout the ages—men and women—have endured suffering for the greater good of all." He smiled. "Not that I consider myself a candidate for sainthood. Besides, I don't think a halo would look good on me."

She appreciated his gentle humor, his willingness to sacrifice himself, but she saw the glimmer of fear in his eyes, as much as he tried to hide it. In the end, the old priest might be able to bear the brutalities inflicted upon him.

But I cannot watch it happen.

She checked a clock on the wall. "I have to get to work."

With a final shake to center herself, she headed over to her pile of books. She already had a general sense of where Hunayn went next. She pictured the fiery river flowing west along the coast of Africa, passing through the Strait of Gibraltar.

"Can I help you?" Monsignor Roe asked, joining her.

She nodded. "I have a lot to do and little time, and I'd appreciate a sounding board for my reasoning before the others get here."

"I'll do my best."

4:10 P.M.

Elena was still buried in texts and notes when voices rose out in the hall. It wasn't just Nehir this time. The woman led Ambassador Firat and Elena's father.

Looks like it's showtime.

She straightened from her work.

For the past hour, she had scoured reference materials, new and old. She had known she would need to produce significant results to satisfy these bastards, more than just picking another stop along Odysseus's voyage. If she failed to impress, the old priest would suffer the consequences. Still, even with Roe's able assistance, the hour had flown by too fast.

The others pushed into the library.

All eyes were on her.

"What do you have to tell us?" her father asked without any preamble.

Elena struggled to organize her thoughts. She stared down at the books and notes stacked around the gold map on the table. Her mind spun with all the bits and pieces of the puzzle in her head, trying to gather them into a coherent, intelligible picture.

Firat pressed her, "Where did Captain Hunayn go next?"

She shrugged. "I don't know."

Which was the truth.

When the map had activated, drawing a flaming river across the northern coast of Africa, she had been focused elsewhere, fascinated as the fiery seam extended past the Strait of Gibraltar. She had failed to note if the tiny silver ship had stopped anywhere else.

Her father's face darkened, his gaze flicked to Monsignor Roe.

Elena lifted a palm. "But," she stressed, "I do know where he *ended up*."

Nehir stepped forward. "Ended up? Are you saying you know where Tartarus lies, where the gates of Hell are hidden?"

She swallowed. "I believe so. At least, I have a pretty firm idea of where Hunayn went to look for it. Especially if he had been following the guidance found in ancient books."

"Tell us," Firat said. "And we'll be the judge."

She nodded. "Hunayn placed great value in the words and wisdom of the Greek historian Strabo, specifically his book *Geographica*. Throughout that text, Strabo makes a case for Odysseus's journey to Tartarus taking place at a semi-mythical city by the name of Tartessus."

"Tartessus?" her father said with a frown. "That sounds a lot like Tartarus."

"Exactly Strabo's reasoning." She drew up her notes. "Here's one mention from *Geographica*. *'One might reasonably suppose that Homer, because he heard about Tartessus, named the farthermost of the nether-regions Tartarus after Tartessus, with a slight alteration of letters.'*"

"Where is this place?" Firat asked.

"According to Strabo and other sources, it lies *'farthermost to the west'* and *'beyond the Pillars of Hercules,'* which was the ancient name for the Strait of Gibraltar." She straightened. "To the ancients at that time, anything beyond the Pillars of Hercules was considered to be ominous, where the sun set and night fell, so if you were going to imagine Hades or Tartarus lying anywhere, it would be out there."

"But where out there?" her father pressed.

"Tartessus was said to lie along the Iberian coast of southern Spain, just beyond the Strait of Gibraltar. A city of great wealth and power." She checked her notes again. "Here's a description from a fourth-century historian named Ephorus: *'Tartessus is a very prosperous market, with much tin carried by the river, as well as gold and copper.'* "

She turned to Nehir. "Why do you think *tin* was so prominently mentioned, even above gold?"

Nehir shrugged.

Elena faced the others. "Because tin is essential to the production of *bronze.* Tartessus was known as a major producer of bronze and the elements to make it." She pictured the horrors released from Hunayn's dhow. "And you would need a lot of bronze if you intend to build an infernal army."

As the others glanced to each other, clearly getting her point, she turned to Monsignor Roe. It was the priest's moment to take the stage.

Roe cleared his throat. "But the city of Tartessus had other stories associated with it. From a very reliable source."

"From where?" Firat asked.

"From the Old Testament."

Elena's father looked to her for confirmation. She simply nodded to the monsignor.

Roe continued: "Many of the books in the Old Testament mention a mysterious city named *Tarshish.* For example, in Ezekiel. *'Tarshish sent merchants to buy your wares in exchange for silver, iron, tin, and lead.'*"

Elena added, "In other words, another mythic city of riches, similar in name to Tartessus."

"Many biblical archaeologists also agree," Roe said. "They believe Tarshish and Tartessus were one and the same."

Firat frowned. "But why does that matter?"

"Because of a swirl of rumors," Elena explained. "About Tartessus, about Tarshish. Going back millennia—from ancient Greeks to modern scholars."

"What rumor?" her father asked.

"It's believed this city wasn't only rich—but that it was home to a society far in advance of its time. Many even compared it to Atlantis."

She let that sink in for several breaths. Glances were shared again.

"Whether true or not," she finally said, "I have no doubt Captain Hunayn went venturing beyond the Pillars of Hercules, following the guidance of Strabo and others, searching for Tartessus, the gateway to fabled Tartarus, a place rumored to be home to an advanced society."

"But where is this place *exactly*?" Firat demanded.

"I can point pretty close," she admitted, drawing a sheet of notes. "Courtesy of a second-century A.D. writer Pausanias, who tells us that Tartessus lies along *'a river in the land of the Iberians, running down into the sea by two mouths . . . some who think Tartessus was the ancient name of Carpia.'*"

"And that helps us how?" her father asked.

"Because modern scholars have studied this description and others," she explained. "They believe Tartessus was somewhere in a river delta between Cádiz and Huelva, along the southern coast of Spain. If you want to find the entrance to Tartarus, that's where it'll be. I can't guide you any more precisely than that."

Elena stood straighter and awaited the group's judgment. They bowed their heads together, murmured excitedly, then turned back to her.

The proud smile on her father's face gave her the answer before he even congratulated her. "I knew you could do it, Elena."

She returned his smile. *Fuck you.*

Her father and the others all left quickly, ready to set sail for the lost city of Tartessus. She dropped and sagged into the leather chair by the table.

Roe joined her, settling his old bones down more delicately. "You think that's where Captain Hunayn truly went?"

She nodded. "I have no doubt."

She stared down at the map. She imagined that fiery river coursing from Vulcano, over to Sardinia, across Africa, and out the Strait of Gibraltar.

"That's exactly where Hunayn sailed to," she said honestly.

But that's not where he ended up.

She lifted her eyes to the library door, a cold satisfaction settling into her. She was her father's daughter all right—a *senator's* daughter. While growing up, she had spent many hours on the campaign trail with her father, standing in the spotlight alongside him, where she had learned how to blur truth and lies to their best effect.

Like now.

She turned and stared out at the African coast. She had needed to buy Joe and the others extra time, so they could hopefully reach the true site of Tartarus first—which meant she had to lead these bastards astray.

But one question remained.

Can Joe and the others figure it out in time?

28

I had better be right.

Gray closed his eyes, plagued by doubts.

His body was pressed deeper into his seat cushion as the Poseidon climbed steeply over the sea, leaving the chaos of Palma behind them. It had taken far longer to escape the island of Majorca than he had hoped.

Commander Pullman had helped coordinate the capture of the submarine, a Russian *Lada*-class boat. All but two of the crew had either died or shot themselves before being captured. The remaining pair were being interrogated, but Gray imagined the two were low-level drudges or hired mercenaries, who likely knew nothing significant, especially about their bosses.

By the time Gray and the others could slip away from the damaged cruise ship and meet up with the Poseidon, the sun had been near to setting. He stared out the window as the plane banked and headed toward where the sun sat on the horizon. He had not even told Commander Pullman where they were going, only to head west toward the Strait of Gibraltar.

Gray hadn't even shared his destination with Director Crowe—or with those traveling with him. Seichan sat next to him, Kowalski and Maria behind, and Bailey and Mac ahead. Gray trusted this team, but he had kept his theories to himself. He feared discussing it on the ground amid the tumult of Palma.

Finally, the plane leveled off at cruising altitude.

Bailey twisted around and glared back at Gray. "*Now* can we talk about where we're headed?"

Gray undid his seat belt. "Follow me."

The group quickly clambered out of their seats. They sidled past the port-side row of monitoring stations. The crew seated there ignored their group and stayed focused on the various glowing screens.

Gray led his team toward the back of the jet, to where a galley offered more space to gather. He carried his e-tablet and the section of the gold coast that he'd pried out of the remains of the Da Vinci map. He placed both on the small counter and faced the others.

"First, let's make sure I'm not crazy," he said.

Kowalski lifted his hand, clearly ready with a wisecrack. Gray frowned at him, and Kowalski promptly lowered his arm.

"Tell us what you're thinking," Mac said.

Maria nodded.

Seichan merely folded her arms, as if already accepting his conclusions.

Gray turned to Kowalski. "You told us before, when the map was activated, that you didn't see where the fiery line ended. Whether Elena did or not, she must've had some inkling of the pattern forming. I believe she was looking for corroboration in those geology texts."

"Corroboration of what?" Bailey asked.

Gray raised a palm, asking to be allowed to finish. "Remember, Elena commented how the flaming route on the gold map looked like a representation of tectonic plates clashing together."

Maria frowned. "But what does that have to do with anything?"

Gray picked up his e-tablet and opened an image he had stored there. It showed a map of the Mediterranean, broken up and divided into the five tectonic plates that underlay the entire region.

The others leaned in closer to study the image.

"What does this look like to you?" Gray asked.

He only got frowns and shakes of heads.

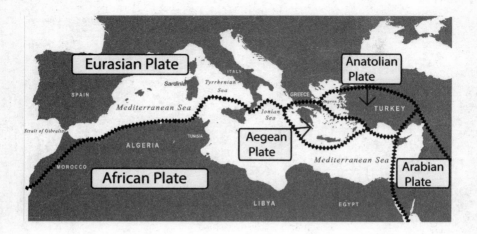

Really?

He sighed, wondering if he wasn't insane after all, seeing patterns that weren't there. Director Crowe had recruited Gray for his ability to see what others couldn't. But what if he'd lost his edge? Rather than noting what was real, was he now chasing phantoms?

Seichan reached to him and squeezed his forearm. Her gaze firmed on him, letting him see her confidence in him. "Show us," she urged.

He reached over and swiped a finger across the tablet's screen to transform the same image—now the winding path of lines between the tectonic plates became dashed, indicating a circuitous route through the geological labyrinth.

He held it higher.

Surely they see it now.

Maria was the first to recognize the pattern. She covered her mouth with a gasp. Then Bailey's eyes widened. Seichan smiled and shrugged, not surprised. Even Mac nodded.

Only Kowalski furrowed his brow. "I don't get it."

Maria tried to explain and pointed to the coast of Turkey. "The dotted line—where the Anatolian plate runs up against the Eurasian plate to the north—starts at *Troy*."

Bailey continued, "From there, it zigzags through the islands of the Aegean Sea, before sweeping south under Greece."

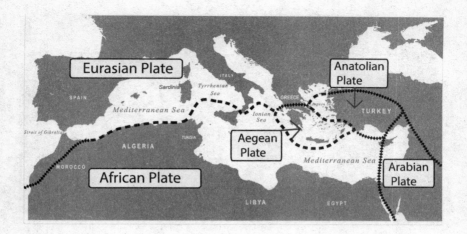

Mac pointed to the Ionian Sea. "And didn't that tiny silver boat spin along that same path to the coast of Italy? Then under the boot and past Sicily to those little volcanic islands?"

"To Vulcano," Kowalski said with a nod. "I remember the flaming river swooping from there to southern Sardinia. Then down to Africa and along its coast. The route looked a lot like what's on your screen."

Gray nodded. "The path of Odysseus's ship appears to be following the boundaries between tectonic plates. At least the route revealed by the map. And maybe even what Homer tried to record in a poetic fashion."

"But how is that possible?" Bailey asked. "How could these ancients know anything about plate tectonics?"

Gray shrugged. "I can only guess. Those same ancients mapped all the volcanic activity of the region, recorded all the major earthquakes in their texts. Perhaps they were able to get some inkling of the pattern of those underlying seismic forces."

Maria offered another possibility he hadn't even considered. "We know the Phoenicians, the Greeks, the Egyptians were far more advanced in astronomy and navigational mapping. They kept records of significant places. The Giza pyramids. The other Seven Wonders of the Ancient World. Even geographical landmarks, like Mount Vesuvius. Maybe by tracking the movements of these major sites over millennia they got some idea of the ground shifting beneath their feet."

Gray knew that was pretty much how modern geologists mapped the movement of tectonic plates: using interferometry to track the changing distances between radio telescopes or GPS to gather positional data of landmarks on the earth and record their movements.

Mac suggested another option, drawing upon his earth sciences background as a climatologist. "Or maybe there were minute magnetic anomalies along these convergent plate boundaries that were detected and mapped?"

Gray nodded.

Could some combination of these be the answer?

Kowalski asked the more important question. "How does this help us know where to go?"

Gray held his tablet higher and showed where the line between the African plate and Eurasian plate continued to the west, cutting through the tip of northern Morocco. He switched over to a topographic map of Morocco with the convergent boundary drawn on it to better make his point.

"Hunayn obviously couldn't take his ship overland *through* Morocco

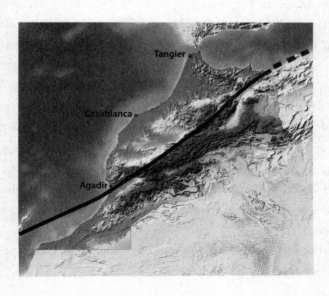

to continue along this path, so he took his dhow *around,* passing through the Strait of Gibraltar. From there I believe he turned south to the place where this tectonic line reemerges on the far side of the Moroccan coast."

Bailey squinted, but slowly nodded. "According to what you and Monsignor Roe discussed, you thought Hunayn was searching for the home of the mysterious Phaeacians."

Gray nodded. "A place described as far away, at the end of the world."

"In other words, beyond the Strait of Gibraltar," Bailey added.

Maria frowned. "But how can we be sure Hunayn ended up going *south,* looking for the continuation of the African-Eurasian boundary?"

"First, the derivation of the name *Phaeacian.* It comes from the Greek root *Phaios,* which means 'gray.' "

"How appropriate," Kowalski mumbled.

Gray ignored him. "The name Phaeacians means 'the Gray People.' Some scholars think this referred to a dark-skinned tribe."

"As in Africans," Mac said.

"And then there's this," Gray said.

He set down his tablet and picked up the golden piece of the map. It depicted the chunk of Africa south of the Strait of Gibraltar. He held it up and tilted it to better highlight the three-dimensional topography sculpted into its golden surface. He ran a finger along a row of ridges that cut across Morocco, a near mirror to what was shown on the topo map on his screen.

"These represent the Atlas Mountains," he said. "Created by the African plate diving down and pushing up the edge of the Eurasian plate. The centermost gold ridge, closest to this subduction boundary, is the High Atlas Mountains, below it the Anti-Atlas Mountains. Between them lies a deep valley. If you look closely, you can see a river draining out of those highlands and emptying into the sea. That's the Sous River basin."

He passed the section of the gold map around so the others could get a better look.

When Bailey got his turn, Gray asked, "What do you see upriver, buried among the High Atlas Mountains near the coast?"

Bailey pushed his nose closer. "I see a little ruby. Is that what you mean?"

"On the map, what do rubies represent?" Gray asked.

Kowalski answered, "Volcanos."

Gray straightened. "I looked it up. There are no volcanos in the mountains where that ruby is sitting."

Maria clutched Kowalski's arm.

"Hunayn marked that spot for a reason," Gray said. "While it might not be a volcano, if you wanted to represent the fiery underworld, a ruby would serve nicely for that, too."

Bailey pursed his lips, clearly bothered by something, which he finally voiced aloud. "But I thought the Phaeacians lived on an *island*."

"No, that's a common misconception," Gray explained. "Nowhere in the *Odyssey* does Homer say they live on an island, only that they live close to the sea."

"Which would fit a city situated near the coast," Maria said.

Voices and footsteps drew their attention out of the galley. Commander Pullman approached with the plane's tactical coordinator. Pullman eyed their group with a deep frown. Clearly he did not like being in the dark and wanted answers, too.

"We're about to pass over the Strait of Gibraltar," the commander said. "I need to know where we're going next."

Gray had already picked a spot, a town near the mouth of the Sous River, the gateway into the maze of mountain waterways.

"Agadir," Gray said. "It's a seaside resort three hundred miles south of Casablanca on the Moroccan coast. We need you to drop us off there. Then stick close by."

Pullman looked like he wanted to ask why, but Gray silenced him with a hard stare. The commander huffed, turned on a heel, and headed off with his tactical coordinator. Pullman groused to his second-in-command. "Feels like we're being hijacked."

Gray turned away. He knew it was risky using this large plane as a transport vehicle versus some private jet, but the Poseidon was equipped with the latest sonar, radar, and tracking equipment. Gray wanted those sophisticated eyes in the air, looking down from above, helping his team below hunt for the lost underground city, for the mythic Tartarus.

"So, we're heading somewhere south of Casablanca," Maria said.

Kowalski grinned. *"Of all the gin joints in all the towns—"* Then he stopped and turned to Maria with a serious frown. "Wait. This Agadir place has gin joints, too, right?"

29

Yes, Agadir had gin joints.

As the rental SUV bumped over a pothole, Maria shaded her eyes against the glare of the midmorning sun. She was still nursing a slight hangover. Her head pounded; her stomach lurched with every sway. Slouched in the front seat, she clutched a thermos of coffee. She suspected a fair amount of her fuzziness was less from the combination of gin cocktails than from the lack of sleep.

By the time the jet had reached Agadir, the plane had to circle as Gray coordinated with Painter in the States to get permission to land at a royal Moroccan air base outside the city. They had finally touched down on a remote strip at midnight. The area had been cordoned off. The story: just an American jet refueling on a base friendly to U.S. interests. Any other information about the new arrivals was kept on a need-to-know basis.

Still, Gray had shuttled their group quickly off the base and over to a nondescript hotel near the ocean. Unfortunately, there had been a bar next door. Both tired and amped, she and Joe had gone over for a nightcap. But one drink became three. Then they retired to their own bedroom for a proper reunion, only falling asleep after three in the morning.

She glanced over to the driver's seat. Joe clutched the wheel with one hand, his other elbow resting on the sill of the open window. He had a stogie clenched between his back molars. He leaned and puffed a stream of smoke toward the window, only to have it blow right back into the SUV. Still, the breeze gusting off the ocean helped clear her head more than the coffee.

Joe looked none the worse, refreshed even, better than would be expected for a guy who'd had only four hours of gin-soaked sleep. Not that they hadn't catnapped on the plane. Still, she felt something had changed in him. They had slept naked, no sheets as it was too hot. Joe nestled against her, enveloping her smaller frame with his bulk, but it felt less possessive than it had a few days prior, more relaxed. She wondered if, over the past months, he had innately sensed the doubts growing inside her. It was as if the more she pulled away, the harder he had tried to hold her, which in turn only aggravated her more. It was a vicious cycle that had threatened their future together.

But that wheel had finally broken.

She knew it—and somehow so did Joe. She remembered where this trip had started. She had hoped that by taking Joe to see the young gorilla Baako, it would rekindle something between them, reopen those cracks in the man's hard demeanor, revealing his more tender side. But she realized Joe hadn't changed. There was always a steadfast well of empathy and compassion inside him, as much a core to him as his bones. It was Maria who had changed, letting her doubts come between them, forcing Joe to cling tighter to her.

She reached over and squeezed his thigh, silently thanking him.

He winced, almost biting off the end of his cigar.

"Sorry." She had forgotten about his healing burn.

She pulled her hand away, but he let go of the wheel, grabbed her hand, and returned her palm to his leg. He patted it and returned his grip to the wheel.

She smiled and settled deeper into her seat, feeling much better, more grounded. Even her headache had passed. She turned to watch the scenery. Rolling white dunes and achingly blue water stretched on one side, and on the other, tracts of green farmlands climbed up in tiers toward the tower-ing peaks of the High Atlas Mountains. They cut a jagged line across the northern sky, crashing into the Atlantic to the west and climbing higher to the east, where several of the tallest peaks—a few over thirteen thousand feet—still glinted with winter's snow.

Closer at hand, the resort city of Agadir grew in size ahead, a lush oasis hugging a long, wide crescent of sandy coast. The resort's colorful promenade—crowded with restaurants and more bars—faced the sea. Palm trees swayed throughout the town, as if beckoning them to rest their weary bones.

She had not expected it to be this green. She had always pictured Mo-rocco as a country of red rocks and desert, but the Sous River valley was a fertile Eden, surrounded and protected to the north and south by the two ranges thrust upward by the clash of tectonic forces below.

From the third row of the SUV, Father Bailey commented on the his-tory of these peaks and their ties to the Greeks. "The local Berbers called these ranges the *Idraren Draren,* or 'Mountains of Mountains,' but the ancient Greeks' name for the place stuck. They believed it was here that the huge-shouldered god Atlas was punished by Zeus to hold up the skies at the edge of the world."

Mac sat next to the priest. "And this is the edge of the world?"

"For the ancient Greeks, yes. Anything past the Strait of Gibraltar was no-man's-land."

And where they believed the entrance to Tartarus was hidden.

Maria stared up at the sharp line of ridges rising ahead. She read the deeper geologic past in the strata of purple, red, and white, the layers of sedimentary rock from prehistoric oceans. She noted the streaks of black basalt from ancient, long-dead volcanos.

Somewhere in that labyrinth of rivers, cliffs, and waterfalls was their goal.

But where?

Luckily, they had more to help them than just a shard of gold map with a ruby affixed to it.

Gray's voice whispered behind her from the middle row, communicating to Commander Pullman, who already had his plane in the air, his crew aiding their search from above via the Poseidon's radar and tracking equipment. Gray had also enlisted Director Crowe to commandeer a satellite pass of the area, using ground-penetrating scans to try to detect hidden pockets that might point to an underground city.

As Gray hung up, Seichan asked the question on all their minds. "Anything?"

Gray huffed, "Unfortunately, *too* much. It seems these saw-toothed mountains have not seen a dentist in millennia. The peaks ahead are riddled with cavities. There are caves and tunnels throughout these ranges."

"Then sounds like we're doing it the hard way," Joe said, guiding them through the town's outskirts, crossing alongside a golf course. "On foot."

His assessment wasn't entirely accurate.

The road ended ahead at a small riverside marina. The green expanse of the Sous widened here, stretching two football fields across to the far bank. An L-shaped dock sheltered twenty slips, packed with sleek pleasure crafts, worn commercial fishing schooners, and several charter boats.

Joe parked in the lot, and they all clambered out of the SUV and gathered their gear, stored in new backpacks. Ever the optimist, Gray had raided hardware and sporting goods stores this morning. He bought flashlights and electric lanterns. Even found caving gear: ropes, helmets, rappelling equipment. Apparently the sport was popular here, what with all those cavern systems. So was canyoning into the deep gorges that hid perfect little oasis gems of cerulean pools and palm trees.

From the back, Joe hauled out their most important bag. He grunted as he shouldered the heavy weapons duffel, loaded with ammunition—along with a short-barreled shotgun, which Joe already called dibs on.

Back at the hotel, Gray had passed around the team's stock of SIG P320s, along with thin ballistic nylon holsters. Only Father Bailey had balked at taking one, but Gray had convinced the priest, telling him, *if you don't want to shoot to kill, at least shoot to defend.*

Joe straightened with his load. "Where the hell's our guide?"

"This way," Gray said and led them from the parking lot to the marina.

The boat they were looking for was tied in the last slip. It was a thirty-foot aluminum cruiser with an enclosed stand-up cabin welded to it. It looked well used and from the polish to its bulkheads and hull, well loved. The captain of the little craft, a young woman—maybe not even twenty—leaned over the stern, tinkering with a raised outboard motor.

She straightened when their group reached the slip. She wore oil-stained coveralls, belted tight at the waist, and a cowboy hat. Her flawless skin was a light ebony, her curly hair a dark cinnamon-brown, her eyes a stunning blue. She looked like she had stepped out of the pages of *Vogue*, but this was no pampered model who worked out at a Pilates studio.

The men around her didn't fail to note her looks, even Father Bailey. All of them were stunned into momentary silence.

Maria took the lead and stepped forward. "Charlie Izem?"

The woman pushed the sleeves of her coverall up, revealing powerful forearms. She reached across the rail to shake Maria's hand.

"That'd be me," Charlie answered, with a hint of a French accent.

Maria guessed she was of local Berber descent, maybe with a little European blood, too.

"From your companions' expressions, you were perhaps expecting a man, *oui*?" Charlie said and waved them aboard with an amused wink. "Or maybe someone older, *non*?"

The others picked up their jaws and climbed into the stern of the cruiser.

"No complaint here," Joe muttered under his breath.

Maria cast him a scolding glare.

Seichan boarded, giving the woman a side-eyed appraisal. Her gaze lingered a beat on the pistol holstered at Charlie's hip, then she gave a small nod of approval.

"You come highly recommended," Gray commented, also shaking the woman's hand. "They say you know the Sous and its tributaries better than anyone."

"My family's been running this river for over a century. And me since I was nine. The Sous, she is temperamental, crafty, mischievous, but we get along. At least, most days."

Charlie stepped over to help Mac with his pack. He had shed his sling but it was obvious his shoulder still hurt. Though he didn't wince or groan, the woman seemed to innately sense his distress.

"How long have you been captain of this boat?" Father Bailey asked.

Charlie surveyed the group, making sure everyone was settled. "Ah, but I am not the captain." She shifted over to remove the stern mooring line. "He is in the cabin, making sure all is ready before we depart. Always busy, that one."

The woman whistled sharply.

From the open door of the enclosed little wheelhouse, a small shape bounded out, rabbit-hopping on its hind limbs, and bracing on its front. The small monkey leaped from the deck and onto Charlie's shoulder as she straightened from freeing the rope.

Everyone was amused by the new arrival—except for one passenger.

Joe groaned and stepped farther back.

10:55 A.M.

What is it about women and monkeys?

Kowalski grimaced. He'd had bad experiences with these little savages in the past. While he had learned to love Baako, at least the gorilla was regular sized and knew sign language—and even so, it took Kowalski a while to warm up to the kiddo. Whereas this little guy creeped him out, with its tiny old-man face, like a wizened apple, and those beady black marbles for eyes.

No, thank you.

While he backed away, everyone else drew closer.

"This is Aggie," Charlie introduced. "Short for *aghilasse*, which means 'lion' in Tashelhit, the local Berber dialect." She made a growly face at the creature, and Aggie mimicked it, showing sharp teeth and long fangs.

Kowalski shivered with disgust.

"See," Charlie said with a big smile, "he's very tough, a real Barbary lion."

Maria examined the monkey closer with the eyes of an experienced primatologist. She checked out his brown fur, which turned more yellow over the belly. "But he's really a Barbary *macaque,* isn't he? Native to this region, endangered, too, as I recall."

"Very much so. Aggie was orphaned. His parents killed by poachers. Barely four months old at the time. He came to a rescue center with a broken arm."

"How old is he now?"

"Shy of a year. So he's got a way to go until he's mature enough to join a troop."

"When is that, around four years for males?"

"Indeed, for sexual maturity, but we'll look to start reintroducing him in half that time."

The two women continued to talk about Aggie in more detail and headed toward the cabin. Besides being an experienced riverboat pilot, Charlie was a zoology student, currently on summer break. But she clearly knew boats, which Kowalski appreciated.

In short order, the cruiser was untied, slipped free of its berth, and headed upriver with a rumble of its outboard motor.

Maria eventually came back to join him, leaving Charlie to navigate up the narrowing channel. "Cute, huh?" Maria said with a grin.

"Charlie? Sure. A stunner."

Maria punched him in the shoulder. "I meant Aggie."

He rolled his eyes and pointed to the cabin. "I heard you call it a monkey. But it's got no—" He motioned to his backside.

"A tail?"

"Without that, doesn't that make it an *ape?* Back in Africa, you kept correcting me whenever I called Baako a monkey."

"Macaques do have tails, only vestigial, maybe half an inch long."

He shuddered. "Somehow that's even worse."

Maria sighed and shook her head. Mac and Father Bailey settled down onto benches along the gunwales. Gray and Seichan stayed with Charlie in the tiny enclosed wheelhouse. The door was propped open, so Kowalski overheard some of their talk, mostly about the river itself.

He only half-listened. He stared out at the chain of mountains, rising in jagged peaks, cut through by tributary streams and cascading water-falls. He caught glimpses of deep wooded gorges, glints of lakes and pools, the sunlit glow of green pastures and meadows.

According to what he overheard, the Sous drained for hundreds of miles out of these mountains, but its flow was strangled and controlled by the Aoulouz Dam, some ninety miles upriver.

Kowalski heard Charlie's view on it. "Before the dam was built in the late eighties, the river was both stronger and more capricious. It flooded regularly—after winter storms or during the snowmelt of spring—but by summer's end, it could fade into a trickle, making it hard for farmers to irrigate. So, while the Aoulouz has certainly tempered the river's extremes, it's also a bit sad to have her so tamed."

Kowalski found himself nodding at this sentiment, preferring nature wild and as little touched by man as possible. *Let a river be a river.* But then, he wasn't the one whose house risked floating away during a flood or whose fields could dry up from lack of water.

Charlie continued with a wave to encompass the entire fertile val-ley between the High Atlas range to the north and the Anti-Atlas to the south. "It's said that long ago, millennia in the past, the Sous used to fill this entire area, making it a bay more than a river."

In the cabin, Gray glanced over at Seichan.

Even from the stern, Kowalski knew what the guy was thinking.

11:17 A.M.

Making it a perfect harbor for a seafaring people.

As the cruiser rumbled up the river, Gray imagined this whole valley flooded with water, mixing snowmelt with salty sea. He pictured a massive fleet anchored here, waiting to lay siege upon the Mediterranean.

In addition to the wide bay, each tributary cascading out of the mountains was likely its own river back then. He examined a stream they passed, leading up to a gorge lined by towering limestone cliffs. The sheer rock walls were set well back from the current flow, suggesting that the chasm had been cut ages ago by waterways much wider and stronger than today.

He checked the e-tablet in his hand, which glowed with a detailed chart of the Sous River system. He had done his best to estimate which tributary led into the mountains closest to the ruby marked on the gold map. He held it out toward Charlie.

"Do you know where this side channel is?"

Charlie took the tablet in one hand.

On her other side, Seichan offered an olive to Aggie. The monkey jumped to Seichan's shoulder to take it, then set about delicately peeling the skin off the fruit and nibbling the flesh around the pit.

Seichan hid an amused smile.

Quickly finished with the olive and spitting the pit aside, Aggie climbed down from his perch and clambered across Seichan's chest. He paused to sniff at one of her breasts, likely noting the slight whiff of milk, even though Seichan had pumped this morning.

Seichan's smile turned into a scolding frown. "No, you don't." She lifted the monkey up and returned the little guy to Charlie's shoulder. "That bar is closed for now."

Charlie passed back the tablet and gave Aggie, who looked deeply wounded, a small squeeze. "It's okay, *mon ami*. I'll get you a proper meal in a bit." She turned to Seichan. "Sorry about that. He's still barely out of his infancy. In macaque troops, the entire group raises their kids. Multiple females will even nurse the same baby."

"Not this wet nurse," Seichan said.

Aggie seemed to sense this rejection and tucked his face against Charlie's neck.

The captain turned to Gray. "That side river you marked. *Oui*, I know it. It is not far, another two miles up. It cuts far into the mountains, but my boat can only motor a mile into the ravine, maybe a bit farther if the snowmelt is strong."

He nodded.

Hopefully that'll be far enough.

Gray stepped out of the cabin to check in with Commander Pullman, letting him know their status. He also double-checked the ground-penetrating radar data from the last satellite pass. He zoomed in on the river gorge they were approaching. Like much of the mountains around here, the peaks and jagged massifs bordering the chasm were riddled with pockets. He picked out a couple of promising spots, but ultimately there was only one way to know for sure.

Go out there and have a look.

He stared at the river, again imagining this valley full of water, creating a massive bay and transforming these landlocked mountains into coastal ranges. If the channel marked on the map had been larger back then, too, it would have made for easy access to the sea.

Finally, Seichan called and waved him back.

He returned to the cabin. Ahead a wide, inflowing waterway entered the green expanse of the Sous. "Is that the one?" he asked.

Charlie nodded and expertly swung the cruiser around and aimed the bow into the mouth of the channel. The current in the narrower tributary proved stronger than the sluggish Sous. The outboard engine rumbled louder; the boat bobbled then straightened. Moments later, they were motoring up the side channel.

Gray leaned down to get a better view of the lay of the land ahead. Cliffs were set well back from either bank, suggesting the channel had indeed once been much wider. Past the band of farmland closest to the Sous, a surprisingly dense cedar forest climbed and spread across the floor of the shadowy gorge.

"Does this tributary have a name?" Seichan asked.

Charlie shrugged. "Nothing that's marked on any maps, but we Berbers have lived here for thousands of years. We have older names for every peak, valley, and rock around here." She nodded ahead. "This is called *Assif Azbar.*"

"Which means what?"

"Roughly *River of Sorrow.*" She glanced over. "For centuries, there have been stories of people vanishing up there. Place is considered to be haunted. Few come this way anymore."

Seichan glanced toward Gray. Her expression was easy to read:

If you're looking for the entrance to Hell . . . you picked the right river.

30

Still trapped aboard the *Morning Star,* Elena stood before the library's half circle of panoramic windows. She gaped at the monolithic limestone rock jutting four hundred yards above the sea. As the yacht passed close by it, the Rock of Gibraltar filled the entire expanse of glass.

"One of the Pillars of Hercules," Monsignor Roe commented beside her. "Easy enough to see how it got its name. Just the sheer size of it."

As the superyacht sped onward, the western side of the Rock came into view, revealing a sprawl of dockyards, piers, and the small city of Gibraltar huddled beneath the limestone cliffs and facing a little bay. She stared farther to the west. They'd be out of the strait in another thirty miles.

A little less than an hour.

From there, the city of Cádiz on the southern coast of Spain was the same distance again—which meant she was running out of time.

Monsignor Roe reminded her, "They'll want some better guidance soon. There are over sixty miles of coastline between Cádiz and Huelva."

She turned to the sprawl of books, notes, and maps spread across the library. Her heart pounded harder. Yesterday she had convinced her captors that the semi-mythic city of Tartessus—a site that much of the ancient world believed was Tartarus—lay somewhere along that stretch of the southern Iberian coast. Today her captors would want her help to narrow that search. Or at least offer some possible sites to explore.

But where?

She had hoped to have more time to come up with possible answers. Unfortunately, the *Morning Star* had a few tricks up its sleeve—or in this case, under its hull. She turned to the windows. With this section of the library cantilevered out from the main superstructure, she could make out the port-side foil cutting through the blue water.

Yesterday, after she had directed her captors here, the yacht had not spared its engines. It had sped away from the Tunisian coast, revealing what the prior three-hour cruise to Africa had not—that the yacht was a hydrofoil, a big brother to the little one that had ferried her here. Once under way at full speed, the *Morning Star* had risen up on twin foils and cut like a silver dagger across the Mediterranean.

Still, even under full power, it took the yacht more than sixteen hours to make the voyage to the strait. Elena had been hoping it would've taken longer, not only for her sake, but also to buy Joe's group extra time to solve a mystery going back millennia.

In the end, though, will it make any difference?

She had no idea if Joe and the others were making any progress. To help them, she needed to keep these bastards searching southern Spain for as long as possible, which meant sending them on a scavenger hunt, one convincing enough to keep them from looking in the true direction.

Even now, she cast her gaze to the south, trying to peer through the ship and down the west coast of Morocco. When the gold map had activated, she had been close enough to see the fiery river pass through the Pillars of Hercules and begin to bend *south*—not north.

She pictured the little ruby she had discovered along the Moroccan coast on the gold map, where according to the geologic record, no volcano existed. Its location was also consistent with the mazelike path between tectonic plates.

The latter still mystified her.

But she was certain about one thing. During Captain Hunayn's first voyage across the Mediterranean—when he sought Tartarus—he must have visited southern Iberia. Maybe he even discovered the rich city of Tartessus. How could he not at least go look for the place? Especially with all the history pointing this way. And if he did discover it, perhaps he learned something from Tartessus that directed him to the true home of the Phaeacians—or whatever that advanced culture was called. She could even guess what it was that he might have learned. From the stories of Tartessus, it was indeed a major bronze producer. Could they have been the ones who supplied the Phaeacians with the bronze necessary to help with the manufacture of the Phaeacians' mechanical constructs? Had the Phaeacians in turn paid the people of Tartessus with knowledge and tech? Was that why the city of Tartessus had been described as being Atlantis-like in advancements?

Elena's mind spun, making it hard to concentrate on the misdirection she needed to build, layer by layer, mixing truth and fiction until they were indistinguishable.

If I fail to deliver . . .

She pictured Rabbi Fine's body crumpling to the ground, the pool of blood spreading. She stared over to Monsignor Roe, remembering her father's threat: *the next death will not be so quick and merciful.*

Knowing this, she left the windows and returned to her stacks and piles of books. Somewhere in there were the answers she needed.

Roe joined her with a sigh. "If we don't figure something out, I fear our captors will lose patience, especially after days of searching the Spanish coast."

"Fat lot of good it'll do them," she said bitterly.

Roe turned to her, a quizzical look on his face. "What do you mean?"

She waved away his question. "Nothing. Just irritated."

He nodded and placed his palms on his hips. "Then where do we even begin?"

"I don't have a clue."

And I need one desperately.

11:31 A.M.

The forty-eighth Mūsā enjoyed the privileges afforded him—not just from his ambassadorship but also from his rank among the Apocalypti. He sat before the remains of a late breakfast, which included Beluga caviar on toast points, eggs with shaved black truffles. The plates and dinnerware were silver and gold.

Over the years, he had used his official role in the Turkish government to grift millions from his own country, from its military, from those who would trade with the United States. From the Apocalypti—with their near-bottomless global financial resources—he embezzled funds for personal gain, while building his own army to serve the cause.

Firat knew the man seated across the dining table did the same. Senator Cargill had his own aspirations. He had siphoned Apocalypti money into his personal campaign coffers—after some diligent laundering, of course. Firat did not begrudge Cargill his share of such riches, nor his ambitions. In fact, if the man ever became president, it would strengthen Firat's ambassadorship as much as it would serve the Apocalypti.

Cargill finished his glass of Syrah and checked his gold Patek Philippe wristwatch. "I should return to the communication room. The morning break at the EU summit must be close to ending. I have a noon panel on economic development in former East Bloc countries."

Firat stood and waved toward the doors of the suite, which occupied the entire top level of the yacht's superstructure. "I understand."

"As to the search along the Spanish coast, I may not be able to stay longer than another day. At some point, I'll need to fly back to Hamburg to take a few face-to-face meetings." He shrugged. "And I believe I've done all I can to motivate Elena."

Firat gave a brief bow of his head. "And we certainly have the tools at hand to keep her properly motivated."

"But I still insist that no harm come to her." Cargill's eyes flashed with an unspoken threat. "Is that also understood?"

Firat bristled but merely bowed his head again. "Of course."

Silently, Firat fumed. To calm himself, he imagined all manner of tortures he planned to inflict upon the woman. The last would be to leave her with Kadir for a night. But first, he would wring all he could from the senator's daughter. After that, after the tortures, the seas would wash away his crimes after he dumped her body. He would blame it on suicide.

What could this *kuffār* do?

The two of them stared at each other, as if each knew the other's heart.

The spell was broken by a knock on the door. Firat nodded to his personal butler, who crossed and opened the door. Nehir stalked in, leading another.

The newcomer pushed past, his face flushed with anger.

What's he doing here? What's wrong now?

Before Firat could inquire, the man blurted out, "Elena Cargill is lying. She's been playing you for fools all along."

12:18 P.M.

Elena already knew something was wrong.

Twenty minutes ago, Monsignor Roe had been dragged out brusquely by Kadir. The two had not yet returned. And now Nehir appeared behind the glass, her face glowing with a self-satisfied smirk that set Elena's heart to pounding. As the library door was unlocked, the yacht lurched, sending Elena dancing toward the bow to keep her feet.

Uh-oh.

Elena glanced out the windows. The *Morning Star* continued to slow, dropping swiftly as its twin foils sank into the sea.

Why are we stopping?

But she knew.

Nehir entered. "Follow me."

Elena had no choice, especially as the woman had come with two armed escorts out in the hall. Elena set down her reading glasses and headed out. Her limbs trembled as she followed. Her mouth had gone stone dry.

Nehir marched her over to the main stairwell and down into the ship's bowels. By the time they left the stairs, Elena could hardly breathe; tension strapped her chest in iron bands. They passed a few of Nehir's fellow Sons and Daughters, but none of them would make eye contact.

At last, they reached a steel hatch that stood ajar. Nehir opened it wider and waved her through first. Even now, Elena wanted to balk. She smelled burning coals. But guns pushed her across the hatch and into a room transported from some circle of Hell.

The walls were black steel. The floor was the same, with multiple drains for easy cleanup. All manner of blades—both small enough to dissect a frog and large enough to remove a limb—lined one side. On another wall hung studded whips, chains, and tools whose uses she was afraid to even imagine.

Across the room, the open mouth of a furnace glowed with a pile of coals, burning in gas-fed flames. It roared as she entered, heating the room to a stifling temperature. Before that fire, a steel X stood upright, angled slightly toward the furnace.

Upon that cross hung Monsignor Roe, his ankles and wrists cuffed in leather to the ends of the beams. They had gagged him and stripped off his shirt, exposing his thin chest, the concavity of his rib cage. His skin was already beaded with terror-borne sweat. His eyes looked with desperation at her, but also pity, as if she were the one about to suffer.

Kadir hunched behind the cross, stirring the coals with a long poker. To either side stood her father and Ambassador Firat.

Elena knew why she was here, what they wanted from her, what they would do to Monsignor Roe. "Daddy, don't do this."

Her father looked mournful but determined. "You are forcing our hand, my dear. You know that. We have it on good authority from an outside source that you have not been entirely truthful with us."

She swallowed, struggling for anything to say. "What . . . what do you . . . ? "

Firat swore in Arabic and waved to Kadir. The giant swung around with the poker, its end glowing a dark crimson. He stepped around the steel cross.

"Daddy, don't," she pleaded.

Her father turned his shoulder to her.

Kadir didn't taunt or tease. With a machinelike coldness, he pressed the end of the poker to the priest's right nipple. Flesh sizzled and smoked. Roe screamed through his gag, his back arching off the cross.

"Stop it!" she yelled. "Please stop it."

Kadir removed the poker, taking skin with it. Roe collapsed back down, hanging limply in his shackles. Tears ran down his face, blood down his belly.

"I *have* been lying," Elena admitted, choking down a sob.

She felt hollowed out, empty. She was too terrified, too guilt-ridden to offer any complicated fabrications. She dared not even try.

Firat stepped closer, scowling at her. "Then tell us where Hunayn truly went, where he discovered Tartarus." The man pointed to Monsignor Roe. "Or next will be his left eye. Then his tongue."

Roe lifted his chin, breathing raggedly. Still, he gave a small shake of his head, urging her not to speak.

Elena ignored him and did as she was told. In halting stops and starts, she explained everything, about activating the map, about what the fiery display revealed, about the ruby discovered along the Moroccan coast.

By the time she was done, she was on her knees, tears flowing down her face.

Her father patted her shoulder. She batted his hand away.

Firat turned to Nehir. "Ready the helicopter. I'll arrange a second one to transport a strike team with you. You'll need to find this place and lock it down. We'll follow behind in the *Morning Star* and be there by sunset."

Elena barely heard any of this. Men freed Monsignor Roe's limbs and removed the gag over his mouth. He could barely stand. Elena regained her feet and stumbled to the old man's aid.

"I'm sorry," she moaned. "So sorry."

Still gasping, Monsignor Roe lifted his head and turned to Firat.

"I told you she was lying."

FIFTH

THE GATES OF TARTARUS

And he bade famous Hephaestus make haste and mix earth with water and to put in it the voice and strength of human kind, and fashion a sweet, lovely maiden-shape, like to the immortal goddesses in face. . . . And he called this woman Pandora, because all they who dwelt on Olympus each gave a gift, a plague to men who eat bread.

—FROM HESIOD'S *WORKS AND DAYS*, 700 B.C. (TRANSLATION BY HUGH G. EVELYN-WHITE. *HESIOD, THE HOMERIC HYMNS, AND HOMERICA*. CAMBRIDGE, MASS., HARVARD UNIVERSITY PRESS; LONDON, WILLIAM HEINEMANN, 1914)

31

The lost city must be here somewhere.

Inside the cabin of the cruiser, Gray studied the satellite scans on his e-tablet. Over the past three hours, his team had stopped at four sites along the channel, where ground-penetrating radar had picked up cavern-ous pockets. But each proved to be a dead end. Literally. Just deep caves that petered out after short hikes.

Doubts had begun to set in.

He fought against them, trusting his instincts.

He shaded his eyes and surveyed their surroundings.

The drone of the outboard echoed off sheer limestone cliffs. The rock walls closed off the gorge to either side, climbing high in stratified layers of purples, whites, and multicolored hues of reds, topped by overhanging lips and broken-toothed edges.

Below and to either side, a dense forest of cedar and Algerian oak spread outward from the banks to the cliffs. As the channel carved higher into the mountains, its path grew more circuitous, its flow interrupted by cataracts. Its color was no longer the sluggish green of the Sous, but a ce-rulean blue of melting snow and spring-fed streams.

Charlie continued to expertly guide her boat up the narrowing channel, but she had to concentrate now. Her chatter had died away; even the macaque Aggie had grown quieter. Occasionally the cry of monkeys reached them, wild relatives of the little one here. Aggie's tiny ears would perk, but he only clung tighter to Charlie.

A new noise intruded, a thumping beat felt in the gut. A helicopter passed by overhead, crossing over the chasm and continuing north. Gray watched it pass. It was the third he'd seen.

"There's a popular tourist spot a few mountains over," Charlie explained with a deep frown. "Paradise Valley, it's called. Very beautiful. At least, it once was. Now it's becoming more and more polluted, like much of the region."

Ahead, disturbed by the noise of the helicopter, an ibis took flight from the shallows ahead and vanished over the treetops.

Charlie's gaze followed it. "There used to be much more wildlife in these mountains," she said with a forlorn tone. "Many have gone extinct. Atlas bears, North African elephants, and aurochs. And more threatened." She gave Aggie a little scratch with a finger. "With my degree, I hope to help stop that from happening in the future. But it's not just tourism impacting the area; more and more mines are opening up throughout these mountains."

"What are they mining for?" Gray asked, glancing again to the stratified cliffs.

"There's a lot of wealth buried here." She scowled. "Iron, lead, copper, silver."

As Gray stared out, he wondered what else might be *buried* here.

Seichan asked a question pertaining to that very matter. "What about uranium? Or other radioactive elements?"

The odd question drew Charlie's attention off the river. Her eyes squinted with suspicion. "Is that why you're here? Are you field scientists for a mining conglomerate? I saw you unpack what looked like a Geiger counter at that last stop."

Gray should have known nothing slipped past their keen-eyed river guide. In preparation for this excursion, he had asked Painter to supply the team with more than just weaponry. Boxed up along with their guns and ammunition had been a small Geiger counter.

Gray raised a hand against the angry look on Charlie's face. "No, I promise. We don't work for any mining company. But why the strong reaction?"

"*Pardon.* My apologies then." Charlie returned her attention to the river. "One of Morocco's major exports has always been phosphate rock. But interest in such deposits has spiked these past few years."

"Why is that?" Seichan asked.

"Because Moroccan phosphate contains *uranium*. In significant concentrations. Three-quarters of the world's phosphate is buried in these mountains. And it's said, the uranium held in those deposits is *twice* that of the entire rest of the globe."

Seichan glanced over to Gray and lifted an eyebrow.

Gray remembered Monsignor Roe's theory about the fuel powering the mechanical constructs aboard the ancient dhow. Roe believed the substance—which Hunayn and his brothers called "Medea's Oil"—could be a more powerful version of Greek Fire.

It was impossible to know for sure, since the recipe for making Greek Fire had been lost to antiquity, though it was generally believed to be some volatile combination of naphtha, quicklime, resin, and sulfur. But one other vital component was calcium phosphate, the main element in phosphate rock.

It made Gray wonder: *Could some ancient alchemist—using the phosphate rock here—have inadvertently enhanced this ancient recipe due to the uranium or some other radioactive contaminant found in these Moroccan deposits?*

A loud, grinding scrape of the boat drew his attention back to the river. Charlie cursed and fought the cruiser away from a submerged rock.

"Getting too shallow from here," Charlie said. "I can't take you any farther."

Gray checked his tablet. "There's another spot we'd like to check. A quarter mile up." He pointed ahead. "Around that next bend."

Charlie throttled down. "I can't risk my boat."

"We'll pay for any damages," Gray promised, knowing Painter would make good on it.

She scowled at him for a long breath, then inched the throttle forward. "*One* more stop."

The cruiser headed upriver, going half speed. It zigzagged around shoals of whitewater as Charlie stuck to deeper water. Even in those stretches, Gray could see the rocks and sand of the riverbed through the clear water. As they continued, the waters grew shallower. Rather than slowing further, Charlie sped the cruiser up.

He glanced over to her.

She never took her eyes off the channel, but she noted his attention. "Planing the hull," she explained. "Faster I go, the more this lady will lift out of the water. Gives me a bit more clearance from the bottom."

It looked like she needed every inch.

Gray gripped the rail along the starboard side of the cabin.

Charlie reached the bend in the waterway and expertly sailed her cruiser around it. Gray rechecked his coordinates on his e-tablet, then looked ahead.

"There," he said and pointed to a deeper pool of dark blue water to the right, where another stream flowed into the channel.

"Got it," Charlie said.

She sped her boat toward the bank, and with a final grind of the boat's keel over rock, slid into the deeper pool.

"Nice," Seichan said.

Charlie cut the throttle and glided the boat's bow to a gentle stop, nudging the nose onto a cushion of sand. She turned to Gray. "Last stop, *oui*?"

Gray looked up the main channel, which ran with whitewater from one bank to the other. "I think we've pushed our luck as far as it can go."

He turned to search up the tiny tributary stream. The clear water ran over polished black pebbles and stretches of brighter sand, passing through a fringe of cedar forest. Upstream, a cascade tumbled over a ten-story cliff.

He pointed to the top of the falls. "See how the rock is scalloped at the cliff's edge, worn by centuries of flowing water over its lip? It's far wider than can be accounted for by the volume of the stream tumbling over the rock."

"That's consistent with what Charlie told us, how this whole area was once far wetter. The Sous River more of a bay. And its tributaries robust torrents."

Mac took several steps away and drew Maria with him. "Look at this." He pointed up toward the cliff and swept to the north. "Follow the cliff edge and what do you see?"

By now the others had returned, drawn by their voices.

"What are you all looking at?" Gray asked.

Maria finally saw it, too. "Other scallops along the rim of the wall."

He nodded. "Long ago, not only was *this* stream larger, but there were others that once flowed down here that have long since dried up. By my count, five."

Mac pictured how this must have once looked, with five mighty waterfalls flooding into a large river flowing down to a wide bay. The whole area must have shone with scores of rainbows. The mist-shrouded cliffs were likely covered in greenery and full of nesting birds. The forests taller, roamed by lumbering elephants and lions.

Father Bailey interrupted his reverie. "Five rivers . . ." he mumbled.

Mac glanced over. "What about them?"

Bailey pointed from the falls back to the channel where the cruiser and its captain waited for them. "Charlie called this tributary *Assif Azbar*. The River of Sorrow. But there was another river that bore a similar name. It struck me before, but I didn't place much significance on it, attributing the association to simple poetic license, especially with the history of people vanishing up here. But now, knowing that another *four* rivers had once flowed through this area, it makes me wonder."

Gray pressed him. "About what?"

"Another river once went by that same name as the tributary behind us. The mythic Acheron. Known to be the river of sorrow, pain, and woe."

The priest turned to the group. "It was one of the *five* rivers that passed through Tartarus leading to the heart of Hades. They were the Acheron, the Lethe, the Phlegethon, the Cocytus, and lastly, the river Styx."

Gray took a deep breath, stepping forward, craning up. "Whether you're right or not, Mac's keen eye has offered us another four places to search. And if those five waterfalls once graced this corner of the chasm, I know where I'd place the entrance to my underground city."

He pointed to the centermost scallop in the cliff.

Seichan drew alongside him. "It appears to be the widest and deepest, too."

Mac pictured a huge waterfall flanked by two more on either side.

Gray clapped Mac on his good shoulder. "That's where we need to go."

32

From the back of the helicopter, Elena watched the city of Marrakesh drop away as their chopper headed off from a refueling stop in the city. As it climbed higher, she spotted a glint of a snow-crowned mountain forty miles to the south. It was Mount Toubkal, the tallest peak of the High Atlas range, rising nearly fourteen thousand feet into the sky.

The helicopter angled away from that notable peak. A second aircraft—an identical Eurocopter EC155—followed behind. Both helicopters headed in a southwesterly trajectory toward those same mountains, aiming for where that jagged range tumbled into the Atlantic Ocean.

Another hour at best, maybe less.

That's how long Elena had to come up with some plan.

She leaned back into her seat. The Eurocopter's cabin held a dozen passengers, mostly the Sons and Daughters of Mūsā, including Nehir, who was seated by the far window, and Kadir, hunched opposite his sister. But directly across from Elena, the traitor Monsignor Roe drowsed within his seat's restraints, his head lolling back and forth in motion with the flight. When he had boarded, his pupils had been huge, indicative of a strong dose of morphine. The large bulge seen through his thin shirt was a thick wad of bandage.

Elena had no choice in making this trip, but from the conversation that the cleric had with Ambassador Firat before boarding, Roe had insisted on coming. He intended to see where his treachery led, believing he could still be of help in pinpointing the location marked with a ruby on the Banū Mūsā map.

The one person she had *not* spotted before the helicopter lifted off the yacht's helipad was her father. There was no final farewell with him. Had shame kept him away or simply matters of state at the EU summit? She wondered if she'd ever see him again. She even felt a reflexive pang at this thought. She still had trouble reconciling the man she had known for thirty years with the one who'd shown his true colors these past two days. It was hard to let go of that past.

And maybe we will meet again.

She pictured the *Morning Star* racing south from the Strait of Gibraltar, flying along the Moroccan coast atop its twin hydrofoils. She knew neither Firat nor her father would miss out being close if anything was discovered hidden in those mountains.

The helicopter hit a turbulent air pocket, jarring up and down, enough to stir Monsignor Roe, who winced and straightened. His glassy eyes noted Elena's dark attention toward him.

"Do not be so troubled, my child," Roe said, his words slurring slightly. "You will help us herald the return of the Lamb to this foul world. The shattering of the gates of Tartarus will mark the beginning of Armageddon. The infernal weapons and radioactive hellfire will be unleashed at hot spots around the globe, destabilizing region after region, igniting war after war, until the very seas are set aflame. Only then will the world be purged of its wickedness and the Lord's throne purified for His return. With His coming, a true and lasting peace can finally be upon us all."

Elena scowled. "Tell that to all those killed at Castel Gandolfo. Tell that to Rabbi Fine."

"All martyrs." Roe waved a hand, dismissing her concern. "Howard knew what he was doing, knew the importance of sacrifice. He even shot his own ear, both to convince the Americans we were kidnapped and to help earn your sympathy."

Elena leaned her head back, suddenly dizzy. *Even Rabbi Fine.* She knew the two clerics had known each other since their university days, but she had never suspected the rabbi was part of all of this, too. Still, she should have. She remembered her father's story, how the Apocalypti had members in all religions, even others who had no faith.

Roe continued: "Your father acted rashly—more in fury than rationality—in taking Howard's life so suddenly. But it was an effective demonstration of our commitment."

Aghast at such coldheartedness, Elena turned away. She had been a fool earlier in the library. Exhausted, she had an unfortunate slip of the tongue. When the monsignor had pressed her about where to search along the Spanish coast, she had said something stupid: *Fat lot of good it'll do them.* It must have been enough to show her hand, to reveal the search for the city of Tartessus had been a ruse. Shortly after that, Roe had taken one of his many restroom breaks—he was an old man. She had no reason to make anything of it. And it wasn't another fifteen minutes after he returned that Kadir had dragged him off again.

I never put two and two together.

"Still, Howard was not the only one who understood *sacrifice.*" Roe glanced down at his chest, heat entering his words. "In your stubbornness, you failed to learn the lesson your father tried to teach you with that gunshot. You still lied. And it was I who had to bear the pain of your deceit."

His eyes found hers again. Only now a fire burned behind the glaze of the morphine. "But *sacrifices* are necessary. I know this well. I was the one who convinced the Americans to bring the Daedalus Key to Castel Gandolfo, to see if it could be useful to us. When it proved not, when the Americans could offer no better insight, I was the one who called down the air strike upon my own head."

Elena noted the fervent passion growing in the monsignor's voice, the speckle of spittle on his lips. The glow in his eyes had turned fanatical.

The pain meds had clearly let loose what the man had hidden for so long, clearly also making him more talkative.

"Only when the Americans proved clever enough to escape the vaults below Castel Gandolfo did my faith in them momentarily return. Needing to remove them from the protective shield dropped around Castel Gandolfo, I brought them to Sardinia, to my ally Rabbi Fine. I wanted to test them one last time, offering what we knew, seeing if they could come up with any new insight. But alas, again nothing."

"So you tried to eliminate them and secure the Da Vinci map."

"And the original Daedalus Key. How could I not?"

"When that failed, you came to Firat's yacht to run the same scam on me."

"Yes, but you proved far more clever." His gaze sharpened, his eyes ablaze with a zealous fire. "You shall see. Soon all my sacrifices will bear righteous fruit. My pain will be my badge when the Lord returns."

She turned away from those fanatical flames. She imagined the monsignor had been a member of the Apocalypti far longer than Firat or her father—two who believed themselves to be either Mahdi returned or King David reborn. Still, neither of them could match the manic zeal in the man seated across from her.

And I've pointed them all to a cache of mythic weapons, along with an unknown power source, that could in the wrong hands ignite a holy war.

She held out one hope.

She prayed Joe and the others had used the bronze rods to unlock their version of the map, that they'd somehow already secured the site.

Don't let me down, Joe.

33

"Over here!" Kowalski called to the others.

The group had spread out along the base of the cliff and gathered toward him.

With his fists on his hips, he studied the stretch of wall. The rocky layers looked like a scattered stack of newspapers, crookedly aligned, some rippled, others torn. The team had already searched the dry spillway closest to the waterfall and had moved on to the next, the centermost of what was once five rivers toppling over the cliff.

This one had plainly been a monster from the size of the divot in the cliff's edge. Easily thirty yards across.

"What did you find?" Gray asked.

Kowalski pointed fifteen feet up the cliff face. "Look at that pile of rocks sitting on that broken ledge. To the left of it, I think there's a crack in the wall."

Gray squinted.

Seichan shaded her eyes. "He's right. I'll go check."

Before anyone could object, she scaled her way up. The strata below the ledge stuck out haphazardly, creating a series of crooked giant steps, offering a crude stairway up to the crack.

"I guess I could've done that," Kowalski groused.

Seichan reached the top and vanished inside. Gray paced a few nervous steps back and forth.

Mac stared up. "If this valley truly had been flooded long ago, the water level here might have reached that ledge. Look at the slight difference in coloration of the rock layers below the ledge compared to above it. They're a more grayish white. Even the lower strata look smoother than those above. Likely worn by waters long dried up."

Kowalski tried to imagine it. He pictured a ship sailing over his head and tying up to the ledge above.

Maybe the guy's right.

Seichan popped back into view and burst all their bubbles. "It's a dead end here, too."

Gray swore under his breath.

Seichan waved. "But I think you all should come up and see this anyway."

Gray cupped his mouth and called. "What did you find?"

"Just come see." She turned and slipped back through the crack.

Gray looked at the group.

Kowalski shrugged. "I could stand to get out of the sun."

With the matter settled, they all clambered up the broken steps. Up top, the ledge was bigger than it looked from below, some sixty feet across. The rock pile filled most of it, likely from an old landslide. Directly above, the lip at the cliff edge had a huge section missing.

Gray led them to the edge of the pile. Kowalski's *crack* was actually an opening between the broken rocks and the limestone wall of the cliff. A precarious boulder had jammed above it ages ago, holding this narrow way open.

Gray went first, then Kowalski ducked under the boulder, holding his breath. Once past it, he hurried into a large cavern on the far side. It was as wide as the ledge and twice as deep. Seichan already had her flashlight out and splayed its bright beam across the arch of roof and the curve of its walls, all a coarse dark brown, a little pocket worn long ago into the rock.

The others crowded in behind Kowalski.

Father Bailey scowled back at the hanging boulder. "Like passing under the Sword of Damocles."

Mac grinned. "It's actually called a *boulder ruckle,* where a rockfall creates a precarious jam of stones. Can be dangerous, but I suspect that particular pile of rocks has been there for several centuries, so it's not likely to fall anytime soon."

"What did you want us to see?" Gray asked, clearly dejected to reach yet another dead end.

"Over here," Seichan said.

She stepped toward the back of the cavern. On the left side stood a row of clay pots, each standing waist-high with little dusty lids on top.

"There's more over there," Seichan said, pointing her beam to the other side, where another cluster of jars stood.

Mac drew closer to one, a grimace carved deep on his face. "These look like smaller versions of what I saw aboard the dhow in Greenland."

"They're amphorae," Bailey said. "Greek and Roman storage pots. For wine, for olive oil."

"Or something far worse," Mac said, straightening.

The priest turned to Kowalski. "Didn't you mention that Captain Hunayn, in his journal, called them Pandora's pots?"

"That's what Elena told me."

Bailey looked at the others. "According to the myth, Pandora was not a real woman, but something artificially created by the god Hephaestus."

"Like those bronze slaves of his," Kowalski said, remembering Elena's story of the mechanical women who served Hephaestus at his forge.

"The gods of Olympus each put curses into a pot," Bailey said. "And gave it to Pandora to deliver to mankind. Sort of a pretty Trojan horse full of death, disease, and misery."

"Definitely matches the description of what was in the dhow's hold," Mac said.

Maria frowned. "But I thought it was Pandora's *box,* not Pandora's *pot.*"

"No, that came about because of a mistranslation of Greek," Bailey explained. "The original Greek word was *pithos,* a sealed jar for storage. But in the sixteenth century, that word got bastardized into *pyxis,* which means 'box,' and it never got corrected."

"Box or pot," Kowalski said. "It looks like we're at the right place or close to it."

"Maybe," Gray said. "But not without checking what's in those jars."

"You want to open one of those damned things?" Mac asked.

Gray stepped forward. "It's the only way we'll know for sure."

Mac tried to block him. "Don't—"

Gray sidestepped him and kicked out with his leg, slamming his heel hard into one of the pots. Even with the guy's considerable strength, the impact only rocked the pot and managed a thin crack.

"Maybe you should heed Mac's warning," Bailey said.

Gray ignored them both and tried again, hitting square into the crack. The pot finally shattered into halves. A black oil spilled across the floor. They all danced away as if a nest of snakes had been let loose.

A strong petroleum odor filled the cavern.

Mac pointed. "That's the same stuff that came flowing out of the pots in Greenland."

"But that's all there is," Seichan commented, the only one to draw closer.

Kowalski followed her. "She's right. No bronze crabs, no green fiery goo."

As a group, they all turned toward the clutch of pots on the other side of the cave. Glances were exchanged, and they all headed over there.

Except for Father Bailey, who stopped to examine a two-foot-high slab in the center of the floor. He ran his hand over a scooped section in the middle. "Like a sacrificial altar," he mumbled.

Kowalski gladly skipped past there.

As they drew near the other set of pots, no one spoke.

A sharp *click-clicking* rose from Mac's handheld Geiger counter. Once closer, it ticked faster.

Kowalski grabbed Gray's arm. "Maybe let's not break these."

5:24 P.M.

Safecracking is all a matter of delicacy.

Seichan passed the hot tip of her knife along the edge of the pot's lid. The heat softened and melted through the wax seal. She scraped a bit loose, then held the blade out toward Maria.

The woman thumbed a lighter, raising a flame.

Seichan hovered the knife tip over the fire, heating it back up.

"Men," Maria commented. "Always going around smashing things. I hope you raise Jack with a little more common sense."

"I'll do my best," Seichan said, hoping that ended up being true. "Though half his DNA is Gray's, so you never know."

Seichan returned to her efforts, working more of the wax free.

Behind her, bored by her meticulous efforts or too nervous to stand idly by, the men had joined Father Bailey over by the slab on the floor.

"What do you make of it?" Gray asked, down on a knee.

"I thought it might be some sort of altar or ritual place of sacrifice," the priest said. "But now I'm wondering . . ."

"About what?" Gray asked.

As Seichan melted through a thicker layer of wax, the top wobbled under her palm. "Got it," she announced, glancing back at the men.

Gray came over, drawing the others. He waved Mac up front. "What do you think?"

The climatologist tested his Geiger counter. "Readings still holding steady. In the safe range, but we don't want to hang around here forever."

Gray nodded to Seichan. "You can do the honors."

She grabbed the lid with both hands. She rocked it back and forth and turned it enough to break the residual wax—then lifted it straight up.

Gasps rose behind her. The clicking on the Geiger sped up.

They all retreated from the glistening green oil filling the pot. It cast out a wan, sickly glow. Seichan crouched, ready if anything horrid should burst or crawl out of the toxic soup. After several breaths, it was clear nothing was coming out.

"I think it's just the liquid," Gray said. "Like the pots on the other side."

Bailey inched forward. "In Captain Hunayn's journal, he stated that on his first voyage to Tartarus his crew only went as far as the city's threshold, due to his lack of supplies. But at that entrance, he collected jars of what he called Medea's Oil and returned home with them."

Hmm . . .

Seichan moved away from the others.

"I don't think it's wise to leave the contents exposed to air for long," Bailey warned. "Hunayn named this Medea's Oil for a reason. According to the mythology of the sorceress Medea, her oil held the secret to an unquenchable fire, a gift given to her by the Titan, Prometheus, who taught her how to store it in *airtight* golden caskets."

"Not unlike these pots," Gray said.

"One of which is no longer airtight," Mac reminded them.

Bailey continued: "It's said her oil—like the legend of Greek Fire—was ignited by water and could not be put out by it." He pointed to the amphorae. "While it's dry enough in here, I fear if exposed too long . . . with these many pots . . ."

"Kaboom," Kowalski added.

"He could be right," Mac said. "Back in Greenland the crabs ignited fairly quickly, but the air was damp and full of ice crystals."

"Then let's close the jar for now," Gray suggested. "At least limit the exposure to any moisture in the air."

"No," Seichan warned. "Not yet."

She reached the back of the cavern and ran her palms over the curve of the dark brown wall. Its surface was coarse, but far too uniform. They'd all missed it, their attentions too caught up by the mysterious jars and altar.

She lifted her steel dagger and pounded its hilt against the wall.

The gong announced her discovery.

She turned to the others. "We're not in a rock cave, but a bronze chamber, long tarnished and blackened with age." She pointed her blade at the pots. "If that's where Hunayn stole his magical oil, then this must be the entrance to Tartarus."

The others hurried toward her and ran their hands along the tarnished walls, confirming her discovery.

"She's right," Gray said, rapping his knuckle to prove it. Others did the same, confirming his suspicion. "It's not just the back wall. The entire cavern is bronze. One seamless bubble of it."

Kowalski raised the question that most needed answering. "Enough with all the knocking. How do we get in?"

Father Bailey returned to the altar. "I . . . I think I know." He turned to them all. "This is a test."

5:30 P.M.

And apparently a timed one.

Gray stared over at the open clay jar. With the jar's seal broken, the glowing oil could ignite at any time. He turned to Bailey. "What are you thinking?"

The priest dropped to a knee by the altar and ran his palm over the depression in the center. "This slab is rock, but I think the shallow basin is the same tarnished bronze."

"But what does any of that have to do with opening a gateway here?" Seichan asked.

"Heron of Alexandria," Bailey said firmly, as if making a point.

No one got it.

"He was a brilliant engineer from the first century A.D. He designed all manner of devices, including the first vending machine, operated by the drop of a coin. Also a wind-powered pipe organ. He wrote volumes of works on the subject that I wager the Banū Mūsā brothers—collectors of scientific knowledge, with a penchant for mechanical inventions—read centuries later. Even Da Vinci references him."

"What does any of that have to do with our situation?" Gray pressed, glancing again toward the glowing pot.

And be quick about it.

"One of Heron's inventions was the means to magically open the doors to a temple using a crude version of a steam engine. A priest would speak to a crowd on the steps of a closed temple, then a fire would be lit in a hearth in front of the place. Once it got blazing hot, the fire would heat a water system buried underneath the hearth. The resulting steam would move pistons, wheels, and ropes, and the temple doors would seem to magically open on their own."

"In other words, a trick," Kowalski said.

Bailey pointed to the basin, then to the back wall. "Like this one."

"How can you be sure?" Maria asked.

"According to Homer, the palace of the Phaeacians was built of solid bronze and the gates into the city, when opened, were said to '*blaze like fiery gold.*'"

Gray began to understand. "If a fire was lit in this altar basin, ablaze with flames from that fuel—" He pointed to the glowing pot containing the secret to an unquenchable golden flame. "Then the bronze here would shine as if made of gold."

Bailey nodded. "That's why I think this is a test. The Phaeacians have given us the tools, the fuel. It's up to us to prove we understand the properties of what's in these jars before being allowed to pass inside."

"What do we do?" Kowalski asked. "Just pour some of that Medea Oil in the bowl and add water?"

"I think so," Bailey said.

Gray shook his head. "No, that's just *one* side of the coin." He pointed to the broken jar on the other side of the room and the black spill around it. "That's the other. Why else place those out here, too?"

"You may be right," Bailey admitted. "But what is that substance?"

The answer came from an unexpected source. "Elena had an idea," Kowalski said. "She called it the pharmacopoeia of Prometheus's Blood."

That can't be right.

It wasn't.

"Do you mean '*pharmaka of Promethean Blood*'?" Bailey asked.

Kowalski shrugged. "Sure, why not?"

The priest turned to the group. "In that same story about Medea—

where she learned the formula for her fiery oil from Prometheus—she also learned the *pharmaka*, the recipe, for a black potion called Promethean Blood. It was derived from the sap of a plant that grew out of the spilled blood of Prometheus. She gave it to Jason to protect him from the fires of the bronze Colchis bulls."

"Like some fire-resistant lubricant," Mac said. "Back in Greenland, the black oil did quench the fires driving those creatures. And I think the oil in the storage pots served as some sort of preservative or insulation, keeping the creatures in an inert form until freed and exposed to wet air."

Seichan frowned. "But what does any of this have to do with unlocking the gate?"

Gray walked back to the altar and looked between the two sets of pots. *Medea developed both the fire and the means to douse it.* He squinted at Mac. *No, not just douse it, but also preserve and insulate the green oil.*

Gray turned to Bailey. "I'm guessing that basin in the altar was not an arbitrary size. If there's some complicated mechanics under it, the bronze bowl likely must be heated to the proper degree."

"I suppose."

"I think we're supposed to add just the right amount of fuel to the basin, likely fill it to the brim."

"Like a measuring cup," Kowalski added.

"But how do you transfer the oil from the jars to the bowl?" Gray said. "There are no ladles or pails."

"By hand," Bailey said, straightening sharply. "That's why the jars of Promethean Blood are here. If we coat our hands with it, then it should insulate the moisture in our palms from igniting the green oil. We can fill the basin handful by handful."

The priest looked around the room, plainly asking for a volunteer to test his theory.

Kowalski groaned. "I'll do it. I'm Sigma's demolitions expert. But if my hands get blown off, I'm blaming you, padre."

Kowalski crossed to the broken pot. A large shard still cradled a pool of the black oil. He dunked his hands to his wrists, coating everything thickly. He then hurried to the glowing pot.

"Be careful," Maria said.

"There's nothing careful about this," Kowalski said. "Let's just hope this black stuff also protects against radiation."

"It might," Bailey whispered. "A draught of Promethean Blood taken before battle was said to protect against all damage, even from arrows and spears. It worked for Jason of the Argonauts."

"Do I look like some mythic superhero?" Kowalski said with a scowl.

Still, Kowalski took a deep breath, then plunged his hands into the glowing green oil. He turned his face away, as if expecting flames to burst forth. But nothing happened. He let out his breath and scooped up a load between both hands. He lifted his arms and waited for any residual drips to stop falling.

"Now what?" he asked.

"Carefully transfer it to the basin," Bailey said.

They all held their breaths as Kowalski walked his glowing load over to the bronze bowl. He bent to pour it in.

"Wait!" Gray said. "Stop!"

Still bent over, Kowalski glowered at him. "What?" he growled.

Gray hurried over to the broken pot and shoveled out two handfuls of black oil. He ran back and slathered it across the surface of the basin. "I don't know if this is still necessary, but if this place was once far wetter, then you probably had to insulate Medea's Oil from touching any residual dampness in the bronze bowl."

"Good," Bailey said. "Better safe than sorry."

Once Gray stepped back, Kowalski glared at him. "*Now* can I dump this load?"

Gray waved everyone else back. "Do it."

With a cringe, Kowalski parted his palms and let the glowing oil flow into the basin. No one moved for a breath.

When nothing happened, Gray waved to Kowalski. "Again."

It took several trips, and Gray helped him, but eventually the bowl churned with the green oil, filled to its brim. Once done, Gray also transferred some of the black oil to the open green pot and covered the glowing oil with a top slurry of the black, hopefully creating a barrier against any moisture in the air, and put the top back on.

Satisfied, he waved everyone to the far side and took the water bottle from his pack. "Ready?" he asked.

He got nods all around and a shrug from Kowalski.

Gray faced the basin. From a couple of yards away, he squeezed the bottle, sending an arc of water through the air. It splashed into the basin.

The effect was immediate.

The entire pool of oil ignited with a blast of smoke and thunder. A spiral of golden flame shot to the roof, splaying across the surface of the tarnished dome. The fountain of fire blazed for several breaths. They shielded their faces from the blinding light and from the furnace blast of heat.

After what seemed like a minute, but was likely only a few seconds, the flames receded. They no longer reached the roof but continued to dance high above the basin.

Kowalski took a step closer. "Nice fireworks," he said and waved an arm beyond the flames. "But nothing is—"

A booming gong sounded, loud enough to make them all duck.

Beyond the basin, the back wall cracked down the middle. With a muffled grinding of distant gears, the two halves slowly drew back, sweeping away like a pair of bronze wings, welcoming them into the darkness beyond.

"We did it," Maria gasped out.

"That's right," Kowalski said, sounding far less pleased. "We just opened the gates of Hell."

34

From the cabin of the Eurocopter, Nehir studied the gorge below through a set of binoculars. Her team had reached the Sous River valley five minutes ago. She had not wanted to waste a minute—not after waiting for so long. She had immediately set course along a smaller tributary draining into the larger Sous River, one that Monsignor Roe had highlighted on a chart, the most likely path to the ruby imbedded in the gold map.

As they flew into the mountains, her heart pounded in her chest. She remembered holding little Huri—*my little angel*—before the child was ripped away. She had just given birth, still in pain, her body covered in sweat, but what joy she had felt when her baby was placed on her chest. Huri had been a hot ember that warmed her all the way down to her heart. She closed her eyes, again hearing her angel wail as she was taken from her arms—until that cry was cut off by the sharp edge of a knife. The same blade that would forever disfigure Nehir. But it was not that scar that pained her the most.

She opened her eyes with a cold promise.

I will hold you again, Huri . . . and my little boy.

The pilot came over the private channel on her helmet's radio. "There's a boat ahead. Beached at the side of the river."

Nehir focused her attention.

Could it be them?

The helicopter swept high. Through her binoculars, Nehir got a good look at a small aluminum cruiser with a tiny cabin. She spotted a woman at the stern, who glanced up, shading her eyes—then returned her attention to an outboard motor. It didn't appear anyone else was aboard.

"Just a local," Nehir radioed back. "Keep heading up."

She continued to search the landscape below. Monsignor Roe did the same on his side. They were searching for any evidence of ancient habitation: a crumble of walls, a broken tower, a bit of foundation. Anything that might hint at the presence of a lost civilization. The plan was to run the length of the gorge by air, then do a more thorough search on foot. The team had access to ground-penetrating radar scans of the region, pointing to possible locations to look, though there were many. She hoped an aerial survey would help narrow the team's search area.

A commotion drew her attention from the passing scenery.

She lowered her binoculars and looked past her brother to the helicopter's cockpit. The copilot leaned back into the cabin and excitedly waved an arm back the way they'd come. His radioed words reached her, full of excitement.

It set her own heart to pounding harder.

"Find a place to land," she ordered. She pictured the little cruiser at the side of the river. "Radio the other aircraft to head back. To land south of that aluminum boat."

She wanted the enemy pinned down between her two forces.

She turned and faced Elena, enjoying the frightened look on the woman's face.

Now it comes to an end.

5:55 P.M.

From the excited chatter between Nehir and the cockpit crew, Elena knew something had drastically changed. But the low roar of the engines drowned out whatever was exchanged. Still, from the savage gleam in Nehir's eyes as she faced the cabin, it was not good.

Elena wasn't the only one to notice this.

Across from her, Monsignor Roe turned from the window and called over to Nehir. "What is it?"

Nehir's gaze remained fixed on Elena. "We just picked up a signal!" she yelled back. "The Americans are already here."

A signal?

Roe stiffened. "How? Where are they?"

Nehir pointed back the way they'd come. "It looks like they've found something."

Elena sank back into her seat, her mouth going dry. She stared across the cabin at Roe. It seemed the monsignor wasn't the only traitor.

Someone else in Joe's group was also a spy.

35

Kowalski zipped up and headed back into the cave. He was followed shortly by Mac and Father Bailey.

Much better . . .

"I'm ready," he announced to the others.

Maria shook her head as she and Seichan readied their gear, clicking on flashlights. "What is it about men who feel the need to pee off anything higher than a ladder?"

Kowalski resented her words. "Charlie's little boat didn't have a bathroom. A guy can hold it for only so long."

Across the cave, Gray stood at the open gate and shone his beam into the depths of Hell. "Look at this," he called back.

The group gathered their packs, picked up flashlights, and joined him.

Behind them, the altar still danced high with golden flames, but their combined beams revealed a sight flanking both sides of the open gateway. They moved past the threshold to get a closer look. Two hulking bronze shapes, twice Kowalski's height, sat on massive haunches, their fronts balanced atop turkey-platter-sized paws armed with silver scythes for claws. Far above, snouted heads hung low, their muzzles resting on their chests, as if asleep. But black diamond eyes remained forever open, staring down at those gathered below.

Bailey mumbled softly, as if fearing to wake the beasts. " '*On either side there stood gold and silver mastiffs . . .* '"

Kowalski recognized the line. Elena had recited it from the *Odyssey*. "The dogs that guarded the Phaeacians' gates."

"This must be them," Bailey said, his eyes shining with awe, reflecting the flames still dancing on the altar. "The story of these dogs must have eventually reached Greece, passed from one generation to another, until ultimately becoming part of Homer's story."

"Which makes you wonder what else might be true," Gray said, sounding both excited and worried.

"Only one way to find out." Kowalski pointed his flashlight ahead, where the tunnel into the mountain curved away. The passage was large enough to drive an Abrams battle tank down its throat.

Before heading out, Gray glanced back to the tarnished bronze cave. "Someone should remain here. If that fire goes out, those doors may close on their own."

Trapping us in hell? Yeah, let's not do that.

"I'll stay," Seichan volunteered.

Gray looked like he wanted to argue. He even scanned the group. But he knew the truth as well as Kowalski. They needed someone to have their back, someone they trusted, especially if all hell broke loose—which, in this case, might actually happen.

Gray finally nodded. "Let's go."

They set off down the dark tunnel.

Maria sidled next to Kowalski and slipped her hand into his. "You do take me interesting places."

"Yeah?"

She nodded ahead. "This time to hell and back."

"Glad you're thrilled." He squeezed her fingers. "But I'm looking forward to the *and back* part."

6:04 P.M.

From the stern of her cruiser, Charlie watched a helicopter roar past overhead and head down the channel. It was a summer weekend, and tour companies were clearly busy ferrying people from the swelter of Agadir to the cool pools and freshwater springs of nearby Paradise Valley to the north.

Still, she felt something was off. The helicopter looked like one of the two that had passed by a minute ago.

If so, why is it heading back so soon?

Could there have been an emergency aboard? As she watched it pass, she heard a change in the timbre of its engines. It circled wider, then lowered, as if trying to land in one of the meadows downstream.

If they're in distress, maybe I should go see if they need help?

She checked her watch. The others had been gone a long time. She had no idea when they were planning to return. She had caught a brief glimpse of them climbing the cliff and vanishing into a cave. Who knew how deep that one went?

She probably had time to motor over to the helicopter, but she feared she might not be able to navigate back to this spot to retrieve her passengers.

And, more important, she still felt something was not right. If there was an emergency, why hadn't the other helicopter come back with this one?

No, something is wrong.

She headed to the cruiser's cabin to retrieve her binoculars, intending to get a better view of that aircraft when it landed.

Aggie chirped at her from his little bed, littered with olive pits.

"It's okay, *mon chéri.*"

She grabbed the binoculars hanging from a hook. Before she could turn and head back to the stern, motion in the woods beyond her bow drew her eye.

She instinctively ducked lower and lifted her binoculars.

In the distance, dark shapes swept furtively through the cedar forest, heading her way. They came with raised rifles. At least nine or ten.

Merde, she swore.

Were they thieves? Cutthroats? Slavers?

As terror iced through her, she thought quickly. She needed to alert the others. But how? She reached to the pistol holstered at her waist. A warning shot into the air might signal her passengers, but it would also alert the enemy that she was armed.

Better not.

As it was, she was already outgunned and outnumbered.

Instead, she unstrapped her holster, searched around, and tucked her pistol under Aggie's bed. The monkey already sensed something was wrong and hopped to her shoulder. Charlie feared for his safety, knowing he'd likely be shot on sight. She carried Aggie to the open side window of the cabin, opposite from the approach of the armed men.

She lifted Aggie and pushed him out. He scrabbled to get back in with her, clinging to the sill.

"No," she scolded and pointed. "Hide. In the forest."

His little face knotted up with fear.

What am I going to do?

Then she had an idea. She had raised Aggie from an infant, nursing him with a bottle. He knew the word *milk* all too well. She had even taught him to fetch his own bottle when it had been time to feed him.

She pictured the woman named Seichan and Aggie's extreme interest in her earlier. She stepped back, cupped one breast, and pointed to the cliffs. "Find momma," she said. "She has a milk bottle for you."

The word had the desired effect. Fear became hope in his face.

"That's right." She gently freed him and pushed him toward the beach. "Go get your milk bottle."

He looked between her and the cliff, hesitating, balanced between fear of leaving her and the hope of a warm meal that always meant safety and love.

"Go on now."

He let out a tiny eek and leaped away. He immediately vanished into the fringe of the forest. She knew macaques had a sharp sense of smell. Hopefully Aggie could use it to follow the trail to the others.

She stared out into the forest, hearing the tread of footfalls on the other side of the boat.

Run, my little lion, run.

6:09 P.M.

Seichan paced in a slow circle around the flaming pyre. She had watched the others vanish down the large tunnel, each of their lights blinking out around the bend in the passage.

How long would they be?

Each time she drew abreast of the tunnel, her ears strained for any hint of a problem. For gunfire, shouts, explosions. But all she heard was the low roar of the fire behind her. It echoed in the confined space, like some trapped beast. At least it was growing less intense. The flames had dropped to the height of her shoulders as the oil in the bronze basin was slowly consumed.

She made another circle.

As she reached the boulder pile, a noise drew her attention to the cave opening. A frantic scrabbling of claws on stone rose from outside. She remembered Mac's description of the bronze crabs.

She crouched, lifting her SIG P320.

From around the edge of the rocks, a small shape bounded into view. It came around fast, bouncing off the wall and hurling toward her. She lowered her pistol as the little brown macaque ran and leaped at her. She caught Aggie in her arms.

The monkey panted, his eyes huge and round, his gaze flicking toward the sunlight.

"What're you doing here?" she whispered.

One furry arm wrapped hard around her throat. He climbed higher, hugging tight to her shoulder, plainly needing reassurance. She carried him to the sunlit crack and cautiously peered out. She knew Aggie hadn't come here of his own volition.

From this height, she could see the beached cabin cruiser—only Charlie had company now. A group outfitted in black combat gear swarmed the boat. More were coming through the woods to the south.

Twenty to thirty.

She knew these were no local thieves or a raiding party.

They found us.

She didn't have time to wonder how. She had a more important task, especially as she spotted someone in the stern of the boat point toward her hiding spot. Those aboard the cruiser started into the woods, heading her way.

She backed into the bronze cave. There was no way she could hold off that number of combatants with a single SIG and a few throwing knives, even with the advantage of height. The others had come with assault rifles and likely grenades. She'd be quickly blown out of this nest. Knowing this and to protect the others, she had only one option.

She stared over at the open gateway.

I need to get that closed.

She hoped Gray was right about the fire keeping the doors open. She holstered her pistol. Balancing Aggie on her shoulder, she crossed to the broken pieces of pottery. She picked up the largest shard that still had a pool of black oil in it. It was heavy, damned heavy, but adrenaline spiked her blood and pounded her heart.

She hauled the piece in both arms over to the altar and dumped the coal-black oil into the basin. It sloshed into the base of the fire, swirled around it, and quickly choked the flames. With the death of the fire, darkness fell over the cavern.

"C'mon, little one."

Seichan ran for the bronze doors and darted through them. She skidded to a stop between the two huge bronze guard dogs and turned. She waited for the doors to close, but they remained stubbornly open.

Was Gray wrong?

She clenched her teeth, trying to judge whether to run after the others or hold her ground and guard the gate. She came to a fast decision.

Better to stay.

She knew a firefight here would alert Gray of danger. So there was no need for her to run down there. But that wasn't the real reason she stayed. She decided to place her confidence where it best belonged.

Gray is not wrong.

She stared into the dark cave, lit by sunlight streaming through the boulder pile. But that wasn't the only light source. The bronze basin in the stone slab glowed a ruddy orange, still red-hot—perhaps hot enough to be keeping these gates open.

Seichan knew the truth.

I have to hold my ground until that cools.

Only then would the doors close.

She shifted to the side and slipped out her SIG.

Can I last that long?

Aggie eeked in her ear, correcting her, reminding her.

Right.

Can we *last that long?*

36

Gray stood at the dark threshold to Hell.

The large tunnel ended at a wide terrace overlooking a colossal cavern. The space looked roughly oval, a quarter mile wide, maybe twice that long. It was hard to get the full breadth of its dimensions. Even the reach of the team's flashlights only offered a shadowy glimpse of the distant wall.

"It's amazing," Maria whispered.

Kowalski grunted his agreement.

The group cast their lights all around.

The cavern appeared to be natural, but long ago its limestone surfaces had been polished to a perfect smoothness. Upon that blank canvas had been carved a continuous bas-relief. A forest of cedars climbed the walls, with monkeys scampering in the branches and larger beasts hiding deeper in the woods, visible mostly by the bronze disks of their eyes. Higher up, inscribed clouds billowed across the roof, swept by falcons and seabirds taking wing. There was even the starburst of a dark sun above, its face an imbedded plate of bronze.

But such artistry was only a fraction of the wonders below.

Standing at the stone rail, the group had a grand view of the city stretched beneath them. It descended in tiers down from the terrace. Many hundreds of homes crowded those steps. Most were single story, both square and round. Others climbed upward in high crooked stacks, like children's toy blocks. But many more rose up into taller sculpted towers with flared tops.

Gray recognized the shape of those last structures. He had seen them before. He focused on one nearby, sweeping his bright beam across its dark surface. "They're near matches to the *nuraghe* constructions on Sardinia. What the Greeks called *daidaleia*."

Gray wondered, *Does this support the idea that Daedalus had originally come from here, shared his knowledge with the greater ancient world?*

"But these structures aren't made of stacked stones," Mac said. "Look at how smooth the walls are. And those dark surfaces aren't *plaster*. Even the roof tiles look made of the same material. Tarnished metal."

Gray nodded. He had already noted the uniform hue to the city, a dark brown, nearly black, making the place look like a hellish firestorm had swept through it, burning every surface, leaving it covered in ash.

But he doubted there was any wood used in the construction here.

"It's all bronze," Gray said.

Kowalski waved to the tunnel. "Like back there."

Mac turned to Gray, his eyes wide and bright, reflecting the light. His words were breathless. "An entire city made of bronze."

"At least plated in it," Gray said, tempering and centering the group. "And only as much of the city as we can see."

The black mouths of tunnels dotted the walls of the tiers, indicating that this space was likely only the town center of a larger subterranean maze, likely a labyrinth worthy of Daedalus. Five of the largest openings were locked behind bronze gates at the top, equidistant from one another. Broad staircases led down from those gates, the steps descending through the city to a dark stone basin in the center. Framing both sides of the stairways were hundreds of bronze statues, standing guard over the place.

It was clear what they were protecting.

Gray shone his light across to the far side, to the city's largest structure. High bronze walls bulged out in a half circle from the other wall, flanked by spiraling, graceful towers that reached halfway to the roof. The gates in the center shone brighter, showing little tarnish.

Gold.

Mac noted the direction of Gray's beam. "I'm guessing that's the palace."

"Where do we even begin to search this place?" Maria said.

"I say we just leave," Kowalski suggested. "We opened the gates to Hell. Found this place. Let's hightail it out of here and let Painter know what we found."

Gray seriously considered this. He knew they had barely scratched the surface regarding the true mysteries hidden here, but perhaps it was best to leave any further exploration to the experts.

This plan was supported by Father Bailey. "Maybe we should heed Mr. Kowalski," the priest warned.

Bailey had wandered off to where a wide ramp led down from the terrace to the topmost tier of the city. But the priest had his back to the dark metropolis, his flashlight pointed at the wall at the top of the ramp. The beam swept over lines crudely carved into the limestone, like some ancient graffiti.

"It's Arabic," Bailey said and turned. "A message left behind by those who fled from here."

"Hunayn and his men." Gray joined the priest at the wall. "Can you read it?"

"Mostly. I studied Arabic, but this script is over a thousand years old."

Maria drew closer. "What does it say?"

Bailey ran his beam like a finger across the lines of Arabic. " *'Here Tartarus slumbers. Walk softly, tread with caution. Do not wake what should forever sleep. Do not tarry, dear traveler. Pestilence is in the very air, curses left behind by Pandora. It drove those who once lived here mad, from peaceful benefactors to maddened conquerors.'* "

Gray wondered if Hunayn was referring to some sort of radiation sickness. Was that why the benevolent Phaeacians of Daedalus and Medea—

who seemed willing to share their knowledge, who helped Odysseus on his journey home—became the destroyers of civilizations, a Sea People leaving a path of ruin behind them, then vanishing?

Bailey continued, " *'For daring to dabble with the gifts of Prometheus, their people of Tartarus became warped, their children born monstrous. They eventually fled, locking their evil and their dread curses behind gates of bronze and never speaking of this place again, letting foul Tartarus fall into myths and legends.'"*

Gray glanced back to the city. To learn all of this, Hunayn and his men must have spent considerable time scouring the place, reading ancient texts of the city's history.

Bailey revealed as much as he continued. " *'Heed the lesson of my reckless trespass. We dared to wake Tartarus, to stir its fiery defenders, and suffered greatly because of it. I only saved the last of us by forcing the city back to its dark slumber. If you should follow in my tragic footsteps, seek the same beyond the palace, where the fires of Hades burn and Titans loom. But Charon will demand his price.'"*

Bailey stopped and explained. "Charon was the old man who ferried souls across the River Styx into Hades."

"But what's that price you mentioned?" Kowalski asked.

"More than Charon's usual coin, it seems." Bailey returned to the wall and continued his recitation. " *'The bravest of all must ford the poisonous lake, one who would forsake his life for his brother. It is how we put Tartarus into slumber. May Allah forever grace Abd Al-Qadir for his sacrifice. In his esteemed memory, I used the knowledge of my brothers—we who call ourselves the Banū Mūsā—to fabricate a final end. So, dear traveler, if you wake Tartarus, know it will be for the last and final time. You have been so warned.'"*

"Then it's signed Hunayn ibn Mūsā ibn Shākir." Bailey sighed and stepped back. "The captain must have left here with his last ship, full of cargo as proof of his discovery and perhaps to warn the world."

"Then the storm blew his ship off course," Gray said. "Gave him time to reconsider whether it was worth the risk to bring that deadly cargo into the wider world."

"He may have also believed the storm was a sign from Allah," Bailey said. "Hunayn had to wonder if the hand of god was punishing him, casting him astray—not unlike his friend Odysseus—all to keep the world safe."

Mac pointed at the wall. "But what the captain wrote there at the end? What was that all about?"

Gray stared up at the inscription. "It sounds like Hunayn rigged some sort of failsafe into the city's systems. Not only to shut it down, but to destroy it entirely, if anyone dares trespass here again."

Kowalski pointed back to the tunnel. "Then let's not do that."

Gray tamped down his burning curiosity and agreed. "We should head back."

With a relieved exhalation, Kowalski scowled at the dark city. "Let's hope we're not already too late."

37

Elena was imprisoned on yet another boat.

She stood in the little cabin of an aluminum cruiser beached at the side of a shallow river. She shared the space with another captive, the riverboat's captain, a young woman in coveralls and a cowboy hat. The stranger kept her arms crossed and a deep scowl fixed on her face.

They were both guarded by Kadir, who stood outside the door at the stern. He was dressed in black Kevlar armor, including a helmet, and carried a massive assault rifle, a weapon equipped with an under-barrel grenade launcher. He also had a machete strapped to his back.

In addition, another two soldiers of Mūsā—a Son and a Daughter—flanked the boat's bow at the water's edge, armed with submachine guns. Those two mostly kept watch on the nearby cliff, likely disappointed to be left behind during the coming assault.

Elena stared through the cabin's front window, watching Nehir lead twenty or more soldiers toward the cliff, her entire battalion—except for those left to guard the prisoners.

And one other.

Monsignor Roe stood in the cabin doorway. He clutched the keys to the riverboat in one hand, which the other captive—a woman named Charlie Izem—kept a close eye on. Roe ignored the captain's attention, his gaze focused on the cliff face. He was likely frustrated to be stuck in the rear, having to wait to see what was discovered.

Elena glared over at him, wanting an answer. "How did you know the others were here? Who signaled you?"

Roe sighed and faced the cabin. "Actually, we wouldn't be here if it wasn't for you, Dr. Cargill."

"Me?"

"You helped Joseph Kowalski escape."

"I don't understand, what does—?"

"A tracker was secretly implanted in his leg, when the medical crew tended to the burn in his thigh." Roe gingerly touched the bandage under his thin shirt. "Trust me, with all that pain, he would not have noticed the injection of the implant. Probably thought it was antibiotics or pain relievers."

Elena pictured the bandage around Joe's thigh. She had thought herself so clever to hide the bronze rods in the folds of his wrap. But apparently, she wasn't the only one who thought to use his injury to their secret benefit.

"We lost track of Mr. Kowalski when he ended up in the water, blocking the implant's transmission. After that, he managed to flee beyond the tracker's range. So, we temporarily lost him." Roe turned again toward the cliffs. "Until now."

Elena sank back against the bridge of the cabin.

If Joe hadn't escaped . . .

Charlie filled the silence, "You are a priest, *non*," she said. "Why is it you help these *bâtards*?"

Roe frowned at her, casting his gaze up and down, trying to judge if she was worthy of an answer. "I am not merely a priest, as you say. I serve the Thomas Church. We are those among the faithful who adhere to the adage *seek and ye shall find*. Which means we refuse to sit passively by. Instead, our members actively *seek* the path that God has chosen for us, as I did."

"To end the world," Elena said.

"To lay the fiery foundation for Christ's return," Roe corrected. "I have seen the atrocities man commits. To each other. To this planet. For decades, as an archaeologist, as a historian, as a prefect of the Church's most secret library, I have observed and recorded mankind's decline. I've watched it grow worse. The end is near. Can't you feel it? The madness, the cruelties. I refuse to sit idly by and wait. I intend to live long enough to see Christ's righteous return, when the world will be cleansed of impurity and depravity."

Charlie crossed her arms, "Ah, *oui,* so you are impatient then. That is your answer."

Elena had to cover her mouth to keep from laughing. She enjoyed the look of dismay on the monsignor's face, which quickly grew to anger, forcing Roe to turn away with a huff.

Charlie mumbled under her breath. "It seems better to fight for humankind than to lie down and wait for God to save us." She glanced to Elena. "*N'est-ce pas?*"

Elena nodded. *That's indeed so.*

But others did not agree with this assessment.

Elena turned toward the cliff, noting small black figures ascending it. She prayed Joe and his friends found somewhere to hide, even if it meant venturing beyond the gates of Hell.

Because she knew one thing for certain.

They're out of time.

6:18 P.M.

Seichan crouched low by one of the bronze doors, near the paw of a giant sculpted dog. Out in the cave, the altar's basin had faded from a brilliant fiery rose to a dull bruise. Still, the gateway into Tartarus refused to budge. Earlier, she had tried forcing them closed, but the doors were locked down by hidden gears.

Alerted by the scrape of boots on rock, she knew she would have to make a last stand here. If nothing else, she would buy the others as much time as possible to get somewhere safe once the firefight commenced.

And at least I'm not alone.

Strong, thin arms strangled her throat. Aggie remained perched on her shoulder, sensing the danger, or at least, Seichan's anxiety. Her heart hammered, and fine sweat covered her skin. A minute ago, she had tried to get the monkey to head down the tunnel, but he kept bounding back, sticking close to her.

So be it.

With her eyes adjusted to the dim cave, the sunlight streaming through the stack of boulders was stingingly bright. She spotted a shadow pass through that radiance, heading toward the larger gap.

Then another.

Here we go.

She shifted her pistol higher, leaning her shoulder against the bronze gate to steady her aim. Then she felt a rumble pass through her body, radiating outward from the door. The gun vibrated in her grip.

She straightened, pushing away from the gate.

The pair of doors began to move with a groan of gears.

Finally . . .

She backed up but quickly noted that the gates were closing far too slowly. The others would soon be inside and through the doors if she abandoned her post. She held her ground and pointed her pistol. As soon as the creeping shadows reached the gap in the boulder pile, she fired.

A single round.

But not at the opening.

She hit one of the pots full of Medea's Oil. The loud gunshot succeeded in driving the intruders away from the cave opening. Unfortunately—as much as she had hoped—the round failed to ignite the explosive load stored in those jars. The pot simply shattered into pieces, dumping a spill of faintly glowing oil across the cave floor.

So, plan B.

Aggie clung even tighter, making it hard to breathe. Seichan retreated deeper into the tunnel to avoid being crushed by the closing doors—which meant she lost her sight line on the cave entrance.

Someone strafed wildly into the space, the rounds ringing off the bronze and ricocheting all around. Seichan ducked low. She blindly returned fire, squeezing her trigger twice, just to keep the others on their toes.

She waited for as long as possible. The two doors were still ten yards apart and closing with an infuriating deliberateness.

C'mon.

Then two dark figures rolled across her view, trying to reach the far side of the cave, planning to set up a crossfire, leaving her nowhere to hide. She didn't bother firing at them. Instead she grabbed her water bottle, used her teeth to unplug the stopper, and lobbed it like a grenade past the doors and out into the cavern. It tumbled end over end—toward the middle of the glowing pool of Medea's Oil.

As it flew, she turned, grabbed Aggie to her chest, and sprinted down the tunnel.

The world exploded behind her in a flash of golden fire.

A blast of superheated air slammed into her back and sent her flying headlong. In midair, she scooped Aggie tighter and twisted to the side. She hit the ground with her shoulder and rolled, protecting the monkey with her body.

When she finally stopped tumbling, she spun around.

The gate remained open, framed by a roaring blaze of golden flames and black smoke. But as she watched, the gap between the doors inexorably closed, pinching narrower and narrower, squeezing the flames.

Still, too slowly.

6:24 P.M.

Nehir crouched on a lip of stratified rock, gasping for air that wasn't on fire. Flames raged in the cave overhead. A boulder tipped over the edge and crashed down the cliff face, coming within a foot of striking her. Stone shards pelted her face as they passed by. The boulder slammed into the other rocks that had been blasted out of the cave in a massive gout of flame and smoke.

Below, four teammates lay crushed and broken beneath the pile. Another three had been inside at the time of the explosion and were surely dead.

She stared up.

Already the worst of the flames had subsided.

Anger—hotter than the fires above—drove her upward. She reached the ledge and peeked into the cave. The heat seared her eyeballs. The hot breath of a dragon, smelling of burnt flesh and oil, swept over her.

Across the cave, lit by multiple flaming pools, movement drew her tortured gaze.

A pair of doors squeezed together at the back.

Then sealed.

She ducked from the heat and pressed her cheek against the cooler stone. *So close.* She choked down a scream and took four deep breaths. She then shifted her helmet's radio closer to her lips. She pictured what she needed, crated in the back of the transport helicopter.

"Send over the rocket launcher."

38

On the dark terrace, Gray gave Seichan a brief relieved hug. "You sure you're okay?"

She nodded and adjusted the monkey clinging to her shoulder. "We both are."

The others crowded close around them.

A few minutes ago, they had all heard the gunfire. At the first shot, Gray had ordered everyone to stick to the terrace and arm themselves. Gray had immediately taken off down the tunnel as more gunfire erupted. Then a huge fiery explosion brightened the curve of the tunnel, followed by a superheated blast of air. With his heart pounding in panic, he had continued around the bend in the passageway. In the distance, he had spotted a thin line of flaming brightness marking the closing gates into the city. As he ran toward them, they sealed, and darkness fell.

At that moment, despair had struck him like a hammer to the heart, stumbling him to a stop. Then a flashlight had blinked on, revealing a small figure rising from the floor.

Thank god.

On the terrace, he took Seichan's hand and faced the group. On the way back to the dark city, she had already explained what had happened, what she'd done.

"What now?" Mac asked, cradling a SIG P320 in both his hands.

The others were similarly armed, except for Kowalski. He had their ammunition duffel over one shoulder, but in his arms he carried an AA-12, an Auto Assault combat shotgun. The weapon's large drum magazine held thirty-two shells, all British FRAG-12s, highly explosive antipersonnel and armor-piercing slugs.

Kowalski had certainly come to play.

Gray motioned back toward the tunnel. "With the gates closed, Seichan has bought us a little time. But we don't know how much. We need to use that time to search for another way out of here, some back door."

Bailey nodded. "The Phaeacians would be too smart to trap themselves inside here if their main gates were compromised. There must be another way out."

"But where?" Maria asked. She waved an arm to encompass the breadth of the dark city. "Who knows how far this place honeycombs out from here? It could be for miles."

Gray shook his head. "No. If there's another way out, it'll be over there." He pointed across the cavern to the towering palace. "The royalty here would've had their own way out of here, somewhere close to them."

Mac grimaced but agreed. "Sounds about right. And didn't Hunayn write that the city's fail-safe system was over there, too?"

"*Beyond the palace, where the fires of Hades burn and Titans loom,*" Bailey quoted.

Only Kowalski voiced a dissent. "C'mon, guys. Does that *really* sound like a place we want to go?"

Gray ignored him and got everyone moving off the terrace and down the ramp to the city's topmost tier. A sprawl of bronze structures at this height created a maze of crooked alleys and narrow, winding streets. But one of the city's main stairways cut down through the levels and lay only a short distance from the bottom of the ramp.

Gray rushed the others to it.

He pointed down the limestone steps and over to where the gold doors of the palace lay midway up the other side. "Down and up again," he said. "Maybe half a mile. But we'll have to move fast."

"What if we can't get into the palace?" Mac asked, noting the tunnel at the back of the stairs, sealed tight with a bronze door. "What if it's all locked up like this?"

"We'll cross that bridge when we get to it," Gray said. "Let's go."

Flashlight in hand, he led the others down the dark steps. The stair-way appeared to be a twenty-yard-wide promenade, similar to the other four that divided the city into larger sections. From the shallow ruts worn into the limestone underfoot, the Phaeacians must have traversed these stairs for centuries, their sandals slowly buffing away the rock.

Gray tried to imagine this city alive and bustling with people. Children running up and down these steps. Shopkeepers hawking their wares. Laughing sailors returning after a long voyage, happy to be home.

But Bailey reminded him of a darker side to the city. "Look at all these statues."

The priest shone his light along the row of shadowy bronze sculptures lining both sides of the steps. Each was twice Gray's height or more. Focused on the task of reaching the palace, he had given the behemoths little attention.

Bailey splashed the beam of his flashlight across one. It was a figure of a man, down on one knee, leaning on a bronze club. When Gray drew abreast of it, he stared up at the figure's face. One bronze eye stared back, with a large black gem for a pupil.

"A Cyclops," Bailey said breathlessly. "And look over there."

His light shifted to the other side, revealing a hulking bare-chested man with thick legs ending in hooves and the horned head of a bull.

"A minotaur," Gray acknowledged.

Mac groaned and gave that statue a wide berth, obviously recalling his encounter with something similar back in Greenland.

"It's like a pantheon of Greek and Roman myths," Bailey said, hurrying along, noting each as they passed. "That massive bronze eagle could be representative of the bird Zeus sent to torture Prometheus. And look at that huge maiden hugging a jar. Maybe Pandora herself. And that pair of hunting dogs crouched as if in mid-lunge. I bet they're supposed to be the hounds that Hephaestus forged for King Minos."

Seichan cradled little Aggie on her shoulder and nudged Gray. She pointed her flashlight at a pair of true giants, twice the size of the other statues. They flanked the steps, each holding bronze boulders in their massive hands. As the two of them passed under their cold gazes, Gray noted the perfect concentric circles of their eyes, the high crown of their head. They had seen those bronze countenances before—only made of stone.

The Sardinian giants of Mont'e Prama.

Kowalski also seemed to recall them. He whispered as he passed between them, "Elena mentioned Hephaestus making a boulder-throwing giant. One that also burned people alive."

Bailey drew closer. "You're talking about *Talos*. The guardian of the island of Crete."

Kowalski shrugged. "Sounds right."

Bailey continued: "Talos was eventually defeated by the sorceress Medea, who used her potions to end his fiery protection of the island." The priest searched all around, his gaze traveling to the other stairways around the city, all lined by more statues. "It's as if Greek history has come to life in here."

Kowalski growled at the priest, "Let's hope not, Padre. I think we should take that Arab captain at his word and *not* wake this place up."

6:48 P.M.

Maria stayed close to Joe's side as they continued down the stone stairs. "Do you think that's possible?" she asked the others. "That the Phaeacians were able to craft all of this on their own?"

Gray looked skeptical.

But Bailey's face shone with little doubt. "I've read deeply into the history of ancient automatons and mechanical devices. The Hellenistic era was full of stories of such artificial creations. Built by Hephaestus, designed by Daedalus."

"But aren't those just myths?" she asked.

"Most of them, of course. But there were also many *historical* accounts. Of Greek artisans, engineers, and mathematicians devising incredible self-moving machines. Not just Heron of Alexandria with his magical temple doors, but countless other men and women. Some known, others lost to history. Philo of Byzantia built his own serving maids. Another constructed a mechanical horse that would drink. Even the gates of the ancient Olympic stadium were said to open on their own, with a bronze eagle shooting high into the air and a bronze dolphin diving low."

Gray still looked unconvinced.

Bailey pressed his case: "The Greeks were far more advanced than most imagine. These were people who were masters of hydraulics, of pneumatics. They invented calipers and cranes, complicated gears and winches, gimbals and pumps. So perhaps the Phaeacians, these seafaring people, gathered such knowledge and built upon it here in safe isolation, *these farthermost of men*. I could imagine them tinkering, experimenting, building, testing. And if they eventually discovered—by accident or design—a potent fiery fuel source, perhaps it gave them the push to make a technological leap forward."

"Until they reached too far," Mac added, nodding to the dark and haunted city as they finally neared the bottom of the stairs.

"Well, they learned something," Joe said. "That's for sure."

Maria considered this. From her study of primitive anthropology, she knew knowledge had indeed passed from one culture to another. As one period of invention died somewhere in the world, another picked it up. In the Western world, the torch of invention passed from the Greeks to the Romans. And when the Roman Empire fell, it moved to the Arab world, igniting their Islamic Golden Age. Then when that age turned dark, Europe again carried the torch forward.

So, was it possible that these seafaring people made this leap all on their own?

Or was another hand involved?

Two years ago, Maria had been involved in another adventure with Sigma, where she met Joe, and where Baako played an important role. Back then, Sigma had come across the trail of mysterious teachers of the ancient past. A people whom Sumerian texts called Watchers, a shadowy group who also appeared again in Jewish texts.

She stared around the dark city.

Is this place further evidence of these Watchers' influence?

Either way—whether self-taught or at the hands of unknown teachers—the Phaeacians had certainly produced miracles.

Both wondrous and monstrous.

At the bottom of the long stairs, the promenade ended at a vast bowl polished into the limestone. It was an empty lake easily a quarter mile across and half as deep. The other stairways terminated here, too. Along the rim of the dry basin was a circle of hundreds of giant bronze fish, the scales dark and tarnished. Each had a high curled tail and was posted at an angle, noses pointed high, mouths sculpted open.

She imagined water spraying high from those open mouths, hundreds of fountains arching into the mirror of a vast indoor lake. Directly overhead was a bronze disk, meant to represent the sun, imbedded in the roof.

She pictured the populace picnicking here under that cold sun, parents watching children splashing in the waters, dancing under the spray of the fountains. She imagined little boats plying its placid surface.

It was indeed wondrous.

But also monstrous.

On the opposite side of the lake from the palace, one final bronze sculpture loomed over the dry bowl. It towered three stories high, perched at the lake's edge but with two clawed forelimbs dug into the dry bed itself, as if it were about to wade in. The creature looked like some monstrous mother to the hundreds of bronze fish, an amphibious beast, with six long necks snaking high over the lake, ending in crocodilian heads.

She stared up at the gaping jaws lined with sharklike teeth.

Okay, maybe kids wouldn't want to come down here to play after all.

And that wasn't the only danger.

Joe pointed his weapon toward the lake's center, where a large drain hole gaped, dropping straight into the earth. "You know, maybe that's the *true* entrance to Hell."

As steep and smooth as the bowl's walls were, no one was willing to go look.

Especially as we're running out of time.

Gray got them moving faster again. He pointed around the edge of the lake, to a narrower stairway that led up to the city's palace. The steps over there reflected the glow of their flashlights.

"Looks like they're gold, too," Mac noted.

"Apparently a red carpet wasn't good enough for these royals," Joe muttered.

They headed quickly around the lake toward those steps—when a thunderous boom echoed over the vast space. They all froze momentarily, sharing glances. Except for Aggie, who chirped on Seichan's shoulder and ducked his face into the crook of her neck.

Joe shook his head. "Sounds like we got company."

39

Aboard the cruiser, Elena ducked as the rocket blasted a hundred yards away. The noise, trapped between the two sheer walls of limestone, was deafening. She straightened enough to see a flume of rock dust and smoke billow from the cave opening.

Lower down, black figures ran out of the woods toward the cliffs.

Elena had already heard what had happened earlier, how Nehir had failed to get through some hidden bronze doors before they closed. Then two men had returned from the helicopter to the south. One had hauled the tube of a rocket launcher, while the other had carried two long rocket-propelled grenades.

From the cabin of the cruiser, Elena watched the soldiers scale the cliff and vanish into the fading smoke. She waited several breaths. No one came back out. Apparently there was no need to fire the second grenade.

They did it.

They must have succeeded in blasting their way through the gates.

Elena turned, worried for Joe and the others. But what she saw next made no sense. Charlie drew a pistol from under a pillow and lifted it as she turned. With both Monsignor Roe and Kadir equally focused on the cliff, Charlie stepped forward and fired.

The first round struck the monsignor in the leg, dropping his thin form away from the doorway. As he fell, the second shot hit Kadir in the head—or rather his helmet. The round ricocheted away, but the impact knocked the man back, tripping him over the stern and into the water.

Charlie grabbed Elena's arm. "C'mon."

They ran out onto the deck and over to the gunwale nearest the beach. The Son of Mūsā posted on that side popped his head up, never suspecting the prisoners were suddenly armed. Charlie was not so lax, having sized up every position. From a yard away, she fired into the man's face. His body flew back, sprawling across the sand.

They leaped over the rail together. Charlie darted toward the front of the boat, ducked low, and fired under the curve of the bow. A scream rose on the far side.

Charlie rounded the cruiser. Elena hurried to follow. Running low, Elena caught sight of Charlie closing in on the Daughter of Mūsā who had been guarding that side. The Daughter was down on her hip, her ankle blown out and bloody. Still, she crawled toward the submachine gun she had dropped in the sand when she fell.

Charlie stalked over and, with cold deliberation, shot her in the back of the head, low, under the edge of the helmet. The woman's body jerked and went limp.

"Grab the rifle," Charlie ordered, covering Elena with her pistol as they retreated toward the woods.

Elena obeyed—or tried to. She reached for the weapon's strap, only to have the sand blast up near it, chasing her off. The chatter of automatic fire drove her away.

Kadir . . .

Charlie fired toward the cruiser's stern, momentarily forcing the giant into hiding. It bought them enough time to reach the dense cedar forest. They crashed through the branches, burying themselves into the cover.

Then the world exploded to Elena's right.

Needles, branches, and bark blasted and pelted into them.

She pictured Kadir's weapon with its under-barrel grenade launcher.

Charlie grabbed her arm and hauled her in the opposite direction— only to be met by another explosion ahead. They dodged away. Kadir might be blindly shelling into the forest, but it only took one lucky shot.

"Run!" Charlie yelled.

"Where?"

"Away!"

Right.

For now, that was all the plan they needed.

Together they fled deeper into the forest.

6:54 P.M.

Thirty yards down the dark tunnel, Nehir heard muffled booms echo behind her. She glanced back to the sunlit cave, still hazed with smoke. The rocket-propelled grenade had blown away one of the gate's doors. It lay crumpled behind her.

Her remaining twenty-two Sons and Daughters gathered with her in the tunnel.

She weighed whether or not to send one or two back to investigate. But as she strained her ears, she heard no further explosions. Satisfied, she turned back around and waved the others to follow. Until she rooted out the Americans hiding here, she wanted every soldier left to hold this place.

If there were truly any problem behind her, she trusted Kadir to have her back—as he had her entire life.

Content with this thought, she ran with the others, rifles raised. From their weapons' rail-mounted flashlights, sharp beams of light lanced through the darkness ahead.

Then a new noise slowed her pace.

Not a boom, this time—but a low, deep, ominous rumble, coming from all around. She felt it in her legs. It shivered all the small hairs on her arms.

What's making that noise?

She lifted a hand, halting the team.

She glanced behind her again. She stared at the sunlit cave, which was almost out of sight as the tunnel curved. Still, she spotted the crumpled bronze door, the relic of their forced entry.

Maybe that was a mistake.

SIXTH

PROMETHEUS UNBOUND

Now of another portent thou shalt hear.
Beware the dogs of Zeus that ne'er give tongue,
The sharp-beaked gryphons, and the one-eyed horde
Of Arimaspians, riding upon horses,
Who dwell around the river rolling gold,
The ferry and the frith of Pluto's port.
Go not thou nigh them.

—AESCHYLUS, *PROMETHEUS BOUND*, 430 B.C.

40

"Forgive us our trespasses," Kowalski muttered.

By the time the group had circled the huge lake and reached the golden stairs leading up to the palace, the entire city had begun to rumble all around them.

"When the others broke in here," Gray said, "they must have triggered some sort of defense mechanism."

"Look!" Mac pointed to the left, toward the highest tier of the city.

At the top of the nearest stairway, the bronze gate that had closed off a tunnel up there had begun to open. Dark water gushed out from beneath the rising door. Kowalski turned a full circle, noting the same was happening at the top of all five main stairways.

As the bronze gates opened wider, the flowing water became a white-water torrent down the steps, transforming the stairways into churning spillways. The strong smell of the sea accompanied the flows, stinging the air with salt and spray.

"Get back!" Gray hollered, pushing them up the narrower gold stairs toward the palace.

To either side, the nearest torrents reached the lowest tier and splashed thunderously into the empty lake basin. All around, the other spillways did the same. Waters swirled across the bowl, slowly filling it.

But that wasn't the only purpose of those streams.

Bailey grabbed Gray's arm and swept his light along the edge of the nearest spillway. Kowalski squinted, noting a line of something blurring there along the banks of the new river, spinning in place, driven by the rushing flow.

"Bronze waterwheels," Bailey said. "Hidden behind the statuary."

Gray frowned but waved them all higher, running for the palace.

"What are they powering?" Maria asked.

The fiery answer started at the top tier. Hundreds of torches burst with golden flames, then more and more, sweeping the full breadth of the cavern—then descending, lighting the place tier by tier.

"They must be pumping Medea's Oil throughout Tartarus," Bailey said. "Their version of gas lines feeding streetlamps."

But it wasn't just the torches being supplied.

Movement drew Kowalski's eye to the left. One of the statues stirred at the water's edge. Plates of tarnished bronze shifted, leaking a glowing green oil from every seam, as if the statue were being pumped so full it couldn't hold any more. As it reached some boiling point, fire burst within it, fierce enough to rattle its form. Flames lapped through cracks in its armor. The explosive force drew the statue straighter. As it turned with a grind of gears, its single eye swung in their direction, the black gem lit by an inner fire.

A Cyclops . . .

But the giant was not the only creation waking. A massive eagle lifted razor-edged wings of bronze. A wolf lifted its head and howled at the bronze sun, flames shooting from its throat. A man-sized cobra reared up with a shuffle of bronze scales, leaking flames as it moved. It shook a wide cowl with a silent hiss, revealing curved fangs dripping with glowing green oil.

All across the city, the statuary awoke, the mythic bestiary stirred.

Mac waved all of them low. "No noise from here," he warned and pointed toward the palace walls.

They'd already scaled halfway up the gold stairs, but the palace doors now seemed an impossible distance away. Especially as Tartarus woke around them. Torches burned everywhere. Creatures waded out of the torrents, leaving streamlets of fire behind in the water. The bronze army slouched and lumbered into the city streets, searching for the trespassers who woke them.

Gray led the others up the gold stairs. Fiery guardians closed in on both sides. Still, with luck and speed, they reached the top. The palace sat perched on the city's middle tier. Its bronze walls curved outward in a half circle, reaching nearly to the steps. Towers spiraled high to either side. The golden doors lay directly ahead, some twenty yards from the top of the golden staircase.

"Stay here," Gray hissed.

He raced low across the open stretch and flattened close against the gold surface. He tried one door, then the other. His frustration glowed in the sheen of his sweat. He turned to them with a shake of his head.

Locked.

"Told you," Mac warned, reminding them all of his earlier fear.

Then it looks like it's time to cross that bridge.

Kowalski stood and raised his AA-12 combat shotgun. He waved Gray to the side—at the same time as something shambled into view on the right. Gray ducked and stayed where he was.

Kowalski stood his ground.

The dark beast was huge, some rendition of a bear, only the size of a dumpster. Its four legs dug bronze claws into the limestone. It had a flat muzzle, with a rounded head and short ears. Fire burned behind gemstones.

Kowalski stayed silent, hoping it might pass if they remained quiet. Still, as a precaution, he lifted his shotgun higher and aimed it at the beast.

The bear's head swung toward him.

Kowalski cursed Mac.

Seemed some of these bastards could *see*—or at least, detect *motion*.

But either way, the damage had been done.

The bear roared in Kowalski's direction, flames bursting out, revealing a maw lined by jagged sharp plates, a literal bear trap.

Kowalski roared back at the monster—and squeezed the trigger on his weapon. Auto-mode unloaded six shells in rapid succession. The armor-piercing FRAG-12 rounds exploded into the monster, ripping away plates of bronze, exposing its fiery heart. One shell flew down its gullet and blasted inside, shattering its inner gearworks. The bear stumbled and crashed to the stone.

Gray ran across and pointed to the golden door. "Get us in there!" He waved to the rest of the group. "Everyone down."

With a grin, Kowalski turned, balanced the gun with its giant drum magazine on his hip, and fired another six-round burst at the gold door. The Frag shells exploded brilliantly against the metal gates. The noise deafened, each blast a punch in the gut.

As the smoke cleared, the doors remained intact.

Dented, scarred, but still closed.

"Behind us!" Maria shouted.

Kowalski turned.

The blasts had been heard.

All across the city, trails of flames had been shifting aimlessly, but now they all turned and flowed toward their position. Closer at hand, a pair of fiery dogs, each the size of a pony, appeared on the golden steps below. Green oil slathered from their jaws, splashing into flames on the steps. The pair stalked up toward the group at the top.

More movement rose to the right and left.

Smoke and fire.

Closing in from all sides.

7:04 P.M.

Nehir reached a high terrace overlooking the fiery city of Tartarus. Flames danced everywhere. Hulking creatures stalked about in cloaks of smoke, blazing brightly with fire from within. Tumbling rivers spilled into the churning maw of a large black lake.

This truly is Hell.

Then a sharp series of blasts drew her eye across the cavern to a mighty castle of tarnished bronze and golden gates. She spotted smaller figures there, lit by firelight.

At long last.

The others appeared to be pinned down before the gold doors as fiery shapes moved inexorably toward their position. Fearing the bastards might escape into the shadow-riven depths of the city and vanish, she turned to her second-in-command.

"Ahmad, bring up the launcher."

The man dashed back and returned with the long black tube of the weapon, already preloaded with a rocket-propelled grenade. She took it from him, balanced it on her shoulder, and dropped to a knee. She steadied her aim and centered the sight's crosshairs on the milling group.

She savored the kill to come and squeezed the trigger—just as something massive rose in front of the terrace, filling her weapon's sight, throwing off her shot. With a blast of smoke and fire, the rocket arced high across the cavern, trailing smoke, then blasted into a section of the city beyond the castle.

Shocked, she fell on her rear and scooted backward.

Before her, a wall of bronze with a bullet-shaped head and rings for eyes rose into view. It ignored her, perhaps blind. It heaved up a huge boulder of bronze, the size of an SUV, over its head.

"With me!" she yelled to her team.

She rolled to the side, onto her feet, and sprinted for the ramp that led down to the topmost tier. Teammates followed, racing with her, pounding behind her.

Then a resounding crash threw her forward.

She hit the ramp hard and tumbled end over end. Once stopped at the bottom, she turned to see the terrace break off the wall and shatter at the foot of the bronze giant. It had smashed away the balcony and now jammed its massive boulder into the tunnel. It proceeded to hammer it even deeper, closing off the only exit.

Once finished—with its purpose completed—it sank to its knees and leaned its bronze forehead against the wall and went quiet.

Nehir gathered her team.

Five were missing or dead.

She stared across the cave, her fury building to a white fire.

I will make them suffer.

41

Following the blast of the RPG, Gray gathered everyone at the top of the gold stairs. He watched the encroaching fiery bronze army turn away from their position at the palace gates, drawn by the rocket's explosion, by the churning smoke. Even now, a tower toppled and crashed over there with a resounding clang of metal on metal.

A moment ago, the two massive hounds on the gold steps had leaped in that same direction, going after noisier prey. But Gray knew this reprieve would not last long.

He glanced around the breadth of the city. In the center, the dark lake was nearly full, reflecting the flames. Its surface slowly churned in a circle as more water flooded down the five promenades. Above it, the six-headed beast stirred, waking more slowly than the smaller creations. Its long necks had begun to snake back and forth; its diamond eyes glowed ruddily, flames lapping from its shark-toothed crocodilian jaws.

From this height, Gray suddenly knew what he was seeing, what was represented here. *Charybdis and Scylla*. The monsters from Homer's *Odyssey*. The former was a monstrous maelstrom, a ship-destroying whirlpool.

The latter was a giant amphibious sea creature that had killed several of Odysseus's men.

But those beasts weren't the immediate danger.

"Over there," Mac warned in a whisper and pointed to their right.

On that side, a good number of the beasts steadily approached. Gray's team was pinned down, in the direct path of that fiery horde as it headed toward the blast site.

We'll be overrun at any moment.

Knowing this, knowing they had no other choice, he grabbed Kowalski by the shoulder and pointed to the golden gates. "We need to get through there. You have another drum magazine, right?"

His teammate nodded. "There's one more in the duffel."

"Then no half measures this time." It felt like letting a rabid dog off a leash, but it was now or never. "Get us in there."

Kowalski's face split with a savage grin. "Everyone down," he warned. "Time for *my* fireworks show."

Gray dropped flat on the stairs, waving the others with him.

Only Seichan remained crouched on her feet. She had their ammunition duffel open and withdrew the team's last two pistols, along with a roll of black duct tape.

He frowned. "What are you—?"

"Buying us a little breathing room." She dashed to the right, toward where the RPG had been fired at a them.

"Wait."

"Get that door open," she called back to him. "I'll be right back."

Then she vanished into the thick shadows.

Kowalski noted the exchange, casting Gray a questioning look.

He nodded to the door. "You heard her. Get that open."

Kowalski shrugged and faced the door. He braced his weapon against his. "Here goes nothing."

The explosive barrage pounded Gray's ears, his head, his chest. On full auto mode, Kowalski's combat shotgun could unload three hundred rounds per minute. Kowalski did not hold back and blasted the last twenty shells of his weapon's magazine into one of the palace doors. Each FRAG-12 round was packed with 3.4 grams of highly explosive composition A5, capable of piercing armored vehicles, bunker doors.

And hopefully these gates.

Kowalski's salvo only lasted a few seconds, as each shell blasted one after the other into the door. When it finally ended, Gray's head rang. He could hear nothing but a dull roaring in his ears.

As the smoke cleared, the result revealed itself. One of the palace gates hung askew from some complicated gearwork that served as its hinges. The twenty explosive shells had knocked the door back, tearing it partially away. But it still stubbornly held, while offering a low, narrow gap under one tilted edge.

Good enough.

Gray didn't bother shouting, knowing all were as deaf as him. He got up and ran low, drawing everyone with him. He reached the broken door and motioned the team through. Maria dove past him. Mac and Bailey hurried through, both men's eyes huge with panic.

Kowalski stripped out the emptied drum magazine and winged it into the fiery city. Gray joined him. They both stared off into the darkness.

Where is Seichan?

7:10 P.M.

With Aggie clinging and shivering on her shoulder, Seichan knelt in the darkness. One of the fiery lampposts at the end of the wide avenue offered enough illumination for her to work.

She quickly duct-taped one of the SIG Sauer pistols to the bronze wall of a two-story home. She positioned the weapon two feet off the ground. She had already strung a twisted length of the same tape across the thoroughfare, gluing the far end to a post on the other side. She then used one of her daggers to trim the rope of tape and pass it around the pistol's trigger.

Satisfied, she stood up. She held two prayers close to her heart: that this makeshift tripwire set across this street would not be spotted in the shadows, and that the enemy who had fired upon them would attempt to use this path to reach the palace. This street—and the other avenue she had already booby-trapped in the same manner—seemed to be the most direct routes from A to B.

At least, I hope so.

With her work done here, she set off back toward the palace, trying her best to stick to the darkest shadows, moving at a fast jog.

Suddenly Aggie's arms tightened around her neck, his little nails digging deep.

Then she heard it, too.

Behind her.

The pounding of bronze on stone.

She glanced back and saw a huge fiery shape round a corner and come barreling toward her, trailing smoke from its massive bulk.

She ran faster, but the clash of metal on rock grew louder, closing down on her. She no longer had the leeway to seek the darkest path to the palace. Instead she sped headlong through the fire and smoke, sprinting straight for her goal. The glow of the palace seemed an impossible distance ahead.

Still, she pictured Jack gurgling and smiling.

She felt Aggie shaking with fear.

She dug in her toes—and ran for all their lives.

7:13 P.M.

Gray stood with Kowalski at the broken gate into the palace. Gray clutched his pistol. Kowalski's earlier barrage had not gone unnoticed. From all directions, fiery shapes closed toward their position.

"Runnin' out of time here," Kowalski warned.

Gray held his breath—then heard a thunderous pounding to the right. He twisted in that direction.

Around the curve of the palace wall, Seichan ran into view, her eyes wild, her breath heaving. "Go!" she screamed at them.

Before either of them could move, a huge bronze horse thundered into view behind her. As big as a Clydesdale, it stampeded after her, its metal hooves sparking off the stone. It came at them with its head low, its mane a line of flames shooting high, trailing a cloak of smoke behind it.

Gray was momentarily struck by its deadly beauty.

Less impressed, Kowalski waved to Seichan. "Through here!"

As she reached them, she grabbed Aggie from her shoulder and dove under the gap in the crooked door. Kowalski followed behind her.

Gray fired at the steed, trying to buy the others a few extra seconds, but his rounds only pinged off the bronze shields of its charging body, mere horseflies nipping at the beast.

The stallion lowered its head further and thundered straight at him.

Gray's ankles were suddenly grabbed in an iron grip. His legs were yanked, and he fell flat and slid backward under the door. Above, the horse rammed its head into the gold door, hard enough to knock it open another few inches. With the resounding impact, fire exploded around Gray, burning his cheek as he was hauled into the palace.

Outside, the steed rose and hammered its hooves against the door, but the gate held for now. Gray understood why the beast failed to get in. As he was dragged into the palace, he saw its doors were a foot thick, likely solid gold.

Gray gained his feet, joining the others gathered in the entry hall.

Kowalski was down on one knee, his ammunition duffel open on the floor, already fumbling another drum magazine into his fearsome weapon.

As the steed outside continued its pounding, Bailey crouched and stared out. "*Hippoi Kabeirikoi,*" he mumbled.

Kowalski scowled at the priest.

Bailey nodded to the gate. "One of the four bronze horses that Hephaestus crafted to pull the chariot of his twin sons."

As the stallion continued to batter at the door, other lumbering shapes could be heard approaching outside, their bronze legs ringing off the limestone, likely drawn by the commotion. Not knowing how long the massive gold gates would hold, Gray got them all moving.

"We need to find another way out," he said. "Hunayn hinted at something behind this palace. That's where we need to go."

Gray led them past the gates, across a short entry hall of tarnished bronze, and into a vast hall. It rose three stories to a domed roof centered on a huge golden chandelier in the shape of a conch shell, its edges flickering with golden flames. More torches lit the walls.

Beyond them rose two tall gold thrones raised on a dais and carved with seafaring images of ships sailing the seas, of large fish with curled tails leaping high out of stylized waves. Behind them climbed a natural rock fireplace, sculpted out of the cavern wall. Its huge hearth danced with oil-fed flames.

Two arched passageways flanked the fireplace, leading deeper into the rock of the greater cavern.

Gray pointed to them. "We should check those out."

"If you say split up . . ." Kowalski warned.

Gray ignored him. He motioned to Seichan, Kowalski, and Maria. "You three check the left. We'll take the right. Stay in sight of one another. Don't proceed into either tunnel. We'll only explore farther"—he glanced at Kowalski—"together."

"Damn straight," the big man said.

Halfway across the hall, noises began to echo all around, rising from the bronze hallways and galleries to either side. A scraping of metal on metal, accompanied by a clinking and rattling.

"We're not alone in here," Mac moaned.

And not just *in here*.

Behind them, the distant blast of a pistol reached them—followed a moment later by more gunfire and the louder explosion of a grenade. The group cast concerned looks all around.

Gray glanced over to Seichan.

She merely smiled with satisfaction.

Apparently her mission a moment ago had not been in vain.

7:22 P.M.

Rifle at her shoulder, Nehir scrambled through the carnage of her team. All around, screams reverberated off tarnished walls. In this corner of Tartarus, the maze of homes and towers, shuttered and locked, offered no refuge. She flattened against the side of a building.

Ahead, blood shimmered in pools on the stone, reflecting the torchlight. Behind her, a Daughter crawled out of an alley—only to have her body jerked back with a loud crunch of bones. A Son ran wild-eyed past her position, panicked and weaponless. As he reached a side street, a bronze bull burst out from there, striking the fleeing man broadside, impaling him on its horns, then vanishing with a thunder of hooves, leaving only the man's screams behind.

A fusillade of grenades erupted a row over.

Nehir stayed low, holding her position. By now she recognized it was *noise* that attracted the fiery guardians, *motion* that drew them to the kill.

A lesson learned too late.

From the broken terrace, she had led her group down to the middle tier of the city, losing two teammates as they forded one of the spillways, before ropes could be properly set. From there she had taken the most direct route across the tier, leading her team into a tight labyrinth of homes and towers.

Shortly after entering, one of her Sons had stumbled over a makeshift tripwire strung across their path. A pistol had blasted, shattering the man's shin. He had fallen with a scream of both shock and pain. But the booby trap's true threat was far more deadly. The gunshot and scream had drawn unwanted attention.

Before any of them could reach their fallen teammate, a winged figure of a harpy had leaped down from the top of a nearby building, like some dread gargoyle come to life. It tore into another of her men, ripping him apart with a fiery beak. The team had driven the beast back, brought it low with a barrage of rifle fire. But the blasts drew other dread shapes hidden in the shadows. More of her team died. Soon gunfire had echoed everywhere, punctuated by tortured screams. The narrow, winding streets and alleys became a hellish hunting ground.

The panicked team had scattered in all directions.

By now Nehir recognized what she needed to do.

Get off this level.

With her back to the wall, she slid down the street, holding her breath. She hugged the rifle to her chest, knowing she dared not use it but not letting it go. She reached the next crossroad and poked her head around. A grenade blasted behind her, startling her, making her tumble into the open. She dropped into a crouch, but there was nothing threatening in sight.

She let out a breath and hurried down the side street. A short distance along, she came upon a gored and trampled body. It was the Son who had been carried away by the rampaging bull. She warily sidled past, her gaze fixed ahead for any sign of the beast.

Then an arm grabbed her from behind, yanked her into a cramped alley she had failed to spot in the gloom. She twisted around and found Ahmad, her second-in-command, standing there with two other Sons. Ahmad held a finger to his lips, having clearly learned the same lesson.

He also waved back at the alley, then pointed down.

Like Nehir, he had also realized that their only hope was to get clear of the war zone, which meant sneaking down to the next tier. She nodded and let him lead the way. He took her by a circuitous route, squeezing sideways at some spots. But the tighter the better. Anything to keep the large hunters from reaching them.

At last they came to a ladderlike stair that stretched from this tier to the next. Ahmad waved her first. She didn't argue and clambered quickly down into the quieter shadows of the lower level. Ahmad followed at her heels, leading the others. As she reached the bottom, she turned around and saw the last member of the group snatched from behind and lifted off his feet.

He kicked and screamed in the clutches of a tall bronze woman. Her beautiful sculpted visage reflected the firelight of the city. The woman turned the Son in her arms and leaned down, as if to kiss him, but not with her lips. From around the tarnish of her face, a dozen bronze vipers lashed out, spitting green oil and fire. They struck the man in the throat and face. Only then did the Medusa straighten and hold her captive aloft. From each snake-bit wound flames danced, darkening the flesh as the fiery poison spread.

Then the Son's face exploded, ripping flesh from skull.

Ahmad grabbed Nehir's shoulder and pulled her into the shadows. She hurried away. Behind her she heard the heavy thud of a body striking the stones as the bronze Medusa tossed aside its prey.

Nehir gratefully vanished into the deeper shadows, silently thanking Allah for sparing her. As she and the two men traced the darkest path across this level, they left the bloodshed and horrors behind them. Nehir stared upward, occasionally catching glimpses of the shining palace and its golden doors.

She now understood the enemy's determined assault on those gates.

They're searching for another way out.

That goal alone spurred her forward. She intended to live. Still, what sustained her the most, what held back the raving terror inside her, was a far stronger goal. She remembered the tripwire and knew who had set up that trap. More than surviving, she had another mission now.

Revenge.

7:24 P.M.

Hiding behind one of the gold thrones, Seichan tried her best to keep Aggie hushed. She let the macaque's arms strangle her throat. Aggie chittered into her neck, while she kept her lips at his ears, shushing softly, soothing him with the warmth of her breath.

Kowalski was less cooperative than the monkey. "That's so fucking wrong," he whispered next to her, his gaze on the main hall.

Maria elbowed him quiet. Gray, along with Mac and Bailey, crouched a few yards away behind the second throne.

A few minutes ago, the group had split up and quickly examined the two stone passageways flanking the tall rock fireplace behind her. Seichan's team had shone their flashlights into the tunnel to the left, discovering only a small shadowy private room off the throne hall. It had not looked promising.

Gray had better luck, waving them toward the other side to join him. But as Seichan's group headed over, the throne hall received a new inflow of guests, forcing them all into hiding.

Out in the grand hall, a motley line of bronze figures continued to parade into the space from the surrounding hallways and galleries. She counted several dozen by now. Earlier their group had heard the figures milling and clanking about in the depths of the palace, slowly working their way to the throne room.

Unlike the bronze horrors outside, the gathering here was human-sized, men and women, the details of their faces long tarnished away. Still, they had been sculpted and plated with long tunics, belted at the waists. The women had braids and flowers entwined in their hair. Several of the men wore tall, crested helmets and carried shields strapped to their arms. This smaller-framed assembly had probably once served as personal staff to the royal family.

Seichan imagined she was seeing the truest representation of the Phaeacians. Sadly, the mechanisms driving these finer constructs must have been more delicate than the larger forms outside. They had not survived the ravages of time as well. Several walked with stilted steps, with limps, or with broken arms swinging uselessly at their sides.

But these men and women weren't the saddest of the lot.

Scattered among them were bronze *children,* some equally broken, hobbling about like toys long forgotten and rusted. In fact, she imagined these constructions might have once been the royal offspring's playmates.

Including blackly tarnished babies—little bronze cherubs, with ruddy hot cheeks and fat limbs—that toddled or crawled across the stone floor of the hall.

Still, despite the assembly's innocuous appearance, the danger was clear. Many remained intact, moving with a determined sharpness. Fires burned brightly throughout the group, heating their bronze surfaces to a smoldering threat. And like all the city's guardians, the assembly here was drawn to the noisy clatter at the palace door. They headed obdurately in that direction, ready to defend the kingdom, likely activated when Kowalski first breached the palace gates.

Gray waited until there were only a handful, mostly broken, left in the hall. Then he waved everyone to follow him. He ran low toward the far stone passageway, ducked into the shadows, and windmilled an arm to urge them to rush over and into the tunnel.

They all followed, moving as quietly as possible.

Once gathered, Gray led them along an arched passageway excavated through the limestone. The tunnel, dotted by a long line of torches, seemed to go on forever. No one spoke until the only sounds were their own footfalls.

"This definitely seems to be leading somewhere," Mac finally whispered.

Father Bailey agreed. "I'd call this heading *beyond the palace,* as Hunayn described."

Seichan felt safe enough to loosen Aggie's chokehold. The monkey protested with sharp eeks. But she shushed him and massaged his back, something that always comforted little Jack when distressed. It seemed to work here, too.

Maria noted her attempt to calm Aggie and held out her arms. "Do you want me to take him?"

Seichan shifted away. "I got him."

Maria nodded, showing no offense.

Gray, though, looked at her with a raised eyebrow.

Seichan ignored him, feeling no need to explain herself. Maybe her desire to keep Aggie with her was born out of some maternal instinct, some hormone-driven mechanism that had control of her actions, as if she were as much an automaton as those figures back there. But Seichan knew it wasn't that. If Aggie hadn't come in time, if Charlie hadn't sent him, they might all be dead. To honor that, she intended to protect the macaque, to return Aggie to his foster mother—that is, if the captain was still alive.

Which was a big if.

42

Charlie crouched at the edge of the forest. She clutched her pistol between both palms, as if in prayer. She certainly needed God's protection. But as the old adage goes, *God helps those who help themselves.* And that was the plan.

Charlie hoped to help herself.

"Be careful," Elena whispered next to her.

Charlie nodded. *That's also the plan.* She stared across the open meadow to the helicopter resting in the green grass and scrub bushes. She had no idea how to fly such an aircraft, but that was not why she had come here. For the past twenty minutes, she had led Elena north through the dense forest. If nothing else, they had shaken the armed giant, Kadir, from their trail.

At least for now.

But Charlie could not count on that luck lasting forever, especially if the armed force should return from their cave exploration and scour these woods. With only two rounds left in her pistol, her plan was to arm up, then continue north into the mountains. She would've preferred to head south toward the distant Sous, but that path was trickier, the way blocked by the stream where she had beached her boat.

The better route was north anyway. The forest grew thicker in the higher mountains, offering more places to hide. Plus she knew one of the two helicopters had landed up here.

She stared over at the aircraft abandoned in the meadow. She needed to reach it, check it for weapons, maybe a radio, then continue onward. Still, she waited a full three minutes, watching for any sign of movement. A dry north wind waved the grass, adding to her anxiety. Finally, she knew enough was enough.

Gotta take the chance.

"Stay hidden," Charlie warned Elena.

Elena nodded and shifted deeper into the shadows.

Charlie straightened from her crouch and ran low across the meadow, skirting rocks and bushes. Her eyes strained for any threat. But there were no signs of motion near the helicopter. Focused over there, she missed it.

Elena did not and shouted from her hiding place. "On your left!"

Charlie trusted her enough to leap headlong and roll through the tall grass. Gunfire blasted from the direction of the river; rounds shredded the grass above her. She caught a glimpse of a giant figure rising from behind a mossy boulder on the riverbank. Kadir must have gone straight up the channel, anticipating her actions. Charlie's more cautious approach had given the bastard plenty of time to set up this ambush.

Reaching an outcropping of rock, she hid behind it.

What now?

She had one moment to think as the giant fired toward where Elena had shouted, likely knowing Charlie offered no threat. Even with a fully loaded pistol, what could she do?

And I only have the two rounds.

She stared over to the helicopter, to the extra tanks of fuel on its undercarriage. She again raised the pistol between her palms.

Just have my back, dear Lord.

Popping out of hiding, she aimed for those tanks and fired. If nothing else, her aim proved true. She noted the spark by the fuel intake cap, heard the ping above the pistol crack. Then she turned and ran like hell for the forest. Unlike Hollywood movies, there was no fiery explosion behind her. She knew there wouldn't be. She had been around enough engines and motors her whole life.

But as she had hoped, someone else had been watching too many movies. From the corner of her eye, she saw Kadir duck behind his boulder after her showy demonstration of her marksmanship. He even cast a protective arm over his face as he dove away.

Her ruse gave her the time to cross halfway back to the forest. Then she spotted Kadir peeking out again, glancing from the helicopter to her. He raised his rifle, but her pistol was already up. She fired at his position, driving him back down for another breath.

It allowed her to reach the forest's edge and dash into the dark woods. She didn't slow, noting Elena crashing alongside her a couple of yards away.

Then the world exploded behind them with a thunderous blast and a heated whoosh of flames.

What the hell? Had the helicopter actually blown?

Then another fiery explosion burst to her right. Another to the left.

Charlie understood as she fled, her body whipped by branches. Kadir was shooting grenades after them again—only these ones were packed with incendiary charges.

She risked a glance back.

A wall of flames grew and spread behind her, quickly becoming a hellish forest fire. The stiff north wind blew the smoke through the forest, enveloping her, heating the air, making it hard to breathe. Elena coughed harshly on her right.

Charlie understood Kadir's intent.

He's herding us back the way we came.

43

At the end of the tunnel, Gray stood before a set of unadorned bronze doors. Even from a foot away, he felt the heat radiating off them. He reached a palm and tested one of the handles. Hot but manageable.

He remembered Hunayn's cryptic warning.

Beyond the palace, where the fires of Hades burn . . .

"Everyone, get back," he warned.

Let's see if this is the right place.

He gripped the handle with both hands and tugged hard. It did not give, perhaps locked like the other gates. But then the door budged. He let out a breath of relief. He braced his legs and hauled on the door, which was solid bronze, half a foot thick, a veritable vault door.

He gasped as he worked it open—not from the effort, but from the intense heat, from the sulfurous stink of rotten eggs that swelled out into the dark tunnel. Still, he heaved the door the rest of the way open.

"Oh god," Kowalski groaned, waving a hand before his face. "This is definitely Hell."

Gray straightened and stared into the cavern beyond. The space was herculean in size, stretching endlessly upward and spreading hundreds of yards to the right and left. Massive stalactites hung from a roof that could barely be seen.

This was not the polished, refined cavern of the Phaeacians, but instead, the home of Hephaestus, a true Vulcan's forge, a vast and steaming industrial workshop.

Gray led the others into the hot cavern.

To either side, a massive mining operation had carved out the walls long ago, leaving behind rough-cut terraces, climbing high, with hills of broken scrap below. Gray imagined that vast operation, pulling much-needed ore, metals, and most important, deposits of phosphate rock.

Gray continued through this area, drawn by a ruddy glow deeper in the cavern. With each yard gained, the temperature rose. The source of the hellish heat became clear.

A fissure split the cavern into two halves. A gargantuan stone slab had been dropped across it long ago, creating a wide bridge.

Gray drew near the fissure's edge and peered down. The drop was endless, as if to the core of the earth. Molten fires glowed far below. The heat became too intense after only a few breaths. He had to back away.

Bailey had looked, too. "Magma," he concluded.

Gray nodded, picturing the Da Vinci map. "This could be a section of the convergent boundary between the African and Eurasian tectonic plates."

"A veritable crack in the world," Bailey said.

Gray headed to the stone bridge, risking the heat, the poisonous air. He climbed to the top of the bridge to get a better look at the cavern beyond the fissure.

The others gathered behind him.

"It's amazing," Maria said in a hushed, reverential tone, as if standing at the threshold to a vast cathedral.

"And terrifying," Mac added.

They were both right.

Ahead, and covering twenty acres, was something out of a Brobding-nagian nightmare, the foundry of some twisted god. The bones of this sleeping factory were a byzantine network of bronze pipes, scaffolded in layers, rising toward the distant roof and diving down into the magma fissure. Across the floor were rows of cold forges. Elsewhere, kilns and ovens towered.

Yet, even here this ancient forge showed signs of waking.

Within the depths of the factory, a scatter of furnaces blazed with golden fire. Several engines rumbled, casting out periodic whistles with blasts of steam. Glowing green oil pumped and bubbled behind clear crystal in tall bronze tanks. Giant valves slowly turned on their own, powered by steam or Promethean fire. Off to the right, a pipe screamed and burst into flames. Several other industrial torches blazed, cloaked in smoke.

"Look," Mac said.

He pointed to the far right, to large open vats, full of shimmering black oil. Pipes ran from those tanks to a mud lake, which bubbled and burped with sulfurous gases. Upon the sludge's hot surface shone pools of the same unrefined oil, apparently the source of fire-defying Promethean Blood.

One mystery among many solved.

Gray got them all moving again, especially considering what they still needed to do: find another way out of here. Or at least some way to put this city back to sleep.

Still, Hunayn's warning played in his head.

If you wake Tartarus, know it will be for the last and final time.

With that ominous warning in mind, Gray headed through the massive foundry. He and the others had seen the handiwork produced by this factory out in the city. But in here, the Phaeacians had hidden their greatest endeavor, their masterworks.

The group treaded lightly across the foundry, as if fearful of waking the bronze colossi to either side. The figures stood ten stories tall, six to a side, encased in scaffolding, bridged by ladders. Though still works in progress, their shapes and countenances were evident enough. Six men and six women. A couple were horrendous in shape, multi-limbed and misshapen. Like some Lovecraftian beasts come to life, true Chthonian monsters.

"The Elder Gods," Bailey murmured. "The Titans of Greek mythology. The twelve firstborn of Uranus and Gaia. Imprisoned by the gods who came later."

"And still trapped here, by the look of it," Maria said. "In a prison made of bronze pipes."

Gray studied one, whose chest lay open. Within that cavity, green blood bubbled throughout a labyrinth of crystal pipes, setting the interior aglow. In the center was a gold and bronze spherical device, not unlike the astrolabe that led them here, but threatening in appearance, especially as it turned with a flash of flame, as if ticking downward.

He pictured this war machine—which he somehow knew it was—marching across a battlefield, its blood surging with radioactive fire, like some walking atomic bomb.

"We can never let this fall into the wrong hands," Gray said. "Into *any* hands."

Gray knew Hunayn must have felt the same a millennium ago.

But what did the captain do?

Gray hurried the group past the foundry, passing under the Titanic gazes of the Elder Gods, to where the cave ended at a small antechamber.

Two fountains of black oil—Promethean Blood—filled stone containers on either side, the excess spilling into catch basins on the floor and draining away. One vat was huge, a veritable Roman bath. The other was small, more like a washbasin.

Between them stood another bronze door, identical to the one behind them, but this one had a small window in it, set with a translucent stone, maybe polished crystal or a crude form of glass.

The view through it was cloudy, but details were clear enough, especially considering what lit the space. Beyond a small bronze landing in the next room stretched an Olympic-sized pool. It was flush to both sides of the chamber. Only this pool was full of Medea's Oil. It glowed a toxic emerald, its surface vaguely stirring, as if hiding some new horror. While its depth was unknowable, considering the scale of everything he'd just seen, Gray sensed the pool was as deep as the Titans were tall.

Mac studied the space with a critical eye. "I wonder if this is the source for *all* of the oil plumbed throughout the city."

"The true heart of Tartarus," Bailey said.

Mac pointed across the pool to an apron on the far side, to a large bronze wheel set into the wall back there. "That could be the main cutoff valve for the city."

Gray leaned closer, cupping his eyes against the glass. "Hunayn mentioned this was where he discovered a way to force Tartarus back to sleep. If that valve did shut off the city's oil supply, the constructs would eventually consume whatever fuel had been pumped into them."

"And then they'd shut down," Mac said.

"Going back to sleep," Maria added.

Mac nodded. "I saw something like that happen to the bronze crabs in Greenland. But not to the bronze bull. Though its bulk surely held a larger supply of fuel."

"But how can we be sure closing that valve will do anything?" Maria asked.

Gray pointed under the valve wheel, to where a pile of bones rested against the back wall, amid scraps of cloth. "I'm guessing those are the remains of Abd Al-Qadir, the one who Hunayn said gave his life to save them all. The captain likely left the body as a warning to whoever dared follow."

Seichan had her turn at the window. "But look to the left. Something looks welded to the wall. Near the valve."

Gray turned his attention to where she indicated. The device shone brighter, not only newer, but made of gold. Even from here, Gray identified a two-foot circular disk, inscribed and decorated in a similar fashion to the astrolabe. The handiwork was easy enough to recognize, its purpose even easier to guess.

"Hunayn's fail-safe," Gray said. He turned to the group, surmising the Arab captain's intent. "I imagine if we shut down that valve to send Tartarus back to sleep, it'll activate the captain's doomsday device."

"In other words," Kowalski said with a scowl, "we're damned if we do and damned if we don't."

Gray turned to the vastness of the steaming cavern, burning with sulfurous brimstone and glowing with Promethean fire. He stared up at the towering Titans and pictured what lay waiting for his group out in the city. He considered all who had died to keep this secret, the many more who had suffered.

Hunayn had been right.

This must end here.

He turned back to the sealed door.

"No matter the risk," he said, "we need to get over there."

7:44 P.M.

With her arms crossed tightly, Maria stood well back as Joe dragged the thick bronze door open. He grunted with the effort but got it open a few inches.

Mac rushed forward and stuck the nose of his Geiger counter through the gap. The device erupted with fierce and rapid clicking. From steps away, she saw the counter's meter flip all the way into the red zone. Illuminated numbers climbed in a blur, finally fluctuating between ninety and a hundred.

Mac yanked his arm back. "Close it! Close it now!"

Joe put his shoulder into the door and slammed it. "So how bad is it?" he asked.

Mac had paled. "Like I feared. The volume of oil, the concentration . . ."

Gray grabbed his arm. "Tell us."

"I'm registering nearly *one hundred* sieverts." When no one seemed to understand, Mac continued. "In the control room at Chernobyl, the staff was exposed to *three hundred*. They took in a lethal dose in under two minutes."

Maria's stomach gave a sickening lurch. She stared through the window toward the pile of bones. "Then we know how that poor fellow over there died. Radiation poisoning."

Mac nodded. "It looks like the only way to close that shutoff valve is to swim across that pool and turn it manually. It's a fatal swim, though. That's if you can even make it across before succumbing."

"Charon's price," Gray said, quoting Hunayn.

Mac looked grim. "You have to give up your life to save everyone else."

The group debated various options—a makeshift boat, stringing a rope—but they all knew they were just marking time until the inevitable.

Joe lifted an arm. "Enough already. I'll do it."

Maria tried to pull his arm down. "Don't be stupid."

"I think that's what I'm best known for." Joe faced the group. "We all know someone's *got* to do it. Gray and Seichan have a kid. Mac has a bad wing. Maria, you're so tiny, you'll burn up before you put your toe in."

"I can do it," Bailey said. He stood beside the large vat of black oil. "I think you're supposed to dunk your whole body in here, as some sort of barrier to help you make the swim across."

Joe joined him. "Padre, I appreciate the offer, but you aren't much bigger than Maria. And I'm not about to send a priest in to do a man's job."

Bailey looked offended, but Joe guided him away from the door.

"Besides," Joe said, "you know all about this mythology business. It's all Greek to me."

Gray stepped forward, looking ready to make his case.

Joe shut him down with a glare. "You know I'm right."

Maria ran up and hugged him. "We could take our chances out there."

"And go where?" he asked. "Even searching would probably get us all killed. Someone's got to go in there and shut this place down."

He freed himself from her and turned to the large vat of black oil, untucking his shirt, preparing to strip down for his dunking.

"Leave everything on," Bailey warned. "The more Promethean Blood between you and the Medea's Oil, all the better. I'd suggest you even soak a scarf and wrap your head entirely."

"How'm I supposed to see?"

"You don't," Bailey said. "You swim blind. It's a straight shot. If you don't think you can do it—"

"I can do it," Joe said.

Gray pulled a set of climbing gloves from his pack and passed them to Joe. "Cover your hands, too."

Joe suited fully up and climbed into the big black vat, spilling oil across the floor. He ducked fully under and stayed there, jostling about, rubbing oil everywhere. The plan was to force the Promethean Blood into every pore, to soak his clothes, to fill his boots.

Maria held her breath while he was under. She wondered if fate was cursing her for her doubts about Joe, about all her second-guessing of their relationship.

Is God punishing me?

Bailey drew next to her. "He may be okay. While Hunayn's sailor probably covered his body with oil, he may not have coated himself as thoroughly as Joe."

Maria grasped at this hope.

"And know I'll pray for him," Bailey said.

I will, too.

Joe finally surfaced and climbed out, a silhouette in black. Bailey soaked a scarf and prepared to wrap his head like a mummy.

"Wait," Gray said. He turned from his study of the washbasin of oil on the other side and pointed back at it. "Why's this here? It's too small to bathe more than a dog in it."

Bailey frowned, unable to answer.

Gray eyed the priest. "One of your stories earlier. You said Medea protected the hero Jason before battle by making him *drink* her potion. That when imbibed, it granted him further protections, from even spears and arrows."

Bailey's eyes widened, and he turned to Joe. "That's right! I doubt even Hunayn thought of that precaution."

Joe looked confused. "What're you getting at?"

Maria answered, hope growing brighter inside her. She pointed to the washbasin. "That's a water fountain. You're supposed to drink from it."

"Shielding both your insides and out," Bailey said.

Gray studied the oil. "Maybe it's got some iodine-like properties that protect organs against radiation damage."

Maria didn't care *how* it worked—only that it *did*.

Joe looked less than thrilled as he stared down into the washbasin. "I'm having second thoughts about *all* of this."

44

Where's that Charon guy when you need him?

As Kowalski stumbled blindly ahead, he heard the door slam behind him, clanging with a note of finality. He reached forward, probing with one leg, then the other, as he crossed the bronze landing. The toe of his boot finally found the lip of the pool.

He breathed hard, sucking the soaked cloth into and out of his mouth, suddenly claustrophobic. He wanted to rip away the wraps, but he knew better. Even blindfolded like this, he kept his eyelids squeezed tight, trying to protect every tender part of him.

He drew closer to the pool's edge. He swore he could feel the radiation emanating from that toxic sea, like waves of heat pressing against him.

His stomach churned, both from fear and from the long draughts of oil the others had forced him to drink. It had tasted like charcoal but weirdly sickly sweet. He had come close to losing his cookies right then and there. Still, he manned up and held it all down.

He sat at the pool's edge and lowered his feet into the toxic soup. It was hot, uncomfortably so, worrisomely so.

If the radiation doesn't get me, I may be parboiled before I get to the other side.

Still, he lowered himself in, careful to keep his head above water. He knew the longer he was in here, the greater his danger. He took another deep breath and kicked off the wall. He glided across the glowing sea, sweeping out with his arms in a breaststroke, frog-kicking his legs. It was harder than he had anticipated. His clothes weighed him down; his boots were anchors on his legs. But at least the oil seemed more buoyant than regular water.

I'm just a big fat water droplet floating on a lethal oil slick.

He continued across. After a minute, he had no sense of how far he'd traveled or how far he had to go. Fear made him suddenly feel sicker. A headache that had been there from the beginning pounded harder. As he continued, nausea rose up, bad enough to burn bile through his chest.

Don't lose it here.

He swept his arms and kicked harder. A wave of dizziness swept through him, making his stomach flip, along with the world. He felt as if he were swimming upside down. He paddled, panicked, afraid of going under. The room spun inside his head. He quickly grew disoriented, unsure if he was even still headed in the right direction. He pictured himself swimming in circles until exhaustion dragged him down.

Already he felt his strength sapping.

Get hold of yourself, he demanded.

Still, he knew what was happening. Mac had explained it all to him. Kowalski again pictured waves of radiation sweeping through him. *It can kill you in minutes,* Mac had warned and ticked off the warning signs. *Nausea, disorientation, headaches.*

Check, check, and check.

Kowalski swam faster, hoping it was all in his head, some psychosomatic bullshit. But he couldn't convince himself of that. Instead he pictured Maria, smiling at some joke, frowning at something stupid he did, which was all too often. He remembered her touch in the night, the smell of her skin, the brush of her hair. He recalled their last night together in Agadir, sinking into her warmth, her breath on his neck.

She was his lamp in the darkness now.

He kicked and paddled, his breath heaving in and out. He would do anything to keep her safe, even cross a toxic sea.

I can do this—for you.

Then something grabbed his ankle and dragged him under.

8:03 P.M.

Maria pounded on the bronze door. With her forehead pressed to the hot glass, she searched the roiling surface of the glowing pool. Halfway across, Joe's body had jerked and vanished into the oil.

Gray had seen it, too. He was at the small fountain, drinking from its black font. He and Bailey had already dunked themselves earlier in the larger tank, to protect themselves as they opened the door for Kowalski and slammed it behind him. Now it looked like Gray intended a rescue operation.

As Gray stepped toward the door, Maria stopped him, blocking him with her body. "No," she said. "That wasn't the plan."

Gray's eyes shone with a fierce determination.

Maria faced that heat.

Bailey grabbed Gray's shoulder. Even Seichan shifted next to Maria, backing her up. They had all agreed they would only try this once, risking only one of them.

"Joe has this," Maria told Gray. "He has this."

Gray clenched a fist.

Maria turned her back on him, leaving the others to deal with Gray.

She stared across the glowing green pool.

Don't make a liar out of me, Joe.

8:04 P.M.

Kowalski thrashed in the oil, struggling to hold his breath, to keep his lips pressed tightly. As he was dragged deeper, he twisted down and grabbed the end of a segmented metal tendril wrapped around his boot. He fought to rip it off, but it only clamped harder.

Fuck this.

He let go of the constricting vine and tugged his laces loose. Then he pried at the trapped boot with his other heel, with both hands. He wiggled and fought. Luckily the foot inside the boot was well greased. The boot finally popped off. He felt it wrench away, towed into the depths.

He kicked the other way, pawing for the surface.

He finally broke through to open air. He clawed the wraps from his face and head. Most of it had already been dislodged. Whatever protection it had offered, it was too late now. The damage was done.

As he swam for the far landing, he opened his eyes, knowing he needed to see. The glow of the pool glared after the minutes of darkness— or maybe it was the radiation causing his eyes to ache. He didn't know, and right now he didn't care.

Maybe the oil over his head was enough. Maybe what he had washed into his eyes when he had bathed in the black oil would protect him. Maybe what he drank . . .

He heard splashing behind him.

A glance back revealed a nest of tendrils shredding the water. His stolen boot was thrown high, bouncing off the ceiling and back into the water. The mass of bronze vines snaked toward him.

He swam faster, choking down bile, ignoring the spin of the room, his heart hammering. He no longer bothered with a cautious breaststroke. He ducked his head and swam freestyle, speeding across the buoyant oil.

Legs kicking, arms digging.

He held his breath, keeping his face down.

He sensed the approach of the wall and peeked up.

Another two yards.

Something brushed the toes on his bootless foot.

He strangled a scream and gave one last burst of speed. He hit the far side, lunged up, grabbed the edge, and pitched over. Like a seal beaching on an ice floe, he slid and rolled across the bronze landing.

He crashed through old bones and struck the wall.

Fuck, fuck, fuck . . .

Out in the lake, a wave surged toward him, led by a churning mass of snaking vines. He cringed, expecting to be snagged and dragged back in. Instead, the tendrils snapped taut, their tips waving at the pool's edge, apparently the extent of their reach. With their prey escaped, they sank back into the depths.

Kowalski grabbed the large bronze wheel and hauled himself up on shaking legs. He paused long enough to flip off the swamp creature and set about turning the stubborn wheel, cranking the valve with all his remaining strength. His arms trembled with the effort. His vision narrowed. Finally, he felt something clank and vibrate the wheel. It would not turn anymore.

Hopefully that's enough.

Because he had nothing left.

Still hanging by his arm, he twisted around and slumped with his back to the wall. He sat atop the bones and didn't care. He dropped his arm, his hand coming to rest on a skull. He patted it.

Yeah, you and me both.

As he gasped, the wall vibrated behind him. He glanced up to the gold device welded to the wall. It had pipes running down from it and through the bronze apron, likely into the pool below. A large gold disk above it started to turn, tick by tick.

That can't be good.

Motion drew his gaze forward. Thick plates of bronze, hinged at the bottom, tilted out from both sides of the room. Chains lowered them until the edges met in the middle with a loud clang, sealing the toxic pool below under this new floor.

Kowalski stared across from one landing to the other. He leaned his head back with an exasperated sigh.

You couldn't have done that earlier?

8:07 P.M.

"What's the number?" Gray asked Mac.

The climatologist retreated from the crack in the door and stared down at the Geiger counter. "With the pool sealed, the levels are down ninety percent in there. Which is still hot, but it should be safe if you're quick." Mac waved at Gray's soaked clothes and body. "Of course, a little extra protection never hurt."

Gray nodded. "Everyone else stay back around the corner."

Bailey stepped forward. "I'll go with you. You may need help with Joe." He lowered his voice so Maria couldn't hear. "He looks in bad shape."

Gray didn't argue. The priest was already anointed in the black oil. "C'mon."

He hauled the door wide enough for them to slip through, then closed it behind them. Across the way, Kowalski noticed their arrival and lifted a trembling arm—then promptly dropped it.

Gray ran forward, his boots ringing off the bronze floor. Bailey kept at his heels. When they reached Kowalski, the priest dropped next to him, looking ready to perform Last Rites. But the big man had some fight left in him.

Kowalski rolled his head toward the device on the wall. "That's your problem."

Gray understood and faced the ticking gold clock of Hunayn's fail-safe. He noted a circle of Arabic inscribed on it. "Can you read this?" Gray asked.

Bailey helped Kowalski up and squinted over at the writing. He tilted his head in order to read it as the clock face slowly turned a tick at a time. "It says *I grant you enough time for your final prayers. So Allah will accept you with merciful grace.*"

Gray had already roughly estimated how much time that entailed. From the circumference of the clock, from the pace of its rotation, he calculated how long it would take to reach the silver mark on the gold dial.

Less than fifteen minutes.

Gray shifted his attention down to a wide gold box that likely housed the fail-safe mechanism. For any hope of disarming it, he had to get it open. He searched its sides but found no means to unlatch or remove the cover. He grabbed the edges and tried lifting it off. He managed to shift it—but that was a mistake.

Even Kowalski noted it as he leaned on Bailey and groaned.

The clockwork dial snapped forward a full third, trimming their time by the same amount. Cursing Hunayn's cleverness, Gray backed away. The device had been booby-trapped against tampering.

"How long?" Bailey asked.

Gray pointed to the far door.

"Less than ten minutes."

45

Elena fled through the burning forest.

Behind her, cedars exploded into torches. Hot smoke shrouded everything. Fires roared all around. She stumbled onward, seeking some refuge, some escape. Her eyes watered, her breath gasped.

Charlie kept next to her, clutching her hand. The woman's face was sheened with sweat, smeared with ash. Tears trailed through them, likely only partly due to the sting of the smoke.

"This way," Charlie urged, tugging her toward where the smoke looked thinner, where the forest was darker.

Elena tripped and staggered alongside her.

Not going to make it.

Then suddenly the trees fell away to both sides. The sun, still cloaked by a layer of smoke overhead, shone brightly.

Elena searched around and immediately knew where she was.

Oh no.

She stared up at the stratified cliff face, at the blasted mouth of a cave a short distance up. It was where everyone had gone, vanished to who knew where.

Elena's feet slowed.

She did not want to follow.

But Charlie left her no choice and clutched Elena's hand even harder. "We need to get out of sight."

Tugged along, Elena realized Charlie was right. With the forest behind them on fire and the river surely watched, they needed to hide, to regroup, to think of some way out of this mess.

Charlie let go of her hand when they reached the cliff face and began to crawl up—then the rock exploded over her, blasted by a line of gunfire strafing above her head.

Charlie ducked and leaped back down, joining Elena on the ground. They both put their backs to the rock. From around the corner of the burning forest, coming up the tiny stream where Charlie's cruiser was beached, Kadir stepped into view, a black armored figure with his rifle raised.

After forcing them here, he had come for the kill.

Charlie tried to step toward the flames and smoke, but Kadir fired at her toes, driving her back to the wall. He marched toward them, closing the distance, making escape even more impossible.

Behind him, another figure appeared.

Monsignor Roe hobbled after Kadir, having followed him from the boat. A white bandage wrapped his upper thigh, stanching where Charlie had shot him during their escape attempt. The priest's countenance was dark, his eyes burning with both pain and fury.

Kadir stopped in front of them with his back to the flaming forest.

Roe called over. "Just kill them both!"

Kadir showed no emotion. As dead-eyed as ever, he simply centered his rifle at Charlie and fired.

8:09 P.M.

Nehir hid alongside the gold stairs that led up to the castle. She sheltered behind a one-story home. Across the steps, Ahmad and the last remaining Son did the same. It had taken them too long to cross the breadth of the city, cautiously sticking to shadows, avoiding any of the fiery hunters, waiting for them to pass.

But Allah smiled upon her and rewarded her caution.

She leaned out enough to catch a glimpse of the palace façade thirty yards above her position. She dared go no closer. Large shapes stirred up there, shrouded in cloaks of smoke, stirring with deeper flames. A spindly-legged spider, as tall as a bus, stalked across the gates, stepping around and over others of its brethren. A smaller figure of a glowing bronze warrior with a helmet stepped to the top of the stairs.

She willed it to stay there—and Allah heard her silent prayer.

The warrior turned and vanished back into the smoke.

Behind Nehir, she heard a faint whistling laugh, so soft she wasn't sure she had heard it. Still, it set her hairs on end. She pulled back into her hiding place and searched around her. Nothing. She glanced over to Ahmad, who still looked toward the palace, plainly having not heard anything. Nehir shook her head and rubbed an ear that still buzzed from all the grenade blasts and rifle fire.

She dropped her hand.

Enough.

She focused back to the task at hand. She and the others needed to get into that castle—either to follow her adversaries to some back door out of here or to hunt them down and exact her revenge.

Hopefully, *both.*

She firmed her hold on her rifle.

Nehir caught Ahmad's attention and signaled him. Her second-in-command turned to whisper in the ear of the man behind him. The other nodded and stepped back, a grenade already in hand. He retreated far enough for a clear throw—not toward the palace but past it. The goal was to use the blast to lure the fiery guardians away from the gold gate.

The Son stared at her, waiting for her final signal.

She gave it.

He reached his arm far back—then screamed.

Something smoldering and hidden back there lunged up in a sudden burst of fire and smoke. It snapped at the Son's outstretched arm, swallowing it whole, ripping it off at the shoulder. Blood spewed high as the man fell forward—revealing a glimpse of the massive bulk of a black dog.

Ahmad tried to get away.

Less in fear of the monster than—

The grenade exploded behind him. The dog's head blasted apart. Shrapnel from both the grenade and pieces of the dog peppered Ahmad's back. But her second-in-command wore full-body armor. Though wounded and knocked to his hands and knees, he crawled out onto the gold stairs.

Nehir backed away in horror.

Ahmad read her face and twisted around.

Behind him, the rest of the huge dog revealed itself, lifting two more heads into view. Diamond eyes glowed with fire; it had flames for tongues. Here was Cerebos, the three-headed guardian of Hell. One snout lunged out and caught Ahmad by the leg and lifted his struggling body high off the ground. The other head snapped onto an arm and shoulder. Then they tossed their necks wide and ripped Ahmad in half.

By then, Nehir had retreated far into the shadows.

She turned away and stared up.

While the plan with the grenade had gone awry, the blast did its job. The mass of flaming forms flowed and clambered down the gold stairs, drawn by the explosion.

She circled wide, steering a path clear of that fiery parade.

Her goal hadn't changed.

She headed toward the gold gate.

8:10 P.M.

Elena gasped as Kadir fired at Charlie.

Charlie cringed to the side, bumping into Elena. The cliff face on the far side shattered with a three-round burst. Shards peppered the two of them, stinging and sharp.

Elena grabbed Charlie's hand. They pulled tighter together.

Across the way, Kadir held his smoking rifle, his head slightly cocked. He had purposely missed her. But there was no leer of sadistic glee at this teasing torture. The giant remained as emotionless as ever, a cat calmly playing with a trapped pair of mice. His actions read more curious than cruel.

Still, eventually the cat kills the mice.

Kadir lifted his rifle again—clearly done with his game.

A heavy scraping of metal on stone drew all their gazes up. Apparently, someone else had heard Kadir's noisy, capricious play. From the cavern, a massive beast leaped out. It crashed heavily between Elena and Kadir with a booming clang of bronze and a blast of smoke and fire. The ground shook with its impact. It landed in a crouch, its front low, its haunches high. A long tail swept across the cliff overhead, raining debris over the two women.

Kadir fired at it, retreating toward the burning woods.

His barrage rang off the bronze.

Charlie and Elena dropped low.

The titanic dog—a huge mastiff of metal—lunged, snapped, and grabbed Kadir before he could escape. This was no cat come to play. The beast reared up and tossed its head high. It threw Kadir's body into the air. The giant cartwheeled, spraying blood. The mastiff roared, casting flames from its jaws, roasting the flailing man in midair.

Finally, Kadir screamed.

The mastiff caught him again and flung his body into the fiery woods.

Panicked, Charlie started for the same forest. But Elena kept hold of her hand and kept her there. Elena lifted a finger to her own lips.

Joe had told her about Mac's experience.

Stay silent . . . don't move.

Charlie trusted her enough to obey.

Another person had never learned that lesson.

Off to the side, Monsignor Roe hobbled away in horror. The mastiff swung toward the motion, the pained gasps. It stalked after the cleric. Roe tried to walk faster on his wounded leg, glancing back, his face shining with terror.

The hunter was also compromised—whether from the leap off the cliff or perhaps injured earlier. Elena remembered the rocket attack on the cave, on the doors inside. Had this been some guardian in there?

The mastiff dragged a hind leg and struggled with a broken elbow.

Elena straightened, watching the slow pursuit. Who would win out? The answer came a few breaths later. The mastiff drained the last of its energy and crashed headlong across the tiny streambed with a jangle of bronze. It sprawled there, neck stretched, mouth open. Its bulk still smoked, remained fiery, but clearly fading.

Roe hopped back around, sagging in relief.

Then the mastiff's body convulsed one final time. From deep in its gullet, it cast out a new horror. Through its gaping jaws, a river of scrabbling bronze-shelled crabs exploded forth. They set fire to the stream, to themselves.

Roe froze in terror.

Then the wave reached him and climbed his body. Sharp legs speared deep into his flesh. His clothes caught fire. He writhed and spun, quickly armored in fiery bronze.

He screamed far longer than Kadir had.

Elena pushed Charlie the other way. "To the boat," she urged.

With the deadly horde momentarily distracted, they needed to reach the cruiser. They fled through the edge of the burning forest, paralleling the tiny tributary, using the smoke and the roar of the flames to hide their passage.

When they reached the cruiser, Elena gasped and turned back upstream.

"What's wrong?" Charlie asked.

She pointed. "The keys . . . Monsignor Roe had them."

"*Mon Dieu*," Charlie exclaimed and hopped aboard. "You don't think I have a spare set? What sort of captain do you think I am?"

Elena followed her aboard.

A damned good one.

46

Six minutes or less . . .

Gray needed every second to pull this off.

The group hit the throne room at a full sprint. Even Kowalski had re-gained his footing, running on adrenaline, though shaky. Still, he hauled his AA-12 with him, holding on to it with white knuckles.

Maria hovered close at his side, Mac on his other.

Bailey caught up with Gray. "Where are you—?"

Gunfire exploded across the throne room, chattering across their path. Ten yards to the right, a figure hid in a side passage, down on a knee, weapon raised at them.

As they all skidded to a stop in the middle of the room, the sniper—a woman—called to them, "Where is the exit? Tell me now!"

Gray knew it was *this* question that had kept her from shooting them outright. She needed a way out of here as much as they did.

Kowalski sneered. "Nehir . . ."

The big man lifted his weapon, reacting with raw fury.

To discourage him, she fired again, closer to the group. Mac yelped and toppled to the side, his leg giving way as a round struck him in the foot. Blood sprayed across the stone floor.

Seichan used the distraction to whip around and fling Aggie through the air at the sniper. Caught by surprise, the monkey screeched like a banshee, arms flailing in the air. Equally caught off guard—and clearly already tense and spooked by what she must have survived to get here— Nehir fell backward, firing wildly at the monkey but missing in her panic.

Kowalski dropped to a knee and unloaded a barrage of FRAG-12 rounds into the side passage. The explosive shells boomed and rattled there, filling the space with smoke and fire.

He shifted ahead to reposition, but Gray followed and pushed the big weapon aside, discouraging Kowalski from shooting again. They might need that firepower later, and they were down to the last drum magazine.

Besides, Seichan was already moving, SIG in hand. She swept through the billow of smoke and out the other side. She gave a shake of her head with a frown.

Nehir had vanished.

Gray checked his watch. *Five minutes.* They had no time to hunt the woman down. He looked over to Mac.

The man wore a pained expression. "I can hop."

Maria already had an arm around his waist. "I got him."

Gray pointed to the exit. "Move it."

Seichan paused long enough to retrieve Aggie. The monkey looked pissed and scared. She extended an arm. "Sorry about that, little one," she said in the same soothing tones she used with Jack.

Aggie chirped, still plainly irritated, but he leaped, scampered up her arm to her shoulder, and hugged close to her cheek.

Gray led the way toward the exit, praying they still had enough time.

"Where *are* we going?" Bailey pressed.

Gray had no time to explain and pointed back at the thrones as they left the hall. "The answer's back there."

Hopefully I'm right.

8:14 P.M.

Nehir dragged her broken leg down the hall of the castle. Her femur stuck through the fabric. Blood trailed behind her. She kept one hand on a wall and shuffled deeper into the palace, seeking the comfort of shadows to hide in.

The only reason she was still alive was a combination of instinct and Kevlar. She had leaped away at the last moment when the American had fired at her. Still, a shell had burst too close, with enough force to shatter her leg. She lost her weapon, but adrenaline kept her moving. First crawling, then eventually standing.

She finally found a dark enough place to collapse, where no fiery torches burned. Along the way, she had noted that the golden flames in the bronze brands along the walls had grown ever smaller, feebler, as if about to be snuffed out.

She didn't know why.

Didn't care.

She sank with her back to the wall, appreciating the cooler darkness. She closed her eyes and leaned her head back. Time skipped a beat as she briefly passed out. A noise woke her. The hallway was even darker now. Her heart pounded in fear.

The sound came from the shadows ahead.

Whistling laughter.

She had heard it before, out in the city. Goose bumps pebbled her flesh. She focused on the source of that laughter.

What is—?

Then it appeared out of the gloom, shedding its shadows.

A glowing bronze boy shambled into view, its head hanging crookedly. It dragged a leg, as broken as hers. Fire and smoke haloed its form. From its lips, frozen in a grinning rictus, another whistling cackle flowed.

The boy came straight at her, perhaps drawn by her gasping breaths.

Once it was close enough, she tried to kick it away with her good leg, but molten hands caught her ankle and tightened. She screamed as fiery bronze burned through Kevlar down to flesh. She writhed, knocking it over on its side. But still it held. Its limbs paddled in the air. Then slowly, like the guttering torches, it stopped and went still with one last thin reed of laughter.

She tried to loosen its grip—then new movement ahead froze her.

Out of the gloom, two new figures appeared, far smaller, but their surfaces glowed even hotter. They crawled toward her, two bronze babies, a boy and a girl.

No . . .

A moan escaped her. She tried to get away, but one leg was shattered, the other trapped, pinned by hundreds of pounds of bronze. She scooted against the wall, turning her face away.

The boy reached her broken leg, then climbed. Each touch burned through the fabric of her trousers, searing her skin. The girl clambered straight between her legs and crawled upward, tracing a fiery path.

Nehir shook her head—not at the blistering flesh, but at what had come for her. Demonic mockeries of her two babies. She cried and writhed. With effort, she could have knocked them away, but even now, she could not bring herself to do so.

If this is Allah's punishment . . .

If this is all I'm allowed . . .

The two bronze babes reached her bosom, melting through her armor, reaching her skin, and continuing to scorch their way down toward her heart.

So be it . . .

She reached her arms and cradled her two children closer. Pain and shock eventually blurred her vision. She stared down at their soft little bodies. Feeling them settle and grow quiet.

My little girl, Huri . . . my sweet little boy.

She held them until they all stopped moving.

47

Four minutes to go . . .

Gray led the others down the gold stairway. All around, Tartarus had grown darker as torches flickered out. He pictured the closed valve, shutting off the fuel source to the city. But dangers persisted.

As they raced down the stairs, Kowalski's weapon fired in bursts all around. The FRAG-12 shells blasted back anything that threatened: a bronze centaur, a sleek hound, a flame-maned lion. Still, even these attacks seemed far more sluggish as the Promethean flames that fueled the guardians dimmed.

Gray noticed that several had retreated to their bronze pedestals, perhaps following some predetermined program to return for refueling when their power ebbed.

He had no time to give these mysteries more than a passing thought. Back at the foundry's radiative pool, he had noticed pipes running from Hunayn's fail-safe device down into the volatile oil. If that pool blew, especially considering all the residual oil still in the city's plumbing, the explosion would end up being the mother of all air-fuel bombs.

It could blow the top off this mountain.

We don't want to be here when that happens.

Gray finally neared the bottom of the golden staircase and checked his watch.

Three minutes . . .

Bailey drew alongside him, followed by Seichan and Maria, who practically carried Mac between them. The climatologist's face was tight with pain, pale with blood loss and shock.

Bailey searched ahead and was astute enough by now to reason out Gray's plan. "How are we supposed to get out that exit?"

"What exit?" Kowalski asked, panting up behind them, still watching for any threat, his weapon braced on his hip.

"Down there." Bailey pointed to the dark lake, to the water still flowing in from five directions to feed the slowly churning whirlpool in the city's center. "Down the maw of Charybdis."

Kowalski frowned. "I've already had my swim for the day, and I don't feel like being sucked down to nowhere."

"Smell the water," Gray said. "It's *fresh* seawater. This is just one big circulating pump. From the ocean to here and back out again."

Mac heard him, perhaps concentrating on their talk versus his pain. "According to a compass reading I took before, this cavern *does* angle toward the sea, but the ocean still has to be a mile off."

Bailey frowned at Gray. "Then how do you propose to—?"

They reached the end of the gold stairs and Gray pointed to the circle of bronze fish around the lake. "We'll take the Phaeacians' subs."

8:16 P.M.

He's finally lost it . . .

Kowalski climbed off the last step and gaped at the huge ring of fish. There were hundreds, each tilted at an angle, as if ready to spray water and create a fountain worthy of Vegas.

Kowalski rushed after Gray. "Why do you think they're *submarines*?"

"As we said before, the Phaeacians were no fools. They wouldn't trap themselves down here without an escape route."

Kowalski pointed to the massive whirlpool. "And you think *that's* their escape route?"

"By necessity, it would have to be centrally located. And that's as *central* as you can get."

"But still . . ."

"Plus, the thrones," Gray added. "Sculpted there in gold, you can see these same curl-tailed fish depicted, plying the seas alongside the Phaeacians' ships."

As proof, Gray took them to one of the bronze fish. It was the size of a minivan, but he found footholds down one flank and clambered up.

Movement drew Kowalski's gaze higher.

Charybdis wasn't the only Greek monster here.

On the far side of the lake, a six-headed crocodilian dragon swung all of its heads toward Gray. Drawn by the motion, their chatter, or maybe Gray's trespass.

"I think you're pissing someone off," Kowalski warned. "And this time, it's not me."

Gray looked up as one of the massive heads dipped low and snaked over the surface toward him. "Everybody up here! Now!"

Kowalski got everyone moving.

But where then?

8:17 P.M.

Two minutes . . .

Perched on top of the bronze fish, Gray discovered a lever along its spine, the end pointing toward the tail. He grabbed it and hauled it around toward the nose. As he did so, he heard a pressure seal pop and the dorsal fin of the fish hinged open, revealing it to be a hatch. He shoved it up and over.

Mac climbed up behind him, his eyes wide.

"Get in," Gray said.

Mac swung his legs to a ladder inside and slid down, landing with a pained groan. Maria followed behind. Then Bailey and Seichan, who still cradled Aggie.

"Move it!" Gray yelled down to Kowalski.

The big guy balanced his AA-12 on one shoulder and hopped his way up the bronze flank. When he reached the top, he looked over Gray's shoulder, and his eyes snapped wide.

"Down!" Kowalski hollered and swung his weapon over.

Gray tried to stop him, but Kowalski fired a burst of rounds past Gray's shoulder. The shells exploded behind him.

Cringing, he looked back.

One of Scylla's heads sat low on the water, its lower jaw gone. Flames shot from cracks and seams. The neck spasmed and contorted, spraying more fire as it pulled the blasted head back across the lake.

"Get your ass in there!" Gray ordered.

Kowalski obeyed, obviously unaware of the damage he had wrought, and jumped inside.

Gray followed, pausing for a breath on the ladder.

Across the water, the five remaining heads of Scylla writhed in fury. Fire and smoke wreathed its form—then it began to climb into the lake.

Uh-oh.

Gray leaped down, pulling the hatch with him. As it clanked shut, he spun a bronze wheel on the door's underside to seal it tight. The group quickly found seats along benches to either side.

Gray headed to the nose of the sub, glaring at Kowalski.

"What?" the big guy asked.

"Scylla's a guardian," Gray informed him. "Intended to protect the populace while they escape. As long as there's no aggression toward it, it'll leave you alone. But now . . ."

"How was I supposed to know that?"

Gray scowled. "Think before you shoot."

Kowalski sulked. "Where's the fun in that?"

Gray reached the front, where Bailey was seated in one of two bronze seats.

The priest twisted toward him. "According to Homer, the Phaeacians' ships were self-guiding." He pointed to a single control, an upright bronze hand crank. "I think this must—"

Despite his earlier words, now was not the time for *thinking*. Gray dropped into the other seat and hauled the crank down.

The entire fish rocked forward, the nose dropping, then slid off its perch and dove into the water. The impact with the lake jarred everyone, but they kept their seats.

Kowalski straightened. "That wasn't so bad."

Then lake water hit green oil. Fire exploded behind them, burning fuel and the seas behind them. Their bronze fish jetted through the water, throwing them all back.

Gray fought to lean forward. The two bulbous eyes of the fish were made of glass or polished crystal. Through them, he spotted Scylla's bronze legs as the beast waded into the maelstrom of Charybdis. He held his breath as the little sub sped through the pylons of the beast's legs, darting and rolling, reminding Gray of what Bailey had just mentioned.

Self-guided.

Then they were in the tidal pull of the swirling current at the lake's center. It caught them and spun their little sub around the bowl of the lake, faster and faster, tighter and tighter. As they flew, Gray caught a brief glimpse of one of Scylla's fiery heads, aflame in the depths, reaching for them.

Kowalski yelled from the back, "I always wondered what it would feel like to be a goldfish flushed down a toilet."

Don't have to wonder any longer.

The fish tipped its nose straight down.

Gray braced himself against the walls to keep his seat, discovering a handgrip on one side. "Hold tight!"

The sub plummeted into the throat of the lake's drain.

A Stygian darkness closed around them. It became impossible to judge up from down, especially as the fish rocked back and forth, sometimes rolling fully around in a stomach-churning spin.

"Lights ahead!" Bailey yelled above the rush of water.

Gray saw it, too, through one of the fish's eyes. A murky brightness in the far distance. He sighed with relief. *We're going to make—*

There was no warning.

An immense force struck the stern of the sub. It blasted the vessel forward, tossing it end over end, throwing them all around its bronze cabin. Worst of all, the sub crashed repeatedly into the rock walls with clangs of a rung bell.

Water burst into the sub as a seam cracked.

As he fought to hold his seat, Gray pictured what had happened behind them. That mother of all air-fuel bombs must have gone off, powerful enough to drive all the water out of the sea tunnel, like Zeus blowing soda out of a straw.

Then brightness burst in through the fish's eyes. The tumbling roll of the sub evened out, becoming a smooth glide that headed upward. The spray of water through the broken seam slowed. Finally, the sub shot out of the waves. Watery sunlight streamed inside as the vessel rocked in the sea.

Gray sat back and let out a breath.

Their little fish had escaped Tartarus.

He said a silent prayer of thanks and stared back at the crew, all battered and bruised but alive.

"How about some fresh air?" Kowalski said. "I may still throw up."

Gray slid out of his seat and shifted back. He boosted himself on the ladder, spun the lock to free the hatch, and tossed the finned door open. Fresh air and brighter sunlight filled the cabin.

Gray hopped down. "Let's get bailing." He retrieved his satellite phone. "I'll see if I can raise some help."

He climbed back up and sidled out of the way, straddling the fish like a wild bronco on the high seas. He speed-dialed Commander Pullman, the closest ally who could help them.

As it rang through encrypted channels, a wide-belled gray jet sped low overhead. He stared up, recognizing it. It was Pullman's Poseidon, appearing as if summoned by thought alone.

The plane continued past them, gliding across the sea—then swept higher, jettisoning a long black tube attached to a red parachute. Gray recognized the weapon.

A Mark 54 torpedo.

Gray searched ahead. The intended target was evident. The only ship out there was a large hydrofoil speeding across the waves.

Then Pullman came on the line, sounding exasperated and rushed. "Commander Pierce?"

"What are you doing?" Gray asked.

"Sort of busy."

"I can see that. But why?"

"Long story. But I was told to tell you Elena Cargill says hello, and Charlie Izem wanted to know if you have her monkey."

Gray struggled to make sense of all of this.

"Maybe I got the last part wrong," Pullman admitted. "The call was dispatched to me through Director Crowe, from a shipboard radio of a riverboat."

Gray rushed to catch up. So, Charlie must have escaped, got word out, and somehow managed to rescue Elena. That was a story he wanted to hear—but later.

"What about the hydrofoil?" Gray asked.

"According to Dr. Cargill, bad guys. That's all I need to know."

As Gray watched, the torpedo hit the water and blasted off in the direction of the fleeing ship. It struck one of the yacht's twin foils and blew it clean off. Running at full speed, nearly thirty knots, the ship skated along atop its one foil—then slowly tipped over. It crashed sideways into the sea, and nosedived hard into the water.

From the coast, a fleet of Royal Moroccan Navy ships steamed toward the site.

Pullman signed off, after getting Gray's fix from his sat-phone's GPS.

Gray stared back toward the mountainous coast. In the distance, a thick cloud of dust and ash swirled into the sunset skies. While it wasn't a new volcano, Gray pictured the little ruby on the gold map.

In the past, Hunayn had done his best to hide this location, to protect his own era—a time of the Crusades and holy wars—against the horrors and hellfire of Tartarus. It seemed history was destined to be repeatedly tested, to be balanced on the precipice of Armageddon over and over again. Sadly, all too often, it was an apocalypse of our own making. It took men like Hunayn—who fought against the darkness—to pull us back from that brink, who were willing to sacrifice all to this cause.

Gray remembered Kowalski's blind swim across that toxic lake. He pictured the bones of Hunayn's shipmate, marking the grave of a man who had made the same deadly crossing. Both men—separated by millennia— had been willing to pay the ultimate price for the greater good of all.

Maybe such brave souls were the world's true messiahs.

Maybe we didn't need to wait idly by for heavenly salvation.

Maybe we were always our best hope.

Gray watched the hydrofoil settle crookedly into the water and pondered the old quote from Edmund Burke. *The only thing necessary for the triumph of evil is for good men to do nothing.*

He stared toward the setting sun, making a silent promise, picturing his young son.

I will always keep fighting against the darkness.

For you.

For all our bright futures.

48

In the flooded stern hold of the *Morning Star*, the forty-eighth Musa swore a litany of curses. The yacht foundered on its side. Multiple fires raged throughout the ship. Klaxons rang continuously.

Firat waited atop a bobbing jet-ski, seated behind one of his Sons.

Across the drowned hold, a team freed the ship's four-man submersible, armed with dual mini-torpedo launchers. The sub's motors started and the craft burbled in reverse toward him. On the other side, the hold's sea doors were already open, facing away from the coast. He heard the engines of approaching military ships, the occasional scream of a jet overhead. The wreckage of the yacht would be seized and overrun at any moment.

I must not be here.

In hindsight, he should have followed Senator Cargill's example. The man had left the yacht at the Strait of Gibraltar, summoned back to the EU summit, needing to address some state matter in person. At the time, Cargill had ranted, disappointed not to be able to make this journey south and rendezvous with the strike team.

But the bastard had gone and lucky he did.

Or maybe the senator's God smiles upon him more than Allah does upon me.

Back at Gibraltar, Firat had been happy to see the man leave. It opened a range of possibilities, including dealing with the senator's insufferable daughter. As if buoyed by his good spirits, the *Morning Star* had made good time, racing along the Moroccan coast. Firat had planned to rendezvous with Nehir's team—or at least, get updated—when he arrived at Agadir by sunset.

He stared through the stern door at the setting sun.

I kept my word.

Unfortunately, by the time the yacht had reached here, he had become worried. Hour after hour had passed without a new update. Finally, off Agadir, with still no word, worry grew to suspicion. He had ordered the ship's captain to speed north as fast as the engines could manage.

His instinct had been right, but his timing poor.

The *Morning Star* had just gained full speed when it was torpedoed from the air and brought down. Now his only hope was to escape. Nothing else mattered.

The submersible finally drew abreast of the jet-ski. He climbed from one watercraft to the other, dropping heavily into a seat behind the two sub operators, two trusted Sons. Firat had the back of the sub all to himself.

Once everything was sealed tight, he pointed ahead. "Go."

The sub's engine rumbled, and the craft glided smoothly across the hold and out to sea. Firat had a moment of claustrophobic panic as water rose up and over the sub's Lexan glass shell. But as the submersible sank deeper, leaving the brighter sunlight for the blue twilight, he relaxed.

He closed his eyes.

The plan was to strike for the coast, where allies would meet him and whisk him to safety. Only then would he contemplate his revenge.

Still, he enjoyed some thoughts of what he would do to Elena Cargill.

Perhaps I'll tape it. Eventually send it to her father.

Still, even such pleasant daydreams failed to dim his worries, his anxieties about what had happened to Nehir's team.

The sub jolted sharply, shocking him out of his reverie.

"What was that?" he demanded.

"We were struck from underneath," the pilot reported. "Maybe a shark. Drawn by the commotion in the water back there. They can do us no harm."

Firat nodded and leaned back, irritated that the pilot felt the need to reassure him in such a condescending manner. The sub bumped again—hard—driving a surprised yelp out of him.

He braced his arms wide to either side and turned to the twilight seas. He caught a flash of fire in the deep below. Was the sub under attack again? Had another torpedo exploded?

He checked the other side—just as something monstrous rose into view. He scrambled back from the sight of it. Its crocodilian head was half the size of the sub. Its unblinking eyes glowed in the darkness. Impossibly, golden flames wreathed its head and traveled in brilliant cascades down its long, snaking neck.

He wanted to believe it was some fever dream, some nightmare that he had yet to wake from. But the crew spotted it, too. Yelling, gasping. The pilot sped away, but it chased them.

"Shoot it!" he yelled.

The crew regained their wits, spun the sub like a skipped stone, and fired both torpedoes. One missed, but the other struck the beast in the neck. The explosion rocked the sub. The seas burst with fire, bright enough to see the decapitated head of the monster fall away and get dragged toward the bottom.

The two Sons cheered their success.

Then on the other side, another of the fiery apparitions appeared, then another, and two more. They surrounded the sub, their eyes burning hotter, their flames writhing and coiling across their forms.

Then they attacked.

The sub was batted, ripped. Huge jaws lined by three rows of shark's teeth crunched into the Lexan bubble. The glass cracked under the pressure. Then the entire canopy was ripped off.

Water pounded into him, flushed him out of the sub into darkness. Pressure popped his ears, crushed his lungs. Then his body was grabbed, pierced by teeth, dragged deeper.

But that was not the worst.

Flames erupted all around him, burning away his clothes, searing his skin, setting his hair on fire. His eyeballs boiled in his skull. He was being burned alive—in water.

He writhed at the pain, at the impossibility, knowing only one certainty.

Rather than finding Tartarus . . .

Hell found me.

49

A month after events in Morocco, Elena stood in the bitter sunlight of an Arctic summer morning. She wore a goose-down parka but felt no need to zip it up. From this mountaintop she enjoyed the cold wind, the frigid bite on her cheeks, the ice in each breath. It made her feel new again, reborn in some way.

Which maybe is appropriate.

Ahead of her, a cliff dropped into the fjord far below. The view looked out across the water to the frozen, cracked surface of Helheim Glacier, a river of ice slowly spilling into the ocean. The bright morning sunlight reflected off it, refracting into rainbows, polishing sections of ice to a dazzling cerulean blue.

It was a perfect spot.

A group of locals from Tasiilaq gathered to pay their respects. Candles were lit, some in hands, more flickering along the cliff's edge. John Okalik stood with his palm resting on his grandson's shoulder. Nuka stared out to sea. Even Officer Jørgen had come to say good-bye.

The village had lost two men who had guarded the tunnel into the heart of the glacier, cousins of John. Their bodies had never been recovered, but she had learned that many found it fitting. According to old Inuit customs, they did not burn or bury their dead, but gave them back to the sea.

Another had also never been found.

Mac returned from the cliff's edge, where he had placed a candle for the lost man. He limped over to her, his foot still in a boot splint, but he was recovering well from his injuries.

"Nelson would hate all this fuss," Mac said, sniffing hard, trying not to let Elena see his damp eyes. "He was the least sentimental man I ever knew."

But you aren't.

Elena took Mac's hand in her own. She squeezed, feeling the heat of his hard palm and fingers, better than any glove. She leaned into him. They had grown closer during the tumultuous aftermath of events in the Mediterranean and Morocco. She knew Mac had been dragged into all of this because of his concern for her. But over the past weeks, something warmer had grown. Who knew where it would lead? But she wanted to find out.

Mac blew out a breath, his voice cracking. "Nelson could argue a mouse out of its cheese. And we certainly didn't agree on most things . . ."

She looked up at him. "But he was your friend."

He sniffed and nodded.

She had come to Greenland, both out of respect for the dead and also to be here for Mac. Still, she hadn't needed much persuading. She had already been here a few days, enjoying the quiet pace of Tasiilaq, away from the cameras, the interviews, the screaming tabloid news.

Her father had been arrested in Hamburg, dragged out of the EU summit in handcuffs and surrounded by a cadre of armed German police and Interpol. The video had played for weeks. Her father now sat in a federal prison, negotiating for leniency, to avoid the death penalty by being cooperative. He had already exposed the upper echelon of the Apocalypti, who were either arrested or driven into hiding. The global hunt continued for the rest, and it would likely take years, if not decades, to truly stamp out every fanatical ember of that apocalyptic cult.

If that was even possible.

Those zealots would not go down without a fight. She had heard how the underground complex in Turkey—a stone's throw from the ruins of Troy—had been firebombed before authorities could secure it. She remembered her glimpse into that vast subterranean library, wondering what historical treasures, some surely dating back to the founding of the House of Wisdom, had been lost forever.

Still, she pushed aside such regrets.

Knowledge is never truly lost.

It moved, shifted, grew, evolved, but ultimately, endured. Even when buried and forgotten, the deepest truths found a way of shaking off the dust of time and revealing themselves again. She certainly knew that now, especially after all she and the others had gone through, following the trail of a long-dead Arab captain to the very gates of Hell.

Singing rose ahead of her, an Inuit song of mourning. She did not understand the words, but the solemnity, the beauty, touched her soul.

Mac drew her closer to the others, allowing her to be part of it.

She came with him. As Mac added his deep baritone, she gazed out across the fjord to the breadth of the Helheim, noting the vast pools of meltwater reflecting the sun. As the Inuit sang, she wondered if they were mourning more than the dead, but an inevitable change to their home, a greater ending to come.

Elena tightened her fingers on Mac's hand, refusing to bow to such defeatism.

She remembered her father's grim warning, about the Apocalypti, about who ultimately supported them: *If you simply believe the world will come to an end and do nothing to stop it, you are one of us.*

Instead, she took strength from Mac, from his passion and dedication, for fighting for these people, for this place, in the face of impossible odds.

The tears she had been holding back finally ran down her cheeks.

But they were not sad, only joyful.

Full of hope for the future.

For all of us who share this beautiful world—this gift from God.

9:09 P.M. EDT
Takoma Park, Maryland

Gray pedaled his road bike hard, then sped around the dark corner onto his street. He panted, sweat dripping down his brow. He had raced the setting sun from the metro station, but he lost this race.

Next time.

Enjoying the last of his ride, he straightened, released the handlebars, and let his bike glide down the street on its own. He balanced the bike's frame by instinct and muscle memory alone. For the past month, he had pedaled home every night, doing his best to get back into fighting shape. He had also returned to the gym and often joined Monk on the basketball court.

But Gray knew he still had a ways to go, especially trying to find that right balance between home life and his responsibilities at Sigma.

The bike wobbled under him, but he corrected it with a shift in his core.

If only it were this *easy . . .*

Maybe it would be eventually. Maybe he just hadn't developed the proper muscle memory as a new father, and once he did, things would get easier. Though, right now, he had a hard time believing that.

And I'm not the only one struggling to find that balance.

He reached his house, a little craftsman cottage. He returned his grip to the handlebars, bounced up the curb, and pedaled to the front porch. The house was oddly dark. Crickets chirped in the bushes. A few fireflies flickered.

He hopped off the bike and carried it one-handed up to the porch. Now that he had stopped, the humidity of a D.C. summer swamped over him, like a wet, hot blanket. He pictured the cold beer in the fridge, believing he'd earned it, even if he lost this race with the sun.

Still, that loss wasn't entirely his fault. Back at Sigma command, Painter had a laundry list of details he needed Gray to address, mostly tied to all that had happened last month.

Over in Italy, Father Bailey was coordinating an international effort to rebuild Castel Gandolfo, but that work took some delicacy, especially with what was hidden below those ruins. Bailey had wanted some guidance on how best to proceed, both to maintain the secrecy of the Holy Scrinium and to safeguard any treasures that might be recovered. Such hesitancy was likely born of a feeling of insecurity. After learning of Monsignor Roe's many betrayals, Bailey seemed to be second-guessing himself.

Gray understood that. He had never suspected Roe was capable of such treachery. He remembered how, upon their first meeting, he had considered the monsignor to be some incarnation of Vigor Verona, one of Gray's most trusted friends in the past. So, he had to cut Bailey some slack for being shaken up. In fact, Gray realized he might have misjudged the young priest from the start. While Bailey certainly did not fill the shoes of Vigor, he might very well grow into them one day.

Maybe.

Gray locked his bike on the porch, waving a cloud of mosquitoes from his sweating face. His work was made all the harder because the porch light was off. He straightened, hearing distant music from a backyard barbecue and the drone of a television across the street.

Whereas his house was silent as a grave.

He turned to the door, his heart suddenly pounding. He quickly entered and found the living room dark. He headed across the dining room. Ahead, there was no sound of clattering cookware coming from the kitchen. He hurried through the swinging doors to check it out.

Nothing.

He clenched a fist. He knew Seichan had been struggling of late. Could she have finally left and—

"Over here!" Seichan called from outside, shouting through the back door from the yard. "You're late!"

Despite the scolding, he sagged with relief and hurried outside.

A picnic blanket had been stretched across the lawn, adorned with large pillows. On top of one, Jack rocked on his back. He was dressed in a blue onesie with a yellow monkey on it. When Seichan had come home with it a week ago, Gray hadn't said a word. Back in Morocco, Seichan had returned Aggie to Charlie with clear reluctance.

On the pillow, Jack tried to grab his toes with a red-faced earnestness. *That's my boy. Never willing to give up the good fight.*

To the side, a low table glowed with a camp lantern. Seichan stood, bent at the waist, her back to him. He enjoyed the view. She straightened and turned around, holding aloft two halves of a cupcake, each with a candle flickering there.

He smiled, getting it. "For Jack's *half* birthday."

She shrugged and drew closer, offering him one.

"I thought you decided not to celebrate it," Gray said as he took the cake.

Earlier, when she had informed him about her decision, he attributed it to some fundamental change in her mind-set about child-rearing and motherly responsibilities, a reflection of her letting go of the need to be a tiger mom all the time.

"It's red velvet," she said. "With cream cheese frosting."

"You made it?"

"Bought it." She frowned. "You think I have time to bake a *single* cupcake? And if I made a dozen, there goes your diet."

True.

She drew him to the picnic blanket, and they settled onto pillows with Jack between them. They made wishes and blew out each other's candles. They leaned against one another, listening to crickets, watching fireflies flit.

"This is nice," Seichan murmured.

"Yes, it is."

She glanced over to him. "For now."

He nodded, recognizing she would never be a mother who only baked cupcakes and planned elaborate half-birthday parties. It was clear she had come to some balance, likely better than him.

"Oh," she said and scooted over to Jack. "Watch this."

She picked up their son, interrupting his ongoing battle to reach his toes, and carried him a few steps away. She then turned, set Jack on his pudding legs, and held him up by his armpits. She waited for him to get his sea legs—then let go.

Jack wobbled like a drunken sailor.

Gray sat up, amazed.

No, she didn't . . .

Jack took one step, waving his arms, swinging a happy rope of drool. Then another step.

Gray opened his arms. "Here, Jack."

His son took another wildly uncontrolled step. Gray caught him before he face-planted into the blanket. He rolled the boy into his arms. Seichan joined them, a very self-satisfied smirk on her face.

"Screw those maternity books," she said.

He grinned at her, placed Jack back on his pillow, and scooped Seichan closer. "Still a tiger mom, I see."

She leaned closer. "Oh, I can be a tiger in other ways, too."

He grinned wider and met her lips.

Now that's what I call balance.

EPILOGUE

Back here again . . .

Kowalski swatted a large fly that tried to take a chunk out of his arm. He stared across the grassland meadow toward the dark fringe of forest in a remote corner of Virunga National Park, a gorilla sanctuary in the heart of the Congo. He sat in a camp chair with a sweating bottle of beer on a small table.

The sun had nearly set on this winter day.

He had spent most of his time here or back at a row of tent cabins behind him. As the hot afternoon wore on, he had watched the shadows stretch steadily across the grass. This was their third day here.

Near the edge of the forest, Maria consulted with Dr. Joseph Kyenge, the sanctuary's chief zoologist. Kowalski watched the Congolese man shake his head and point toward the forest. The guy was plainly giving up for the day. There was still no sign of Baako, the western lowland gorilla whom Maria had released into this jungle two years ago.

Maria's shoulders sagged.

Kowalski frowned and shook his head. It seemed like young gorillas were like teenagers. Always disappointing their parents. Wanting to spend more time running around with their friends than at home.

Maria started back toward Kowalski.

He stood up with a groan, ready to console her as he had the prior two nights. Since events half a year ago, they had grown even closer. He couldn't say why, only that something seemed to have broken between them, a barrier he hadn't even known was there.

Before Maria could cross the meadow, Kyenge called to her. "Dr. Crandall, wait!" The zoologist pointed back at the forest. "Come see!"

She looked at Kowalski, hope brightening her face. As she turned toward the jungle, Kowalski hurried across. If this was a false alarm, she'd be crushed. He intended to be there for her.

He reached her side, and they returned to Kyenge together. The zoologist stepped back, a huge smile on his face, and waved an arm as if introducing a debutante.

From the leafy fringe of the forest, a frond was pushed aside by a leathery palm. A muscular shape bulled into view, leaning on the knuckles of one arm. Dark eyes stared at them. Almost shyly, the large gorilla left the forest and stepped into the sunlight. He sank to his haunches, his bullet of a head down, as if ashamed, a teenager who had missed his curfew.

"Baako," Maria said, "you're here."

The young gorilla lifted his face enough to show his eyes. He raised his hands and signed to her.

[*Mama*]

Baako's furry black brows remained pinched with worry. His lips were stretched taut, almost a wince, showing a hint of his white teeth.

"Oh, Baako, it's okay."

Maria rushed over and hugged him. She did her best to console him, but she had difficulty getting her arms around him. Baako had nearly doubled in size. She tickled him, teased him, scratched him where she knew he liked it best.

Kowalski frowned.

Wait, she does that to me, too.

Baako relaxed, his shoulders dropping, letting out a series of short wheezes, the gorilla version of laughter. Finally, Maria leaned back and held out an arm toward Kowalski.

"Hey, kiddo," Kowalski said, lifting a hand.

Baako's greeting was more exuberant.

The only warning was a quick sign.

[*Papa*]

Then Baako bolted forward and tackled him. Kowalski felt like he'd been hit by an NFL lineman. Still, he took it happily. They rolled across the grass until both were wheezing. Baako from laughter. Kowalski because he was out of breath.

Kowalski ended up on his butt and smiled at Maria. "Our boy's sure gotten big."

Over the next half hour, their greeting went from energetic cheerfulness to a quieter time of reflection and reunion. They signed silently to one another, huddled close together. Baako shared stories of the jungle, of other gorillas. Eventually they settled to simple touches and murmurs of affection.

To the west, the sun had sunk below the horizon, leaving only a rosy glow. Campfires were lit near the tents behind them. A swash of starlight crowned the skies overhead.

Kowalski knew there was no better time. He had his whole family gathered here. He reached into his pocket and removed a ring box. It wasn't the same one he had first carried here half a year ago. He had lost that one and spent a good chunk of his savings to replace it.

Just as well.

He knew he wasn't that same man from six months ago. He stared over at Maria, who hadn't noticed what was in his hand. She remained focused on Baako, her smile wistful and happy. She was also not the same woman. Their relationship felt brand-new, forged stronger in those hellish fires.

He swallowed and lifted the box.

She finally turned; so did Baako.

He used a thumb to flip open the box. "Maria Crandall, would you do me the ho—?"

She tackled him, hitting him harder than Baako. The gorilla joined them, likely thinking it was another game. Luckily, he snapped the ring box closed before getting knocked on his backside. Maria ended up sprawled on top of him.

"I take it that means yes?" he asked with a wince.

"You are such an ass." She leaned down. "But my ass forever."

Holding his face in her hands, she kissed him.

After a time of whispered plans, of smiles and laughter, and quiet moments of shared tenderness, all three of them lay on their backs in the grass. With the daylight waning, they stared as the stars peeked out and listened as the jungle settled into evening birdsong and the distant cries of nocturnal hunters.

Maria finally rolled on her side, kissed his cheek, and pointed to their tent cabin. "I'm going to grab us a couple of beers."

He leaned his head back with a happy sigh. "I knew you'd make a good wife."

She punched him and left.

Baako took advantage of some private father-son time. He sat closer, looming over Kowalski. Baako sniffed at him, picked at his clothes as if searching for something. He had done this periodically during their reunion.

Still on his back, Kowalski signed to him.

[*What are you doing?*]

Baako sat back, then tapped the middle finger of his left hand on Kowalski's belly, the right middle finger on his own hairy brow.

[*You sick*]

Kowalski sat up and pulled the gorilla's hand down. He glanced back to the cabin, but Maria was still inside. He had only gotten the final medical report last week. Painter knew but respected his privacy, allowing Kowalski time to fully digest it.

It seemed he had not entirely escaped Tartarus unscathed. While the

Promethean Blood had protected him from the worst of the radiation, it couldn't stop everything. The medical report had a lot of jargon and numbers, but it all boiled down to three lines.

MULTIPLE MYELOMA.

STAGE 3.

LIFE EXPECTANCY: TWO YEARS.

But one oncologist had cautioned about that prognosis.

If you're lucky.

Kowalski noted the concerned crinkle around Baako's eyes. That worried look was why he hadn't told Maria yet. He would, but not now. Not when she was so happy, when everything was going so well between them. Maybe such silence was foolish, even selfish, but he needed time to process everything first.

Kowalski signed to Baako, knowing the gorilla would believe him, knowing it was easier to lie in sign language.

[*Papa is fine*]

Baako stared at him, then hugged him hard. Kowalski patted him and rubbed his back in reassurance. When the gorilla finally let Kowalski go, Baako looked relieved, much happier again.

Good.

Kowalski turned to the cabin and saw Maria pop out, carrying two bottles of beer. He waved an arm.

Baako trotted to greet her, as if she had been gone for days.

Or maybe it was something else.

Maria struggled to keep a bottle of beer from Baako.

"You're too young," she scolded. "Maybe when you're twenty-one."

Kowalski smiled.

She joined him with an exasperated happy huff. Framed in starlight, she stared down at him. "What's that grin all about?'

He smiled wider. "Because I'm the luckiest man alive."

And I intend to stay that way.

Author's Note to Readers:
Truth or Fiction

We come to the end of another odyssey. Maybe not one sung by ancient Greek choruses, but hopefully one that entertained well enough. In the past, Homer had mixed facts and fiction. He told the tale of the historical fall of the Troy, but he layered in myth and magic. Unlike that great bard of yore, I will attempt in these last pages to separate the truth from fiction found in my story, while perhaps letting a little light into my own writing process.

Let's start with the two bibles that I found immensely valuable in crafting this tale. Of course, countless other volumes were consumed, picked apart, and studied, but these two books I found not only informative and inspiring but also damned good reads. So, I encourage everyone to check them out.

The first delves deep—and I do mean *deep*—into the mythos of what lies underground, why we look there, and why it continues to fascinate us. I read it not intending to use it as a research text, but simply from my love of caving. But in the end, it moved me enough to write this novel and challenged me enough to write it *better*. What more could anyone ask? Please check it out:

Underland: A Deep Time Journey, by Robert Macfarlane

I picked up the second bible for research and references, but I got lost in the wonderful writing, and was awed by the concept, and ultimately I found this book instrumental to the core of this novel. Still, my story barely scratches the surface of ancient technology, the blend of myth and science, that can be found in the following work. If you would like to know much more about the historical details and speculations raised in my novel, do read this book:

Gods and Robots: Myths, Machines, and Ancient Dreams of Technology, by Adrienne Mayor

That said, let's do look deeper into the history raised in *The Last Odyssey.* And we'll start all the way back in the Greek Dark Ages (from 1100 to 800 B.C.), what has been called the Homeric Age.

Homer's *Iliad* and the *Odyssey*

I hinted at the true history buried in the myths of these two epic poems at the start of the novel. But I was not the first to explore that line between fact and fiction found in those stories. One of the earliest was the Greek historian Strabo, who in his travelogue of the ancient world—his multivolume masterwork *Geographica* (from 7 A.D.)—sought to do what I did in my story: to try to map out Odysseus's fateful journey across the Mediterranean. Much of the speculation raised in this book (with the exception of the role of tectonics) came from Strabo's texts.

World War Zero

Archaeologists and historians readily accept that there was a major Mediterranean-wide war that led to the downfall of three major Bronze Age civilizations: the Greek Myceneans, the Egyptians, and the Hittite kingdom of Anatolia. This conflict has been dubbed "World War Zero." It was a corner of this war that Homer related in his twin epics. What remains a mystery that continues to today is: *who* attacked those civilizations and brought about the Greek Dark Ages? The prevailing opinion is that it was the enigmatic Sea People, but even their identity remains clouded in speculation. Some believe they were a coalition of various tribes, others that they belonged to another Anatolian kingdom called the Luwians. I, of course, have my own opinion on the subject, which is shared in this novel.

The next section I'd like to tackle revolves around ancient knowledge, technology, and science. Let's break it down into pieces.

Banū Mūsā brothers and Ismail al-Jazari

The Islamic Golden Age ran from the ninth to the thirteenth century. The three Banū Mūsā brothers were scientists and engineers at the beginning of that age, and Ismail al-Jazari continued on their tradition of innovation and design near the end. As related in this novel, the Banū Mūsā brothers did indeed preserve and build upon knowledge that was nearly lost following the fall of the Roman Empire. Though the *fourth* Banū Mūsā brother—Hunayn—is my own creation, much of his actions, interests, and skills were patterned after the three historical figures. It is also known that Ismail al-Jazari—who is sometimes referred to as one of the "fathers of robotics"—was greatly influenced by those three brothers' work. As was someone else—

Leonardo da Vinci

Volumes of work have been written about Da Vinci, but one of the best is Walter Isaacson's *Leonardo da Vinci,* which both humanizes the man and offers insight into his genius (do read it). So, I won't go into great detail here. But as the Islamic Golden Age ended, men like Da Vinci did indeed pick up the torch that was nearly snuffed out, conserving and building on the knowledge of the Islamic world. Other details about Da Vinci in this novel were also based on real events. Leonardo did lug his poor Mona Lisa from country to country. He did perform anatomical dissections to better hone his paintings and sculptures. He also was called upon and commissioned by the French king—François I—to craft a mechanical golden lion, following the sacking of Milan.

On to some specifics:

Arabian Dhow

The ship locked in ice at the beginning of the story is based on a Sambuk design. These large dhows were not only *oceangoing* but often *exploratory*. The Islamic world should be thanked for all their many contributions to navigation, mathematics, and astronomical studies. Including one very important element of this novel—

Spherical Astrolabes

Oxford University's History of Science Museum was kind enough to permit me to use the pictures in this book of the only known example of a *spherical* astrolabe. The technology and use of such devices found in this novel is accurate, from the universality of these astrolabes to the rods used to "program" them to different latitudes. Even the name inscribed on their astrolabe was a bit of serendipity. I had already been writing about the Banū Mūsā brothers in this novel, and lo and behold, who had signed the astrolabe at Oxford University: someone named Mūsā. Read into that what you'd like.

Ancient Automatons

Ah, now we're getting to the crux of my story. It seems we're always underestimating the technology of ancient peoples. They keep surprising us, even now. I had a chance to study the Antikythera mechanism at the National Archaeological Museum in Athens, a Greek device dated to the first century B.C. It was discovered aboard a shipwreck in 1901, but it would take until we were developing our own computers that the mechanism's purpose and design became known. Most archaeologists now accept that it is the first known analog computer.

Still, the litany of amazing Greek automated designs is astounding. So much so that the Greeks incorporated them into their legends of Hephaestus and Daedalus (who some speculate could have indeed been a historical figure). But historians and archaeologists have documented countless designs of self-operating mechanisms, cunning automatons, and yes, those "Ingenious Mechanical Devices" of the Banū Mūsā brothers and Ismail al-Jazari. I could fill pages on this very subject, but luckily someone already did. I'll refer you to the second of the two bibles listed above.

Greek Fire and Promethean Flames

Those Hellenistic pyros did invent a great war weapon known as "Greek Fire." It terrified sailors and was critical to winning many battles. The infernal liquid was said to be ignited by water and could not be doused by it. Unfortunately (or maybe *fortunately*), the recipe for making Greek Fire has been lost to antiquity. Speculations abound regarding how it was crafted.

This novel touches upon similar concoctions found in the myths and stories surrounding the sorceress Medea, who helped Jason of the Argonauts defeat all manner of fiery mechanical automatons, from Talos of Crete to the Colchis Bulls. It is said she did develop two important potions: Medea's Oil (which possessed the secret to an unquenchable fire, a gift from Prometheus, and very much like Greek Fire) and Promethean (what I called "Promethean Blood" in the novel, which was a black potion that could grant one resistance to fire, and if consumed, the ability to ward off arrows and spears). It made me wonder: If Greek Fire was historical—and very much like Medea's Oil—could Promethean Blood be real, too?

Tartarus/Tartessos/Tarshish

The section in the novel relating to the myths and historical history of the three abovementioned cities is as accurate as I could make it. The Greek historian Strabo also believed that Homer's Tartarus and the rich Spanish city of Tartessos were the same place. And later others believed the biblical city of Tarshish was just a new spelling of that same mysterious metropolis. Even the speculation about all three cities being home to an advanced civilization was not born of my own imagination, but instead, based on more scholarly (and controversial) research.

Tectonic Plates

The map of tectonic plates used in this novel is accurate. What I found again to be a bit of serendipity was how many of Strabo's theories regarding the true locations of the mythic islands and ports of Homer's *Odyssey* ended up falling along the line between the African tectonic plate and its Eurasian neighbor to the north. Does this mean anything? If you read this novel, you know it does.

Okay, that's enough of history and ancient science. Let's address a few locations.

Iceland

Maria and Kowalski do spend a bit of time soaking in hot water before they find themselves in real hot water. I was lucky enough to spend an afternoon enjoying the Blue Lagoon's Retreat. To honor that, I tried to be as accurate as possible, but then again, I did have a few of those green banana/rum concoctions, so go check out the place yourself. I suggest you read *The Last Odyssey* there. On a minor note, the United States does operate a group of P-8 Poseidon jets out of Iceland to aid in tracking and hunting submarines. And considering this novel delves into Greek history and Sea People, how could I not feature military planes named after the Greek god of the oceans?

Helheim Glacier and Greenland

Most of the details and specifics of this part of the novel are true, from the Red House hotel in Tasiilaq to the dynamics and threat to Greenland's glaciers. While I've never personally rappelled into one of those frozen whirlpools called a moulin, I did consult a caving buddy who did. After his harrowing story, I'd rather take my chances with a fiery bull. On to one final bit of serendipity. I knew from the start of this book that I was going to freeze an ancient dhow in a Greenland glacier, in a book about the hunt for the true location of mythic Tartarus, the Greek Underworld. And what is one of Greenland's largest glaciers, one of its most threatened?

That's Helheim Glacier, named after the Nordic "World of the Dead." So, take what you will from that true detail.

Turkish Underground Cities

Elena and Kowalski are briefly imprisoned in an ancient subterranean Turkish city. I based that description on a real site, the Derinkuyu Underground City. Now, while I don't believe there is such a lost metropolis within a stone's throw of Troy, archaeologists have, in fact, discovered more than two hundred troglodyte-cave cities throughout Turkey—so why not one on the outskirts of Troy?

Castel Gandolfo

My Italian publisher was kind enough to invite me to speak in the small village of Velletri, outside of Rome. It's a village with a long literary history. If you ever go there, eat at Casale della Regina. You will thank me. Velletri is also a short hop to Castel Gandolfo, and I was able to do a tour of the pope's summer palace. It was that visit that convinced me to include it in this novel—so, please accept my apologies for blowing it up. Again, based on that visit, I tried to make the descriptions as accurate as possible. A few fun facts. The palace is indeed built atop the ancient ruins of Emperor Domitian's villa. The summer palace has a long and rich astronomical history, including the new and old observatories, and a great museum pertaining to astronomy. The story of the "Pope's Children" is also historically accurate. As to the Holy Scrinium, the original traveling library of the popes, it truly did exist and was said to hold rare treasures going back to the founding of Christendom. Does it still exist? Is it located in ancient Roman vaults beneath Castel Gandolfo? Unfortunately, that was not part of my tour.

Sardinia

The Italian island of Sardinia has a rich archaeological past, which I touched upon in this story. The details of the Noro Stone and the Giants of Mont'e Prama are accurate, though some of my speculations regarding them are born of my own imagination. The ancient *nuraghe* fortifications and buildings are real, as are their ties to Daedalus, who is indeed said to have resided on the island after he fled from King Minos—and why those ancient ruins were called *daidaleia* by the Greeks.

Morocco

Moving south to Africa, Morocco is fascinating both geologically and historically. The convergent boundary between the African and Eurasian tectonic plates does run straight through the country and gave rise to the Atlas mountain range. One of its main exports is indeed phosphate rock, one of the chief ingredients for making Greek Fire. Also, their phosphate deposits are rich in uranium. It is estimated that the phosphate rock in Morocco holds twice the amount of uranium as the rest of the world. So, if you want to make potent Greek Fire, build your foundry in the Atlas Mountains.

Finally, let's discuss the end of the world.

Apocalyptic Cults

I'm fascinated by all the ways various cultures view the end of the world. Especially in regard to the visions that are common among them. Of course, the Apocalypti—a confederation of cults, both religious and otherwise, whose goal is to trigger Armageddon by any means necessary—is purely of my own imagination. That said, it is worrisome that there appears to be a growing zealous view that not only are the end-times near—but that we should do everything politically and militarily possible to make sure it happens in our lifetime. That trend is growing in support both across the Islamic world and among Western nations. So, while the Apocalypti cult is fiction, their existential threat is real.

I love this world—this wondrous gift to humanity—so let's not be so quick to burn it down. Of course, I've been blowing up UNESCO world heritage sites for more than twenty years; therefore, I might not be the best advocate for this position.

There you have it. I hope you enjoyed this latest Sigma adventure. As you might suspect, there is much more to come. But for now, we'll let Gray and company recuperate, have a few drinks, and spend some quality time with their families.

Because that's what I'm going to do—and you should, too.

Rights and Attributions for the Artwork in This Novel

p. 101—Spherical Astrolabe B

© History of Science Museum, University of Oxford, inventory #49687

p. 127—Papal Cards

Designed by author

p. 153—Sketch of Vault

Designed by author

p. 183—Sea People Map

© 2011 David Kaniewski, Elise Van Campo, Karel Van Lerberghe, Tom Boiy, Klaas Vansteenhuyse, Greta Jans, Karin Nys, Harvey Weiss—"The Sea Peoples, from Cuneiform Tablets to Carbon Dating" (from PLOS ONE)

From PLOS ONE, an open-access article distributed under the terms of the Creative Commons Attribution License, which permits unrestricted use, distribution, and reproduction in any medium, provided the original author and source are credited. "© 2011 Kaniewski et al. This is an open-access article distributed under the terms of the Creative Commons Attribution License, which permits unrestricted use, distribution, and reproduction in any medium, provided the original author and source are credited."

https://en.wikipedia.org/wiki/Sea_Peoples#/media/File:Map_of_the _Sea_People_invasions_in_the_Aegean_Sea_and_Eastern_Mediterra nean_at_the_end_of_the_Late_Bronze_Age.jpg

p. 184—Egyptian Sketch

Public domain

https://en.wikipedia.org/wiki/Sea_Peoples#/media/File:Medinet _Habu_Ramses_III._Tempel_Nordostwand_Abzeichnung_01.jpg

p. 186—Giant of Mont'e Prama

Purchased with Enhanced License from Shutterstock